CURSE QUEEN

Forbidden Forest 4

AMBER ARGYLE

Book Cover Design by Melissa Williams Design

First Edition: January 2021
Library of Congress Cataloging-in-Publication Data
LCCN: 2021900724

Argyle, Amber
Curse Queen (Forbidden Forest) – 1st ed
ISBN-13: 978-1-954698-01-7

TO RECEIVE AMBER ARGYLE'S STARTER LIBRARY FOR FREE, SIMPLY TELL HER WHERE TO SEND IT:
http://amberargyle.com

To Derek,

For letting me put my cold feet on your legs at night.

For not complaining when I ask you to pop my bad back daily.

For making a gourmet cake every year for my birthday.

CHAPTER 1

REVENGE

High Lady Eiryss slipped around dancing pairs, narrowly avoiding Lord Darten's gaze—if she met his gaze, propriety would demand she dance with him. She didn't have time for another dance. Not before the toasts. And she could not endure another hour of his droning on and on about the cursed history of magic.

She reached a table set along the perimeter, slipped the vial from the folds of her skirt, and poured the colorless liquid into two glasses. The champagne bubbled and foamed before settling again. She dropped the vial to the bark and crushed it beneath her boot—she couldn't be found with it later.

"What are you doing?" came a voice, the breath warm against her neck.

She whirled to find Ramass directly behind her, one eyebrow cocked. His curly red hair had been mostly tamed into a queue at his back. He wore royal black, which complemented his pale skin and freckles and made his gray eyes almost appear blue. His shoulders were wide and muscular, his waist narrow.

"Light," she swore. She grabbed his sword-calloused hand and pulled him away. "We can't be seen here."

"Eiryss," he said warningly.

Back amid the dancers, she placed one of his hands onto the curve of her hip and lifted the other into position. "You danced with me the entire song. At no point did you see me go anywhere near Iritraya or Wyndyn's glasses."

He rolled his eyes and took the lead, maneuvering them around the dais at the center of the kaleidoscope of dancers. The font, with its wicked sharp thorns, sparkled in the middle and was guarded by sacred tree sentinels in their silver and white livery. Only royalty, the Arbor, or an initiate receiving the thorns that would form sigils were ever allowed upon the dais.

"What did you do?" Ramass asked.

She smirked. "You'll see."

He made a sound of exasperation. "Eiryss, now is not the time for one of your pranks."

Oh, it was the perfect time. No way either girl could best this.

"Why do you insist on this childish feud?"

She leveled a stony gaze at him. "You haven't had to endure them." The two cousins had been insufferable for the entire year. Ever since Hagath had graduated from the Enchantress Academy a year ahead of Eiryss, leaving her outnumbered and alone.

He looked away from her. "Don't turn those brown eyes on me."

Why not, when they always worked? She sniffed and changed the subject. "Where's Ahlyn?"

Ramass's jealous gaze immediately zeroed in on their princess, where she danced with the Alamantian king. "Busy being a princess."

Where the princess's features were light, the foreign king's were dark. Where her dress was suitably sober as the night sky, his layered tunic was a garish shade of green. All the Alamantians wore bright colors and laughed too loudly—like flashy birds screeching for a mate.

Not that anyone could blame the king for wanting to monopolize Ahlyn. The princess had rich golden hair, sapphire eyes, a slim build, fine features, and perfect, dainty teeth. Not to mention unending power. Half the Valynthian aristocracy was in love with her.

The truth was Eiryss didn't really like Ahlyn. Certainly not because the princess was beautiful or because she spent more time with Eiryss's friends than Eiryss did—especially since Ramass had decided he'd fallen in love with her. But because the girl was sulky and delicate and never did anything wrong. And worse, the Silver Tree had chosen her to become the next queen.

Eiryss pinched his arm to get him to stop glaring daggers at the visiting king. "I might be able to scrounge up another vial." *Maybe some could accidentally end up in Ahlyn's glass as well.*

Ramass huffed a laugh, one side of his mouth quirking up. "Things are tense enough as it is."

Feeling like she'd won a victory with that lopsided smile, she swirled under his raised arm, her skirts flaring, and came back to his embrace. "My father won't let the wicked Alamantians hurt you."

"Your father isn't infallible."

"Of course he is." Her father was a legend. No one had bested him in any test of skill in twenty-five years.

As the last song faded to silence, the pair of them reached their own table—the plates of food having been cleared away by the servants. Champagne sparkled beside her name card. She sighed. She would never be able to drink from an unattended glass again. She took it in her hand.

3

Hagath slipped in beside her and picked up her own glass. Her friend was the female version of her twin, Ramass, right down to the blue eyes, freckles, and wild red hair—though she made every effort to tame it. She wore her dress healer robes—dusty blue with silver embroidery. Her boots were wet, which meant she'd only just arrived, and in a leaky boat at that.

"Couldn't your father get you out of working tonight?" Eiryss asked. He was the king, after all.

"I didn't ask." Hagath always insisted on doing everything on her own merit, which was silly. Let one of the lower-caste healers take the night rotation—they needed the money, after all. And she had proved her merit a hundred times over.

"Couldn't miss the ceremony, dear sister?" Ramass asked.

Hagath waited until an Alamantian woman passed out of earshot before leaning close and dropping her voice. "I promised Ahlyn I would be here if I could manage to slip away. You have no idea how nervous she is."

Ramass's expression immediately soured. "Had I been forced to play hostess to that vile king, I would be nervous too."

Accompanied by King Dray, Ahlyn moved past them. As high nobility, Eiryss and her friends would normally have a place at the base of the dais, but her father had insisted they stay by the tables to the right—just in case anything went wrong. It wasn't ideal, but they were still close enough to hear the princess murmuring politely to a question Dray posed.

The king's eyes flicked to Eiryss, who dropped his gaze like she would a hot coal. She pushed her fingers down the plush skirts that began as the deepest navy and darkened to black at the base. She wore sapphires and diamonds at her ears and wrists. Her thick blonde and silver hair had been twisted into a prim knot, a glowing lampent flower tucked behind her ear. If she moved too fast, she caught flashes of color chasing each other along the edges of the petals.

Her attention was drawn back to Ahlyn and Dray as they climbed the dais to stand before the wicked thorns surrounding the font and took their place next to King Zannok. Like his children, the king's hair was red, his skin freckled, and his eyes blue, though wings of white framed his temples and lines bracketed his mouth and fanned from his eyes. He had aged well, his body still strong and honed from years of weapons training.

"On behalf of Valynthia," Zannok said, "I am pleased to welcome King Dray and his delegation to our beloved city."

Delegation, ha! There wasn't an enchanter among the Alamantians under fifty—the older ones always had the strongest magic—while each of the enchantresses was in their fighting prime. More an army unit than a delegation, they could easily assassinate the king or the princess, though they would all immediately die for it.

Of course, Eiryss's father, Undrad, had prepared for just such violence. Her brother and cousin, Rature and Vicil, had followed Princess Ahlyn all night as "chaperones." Undrad trailed the king—as the son of the previous queen, it was his duty and his honor. And there were far more honed Valynthian enchanters and enchantresses than even Dray had brought.

The men of her family were a fine sight in their best tunics, their leather mantles—peaked at the front, back, and shoulders—proclaiming their house and status. Mantles nearly identical to the one Eiryss wore, aside from the differing jewels that hung at each of the peaks.

Her father's hair was pure white. Vicil's and Rature's blond hair had already started to gray at the temples. It was a common family trait—one Eiryss hadn't escaped. On her brother and cousin, it somehow lent them an air of authority, while she just looked odd.

Her father nodded to Jala, the strongest enchantress in decades—though as queen, Ahlyn would soon surpass her. The faint silver gleam of her sigils showed that she was ready to shield the king at a moment's notice. She didn't look worried though. If anything, the woman seemed bored.

If the Alamantians tried anything, they'd find themselves outmaneuvered and outmagicked. Though Undrad doubted they would attempt anything tonight; he wouldn't have let Eiryss attend otherwise. He'd seen to it that she had weapons training, but she'd decided long ago to be a healer. She'd realized it after she lost her second batch of abandoned baby birds and cried for three days straight. She simply wasn't made for killing.

King Zannok raised his glass to Princess Ahlyn. "And to our princess, at the approach of the first anniversary since the Silver Tree chose her as my heir."

King Dray lifted his own glass. "To the princess." He was in his mid-thirties with sharp features, dark skin, and straight black hair. Even tied, it hung halfway down his back. His mantle was peaked at the shoulders, the jewels at the four points fire opals. The White Tree had been beautifully wrought at the center of the mantle in opal and gold. His ring bore a green serpent, knotted and eating its own tail. The symbol for his line.

Ahlyn inclined her head. King Zannok tipped his glass to his lips and drank, the cue for the rest of them to do likewise. Eiryss took a sip while looking toward Iritraya and Wyndyn, who tasted their own champagne, none the wiser. Suppressing a grin, she quickly looked away again.

King Dray took Ahlyn's hand. Her magic flared, the raised lines of her sigils gleaming silver.

If Dray was bothered by her obvious mistrust, he didn't show it. "I have heard rumors of your strength, Princess Ahlyn. They have said that your monarch sigils have grown strong and true—that after a few months more, they will have grown strong enough for you to become queen."

All this was true, yet it wasn't seemly for Dray to say it. For as Ahlyn's power grew, Zannok's faded. He'd been a good king—a great one, even—and like a dear uncle to Eiryss. He deserved more respect than to have his swift fall from power flaunted before the most powerful people in two kingdoms.

To his credit, King Zannok showed no outward signs of the insult, except for perhaps the tremor of champagne in his glass. Dray went on—he was either oblivious or indifferent to his gaucherie. Eiryss would bet on the latter. "After spending this evening with you, I can see that those rumors are true. I have come to make an alliance with the Valynthians, one that will bind our kingdoms. No more Alamantians. No more Valynthians. But a new people."

He reached into his pocket and withdrew something. Valynthian guards and magic wielders tensed. He opened his hand to reveal an opal the size of a small bird. Eiryss's mouth fell open. King Dray wasn't going to attack. He was proposing, offering Ahlyn a jewel to hang from her own mantle. She gaped at the opal, then at Dray, before her frantic gaze landed on Ramass.

Ramass was already moving. Hagath snatched his arm and shot Eiryss a look. Catching her meaning, she grabbed his other arm, spilling most of her champagne on his sleeve in the process.

"She's not going to accept," Eiryss hissed through clenched teeth. Of course she wouldn't. No Valynthian would debase themselves by marrying an Alamantian. Especially not their blasted king.

"Release your sigils before you start a brawl," Hagath whispered.

Eiryss hadn't noticed the buzz of his sigils under her palms, but she felt them now. Ramass hesitated, clearly torn.

"Ahlyn can take care of herself," Eiryss said.

He eased back a step, his sigils going dark a moment later. Eiryss didn't trust him enough to let go of his arm. Her gaze swung back to the dais. To the king who dangled peace between their kingdoms. For a price.

"You think to force our hand?" King Zannok said coldly. "Bully our princess into marrying you?"

The Alamantians were already pressuring King Zannok into giving magic to the rabble. Imagine, their next monarch could be wallowing in the mud right now. And Eiryss would have to bow and scrape before them. Such debasement wouldn't stand. Not in Valynthia. Especially not after one of their cities, Oramen, had tried to secede from Valynthia to join the Alamant.

And the Alamantians had welcomed Oramen with open arms.

That had set off skirmishes and threats until the Alamantians had decided to back off and offer these peace talks. *They thought to make Valynthia and the Alamant one?* Eiryss snorted. *More like destroy us from the inside out.*

"War between our people is coming. You know it as well as I." Dray eyed the males of Eiryss's family as if he'd seen right through their fine clothes to the soldiers beneath. He looked back at Ahlyn. "We can still stop it."

The princess took a step back. "I will never marry you." Her eyes again shifted to Ramass.

Dray followed her gaze, moved closer, and said something Eiryss couldn't make out. Then he lifted his glass. "To Ahlyn—a queen who holds the future of our kingdoms in her hands."

He drained his glass. For a time, there was silence. Belatedly, everyone realized they were supposed to drink after the monarch's toast. Instead, Eiryss set down her mostly spilled glass in disgust. People murmured, some in outrage.

King Dray bowed to King Zannok. "My delegation thanks you for your hospitality. Please accept our gifts of friendship." He gestured, and men came in, bearing casks. "Wine from our best vineyards."

Ahlyn opened her mouth, closed it, and cleared her throat. There was still protocol to observe—the girl knew it better than any of them. With a deep breath, she regained control over herself. "We have gifts for you as well, King Dray."

Bolts of finely woven material, far superior to anything the Alamantians had, were brought out. All of them were in suitable somber colors, as well as royal black—a great honor that the foreign king didn't deserve.

"And now," the king's scribe said with a pointed look at Iritraya and Wyndyn, "as a show of good faith, two of our girls will sing your Alamantian anthem." Both girls hurried to the front of the crowd and stood before the dais. As the band began the boisterous anthem, the cousins opened their mouths to sing, exposing azure teeth and indigo tongues. Unabashed as their singing was, they clearly didn't know.

Despite everything, a wicked grin spread across Eiryss's mouth, her crooked teeth bared for all to see.

Ramass's head whipped toward Eiryss. Hagath narrowed her gaze. More and more people turned to look at Eiryss, whose lips slammed over her teeth. She adopted her most innocent expression. Curse the light and all who followed it. Her reputation ruined her even without evidence. She shifted uncomfortably— she hated the attention of so many people.

Clearly baffled, Iritraya and Wyndyn belted out all the louder. People, Alamantian and Valynthian alike, began to laugh. The tension eased, seeping away like snow before the hot sun. Confused, the two girls exchanged baffled looks. Their eyes widened as they took in the other. Both pointed. Iritraya's hand slapped over her mouth, her singing dying with a clap. Wyndyn followed a beat behind. The two girls rushed toward the bathrooms on the upper branches.

They could scrub all they liked. The blue wouldn't come all the way off until sometime tomorrow. It took everything Eiryss had to hold back an unladylike snort.

King Dray held out his hand to Ahlyn. Biting her lip to keep back her smile, she took it. The two danced, and even Eiryss had to admit they made a beautiful couple who would probably make even more beautiful children.

Movement caught her gaze. Her father's eyes locked on her. He said something to one of his soldiers in brocade velvet and headed toward her.

"Time to go," she said.

"Eiryss," Hagath hissed after her.

But Eiryss was already a quarter of the way to the stairs that would take her to the dock at the base of the tree. Moments before she reached the archway, her father's hand locked around her arm, and he pulled her up one of the side branches until they were out of sight and out of earshot.

He released her. "Eiryss," he said firmly. "You're seventeen—far too old for such pranks."

She kept her gaze fixed on her feet, shame swirling inside her. "They deserved it."

"And now they will retaliate. Then you will retaliate. On and on and on. When will it end?" He looked out over the water beneath them.

Above them, the vault shone like a bead. Through Valynthia, cities gleamed under the domed vaults, so named for their impermanence. Eiryss imagined that from above, they would look like pearls strung through a necklace, with the capital city of Hanama the largest and most lustrous.

With the vault in place to keep out the weather, the lake was like black glass, reflecting the tree perfectly. Only the rainbow-pulsing fish swimming among the branches distinguished the truth from its reflection. If she unfocused her eyes, she could almost pretend they were birds.

The shadows in the hollows of Undrad's face made him look haggard. If there was a war, her father would lead it. And instead of protecting the king, he was chiding his wayward daughter.

"I'm sorry," she muttered.

"What have you been training for years to do?"

Here came the lecture. "To serve our people."

"And why must you serve them?"

She sighed in exasperation. "Because I'm in a position of power."

He pulled her into his arms, holding her tight. "Ah, my girl. I'll speak with Iritraya's and Wyndyn's fathers tonight. We'll make sure a cessation of hostilities is negotiated and sealed with iron."

She buried her head into her father's chest and let the familiar smell of him—like old books, steel, and magic—comfort her. "I should have come to you."

He chuckled. "Sounds like you were dealing with it pretty well on your own."

She sniffed and wiped her eyes. "Of course I was."

He tugged the flower from behind her ear. She'd crushed it when she rested her head against him. "You're going to be a formidable woman. I'm a little worried for your enemies."

She smiled, and for once she didn't worry about keeping her teeth hidden behind her lips. They matched his, after all. He motioned for her to follow him.

"Just give me a moment," she said.

He studied her before handing her the lampent. "You have to stay at least a couple more hours, but don't wait for me after that. I imagine the council will be chewing at Dray's proposal all night."

The Council of Lords and Ladies—a bunch of old men and women who had nothing better to do than stir up trouble.

He left her. She released the flower, watching as it fell helplessly toward the dark water. It landed, spreading ripples that changed the tree's reflection, then bounced back and changed it again. A discordant ripple, and the flower was pulled to the depths by an unseen predator.

Taking a deep breath, she went back to the gala and came face-to-face with Ramass.

"Did your father toss you into the lake?" he asked.

"Clearly."

"You deserve it."

"Always." She looked about for Hagath and found her hurrying toward the exit, a flushed acolyte beside her. A lower-caste acolyte. The girl definitely hadn't been invited to the gala, which meant she'd come to fetch Hagath.

Eiryss's heart sank. She'd hoped to spend the evening with her friend. But clearly, one of her patients had taken a bad turn. With Hagath working all weekend, Eiryss didn't know when she'd see her friend again.

"Come on." Ramass took her hand, and she sighed.

At least I still have Ramass.

He led her to where everyone was dancing. They hadn't finished their rotation when King Dray approached them, Ahlyn's hand slipped through the crook of his elbow. He was more than ten years her senior and a widower. Rumor had it that his two sons were the terror of the Alamant. He bowed to Ramass. "Lady Eiryss, might I have a dance?"

Ramass abandoned her like she'd suddenly turned rancid. He and Ahlyn were dancing before Eiryss could formulate a protest. King Dray held out his hand.

Light, she couldn't think of a way to politely decline. She pressed her palm into his, wincing a little at his moist grip. He spun her about, clearly an excellent dancer.

"I'm surprised you remembered my name," she murmured at his chest. He'd met all the high nobility before dinner, but there were a lot of them.

"I wanted to thank you."

She resisted the urge to shoo his hand off her hip. "For what?"

"Lightening the mood earlier."

He was thanking her for easing the tension with her prank. Heat climbed up Eiryss's cheeks. Who had told him? Ahlyn? The little traitor. "I don't understand your meaning."

His eyes flashed with amusement. "I'll take what help I can, even if that wasn't your intent."

What harm was there in admitting her guilt to a foreigner? "Had I known that, I would have saved my revenge for later."

He tipped his head back and laughed. *He really isn't too bad looking,* she admitted ruefully. But his flawless, dark skin and black eyes only made her distrust him more, and she hadn't thought that possible.

Eiryss caught sight of her father watching them from where he stood next to the king, his expression dark, one hand on the hilt of his sword. She flashed a smile at him to let him know she was all right.

Dray followed her gaze. He spun her deftly and then pulled her back into his arms. "Your father is a legend, Eiryss, even among the Alamant. Is it true that he is as honorable as he is skilled?"

You have no idea. "Why don't you ask him yourself?"

"I would, but he never leaves the king's side."

Her eyes narrowed. "And what would you have to say, King Dray, that you couldn't say in front of my king?"

He twirled her again and again so that her head spun, before settling her against him—close enough that the line of her hip touched his. "Just a friendly meeting between commanders."

Mercifully, the song came to an end. She backed away from his arms, relieved to be free of his touch. He caught her hand. She felt the press of paper between their palms. "Will you give this to your father?"

This was not the first time someone had used her to gain access to her father, and she had strict instructions to always pass the information along. "Very well," she sighed. She slipped the note into her pocket and bowed only as low as she had to. "King Dray."

He inclined his head. "I hope to see you again soon, Lady Eiryss."

She gave a tight smile and backed away to the outskirts of the dance floor. With Hagath gone and Ramass occupied, she scanned the room for someone else to spend the evening with. Instead, her gaze snagged on Wyndyn and Iritraya, who shot daggers at her. Biting her lip, she caught sight of a familiar figure moving along behind the tables. Her gaze lightened on Kit in his Silver Tree guard uniform.

He was her brother's age, a good dancer, an excellent kisser, and very pretty—even if he was far enough beneath her station to never be an equal. There were a very select few of acceptable rank to court her. Lord Darten and his droning, for instance. *Gah! I'm never going to marry.*

Judging by the way Kit was heading toward the exit, he'd just ended his shift. Eiryss angled to intercept him. She timed it so she popped out in front of him, her grin so wide it was hard to keep her lips together over her teeth.

He started and began to smile before glancing around nervously. "Eiryss."

She grabbed his hand. "Come on. We're going to drink all the king's wine and dance until they make us go to our hometrees." She picked up a glass and pushed it into his hands.

He looked around nervously. "Eiryss, you know I'm not high nobility."

"I am." She tipped the wine to her lips. It was actually very good—hints of rose and apples—so the Alamantians could at least do one thing right. "Only the king's and Ahlyn's family outrank me. None of whom will bother with me bringing a friend."

He didn't look certain. She lifted the bottom of his glass. "Come on. It's hours yet before I can go home." She watched his mouth pinch in uncertainty. Watched as he finally gave in, lifting the glass to his lips and licking the traces of wine away.

She smiled, planning to take full advantage of those lips later. She finished the rest of her glass and pulled him among the other dancers.

CHAPTER 2

TRAITOR

L ight flooded Eiryss's chambers. The magical doorpane
shivered as Ramass pushed through. A lampent flower
cast shadows that made his copper hair gleam auburn. He
still wore his royal-black dress tunic, the Silver Tree embroidered on his chest.

Judging by the ache thrumming at the front of her head,
she'd had too much to drink last night. Or this morning. *Is it still
morning? Must be. I'm too tired for it to be afternoon yet.* She
groaned and buried her head in her soft blankets. "Go away."

"Get up."

It had been a while since she'd heard that command in his
voice directed at her—probably the time they'd put eggs in Mistress Tria's seat cushions. Dripping egg whites covering her
backside, the woman had nearly caught them peering at her from
the magical panes above her office. *Move! Move! Move!* he had
demanded.

Instantly alert, she sat up and looked more closely at Ramass. His haunted expression stole the breath from her throat. She shoved back the covers, the wooden planks cold against her bare feet. "What's wrong?"

He hauled open the doors to her armoire. "Get dressed. Quickly."

He grabbed the first dress he found and thrust it at her. The fine gown from the gala last night? Far too fancy for trouble. She reached past him for her simple day tunic, slipping it over her silk shift rather than stripping in front of him.

"What did I do?" This wasn't about Iritraya and Wyndyn. She flipped through the lists of pranks she'd managed to get away with. She couldn't think of anything that warranted an emergency morning visit from her friend.

Ramass started going through her bookshelf. "Is there anything here that would tie you to Alamantian sympathizers?"

She blinked at him in confusion. "Sympathizers?" Beneath her, the floor swayed hard enough for her to stagger. By the light, what was going on? She stepped to the magic pane, spreading her fingers across its surface to shift it to clear. The sound of whipping branches flooded her chamber, which explained why the floor rose and fell like a ship in a storm. The enchantresses must have taken the vault down.

But why?

The troubled sky and slate horizon proclaimed it very early morning. On the angry lake, a boat full of constables appeared through the thick fog to bump into her hometree's dock. They disembarked and filed up the tree's splayed roots toward the stairs that wound up the tree's trunk toward the living areas.

"Eiryss," Ramass snapped.

Light, what did I do? She pressed the heel of her hand to her head and tried to think, but she was exhausted and hungover and maybe still a little drunk.

"They think I'm a sympathizer?" she asked in disbelief. "I hate the Alamantians as much as anyone!"

Ramass chucked one of her books across the room. It slammed into a magical panel, sending it rippling. "The truth doesn't matter anymore!"

She gaped at him. "Light, Ramass. What's wrong with you?"

He gripped her bookcase, his eyes screwed shut. He panted, hands opening and closing as he reeled in his temper. "Do you have anything or not?"

She shifted the pane back to opaque but didn't mute the sound. "That king handed me a letter to give to my father." She hurried to her nightstand, where she'd placed it last night, meaning to give it to her father in the morning. She pushed aside the jewels she'd dropped into a careless heap and picked up the folded paper.

Ramass tore it from her fingers and ripped it open—her father would be furious. "Get dressed, Eiryss!"

She'd forgotten her trousers. She shoved her feet through. "What does it say?" She tugged on her soft leather sandals, lacing them up her wide calves.

"It asks for a meeting between Undrad and Dray." Ramass tucked it inside his shirt and under his belt. "You never had it," he said curtly.

He went about the room, tapping her potted lampents, making them pulse brighter, colors chasing one another along the edges of the petals. Only then did she notice his muddy boots. Had he left Valynthia? For there was no mud in a city of trees growing out of a wide lake. One more lampent, and she could make out the color—not the brown of dirt, but the rust of dried blood. The bases of his boots were saturated with it.

She had a sudden memory. Her seventh summer. The metallic smell of blood pressing against her face like a living thing as she'd opened the shed's door. The flash of black eyes as the panthyrn had looked up at her, pieces of one of the baby inverns gripped in its teeth. She'd screamed and lunged, determined to wrest it from the predator's mouth, but it slipped out a hole it had chewed through the boards and disappeared.

Only then had she realized she was stepping on the bodies, the blood soaking through her boots. They were all in pieces—the mama invern with her droopy ears was the only one still recognizable. Eiryss couldn't even stroke their soft white fur to say goodbye. She'd screamed—the sound grating and high pitched—until her father had come for her, scooped her in his arms, and shut the door firmly behind him.

Ramass gripped her arms and called her name. Not the first time he'd done so, she realized. "Anything else. In your family library? Anywhere?"

She was suddenly cold. "My mother might—"

"Ture is checking her rooms."

She opened her mouth. Closed it again. Her brother, Rature. Checking her mother's rooms. He shouldn't be back from guarding the princess for hours yet. Something was wrong. Something far worse than a letter from the Alamantian king. "Ramass, why is there blood on your boots?"

He jerked away as if she'd burned him, his eyes wild. He looked dangerous. And terrified. "I'm going to protect you. I swear it."

Suddenly afraid, she took a step back. "Whose blood is it?" Ramass's hands shook. Stoic, unflappable Ramass never shook. "Is it Ture? Or Mother?" Her health had been steadily failing, which was why she hadn't attended the gala last night. But if it were her mother, why would Ramass be here? Why the blood? It had to be her brother.

Dozens of footsteps thudded up the stairs. One of the maids yelped. Eiryss grabbed Ramass's tunic in her fist. "Tell me."

His eyes closed, he gathered himself with a deep breath. And then he finally looked at her. "It's Undrad. He's been accused of treason against the king."

Her father? She nearly laughed in relief. Her father and King Zannok had been the best of friends since the early days of their military training. And while her father and the king sometimes argued about rights of the common man, her father would never actually side with the Alamantians. So that's all this was. An argument that had gotten out of hand.

She released him. "What happened?"

He shook his head in frustration and passed a hand down his face. "I can't... can't tell you."

"Just say it."

His face went red, a vein standing out in the center of his forehead. "I-I can't."

She wished he'd stop overreacting about all this. "My father would never betray yours. I'm sure this is all just a misunderstanding between friends." The king and her father might not speak for a few weeks, but one of them would eventually apologize.

Ramass held her gaze. "Undrad has been gravely injured."

He is serious. She didn't want to know. She had to know. "How injured?"

He slowly shook his head, his expression grim. "He was stabbed in the liver."

How out of hand had this argument gotten? "How bad is it?"

Ramass hesitated. "He lost a lot of blood."

He thought her father would die. He was wrong. Father was the strongest man she knew. He still regularly sparred with much younger members of the guard. And beat them soundly. Just last year, he'd broken his arm. It had taken Eiryss and Mother three days to convince him to let the healers look at it. He'd continued sparring, one-handed, and still managed to beat all the recruits.

Livers could heal. Her father's *would* heal.

She grabbed her cloak and headed for the doorpane. Ramass blocked her. "Where are you going?"

"To see to my father." They would have taken him to the healer's tree. Hagath was still working. She was a talented healer. She would see Father to rights.

"Only the healers can see Undrad," Ramass said.

"That's ridiculous." She tried to push him out of her way. He didn't budge.

"Eiryss, you must listen."

To what? He hadn't even told her what had happened yet! "My father would never betray his king. And your father would never keep me from mine."

He gripped her arms and shook her. "There are witnesses. Four of them."

Witnesses to what? "They're lying!" Her head pounded with the shout, reminding her she'd had too much wine last night.

Constables stepped into her chambers without bothering to ask for permission. Fin stood at their head. He froze, his eyes going to Ramass's hands gripping her arms. Ramass quickly released her. She stepped back, straightening her tunic.

"Sir," Fin said. "What are you doing here?"

Constables spread throughout Eiryss's chambers. She straightened indignantly. "Get out!"

No one dared look her way.

Ramass's expression shifted to that cold mask he wore when commanding inferiors. "I came to inform my friend of the charges against her father."

Fin's mouth thinned. "You will not interfere."

The guardsmen pawed through her underwear and rags. They shook out her books. One even inspected her chamber pot. Humiliation heated her cheeks. By the light, her grandmother had been queen. She was Lady Eiryss. Not some commoner.

She straightened to her full height. "Get out. All of you." The constables would not return her fierce gaze. Cowards. "My father is the king's head guard, marshal of our armies, and an esteemed member of the council. He would never do this!"

She still wasn't sure what "this" was. She certainly wasn't going to ask Ramass while the constables going through her underthings.

Fin's expression turned pitying. "There are four witnesses, lady." His voice dropped. "I'm sorry."

Lies that Fin clearly believed. How had she ever let the fool kiss her? Now she had to grit her teeth to keep from berating him. Well, she wasn't going to stand here and watch while they abused her things. "My mother. I have to see to my mother." Her health was already so fragile. What would this do to her?

Eiryss turned away. Fin reached for her, his fingers closing around her arm. She jerked out of his touch. "Don't!"

Fin's gaze dropped. "I'm afraid you'll have to be searched, lady."

"Absolutely not," Ramass said.

"You will as well, sir."

"I outrank you."

Fin didn't waver. "Not in this matter."

What would happen if Fin found the letter tucked inside Ramass's shirt? Ramass's gaze met Eiryss's. Years of getting in and out of trouble together let her decipher the message there: distraction. Gah! She always had to play the part of the distractor because she was so blasted good at it.

Taking a deep breath, she rounded on Fin, her finger stabbing into the center of his chest as she bore down on him. "You will not lay a hand on me." Fin gave way before her. She still outranked him. He wouldn't dare do anything else. "Your men will get their grimy paws out of my underthings." Another poke. "And you will quit my chambers at once!"

The constables all stopped what they were doing to watch. Good. That meant they weren't paying attention to Ramass.

Fin sidestepped another poke. "I'm sorry, lady, but I must search you."

"You will not! I will speak to the king himself about—"

The very picture of ease, Ramass rested a shoulder lazily against the armoire. "Lady Eiryss, let him."

Ramass had managed to dispose of the letter, then. She pretended to waver before setting her chin. "Afterward, you will leave my chambers. And you will *never* touch me again." Not that he'd ever had any real chance with her. A constable was so far beneath her station as to be laughable.

Fin bowed, catching her double meaning. "As you say, lady."

She held out her arms, head tipped regally to the side. Fin's touch was perfunctory. It could be little else with Ramass glaring at him, his sigils glowing silver. Still, her cheeks flamed when his hands brushed under her breasts, and she had to resist the urge to hit him.

Finding nothing, he bowed. "I am very sorry."

He turned to Ramass, who held out his arms with a murderous expression. Eiryss couldn't help but hold her breath when Fin's hands passed over Ramass's middle. But they didn't pause, thank the light. She forced her exhale to come out evenly.

Ramass noticed and cocked a little triumphant grin. Gratitude surged through her. If not for Ramass, she would have faced this alone. How had Ture and Ramass even known this was going to happen?

Fin bowed deeply and motioned for the constables to leave. Another pressed in against the tide. "The men have finished everywhere but the library, sir."

Fin nodded. "I'll join you in a moment." When the room had emptied of all the constables save himself, Fin turned to her. "If you try to leave the city, you will be arrested."

Light save her.

"For what?" Ramass said.

"It's for her own protection," Fin said.

"Protection from what?" she cried.

"Get out, Fin." Ramass had that look about him—the look that said he was about to lose that famous temper of his. Eiryss knew it well. It appeared Fin did too. He retreated without a backward glance.

She made to follow him out, but Ramass held her back. "I never liked him." He poured a glass of water from the pitcher on her table and stirred in some of the headache powder she kept in a jar on her vanity. He held it out to her.

"I've kissed him before," she admitted ruefully as she took it from him. She'd kissed a lot of boys before.

Ramass started. "You have terrible taste in men."

She gulped the medicine down, bitterness sliding down her throat to sit uneasily in her belly. She set the cup down, headed toward the doorway, and shot him a sardonic look over her shoulder. "Clearly. I'm friends with you."

"Yes, but my handsomeness more than makes up for it."

She clung to their banter, grateful for something to center her.

They walked through the magical doorpane that kept out the weather, the feeling akin to passing through liquid glass—cold and wet, with a mineral taste on the back of her tongue. Instantly, a brisk wind blasted Eiryss in the face, along with the rushing sound of the branches. The vault should be up—it was always up in the winter. It kept the trees from freezing.

"Why isn't the vault up?"

"I don't know," Ramass said.

The turbulent lake was already littered with triangular leaves and broken branches. The enormous trees would freeze and suffer wind damage, not to mention all the platforms that would break—they were too brittle to handle so much motion.

Eiryss had been born and raised in the trees of Hanama. Easily shifting her weight to the rolling motion, she crossed the bridge to her mother's room. One level down, all five servants had lined up in the common room. In the branches high above, even their rooms were being searched. Constables carried crates from her father's library toward the main bridge.

They wouldn't find anything. Of that much she was certain. Still, worry shot through her. *Father will be fine,* she chided herself. *Livers can heal, and he's the strongest man I know.*

Her mother's room was in similar disarray as Eiryss's. Eyes red-rimmed as if he'd been crying, Ture stood beside their mother. She sat on her bed in her nightclothes, her canes toppled haphazardly at her feet, as if she'd tried to use them to stand and then collapsed and couldn't be bothered to pick them up again. Her blonde hair was tied in a neat bun to keep it out of her face while she slept. Her pale skin seemed paler than usual. She was somehow smaller—as if something vital inside her had shattered.

Eiryss knelt before her mother and gathered up her too-thin hands. "He'll be all right, Mother. He always is. The king will see the witnesses are lying."

Mother passed a fragile hand down Eiryss's silver-blonde hair and said nothing. Eiryss hadn't seen her like this since her mother, the queen, had died. Eiryss looked up at her brother, silently pleading with him to do something. His eyes, the same warm brown as her own, looked away.

"Mother?" Eiryss's voice wavered.

Mother took a shuddering breath and looked to Ramass. "King Zannok is all right?"

Ramass's hands opened and closed to stave off the temper Eiryss saw building in him. "Yes," he said in a strangled voice.

Her mother breathed out in relief. "Then I'm sure this can all be sorted. A fight between old friends, nothing more."

"I haven't been able to tell you everything," Ture whispered to their mother.

Eiryss sat beside her. "How could it possibly be any worse?"

"My father survived the assassination attempt," Ramass said bitterly. "Princess Ahlyn did not."

Assassination attempt? Eiryss could only stare at him, dumbfounded. Her father had tried to kill the king? And Ahlyn? That was impossible. And Ahlyn couldn't be dead. Eiryss had seen her only a few hours before, dancing with King Dray. And her father—his duty was to protect the king and princess. He would never hurt them.

This all had to be a misunderstanding. "Why didn't you say anything before?" Eiryss cried.

"With the constables coming?" Ramass asked.

He'd only told her about her father after she'd noticed his bloody boots. His discretion had allowed her to keep her dignity in front of the constables. To think instead of being over-whelmed with the horror that now threatened to suffocate her from the inside out.

"She died of poison before midnight," Ture choked.

Eiryss latched on to "poison" like a drowning woman. If they were poisoned, no one could know for certain who had done it.

Ramass wiped furiously at the tears that escaped. He had lost Ahlyn and put aside his grief to keep Eiryss safe. She didn't know how he was standing, let alone protecting her. Numb, Eiryss frowned at him. "Ramass, I'm sorry."

The resolve he wore like a shield wavered, but it did not break. He cleared his throat and met her gaze. "Hagath was poisoned as well. The healers hope she will survive."

Hagath... no!

No wonder Ture was crying. Hagath was to him what Ramass was to Eiryss. Only instead of getting in trouble, Ture and Hagath were always tattling on them.

Accusations of attempted murder was one thing. But to kill the princess and nearly kill Hagath? All of Eiryss's petty jealousies about the princess hit her hard. Ahlyn hadn't earned any of them. Eiryss stood and promptly collapsed back on her seat. By the light, how had this all happened in one night? She bit her fist, using the pain to keep from sobbing.

No. Her father would never *do* this. "Father has every reason to keep Ahlyn safe." She glared at her brother and Ramass. "Someone is lying."

"Where are these witnesses Ramass mentioned?" Mother cried. "I will see them imprisoned for these lies."

Ture choked. "It's us."

Eiryss gasped. "What did you say?"

"Start from the beginning," Mother said coldly.

CHAPTER 3

WITNESS

Ramass and Ture looked at each other, hopelessness and despair plain on their faces. Finally, Ture spoke. "Vicil and I guarded the princess's door. Hagath and Ahlyn were drinking and talking. And then Ramass came."

That didn't make sense. "Hagath would have never left her patient," Eiryss said.

"Ahlyn asked for her," Ramass said. That sounded like Ahlyn. "I arrived shortly after. I wanted to talk to Ahlyn about King Dray's proposal. She started sweating and feeling sick. Luckily, Hagath was there and recognized the symptoms."

"It was the wine," Ture said. "Vicil went for help and—" He broke off, sobbing into his hands.

Not soon enough to save Ahlyn. Eiryss placed her own hand on her throat. She'd drunk the same wine, though clearly her cask hadn't been poisoned or she'd already be dead. Though, if she'd received her secret wish to be the next queen, she would be.

Ramass choked on a sob and then caught hold of himself. "By the time a healer arrived, it was too late. Hagath hadn't consumed as much poison. We think she took the antidote in time."

Eiryss bit harder down on her knuckle. *How had they even known what antidote to give her?* Her mind raced through dozens of poisons, some which could show very similar symptoms and yet need entirely different treatments.

Light, this couldn't be happening. It couldn't. *Charcoal. Charcoal is always a good option. Maybe they gave her charcoal.*

Blood dripped down Eiryss's hand. She'd bit through the skin over her first knuckle. Ramass swore and grabbed a handkerchief, pressing it against the wound. The throbbing was a relief from the anguish inside her.

"Ahlyn was poisoned," Mother said. "Yet you said my husband split his liver."

"The king was called for, same time as the healers," Ture said. "Zannok and Undrad arrived just after the healers left." He opened his mouth as if he would say something else. His face reddened, and he shook his head. He and Ramass exchanged defeated looks.

Eiryss didn't understand the exchange.

"That's when Vicil got back," Ramass finally said. "He stopped at the sight of Undrad, his face going pale. He told us he'd seen Undrad pour something into Ahlyn's wine and replace the cork. Undrad ran. The king tried to stop him. Undrad was wounded in the exchange. We thought him dead at first. The healers said his liver split."

Eiryss heard, but she didn't understand. Couldn't understand. She latched on to something, anything. "There is no way the king could best my father in a fight."

Ramass and Rature exchanged another unreadable glance.

"Ture," Mother said. "Is this true?"

"I saw Father attack the king," he choked out. "As did Vicil and Hagath."

"And me," Ramass said through clenched teeth.

No. Oh, light, no. All the breath left her. Suddenly dizzy, she braced her head in her hands and leaned over her knees. She was not going to pass out. She wasn't the type of girl who passed out.

"Why?" Mother breathed. "Why would Undrad do this?"

"Who else would want to kill our princess and king besides the Alamantians?" Ture asked, eyes pleading.

"Father would never ally himself with the Alamantians," Eiryss cried. There had to be another explanation. There had to!

"Ahlyn refused to marry their king?" Mother asked.

Rature nodded.

Suddenly, Eiryss understood. After Ahlyn had rejected their king, the Alamantians would need someone on the inside. Someone who knew which casks would go to the princess. Someone to poison them.

No. No, this can't be happening.

"A contingent was sent to arrest Dray and his party, but they were already gone, having slipped out right after the party."

"How?" Mother asked.

"The vault's down," Ture said. "They cut through the defensive walls."

The Alamantians had come under the guise of peace. Instead, they'd killed their princess, tried to kill their king, and destroyed the vault that protected them from outside forces. All of it had been orchestrated by King Dray—Dray who had danced with her. Touched her. All the while plotting her people's—her family's—destruction.

She suddenly remembered the dark look her father had worn as he'd watched her dance with Dray. "Dray must have threatened to hurt me... our family." Rage burned through her hurt. He was behind this, and she would kill him for it.

Her mother nodded. Ramass and Ture watched her with hopeless expressions, like they didn't believe her.

She pushed to her feet and paced. "Don't you see? Father would do anything to protect us. He isn't a traitor." Eiryss glared at Ramass, daring him to disagree with her.

Ramass stared at her as if willing it to be true.

She would prove her father's innocence. She would clear her family's name. She knelt before her dearest friend. "Let me talk to him when he wakes. If I could just—"

"Only the healers are allowed to see him," Ramass said gently.

"There has to be a way," Eiryss said.

"Eiryss, fetch my canes," her mother said. Eiryss picked them up, pushed them into her mother's hands, and helped her to her feet, arms around her waist and elbow to steady her. Mother shuffled on numb feet—she'd lost the ability to feel them months ago. She banished the windowpane completely, letting in a stiff breeze, and stared toward the Silver Tree, its light fading against the coming dawn.

Eiryss studied her mother's face, the fine lines at the corners of her eyes and mouth. Her hair had once been thick and glossy, spreading in a silky curtain across her back. Now, it was as thin and brittle as the rest of her. The night before, her mother had helped cinch up the dress around Eiryss's small waist.

"Full lips and wide hips," Mother had teased as she'd bumped her even larger hip against Eiryss's. They'd both laughed, Eiryss covering her crooked teeth with one hand. Her mother had tugged it down. "Never be ashamed of your faults. They make you unique."

"Beauty isn't important, Eiryss." Her father had stepped into the room, looking so handsome in his dress uniform. "Power is—what do I always tell you?"

She held in her sigh. Father read too many dusty tomes on philosophy. "Power is the blade of change—a blade that cuts both ways."

H had kissed her forehead. "And you, my dear, will change the world."

Eiryss blinked hard, twin tears plunging down her cheeks. Last night felt like such a long time ago.

"We must appeal to the king," Mother said. "Beg him access to Undrad."

"Zannok won't see you," Ture said.

Mother's gaze shifted to Eiryss. "He will see her."

Ture wiped his face with that infernal handkerchief he carried with him everywhere. "I'll go."

Mother eyed him, lips pressed into a thin line. "No. Eiryss has always been his favorite."

It was true. When she was a child, Zannok always bought her practice weapons and herbs for her potions. Now she was older, he sent boxes of hair ribbons and gowns for every king's gala. And he always saved the second dance for her, right after Hagath.

Mother squeezed Eiryss's hand. "Beg the king to let us see your father. To spare his life."

Eiryss nodded and hurried to her room, Ramass following her. Standing before the mirror, she undid her falling-out bun and tied back her long waves with one of the king's ribbons. She fetched the cloak the King had sent her for her birthday last year—a fine sapphire blue trimmed in gray fur.

aass watched her from the doorway, one foot cocked against the carved sill. The very picture of ease, though the intense way he watched her said otherwise. "Eiryss, I'm saying this as your friend. Stay here. Where it's safe."

"Don't start."

He sighed in defeat. "You're going to want boots."

She switched out her sandals and pushed past him. He fell in behind her.

As soon as she reached the common room, their butler, Belgrave, sidled in beside her. He was thin and stooped, ears and nose seemingly too big for his wizened frame. Arthritis gnarled his hands and shuffled his steps. "What does Lady Emlon wish I should say to the servants?"

Eiryss didn't know what her mother would want, so she said, "For now, nothing."

"I'm sure that's the best course, Lady Eiryss." His disapproving frown said otherwise.

Belgrave had started the maids on their morning chores at least. Polishing rags in hand, Grenda and Shila stared in the direction of the library, where constables could be seen through the clear doorpane, combing through every book.

"Back to work!" Eiryss snapped. They jumped back to their tasks. "I expect discretion from our servants, Belgrave."

"Of course, lady."

Marinda hustled up the stairs with a few slices of berry-stuffed bread, as well as glasses of hot tea. "I'm sorry, lady, lord. I haven't had time to make breakfast yet."

Ramass took the larger slice. He always did.

Eiryss took her portion gratefully. She doubted she could stomach more. "Thank you, Marinda."

Eiryss and Ramass drank the tea all at once, handed the cups back to the woman, and ate the bread as they crossed to the elaborate entrance where four of Ramass's men waited. Beyond them was the bridge that connected Eiryss's hometree to the others. Made of beautifully woven branches, it swayed with the wind.

They passed through the barrier. The wind slammed into her. She ducked her head, her cloak streaming to the side. All around, lampents curled in tight. Mist from steaming whitecaps stung Eiryss's exposed skin. The water gleamed white, black, and violet—the last from the algae that glowed purple when disturbed.

Winded, wet, and wind-lashed, Eiryss and Ramass finally reached the king's tree a half-mile away. She stepped through the dome in relief and found a drier bit of tunic to wipe the moisture off her face.

"Your cloak, lady?" a servant asked.

She debated—the dripping cloak chilled her, but the reminder of her friendship with the king was too important. "No. Thank you."

The woman bowed away.

The entrance guardsmen watched her through narrowed eyes. "Marshal Ramass, should she be here?"

Marshal. Light. Her father had been stripped of his command. The position had fallen to Ramass, as the son of the king.

Ramass stiffened at the title. "Always." He motioned for his men to wait for them and strode under the arch, Eiryss right on his heels.

Once they were out of earshot, he pulled Eiryss to the side and stared at her, his eyes red-rimmed and bloodshot, and she remembered that he hadn't slept at all. That his sister was gravely ill, and the woman he fancied—he didn't love her; Eiryss was certain he didn't love her—was dead.

The look he gave her—as if he were peering into her soul—made her nervous. "Lady, tell your mother the king wouldn't see you and go back."

He only called her lady when he wanted something from her. "I can't do that."

"h fallout from this night… I'm not sure I can protect you from it."

It wasn't just the king who could topple her family. The Council of Lords and Ladies or Arbor Enderlee could crush them. "Someone is using my father. I'm going to find out who.

I'm going to make them suffer and clear my father and my family. I will make this right."

"What if you can't?" he whispered.

"I have to try." iys pushed past him, taking the walkway that cut through the main branches. She'd never seen so many guardsmen. They stood at each junction and doorpane to the many platforms of the king's tree—all of them opaque and shaped much like the closed lampent blossoms. Their eyes tracked her every step, bodies tense, as if she were a threat. Which was ridiculous. She was months away from her thorns, and her swordsmanship was far inferior to theirs.

You are the granddaughter of a queen, her parents always reminded her. Hierarchy in Valynthia was based on how closely you were related to the last monarch. As Eiryss's grandmother had been queen before Zannok, her family was the third most powerful in the kingdom. They'd been the second before Ahlyn's ascension. Light, she'd resented the girl for it. And now she was dead.

Eiryss lifted her chin, the guards' slight beneath her notice.

She and Ramass passed through the common room with its massive, round dining table and comfortable chairs before the fire. They branched off to the right, crossing a wide branch. Above was a round platform, the beams coming to a point at the center of the roof. Eiryss had always thought the council chambers looked like an elegantly pointed hat.

The vague shapes moving beyond the opaque barrier made it clear the room was teeming—a strange sight this early in the morning. Especially the morning after a party that, for some of them, had only just ended.

The guardsmen posted at the doorpane twitched toward their weapons. One look from Ramass and they stilled, but their bodies did not lose their lethal grace.

Ramass paused at the entrance and ran a freckled hand over his windblown hair. Following his lead, Eiryss smoothed her own hair. She'd always hated crowds. Especially when those crowds were filled with people who would love to see her whole family fail.

"You don't have to do this."

"I do."

They stepped through together.

It appeared every able-bodied member of the Council of Lords and Ladies was present. And unlike their typical arguing, they had fallen silent. Some hadn't even changed from the party the night before, giving them a look of rumpled elegance. The gray military uniforms and raised sigils marked the enchanters. In contrast, the healers wore dusky blue. Maps and documents had been spread across every table, though no one paid them any mind. They were all too busy watching the king, who stood in the back of the room before a soaked, dirty man whose back was to Eiryss.

Wearing the pine green of the enchantresses, Arbor Ender-lee sat beside the king, watching the man with an inscrutable expression.

Servants in gray bustled about the room, pouring cups of strong, hot tea. Someone had even found a brazier, heat shimmering from its surface. The warmth hit Eiryss in a wave—she hadn't realized how chilled she'd become.

It was cold. In Valynthia. The city of eternal summer.

Despite her shivering, Eiryss broke out in a cold sweat at the sight of the council. There wasn't a single member who wouldn't benefit from her family's demise. Together, they held nearly as much power as the king.

Gritting her teeth, Eiryss maneuvered through the press toward him. One after another, the descendants of past monarchs turned gazes of silent disapproval on her.

"I sent enough enchantresses to break through their dome ten times over!" King Zannok said to the dirty man.

"Fifty Alamantians left your entire company unconscious in the dirt," Arbor Enderlee said to the man, her dark eyes flashing. She was unusually young for an Arbor—only in her mid-thirties. Her long dark hair hung in a straight seam down her back and her deep-green Arbor uniform was perfectly pressed. "That's not possible."

The dirty man shook his head. "Their magic—it's stronger, Majesty. Unnaturally strong."

Zannok slapped the table. "I want Dray dead for his crime. No quarter. No negotiation. You will find them and kill every last one of them. His entire company. Now!"

The man bowed and turned. Eiryss recognized him—one of Father's top commanders. He froze at the sight of her, eyes going wide. Regaining his composure, he pushed past without so much as a nod of acknowledgment. Another insult she was forced to ignore.

King Zannok followed the gazes of the council to her. "Eiryss," he breathed. He came around the table and made to put his arms around her.

Ramass stepped between them. "Your armor," he choked.

The king looked down at himself. At the faint gleam of silver visible along the edges of his body. Hugging him would be like hugging a glass statue. She'd never known the king to use magical armor inside his own home. But sure enough, his personal enchantress, Jala, stood at the back of the room, her sigils gleaming through the same diaphanous dress she'd worn last night. Her hair was still in its elegant updo, which Jala somehow made look fetching even though it was falling out. Everything from her sultry gaze to the way she cocked her sensuous hip invited men to stare, which they frequently did.

The king shrugged helplessly and whispered so softly only Eiryss could hear, "I'm so sorry, child."

For nearly killing her father? For the devastation that had been wreaked on her family? "You don't need to apologize to me." He'd done everything he could to spare her family. "None of this is your fault. It's the Alamantians. Dray."

The king stepped back and said to the entire room, "We will make the Alamant pay. I swear to you; Dray will die for what he has done."

From the council all around her, a grumbling snarl rose, more animal than human. Dray had killed their golden princess, and they clearly hated him for it.

"My father is the most honorable and loyal and good man in all of Valynthia." Tears smarted Eiryss's eyes. "He must have been threatened, my king. There is no other explanation."

Zannok stiffened and gestured vaguely to the people in the room. "Continue without me." He led the way toward a side doorpane. When Jala made to follow him, he waved her back. Her lips tightened in disapproval, but she obeyed. On the other side, Zannok leaned toward Ramass. "Were you there in time?"

Ramass blanched. "Not for the library."

King Zannok swore. Out of sight of his council chambers, he leaned heavily on the railing. "Eiryss, I'm sorry. I tried to delay the constables. Tried to intervene on your family's behalf with the council. I don't know what more I could have done. I don't know how things could have turned out differently."

"Is he talking? Did he tell you they threatened his family?"

"If Undrad had been threatened, he would have told me. We would have figured it out." He shook his head. "When he came at me with his blade, his eyes were clear, as was his intent. He would have killed me." The king looked lost. What must it be like to stab a man who was like a brother to you? But she could find no anger for the king. He'd only defended himself.

Ramass choked, his hand over his mouth like he might vomit. Was he reliving that horrible moment?

Light. Father really did this. If all this was true, her own father had nearly killed her best friend's sister. Had killed Ahlyn. The king clearly believed her father wasn't coerced or poisoned, but he wasn't a healer. He didn't have her training. "I'd like to see him myself."

King Zannok wouldn't meet her gaze.

"What has my father said? What was his explanation?"

Zannok shot his son a look full of something she couldn't read. "Nothing. He won't talk to me. He won't talk to anyone."

Someone had betrayed him. He clearly didn't trust anyone. "Perhaps he'll speak with me? Mother?"

"Meeting with him will cast suspicion on your entire family," Zannok said. "Please understand, keeping you from your father is the only way I can protect you."

If her father refused to defend himself... She looked between Ramass and the king. "What will happen to him?"

Zannok stared out at the Silver Tree as if searching for answers. Ramass wouldn't meet her gaze.

Treason. Murder. Her father would die for it. Eiryss wasn't above begging. Not for this. She dropped to her knees, hands spread in supplication. "I beg you. Save him."

"Eiryss, get up," Ramass pleaded, his voice breaking.

King Zannok suddenly looked old. "As long as he doesn't confess, I can keep him alive. That's all I can promise for now."

Ramass reached down and pulled her to her feet. He didn't let go of her hand.

"You're like a daughter to me, Eiryss," Zannok said. "I will help your family in any way I can. Take care of your mother for me?"

Tears in her eyes, she nodded.

Zannok started back the way they'd come, pausing by his son. "I need you beside me, Ramass. See Eiryss is sent safely home. Join me in the council chambers. Take your command."

Her father's command.

Ramass wouldn't meet his father's gaze. "I don't want it."

"Your kingdom needs you," the king said gently.

Ramass's jaw worked, his gaze fierce as the king strode away.

Eiryss held her head in her hand. "Light."

Ramass rubbed his face. "This is so much bigger than us."

He was right. Of course he was. Assassinations, one of them successful, would change everything. "Whatever happened last night... it means war." All her friends. Her dozens of cousins. Her own brother. Ramass. They would all go to war against the Alamant. By the time she finished her training at the academy and received her own thorns, it would all be over. As would any hope she had of revenge.

Eiryss's gaze settled on the blood on Ramass's boots. Her father's blood. She looked back the way they'd come. They had to go back through the council chambers. Through all those people who saw her as the daughter of a murderer and a traitor.

She hated crowds on a good day. But this... Better to get it over with. She released Ramass's hand, clenched her fists, and marched down the corridor and into the council chambers. The men and women inside were clearly waiting for her to reappear. Their gazes were filled with pity or disgust or both. Whispers rose from behind as she passed.

"Poor child. She's lost her father and her station in a single night."

"Don't feel sorry for her. Her father has just catapulted us into a war."

"She's a spoiled, willful child—always has been."

Much as she'd always hated it, she was used to being the center of attention. This was so much worse.

You are the granddaughter of a queen. Her mother's words rang through her.

She forced herself to straighten. Head high, she crossed the room. Only the king did not watch her progress.

"How could her family not know?"

"Who's to say they didn't?"

"I hope they're banished."

Banished. Eiryss faltered.

"Five more steps, Eiryss," Ramass whispered. "Then they won't be able to see."

But Eiryss had to see the truth. Had to face it.

One.

Her father was a traitor.

Two.

The princess was dead.

Three.

Hagath could still die.

Four.

So could her father.

Five.

They could all be banished.

She stepped through the barrier. Servants and guards stopped to stare at her. Everything seemed too big and too small at once. She couldn't catch her breath. Couldn't... Blackness edged the outside of her vision.

Ramass's arm snaked around her side, the smell of him flooding her. "Breathe, Eiryss. Breathe."

The blackness circled in. She sagged against him. Ramass bent down, one hand going under her knees to lift her into his arms. He sat on the rail and shifted his legs to the other side. The mineral taste of the barrier, then they were on the other side. He carried her out of sight behind a branch.

The wind cut through her, and she gasped in a breath.

"No one can see us here." Settling her back on her feet, Ramass held her so tight it hurt. He seemed to need comfort as desperately as she did.

The dark receded, but she could feel it waiting for her just out of sight. "Is there any way you can sneak me into his room?"

"I would if I could."

"Can I at least see Hagath?"

"The healers won't even let me see her."

Hagath must be so afraid and alone. Tears welled in Eiryss's eyes. Her breath hitched.

"Don't, Eiryss. Please."

She dug her thumb into her bitten knuckle, letting the pain chase away the tears.

"My Lord Ramass." Jala's voice was full of sex and venom.

Eiryss and Ramass peeked around the branch. Jala, the king's enchantress, stood waiting, two constables behind her. Someone must have seen Eiryss and Ramass duck in here. Eiryss slipped out of Ramass's arms and turned to discreetly wipe her face. Ramass cleared the emotion from his throat, his hands clenched at his sides.

They both stepped into view.

Jala's blue, kohl-lined eyes made a slow appraisal of Ramass, as if seeing him for the first time. "I suppose it's *Marshal* Ramass now."

Light, the woman chased power like clouds chased wind. And really, she was a decade and a half too old for him anyway. The only reason the woman was the king's enchantress was the sheer power of her magic.

"What is it?" Ramass said stiffly.

Jala rested a hand on her cocked hip. "The king needs you. Now. These men are to escort Lady Eiryss back to her home-tree."

Escort her. Like she was a criminal.

Ramass's mouth tightened, anger flashing in his eyes. "Is that really necessary?"

Jala made a study of her long nails. "You'd have to take that up with the council."

If Eiryss's family was banished from Hanama, the whole council would rise a level in the hierarchy. They would see this as a chance to finish them off.

Ramass turned his back on the men and leaned toward her. "I hid the letter behind your armoire," he whispered, his voice hoarse. "Burn it." He walked backward the way they'd come. "I'll send word as soon as I know anything."

"When you see Hagath, tell her I'll visit when I can."

He nodded before turning. The constables motioned for her to precede them. She had an unaccountable urge to run. Quashing it, she moved past them, back to the colonnade. The constables stayed on her heels—not quite touching her, but making it clear they would. That they would even consider it was unthinkable.

You are the granddaughter of a queen. This time her father's voice echoed through her.

She lifted her chin and kept it high the entire way home. At the archway that separated her home from the bridge, the constables took up residence. There were already two more posted at the docks.

Jaw clenched so tight it hurt, she hurried to her room and peered behind the armoire. No slip of paper hid in the dusty shadows. Bracing herself against one of the posts, she pushed. An unholy squeal sounded as the armoire slid across her floor.

She searched behind it. Under it. Emptied it. Sweating and cold, chest heaving, she slid down the wall and sat on her haunches.

The letter was gone.

CHAPTER

DESPAIR

"Lady Eiryss," Belgrave gasped from outside her door-pane. "Come quickly."

Pushing herself to her feet, Eiryss hurried from her chamber to find him panting hard, one arthritic hand over his chest. He was too old to be rushing about delivering messages. Where were the maids?

"What now?" she asked.

"Your mother has had a fit."

How many times had Eiryss heard those words over her lifetime? A hundred? Two? And yet it always set her heart to racing.

Eiryss swore and ran past him toward her mother's chambers. "How long ago?"

"I tried to intercept you when you arrived, lady," he called after her. "I'm sorry."

"Where are the maids?" Eiryss pushed through her mother's dome before Belgrave could answer. Her mother lay crumpled on the floor. The air smelled sharply of urine.

Ture paced beside her, looking helpless. "Father?"

"As long as he doesn't confess, Zannok thinks he can keep him alive." Ture had seen their father attack the king? Perhaps he'd noticed something off about their father. "Did Father seem sick to you?"

"No." Ture's voice came out strangled.

Fighting the despair welling inside her, Eiryss knelt next to her mother, who was fast asleep in her wet clothes. "Why hasn't she been changed and put to bed?"

Ture stared at his empty hands. "Grenda and Shila are gone."

"What do you mean they're gone?"

Belgrave asked for entrance.

"Come," she called.

"I tried to tell you, lady," he wheezed. "The two serving girls have gone."

"Gone where?" she demanded.

"They have abandoned us," Ture said.

How dare they! Had they not already left, she would have them flogged. Eiryss took a steadying breath. She was a healer in training. She'd done this hundreds of times. "Ture, help me change her. Belgrave, fetch water and soap from Mother's bathing chamber."

Belgrave shuffled quickly away.

Ture looked away. "She's my mother."

Eiryss tugged down her mother's trousers. "Stop being utterly useless."

He abruptly headed for the door. "The king has already sent for me. I'm to report to his hometree. I was just waiting for you to see to Mother."

Eiryss gaped at him. "Sent for you? Why?"

He wrapped his cloak around his shoulders. "I'm to captain one of his armies."

"What?" she said in disbelief.

He looked hurt. And guilty. "I am not completely useless."

She wasn't allowed to even leave the city, and yet the council had approved her brother's promotion to captain an army? It didn't make sense... unless Ture had found a way to prove his loyalty without question.

She stilled, realization washing over her in a cold wave. Her father was the best fighter in all Valynthia. Her brother was a close second. "You stabbed Father." It had never been the king. All along, it had been Rature.

Ture paused before the doorpane, his shoulders slumped. "I did what I had to."

She lunged at him. He half-turned, and she landed a punch to his jaw that sent him reeling. Sharp pain bolted through her wrist. She swung again. He deflected her, stepped into her guard, whipped her around, and pinned her against his chest.

"I did it for our family! To save us!" He was crying again.

How dare he cry! Gripping his arms tight, she leveraged herself up and kicked him with her heels. "He's our father!"

He dropped them both to the ground, his legs wrapping around hers. Her father was marshal—had been marshal. He'd taught her to fight, but Ture had fifty pounds of muscle on her and a lot more training.

"What would you have had me do?" he whispered. "What else could I have done?"

She head-butted him. His arm came around her neck. She tried to pin her chin to her chest, but he leveraged her head up and squeezed her windpipe. "Please don't tell Mother."

She couldn't answer. Grayness closed in on her. She tried to buck and twist her hips. Tried to shove an arm between them. But she couldn't keep her head upright. It slumped slowly backward, the blackness consuming her.

"I'm sorry," he whispered. "Light, Eiryss, I'm so sorry."

Eiryss opened her eyes to find her face mashed into a puddle of her own drool. Her head ached fiercely. Things slowly came into focus, the color returning one shade at a time.

Ture was gone.

"Lady?" Belgrave set down the basin of water and hurried toward her. She must not have been out longer than a minute or two. He hovered anxiously—if he got down on the floor, he couldn't get up again. "Oh, tell me you haven't started having fits like your mother?"

He hadn't seen anything. His hearing must really be bad if he hadn't heard it either. She coughed, wiped her mouth with the back of her sleeve, and pushed herself up. What had just happened… ? She couldn't deal with it, not on top of everything else. She dug her thumb into her injured knuckle, letting the pain focus her.

All of this was only temporary. As soon as she cleared her father's name, she would put the council in its place. She'd hire new maids—and make sure no one ever employed the old ones. People might look at her family with suspicion, but that wouldn't last. Her father was stronger than their suspicion.

Belgrave reached out to steady her. Instead, she ended up steadying him.

"I'm fine, Belgrave. Don't tell Mother." He opened his mouth to say something. She cut him off. "Send the boy in to help me lift her." He wasn't much of a boy. Fifteen and enormous. He fished for their family, tended to the tree, and carried Mother when she couldn't manage on her own. Eiryss could never remember his name.

"Turbill is gone, lady."

Eiryss swore. Belgrave's mouth tightened in disapproval. He should be used to her cursing by now. Eiryss rubbed her throbbing forehead. She added hiring a new boy—one with an easy to remember name—to her list of things she needed to accomplish. "First, mix me some headache powder—you take some too. Then send Marinda in."

He limped out the door. Eiryss fetched the basin, soap, and cloth Belgrave had brought. Her mother woke when she started tugging on her clothes. She looked at Eiryss with bleary, uncomprehending eyes. She wouldn't remember that her son had confessed to stabbing her husband. Or that her daughter had attacked her son. Or that her son had choked Eiryss into unconsciousness.

Ture had asked Eiryss not to tell Mother. She might find out sooner or later. But looking at her mother now… Perhaps later was better.

Or never.

Eiryss hummed as she worked—she found it soothed her patients. Marinda arrived in time to help dress Mother in a soft nightdress. They helped her stumble to the bed, where she immediately fell asleep.

Marinda had brought Eiryss a late lunch, which she had little appetite for. She nibbled at the edges of it and looked around the disaster the constables had left behind. She spent the rest of the day putting the room back to rights. Her mother woke long enough to eat some dinner and use the privy before falling back in bed. Eiryss curled around her softness. Only then did she notice her mother's speaker sigil—stars peeking out between leaves and branches—gleaming silver on her upper arm.

Barrier magic had eight sigils, wielded by women in Valynthia and men in the Alamant. Weapons magic had two sigils and was wielded by men in Valynthia and women in the Alamant. Ten basic sigils and ten basic notes. But there were other sigils, just as there were sharps and flats. Seers and binders, bearers and speakers for the dead, dreamers and emotives, just to name a few.

Her mother was a speaker for the dead—the Silver Tree took the memories of the dead and gave them back through the speakers. Most were random recollections of those long since passed—a woman singing as she'd washed dishes, a boy feeding fish, an old man dancing with his granddaughter. Rarely were they of important events. The Silver Tree didn't seem to think a pivotal battle to be as important as the brush of a mother's hands through her young son's hair.

Eiryss waited, watching her mother's eyes move behind her lids as she experienced a memory of the dead. She knew when the vision had ended because the silver faded along with the slight buzz that always accompanied an open sigil.

Her mother blinked, her focus sharp. But that focus wasn't on the here and now. "What did you see?" Eiryss prompted.

Her mother shuddered, and Eiryss knew.

There were other memories. Darker ones. Memories of murder and betrayal and abuse. They didn't come often, but they were devastating when they did.

Mother lifted her hands and covered her eyes. "I saw an old, broken woman in her bed. Her son covered her face with a pillow and suffocated her."

Like her brother had killed their father. Bile rose in Eiryss's throat. Why did the Silver Tree force such evil upon her sweet mother? "Recently?"

Mother shook her head. "Judging by the style of clothing, it was long ago."

Above, the storm broke, raging against the panes and thrashing the tree beneath them.

Eiryss woke the next morning drenched in her mother's urine. Swallowing her curses, she padded to the bathroom and cleaned up. The branch dipped and swayed, the motioned making her nauseous. She hadn't slept much the night before and her head ached. Dressing in one of her mother's tunics, she mixed more awful pain powder in lukewarm water and took a bitter swallow.

She glanced at herself in the mirror and couldn't look away. She was not beautiful—she'd heard it whispered enough when they thought she couldn't hear to know it was true. Her feet were too large, as were her hips and legs. Her breasts were too small. Her face was fine enough—symmetrical and delicate—until she spoke and revealed her crooked teeth. Her blonde hair would have been lovely—it was thick with a gentle wave—if not for the streaks of silver.

With a huff, she tipped the mirror up. *Never stopped me from getting what I want.* Power had always more than made up for anything she might lack. But if that power was gone… what exactly did she have to offer?

Muttering, she fetched Marinda to help her bathe Mother again.

Mother had a hard time waking. "It wasn't a nightmare?" she breathed. "Your father…"

"No." Eiryss cleared the rasp from her throat. "It was real."

Her mother's eyes slipped closed, tears leaking out the corners. "Were you successful with the king? Where's Ture?"

At the mention of her brother, Eiryss rubbed her throat. *Ture probably has more bruises than me,* she thought in satisfaction. "The king won't let us see Father. He thinks it's for our own good. To keep us above suspicion." She explained what happened, leaving out that Ture had stabbed Father. She still couldn't find the words to tell Mother. At least not until she was better.

A gust of wind hit their hometree. The whole platform rocked, and one of the vases shattered, shards scattering across the room. Eiryss went to clean it up and paused to look toward the healing tree three trees over. Rain lashed against the panels, which made them ripple like water and obscure her view. Lightning streaked across the violent sky. The whole tree dipped and swayed beneath them like a boat in a stormy sea.

"They should have had the vault up by now," Eiryss said.

She felt her mother's gaze on her. "Have you slept? Eaten?"

Eiryss rubbed her dry eyes. "Some."

Sighing, Mother struggled to push herself up to sitting. "Send in the maids."

Eiryss helped her. "They're gone. The boy as well." How had she forgotten his name again?

"What?"

Eiryss shrugged helplessly. "After we clear Father's name, we'll hire new servants. Better servants." She just had to find a way to prove he'd been coerced. After all, if they could damage the vault so thoroughly, what might they have done to Eiryss or her family?

Her mother's mouth tightened. "Marinda? Belgrave?"

"Still here. But there are four constables, two at the bridge and two at the dock."

"The council's doing?" Mother asked.

Eiryss nodded.

Mother's face went white with fury at the insult. "You must go to the Arbor."

"What can Enderlee do?"

"The healing tree is under her domain, is it not?"

Eiryss straightened. "You think she could grant me access to Father?"

"If anyone can, it's her. And she can make sure no one knows you were there. That way our family remains above suspicion and we can speak with your father."

Eiryss hurried to pull on a pair of borrowed trousers.

"Eat something first," Mother said. "Put on your novice robes and braid your hair. Send Marinda in to help me."

Eiryss would convince the Arbor to let her see her father. He would tell her what she needed to know to clear his name. This entire nightmare would end. She hustled for the door.

"Eiryss," Mother called. "You are descended from five lines of monarchs. Your grandmother was a queen. Never forget it."

Her grandmother had ruled for an unprecedented fifty-six years. Eiryss couldn't have been more than five, but she still remembered the ceremony where her grandmother had handed over the power of the kingdom to Zannok.

Eiryss straightened to her full height and nodded. Cool seeped from the floorboards as she made her way from her mother's room. Hanama was not made for cold—the vault had always protected them before.

From a heap on the bottom of her armoire, Eiryss pulled out the old woolen coat she used when she left the protection of the vaulted city in winter—the last time had been during winter break when she had gone on sleigh rides with Hagath, Ramass, and Ture. Hay was still stuck in her gloves. She pulled them over her numb hands and tugged on her boots. In the kitchen, she forced down a small breakfast of boiled lallo eggs and lake greens.

At the archway, she eyed the two constables, simultaneously relieved and uneasy that she didn't know them. She almost asked if they would try to impede her. But someone of her rank didn't dignify their insulting presence by asking questions.

She strode past them, hoping they wouldn't stop her. Thankfully, they fell into line behind her as she headed toward the archway. She decided to pretend they were hired to guard her as she left the protection of her hometree. She ducked against the wind, her body naturally adjusting to the sway of the bridges.

Her feet traveled the well-worn path to the Enchantress Academy, where she'd been a student since her tenth year. Nearer the academy, all the merchant stalls that catered to the students were empty—a few had even broken from their tethers to block the bridge. Muttering about the incompetence of the vendors and the city's servants, Eiryss stepped over and around the rubble toward the nearly opaque doorpane, which meant the domes had been strengthened against the storm.

Nearly soaked, she stepped through the vaulted archway, her ears feeling stuffed. She popped them and hung her coat next to a brazier. She couldn't remember ever seeing a brazier inside the academy—they must have brought them in from the manors beyond the vault.

Rubbing her arms against the chill, she entered the ring of eight trees, the branches woven seamlessly together. After seven years, the beauty of the winged arches and shimmering panels was lost to her. Her first four years as a student, she'd worked on perfecting basic enchantress theory and practice. The last three, she'd specialized as a healer's novice. As a noblewoman, she was expected to take basic swordplay, though she'd only taken the required courses. Her father had taught her after all.

She headed toward the library, from which the Arbor's office branched off. The constables trailed behind. For a place usually bustling with activity, Eiryss didn't see a single enchantress or novice about. Even the towering library was empty. Perhaps they were in mourning for Ahlyn?

"Eiryss?" Head Mistress Tria came from the Arbor's wing. She was a rotund woman with short, curly gray hair and pale blue eyes. Those eyes shifted between the constables and Eiryss. "What are you doing here?"

Eiryss inclined her head in a show of respect. "I've come to speak with Arbor Enderlee."

The constables and Eiryss jumped out of her way as the older woman cut right through the center of them. "We have a bit of a problem on our hands, Eiryss. Go home."

Eiryss hurried to catch up. For a short woman, Tria moved fast. "I must speak with her, Mistress."

"That is not possible."

Eiryss would see her father. She would clear his name. Restore her family's honor. "Mistress, you taught my parents. You've overseen my education for years. You know we're not traitors."

Tria sighed. "It's not a question of your loyalty, lady. I'm heading to the Silver Tree. Princess Ahlyn is laid out in state and all the enchantresses and novices are there."

All the enchantresses and novices except for Eiryss. "Why was I not informed?"

Tria frowned, the deep lines bracketing her mouth severe. "You know why."

Eiryss winced. If she accompanied Tria, she would have to face everyone. All her classmates and teachers, as well as every enchantress. But her father was gravely injured. If he died, she'd never had a chance to say goodbye. Never find out why he had done this monstrous thing. Never clear his name—their name.

"You can't actually stop me," Eiryss said softly. She had learned early on not to pull rank with her teachers. They had ways of making her pay for it—extra assignments, poor grades, complaints about her willfulness to her parents. Power was a blade that cut both ways, as her father always said. Now was a good time to risk wielding it.

Tria stiffened, clearly affronted. "This is not the time, Lady Eiryss. And the lake is not something you want to cross without good reason." The only way to reach the Silver Tree was by boat; bridges were not allowed anywhere near it.

"Then why did you cross it?" She was sopping wet—she'd come from the Silver Tree.

In answer, Tria held up the Arbor Flute—the most powerful flute ever made. Eiryss had only ever seen it for the first time at Ahlyn's coronation. Something was very wrong if they were bringing it out now.

"I'm coming," Eiryss said.

Tria's jowls trembled as the woman worked her jaw. "Foolish, entitled girl."

At the docks, one of the bigger boats waited for Tria, enchantress guards in deep green tunics inside. The lake's swells slammed into the dome with a slap before slowly filtering through.

One of them helped Tria climb inside the rolling boat. "Where's your coat, child?"

She hopped in after Tria. "I'll be fine, Mistress."

One of the constables moved to step into the boat. "There isn't room," Tria pointed out. "Give me your coat. Wait for Eiryss at her home. I'll see she makes it there safely."

"Mistress," one of the men said. "We are not to let the girl out of our sight."

Tria snapped her fingers. "She's not going to escape into the wilds, boy. Coat. Now."

Eiryss swallowed her snicker. No one disobeyed Tria after she snapped her fingers.

The men grumbled, but one of them gave her his coat. Eiryss pulled it on—the musk of a strange man enveloping her— and rolled up the sleeves so she could work a paddle.

"Thank you, Mistress."

"Pull the hood over your face. It's better if no one sees you."

Obeying, Eiryss glanced back at the dock. The constables were already headed back to the main level. She hoped they remembered to grab her coat on their way back.

The boat rolled as they left the protection of the dome to the rough waters beyond. They strained against their oars as the boat mounted a swell. Eiryss braced her feet and paddled furiously as they came to a near standstill at the top before rushing down.

Heart in her throat, she gritted her teeth and refused to squeal. They rushed up the other side, Eiryss stomach clenched tight. It was foolish that bridges weren't allowed to be built to the Silver Tree! When her father was back in power, she'd insist the oversight be remedied.

"Why haven't you put up the vault?" she cried over the storm.

"The magic," Tria said, her gaze fixed on the Silver Tree. "Something's wrong."

CHAPTER 5

SILVER TREE

Music poured down from above. The enchantresses were finally raising the vault. Eiryss staggered from the still heaving boat, which pitched and rolled beneath her. She headed up the dock after Tria and the enchantress guards. Violent water slammed into the dome and seeped past, flooding up to her waist and pushing her toward the edge of the pier.

"Help her, or you'll be fishing her out of the lake," Tria cried to the guards.

Hands gripped Eiryss on either side. Holding onto each other for balance, the three of them reeled onto the flooded roots. The wave retreated, undercutting Eiryss's feet and trying to drag her under. To force her away from her purpose.

All her life, her father had supported her. Now it was her turn to return the favor. She wouldn't fail. Not when she was this close. She dug in, refusing to be swept away. The heavier guard's grips tightened. The pull of the water lessened. She managed to catch her balance when the guard to her left slipped. She braced herself, hauling him back up. Together, they sloshed up the stairs. They were nearly to the enormous archway before they were free of water.

The guardsmen immediately released her.

"Thank you." Careful of the stingers, Eiryss pulled a sloppy, gleaming tenterfish off her borrowed coat and tossed it back into the lake.

They murmured something before going back to fetch Tria, whose hair was plastered to her head. The men waited for the wave to retreat before one of them threw Tria over his shoulder and ran for it.

The man set her down next to Eiryss. She staggered back, panting.

He rested his hand on her arms to steady her. "You all right, mistress?"

She tried to pat his shoulder and only managed to reach his upper arm. "Yes, my boy. Thank you."

He stepped back, eyeing Eiryss before moving on ahead of them.

"I'm not making that trek again." Tria wrung out her tunic. "I don't care if I have to sleep in the Silver Tree." Boots sloshing, she marched past Eiryss, who lurched behind her, her sea legs not adjusting well to the stillness at the base of the Silver Tree.

Stairs wound up the enormous trunk that sparkled like frost in early morning light. Deep inside the tree, shapes shifted—the souls of their ancestors. Soaked and shivering, Eiryss braced herself against the tree and sent up a prayer to her grandmother to watch over her. To help her save her father. Was it just Eiryss's imagination, or did the shapes move in response?

The music grew louder, echoing through the dome. At the top of the steps was another grand archway leading to the main platform, where the branches splayed out, creating a natural bowl shape that Eiryss had danced across the night before.

Now, masses of enchantresses and enchanters spilled out of the archway, down the steps, and filled the boughs like overripe fruit. It should only take around a hundred or so to raise the vault. Yet Eiryss guessed every enchantress inside Valynthia had been called upon.

Not wanting to be recognized, Eiryss pulled the hood down low. The guards forced their way through the press of bodies. Eiryss gripped the back of Tria's coat so as not to be left behind.

Thankfully, the crowd was too intent on the Arbor standing atop the dais to pay much attention to Eiryss. The massive emerald that hung from her mantle of office swung above her chest as she led the combined music.

Finally, Eiryss and Tria reached the stone-faced sentinels surrounding the front. They parted before Mistress Tria. Eiryss wasn't sure whether to be relieved or disappointed that Kit wasn't on duty—she could use a friendly face. But then, what if his face wasn't friendly anymore?

"Stay here," Tria said before climbing the steps.

As soon as she moved out of the way, Eiryss caught sight of Ahlyn lying in state at the base of the font. She wore a royal-black gown, a black blanket crusted with shadow diamonds and night opals clutched in her lifeless hands. Lampent flowers had been tucked all around her. A blanket had been rolled beneath her chin to keep her mouth from falling open. And her face... Whatever had made her Ahlyn was gone, leaving behind a waxy shell.

She was clearly dead. Eiryss had known, but seeing it... She suddenly remembered the day Arbor Enderlee had proclaimed that the Silver Tree had chosen Ahlyn to carry the monarch sigil—not a seed, but a graft of the Silver Tree himself. The next day, Ahlyn had received her monarch sigil, seeing her for the first time in royal black, a train of rippling lampent flowers trailing behind her.

The powerful of Valynthia had parted as Ahlyn had approached the font. Enderlee had handed her a chalice of the sap that collected in the basin. She drank.

She'd been radiant as she'd pressed her palm into the wicked sharp tip of the conduit thorn. Her blood had shifted through the font, settling in a thorn that had turned dark with her blood. Her thorn—a piece of the Silver Tree that would accompany her for the rest of her life. She'd broken it off—the snap loud in the utter silence. She'd shifted her hair over her shoulder and turned her back to Arbor Enderlee, who'd slipped the sharp point into the skin between her shoulder blades, a single bead of blood cutting across her perfect, pale skin and disappearing into the fabric of her dress.

Thorns usually took days—even weeks—to grow to a full-sized sigil. But Enderlee took the Arbor Flute—the most powerful flute to have ever been made—and played an impossibly complex song. The thorn instantly took root, growing just beneath Ahlyn's skin. One branch at a time, a rendering of the Silver Tree flared to life across her back. She hadn't winced at the pain. Instead, she'd thrown her head back as if enraptured.

Even with the flute, the sigil should have only grown a few finger widths, but by the time Enderlee had finished, it was half grown. Though the music had ended, Ahlyn continued swaying to music only she could hear—the song of the Silver Tree.

Expression unreadable, King Zannok had taken the mantle from Ahlyn's mother and slipped it over the girl's head, the jewels at the peaks swinging with motion. Then Ahlyn had opened her eyes—the blue swallowed up by black—and looked out over the crowd, Eiryss had dropped to her knees with the rest of them, bowing before their new princess.

Just like that, Eiryss was less. Less powerful, less important, less adored. She had been jealous of Ahlyn from the start. Oh, she'd masked it well enough, but Eiryss knew what had been in her heart. She'd resented the girl's intrusive friendship with Hagath and Ramass. Resented her for forcing Eiryss's family down a level in the hierarchy. Resented her beauty and power.

Ahlyn hadn't deserved any of it.

Even now, Eiryss didn't grieve for the girl or her family but for herself. Even Eiryss's grief was selfish. She hunched over and gasped for breath; glad no one could hear her choked sobs over the music. She couldn't do this. Not here. She bit into her knuckle. Blood welled, out of sight beneath the bandages. The pain cut through her, drowning out her despair.

Having brought herself under control, Eiryss was careful to avoid looking at the princess again.

From the inside of her coat, Tria pulled out the case for the Arbor Flute. Made from the sacred wood of the Silver Tree, it had been carved by a master centuries ago and was usually only used to find the next monarch and in a royal embedding ceremony.

Yet they had brought it out today.

Sigils gave an enchanter or enchantress magic, but the musical instruments carved from the sacred tree allowed the enchantress to communicate with their sigils to weave complex enchantments. The Silver Tree was male, so weapons magic went to the men and barrier magic went to the women. It was the opposite in the Alamant, as their tree was female.

Though theories abounded, no one really knew why. It just was.

Enderlee opened the case and removed the flute, the stars carved into the wood glittering with inset gems. From the platform all the way up into the high boughs, thousands of enchantresses and enchanters stilled, their silver sigils gleaming to life. She pressed it to her lips.

The moment Tria moved, enchanters and enchantresses lit their sigils—an enchantment this large required both male and female magic. The melody directed the magic, weaving the gleaming streamers into a complex sphere. Tria smoothed loose threads and fixed mistakes. It was a rare gift—the ability to weave magic with one's hands.

The music resonated like a massive mountain capped in enormous trees. Rivers swift and wide cut through. Impenetrable, massive, unassailable.

When Tria was satisfied, she made a throwing motion. The vault expanded, encompassing the Silver Tree and pushing farther into the violet and black lake. Eiryss had seen this many times, and still, awe filled her. This was the unity and majesty of her people. This was Valynthia.

But something went wrong. Cracks appeared in the vault. Cracks through which the storm seeped through. As one, the enchantresses flinched, as though something had collectively pained them. The vault shattered with a sound like thunder, and broken magic rained like fallen stars that guttered to silver ash before blowing away on the stiff wind. Enchantresses and enchanters alike gasped or gaped or cursed. The woman next to Eiryss began to cry.

"Something's wrong with the magic," Tria had said.

Eiryss suddenly understood. This was not the first time the enchantment had broken. Judging by the numbers of enchantresses or enchanters, it wasn't the first time by a long shot.

Light, how could the magic fail? And on the eve of war.

Mistress Tria said something to Enderlee, who stiffened and scanned the crowd, gaze landing on Eiryss. She called to one of her enchantress guards, said something, then disappeared down the steps on the other side of the dais.

The female guard ordered the sentinels before Eiryss to let her through. They turned sideways. She slipped between them. They turned back, shoulders touching, sealing her in. She followed the guard around the altar, bypassing the dais and font, with its hundreds of thorns glistening razor sharp.

Tria and Enderlee waited on the other side. Out of view of most of the enchantresses. Hopefully, those in the high boughs wouldn't be able to make out faces.

Arbor Enderlee didn't even wait for Eiryss to reach her before speaking, "Your father hasn't said a word since he came to us. Can you get him to explain what he's done to the magic?"

Eiryss's eyes fluttered shut. He was still alive—she hadn't realized how terrified she'd been that he would pass without her even knowing. Then Enderlee's other words caught up with her. But she couldn't make sense of them. "What?"

Arbor Enderlee gestured around them. "Our magic is broken, Eiryss. Has been since the assassination."

Light. The vault. And the fifty Alamantians with their treacherous king who'd inexplicably escaped the much stronger numbers King Zannok had sent after them. "You think my father had something to do with this?" *Impossible!*

The woman's gaze hardened. "The day after your father attempts to assassinate our most powerful magic wielders, the Alamant gathers her armies and our magic fails. So yes, I think your father had something to do with it. At the very least, he knows something."

Eiryss gripped her injured hand and squeezed. The pain centered her. Focused her. "Why haven't we been called in to speak with him before now?"

"The king won't allow it. He's too busy trying to protect you."

She gathered herself. "Is my father going to live?"

"No one's told you anything?"

Lips pressed in a thin line, Eiryss shook her head.

"Barring infection, I believe Undrad will make a full recovery."

He was going to live. And as long as he lived, he would see this whole mess put to rights. Just as soon as he was well. But until then, it was up to Eiryss.

The Arbor stepped closer, her voice dropping. "The council is demanding the truth be tortured out of your father. The king is fighting them with everything he has, but I'm not sure it's a battle he can win."

Tortured. In his weakened state... "He wouldn't survive it." Eiryss wavered on her feet, her hand gripping Enderlee's robes to keep from sinking to the floor.

Enderlee's hands steadied her. "Undrad is on the northern side, near the middle. One of the roof panels will be passable tonight. If you're caught, I'll deny all involvement."

Grim determination rushed through Eiryss. She could not fail. Not now. "Thank you, Arbor."

Unnamed guilt flashed in the other woman's eyes. "I'll see someone sends you updates on your father's health. Now go home before you start a riot." She started back up the stairs.

One of the enchantress guards appeared at Eiryss's shoulder and gestured for her to follow. She did, casting one last look at Ahlyn's body. Tears welled in her eyes. "I'm sorry," she whispered, her words swallowed by the swelling of music.

CHAPTER

TEMPER

Arms shaky with exhaustion, Eiryss pushed herself from the boat onto the king's pier. Enderlee had told her to go home, but thanks to Tria, Eiryss had shaken the constables. She needed to take this opportunity to tell Ramass about the missing letter and solicit his help sneaking into her father's sick room. And she wanted to see Hagath.

Thankfully, the lake had settled, so water didn't batter her legs—she wasn't sure she had the strength to fight another current. She looked back at the enchantress guards who'd brought her back. "I'll take the bridges."

The two men nodded and pushed back into the lake. The king's guards blocked her entrance from the dock to the tree. She drew up in shock at their daring. "I need to see Ramass." He was the only one she could trust to help her break into her father's room.

"I'm sorry, lady, none besides the council and Arbor are presently permitted."

Anger and disbelief formed a maelstrom inside her. "Do you know who I am?" Even before the words had fully left her mouth, she realized that might be the exact reason she'd been barred.

"No one is permitted," the other guard repeated.

Steeling herself, she glared at both. "Is Ramass here? Does he know you won't let me in?"

"He's in meetings, lady."

This was more important than any meeting. "Ramass!" she called into the boughs. "Your guards are being ridiculous! Get down here and let me up."

From above, dozens of eyes peered down at her—mostly servants and guards. Eiryss tapped her foot to show them she wasn't uneasy. Ramass didn't answer.

One of the guards crowded her. "Since your escort has gone, we will see you to the bridges."

"Ramass!" she called louder than before.

From the council chambers, Ramass peered down at her, rolled his eyes, crossed the boughs, and dropped down on a pulley rope to about ten feet away. He'd exchanged his royal black for the silver uniform of the enchanter elite. His mantle proclaimed him marshal—her father's mantle. At the sight, something cracked inside her, breaking open and bleeding in a puddle around her feet.

He gave her an exasperated look before facing the guards. "Let her pass."

"My orders—" began the taller of the two.

"I said," Ramass barked. He let out a breath and said in a calmer voice, "Let her pass. As always, Lady Eiryss is welcome in my home."

"But, sir—" began the shorter.

Ramass's sigils gleamed silver. "I won't say it again."

He was about to lose that famous temper of his. She gave him the look that said he'd better calm down, but he was too busy staring down the guards to notice.

The two men exchanged uneasy glances. Eiryss huffed, one eyebrow raised imperiously. The guards parted, and she marched between them. Ramass released his magic, the silver sigils fading.

"My father," she said low so that guards wouldn't hear. "Did you know they mean to torture him?"

Looking suddenly exhausted, he passed a hand down his face. "We have been fighting the council about it all morning."

Light. She had to stop this. "You have to get me in to speak with my father."

"It's taking everything we have just to keep them from shoving hot knives up his fingernails."

Eiryss gasped and hunched over, the words a blow to her stomach. "Then we sneak in."

Ramass gripped both her arms, his gaze intense. "Try anything, and you'll end up in prison with him! Swear to me, swear upon his life and mine, that you will let me take care of this." His grip hurt. She tried to squirm away. He squeezed her harder. "Swear it!"

"I swear!" she shot back, wounded that he'd opposed her.

Ramass stared into her eyes, as if trying to see the lie. He released her and stepped back, casting a glance at the guards who were trying very hard to watch them without appearing to watch them. "Did you burn the letter?" he murmured under his breath.

She rubbed her sore arms. "It wasn't there."

"Did you look under? Because—"

"I looked everywhere."

He rubbed his eyes. "I'll see what I can find out." He gripped the rope as if to go up.

She glanced past him, to Hagath's room. It was hours until dark and her chance to sneak into her father's room. She had time to visit her friend. "Hagath. I want to see her."

He made a sound low in his throat. "I don't have time for this."

He'd endured an assassination, attempted assassination, and the death of a woman he'd fancied himself in love with. Judging from his bloodshot eyes, he'd slept even less than she had. Because of all this, she decided not to kill him. Yet.

"Ramass," she said in warning.

He made an exasperated sound. "King Dray made it into the Alamant. His forces attacked Lias Lamoren this morning. Our defenses are floundering."

As marshal, the weight of the entire war now lay on Ramass's shoulders. She shifted her weight uncomfortably. "She's all alone."

With a sigh, he motioned for her to get on.

She stepped into the loop and gripped the rope.

"Up!" Ramass called.

The counterweight dropped, sending them shooting up and leaving Eiryss's stomach far behind. They raced toward the boughs, the color and shape of the leaves coming into focus. They stopped abruptly and spun aimlessly as the servant who worked the system hooked the rope.

Hagath's wing was just to the left. At the sight, worry for her friend exploded inside her. Eiryss stepped off first and took off at a run. Two guards stood before Hagath's chambers.

One held out a hand. "Lady."

She was too close to stop now. And they wouldn't dare touch her. She tried to slip past them. One of them pushed her. She stumbled back. Ramass caught her. The seething, hateful looks the men gave her…

"How dare you touch Lady Eiryss!" Ramass shifted her to the side and shoved the guard into the post, pinning him there with an arm across his throat.

Eiryss's mouth fell open. Ramass losing his temper usually resulted in shouting. Never violence.

The man glared at Ramass indignantly. "Lady Hagath is too sick to be disturbed."

A petite older enchantress in healer blue stepped from the room, her gaze lighting on Ramass. "What is going on?"

Ramass's magic sword flickered in and out of being in his hand as he struggled to rein in his temper.

"I know you're going through a lot," Eiryss said through gritted teeth. "But this is not the way to deal with it. Take it to the training platform."

"If you wake my patient," the enchantress said in a firm voice, "You'll have to answer to me."

It was not an idle threat. Enchantresses were the law when it came to their patients.

Eiryss grabbed Ramass's arm and tried to drag him away. He wouldn't budge, blast him. Eiryss punched his arm. He turned to her, his expression full of rage. Him and his blasted temper.

"Back. Down," Eiryss said through gritted teeth.

For a moment, she worried he wouldn't. Finally, he let out a long breath and released the guard.

The healer relaxed. "She's resting."

"I could sit—" Eiryss began.

"She's too sick, lady," the healer said firmly. "She needs absolute quiet."

"Is she still vomiting blood?" Ramass asked the healer.

Blood? Oh, light. Why didn't he tell me Hagath was so bad?

The enchantress softened. "Not for an hour or so."

"Is she going to make it?" Eiryss said in an impossibly small voice. She couldn't bear to lose Hagath too.

"I don't know." She shot Ramass a withering look. "Both of you need to leave. Now."

Ramass turned on his heel and stalked away. Eiryss followed him to a training platform in the lower trunk. Just far enough away to make an epic splash was the turbulent lake. He stripped his tunic. His body was heavy with muscle, freckles thick where sun directly touched him and lighter where it glanced off his skin. The sigils gleamed, silvery thorns and leaves like blades that circled both his wrists halfway to his elbows. Magic filled his palms with his sword and banded his shield to his arm.

"Ramass."

He turned, light catching the red-gold hair of his chest. Light, he was beautiful. And he was moments from losing his tightly held control.

She stepped forward, tracing her fingers gently across the edge of his shield—the buzz of magic dancing across her sensitive fingertips. It was like stroking glass and light. Like holding a lightning bolt.

He shivered—all magic wielders could feel touch through their magic. "She's going to be all right."

His weapons flickered and died under her hands—this is the closest she ever came to magic of her own, and her body ached with the lack.

His sigils went dark a moment later. He picked up a wooden practice sword and a shield. "Come at me."

They hadn't done this in a very long time. "You've had years more training," she mumbled. She hated losing.

"I'll only defend."

She perked up. She wouldn't mind beating him senseless. She snatched a pair of swords and charged before he could set himself. She swiped low with one sword and stabbed with the other. He easily blocked her stab with his shield and her swipe with his sword. She feinted and struck at his side. He had an easy opening to counterstrike. He didn't take it.

Instead, he simply blocked. Over and over again, she struck and thrust and jabbed. Finally, *finally*, she managed a hit on the outside of his arm.

"You're angry with me," he said.

She feinted to the right and jabbed with her left. "Brilliant, that's what you are."

He blocked her. "Very angry."

She spun around, her kick landing on his thigh. "You shouldn't have attacked that guard."

He grimaced. "He touched you."

"He was just doing his job!" Eiryss shouldn't have tested the man. "And you shouldn't have lied to me about Hagath."

"Ah, so that's the real reason you're upset."

Abandoning form, she swung two-handed at his skull. He whipped his shield up and out, easily disarming her right hand, and stepped into her guard, his wooden blade pointed at her throat.

Her hands smarted where the sword had been ripped away. "You said she would be all right." She spoke in a whisper because saying it aloud made it real. She sagged, her second sword falling with a clatter, and broke down.

Ramass's weapons dangled from his limp fingers. He tossed them toward the chest and missed. "Oh, Eiryss, I was just trying to spare you."

"Don't!"

He gave a rueful nod.

She tried to master herself and failed. "I'm not the crier. Rature and Hagath are the criers."

He sniffed and wiped at the tears welling in his own eyes. "Clearly."

She smacked his arm. With a strangled chuckle, Ramass pulled her against him. She cried until her eyes were swollen and her head threatened to explode. His tears dripped into her hair. She'd slowed to hiccupping when someone cleared their throat.

Eiryss jerked up in surprise. Jala stood at the entrance, one eyebrow raised. "Is that all you two do? Hug and weep?"

Embarrassed, Eiryss turned and wiped her cheeks.

Ramass brushed each cheek against his shoulders. "What?" he said gruffly to cover his own embarrassment.

Jala glared at him. "Your father seems to think I'm a courier. He has requested your presence at once, *Marshal* Ramass." She sashayed away.

Ramass stared up at the council chambers with the look of a man facing down an enemy army alone. "I have to go," he said, his voice heavy with resignation.

"Will you send a servant when Hagath wakes?"

He nodded. "Go home. Try to get some sleep. You look as miserable as I feel." He sucked in a great breath and trudged up the stairs without looking back.

The constables visibly relaxed as Eiryss passed beneath the arch of her hometree. She was so tired it was hard to put one foot in front of the other.

She stripped off her borrowed coat and handed it back to its owner, glad to be rid of it. "Did you remember to fetch mine?"

He held his dripping coat with two fingers, as if it had been worn by someone with the plague, before hanging it on a branch. "Your servant has it."

He didn't deserve her thanks. Not when he had no business being here in the first place. She stepped between them. Belgrave met her at the main platform.

"How's my mother?" she asked.

"Waiting for you in her rooms, Lady Eiryss. Shall I have an early dinner brought?"

She'd managed to miss lunch entirely. "Yes, thank you."

Belgrave shuffled toward the kitchens. Eiryss trudged up the stairs to her parents' wing. She paused at the doorpane to her father's library. His books lay strewn about. His chair was up-ended. One of his lampents had been tipped over, dirt scattering across the pale gray wood.

With a heavy tread, she stepped inside. His library smelled like him. Like books and oiled leather and steel. She knelt beside the plant, scooping dirt into the pot. Granules fell between the cracks in the boards, cold creeping up.

She set the plant upright on his desk and tapped the petals of the lampent, sending colors scattering along the edges. The light from the flower illuminated all the books that needed re-shelving. The papers dotting the floor. The maids should have had this cleaned up by now. Maids who'd abandoned them yesterday.

Was it only yesterday? It seemed a lifetime ago.

She blinked away tears and paused at the doorpane, shifting it to opaque so she wouldn't have to face her father's things again. She paused, gathering herself before stepping into her mother's rooms.

Emlon sat in the bed, in nearly the same position Eiryss had left her. Her quill scratched across the paper tacked to the writing board on her lap. The side of her palm was stained black with ink. On her nightstand, a dozen letters had been sealed with her family crest.

Even bedridden, her mother was far from helpless.

"Who have you been writing?" Eiryss asked.

Mother started, her quill scratching across the paper. She swore.

"Sorry," Eiryss mumbled. "I didn't mean to startle you."

"It was a draft anyway." She started writing again. "The letters are for our family and allies. Though finding someone to deliver them has been difficult." She visibly braced herself. "Will Enderlee help us?"

Eiryss hesitated. If she were caught sneaking in to see Father, she could be branded a traitor. More likely, the king and her family name would protect her. Still, she doubted her mother would take the risk.

"She won't help us." Eiryss was surprised how easily the lie rolled off her tongue.

Mother's eyes clenched shut. "Then we must rely on our family to put pressure on the rest of the council. Come. Help me write more letters."

Eiryss sat at the desk and pulled out a fresh sheet of paper. "Who's taking Father's place on the council?"

"Vicil."

The other member of their family present at the assassination attempt. Eiryss's hand tightened on the quill. "Is he qualified?"

"Not by half," Mother huffed. "But the King insisted."

Eiryss dipped the quill tip and watched the black ink seep into the core. Just like the dark that had seeped into her life. She slumped against the table, burying her head in her hands.

"If it's the last thing I do, I will see him free, Eiryss," her mother said gently. She let out a heavy sigh. "Ahlyn's funeral is tonight."

Ahlyn's waxy, beautiful face. The flowers around her. And tomorrow, a procession would take her body to the portal. Her parents and siblings, aunts and uncles, cousins and friends would lead it. Just like the day not so long ago when Ahlyn had had her embedding ceremony.

Only this time, she was dead.

Eiryss imagined Ahlyn's family. Their accusing stares and uncontrolled weeping. "You don't expect me to go?"

"Vicil will represent our family." Mother's quill scratched the final words across the paper. She tore it out and tacked up another sheet. "Tomorrow, you will continue your training at the academy as if nothing had happened."

"And Father?" Eiryss asked.

Mother lifted a trembling hand to cover her mouth. "The best we can hope for him now is his banishment."

Eiryss couldn't accept that. She wouldn't.

CHAPTER 7

STEALING

Knowing she had to wait until everyone was sound asleep, Eiryss delayed until, the lampents in the other trees faded, one after another. It might be better to wait until the hours before morning, but visions of her father being tortured would not leave her. Unable to bear it a moment more, she changed into her darkest gray tunic and trousers and hid her pale hair beneath a wrap.

Moving on silent feet through her hometree, she stole into the supply room and sifted through the tools the boy used to care for their tree and the cleaning implements the maids had used. She took the hook and lines that the boy used to secure himself while in the highest branches and hid them under her cloak.

It was bitterly cold out, her breath misting the air before her. The fog was heavy and dense, a drizzling rain misting her cheeks. To avoid the constables, she threw the hook to a neighboring tree and swung out over open water. She climbed the boughs, gathered her equipment, and took to the bridges on the other side.

It was never completely dark in Valynthia. Potted and natural growing lampents made that all but impossible. But thanks to the storm, there was no moon or starlight, and the drizzling rain made a perfect excuse to hide beneath her hood.

Ahead, a knot of her classmates staggered into view. Eiryss caught a fleeting glimpse of Iritraya and Wyndyn and ducked her head low. They passed by without giving her a second look—after all, she was dressed more like a servant, and they were always invisible. The group smelled like a party, like alcohol and yeast. But their somberness and the tight way they bunched together spoke of grief.

Iritraya was crying softly. So not so much a party as a gathering to mourn the princess. Eiryss hadn't been invited. Hadn't even known it was happening. Eiryss, the highest noble in the entire academy, had been purposely ignored. Rejection and humiliation sank heavily through her middle. Tears filled her eyes.

She gritted her teeth. She didn't care what her classmates thought of her, or if any of them were her friends. She had her own friends and her family. And when she exonerated her father, she wouldn't forget those who had abandoned her.

It was only as she reached the bridge to the healer's tree that she hid in the shadows. She spotted a couple of healers and servants in dull green as they moved through the tree with a potted lampent in hand. She wouldn't be able to slip undetected into the tree through the front entrance. Too many people moving about—and all of them would recognize her in an instant.

Undrad's chamber was easy to spot—only a third of the tree was occupied—all on the lower levels. Her father's room was higher than the rest and isolated. It was silver, meaning it was impassable to all but the healer who'd put it in place. Enderlee had promised one of the top panels would be passable, though Eiryss couldn't detect which one from this distance.

Eiryss slipped into a hometree—the occupants none the wiser—and climbed into the high branches, where she sent a dozen four-armed wailer vites calling out in protest as they scrambled away. She didn't worry about the noise. The occupants likely had the magical barriers set to silent. And even if they didn't, the dozen different types of vites and birds were always making noise in the boughs.

Far above even the maids' chambers, Eiryss tossed her hook toward the branches of the healer tree. It caught on something on the first try but did not hold when she tugged on the rope. She jerked it free. It landed with a distant splash—not an uncommon sound in a lake teeming with fish. She gathered the rope— dripping from the lake—and tried again. And again.

On the fourth attempt, the hook held. She climbed higher— to where the branches bowed dangerously beneath her feet—and attached her end to a sturdy branch, tightened the line, and placed the hook with handles over it.

She looked far below, at the algae that tinted the crashing waves violet. Water or no, a fall from this height would kill her. She had tugged on the rope on the other side, but the only way to know for sure that it would hold was to jump.

Still, she wasn't frightened. A thrill shot through her middle. She loved heights. Loved the freedom and the undeniable feeling that she was alive. She wiped her damp palms on her trousers, donned fitted leather gloves, took hold of the leather-wrapped handles, and pushed off. She whooshed through the branches, getting a face full of leaves, and burst out into the open, her silhouette nearly invisible against the dark sky.

The line sagged, easing her to a halt halfway to her destination. Tucking away the metal hook, she gripped the line and climbed hand and foot the rest of the way. She breathed a sigh of relief when she reentered the cover of the healing tree's canopy and pushed through smaller branches until she reached one that would hold her weight.

She slipped forward until the branch grew thick enough for her to let go of her line. She abandoned it for now—she was high enough up that her line should be safe from discovery.

Holding onto nearby branches for support, she descended until she reached the uppermost pathways and the first small, individual rooms. This was where the healers kept the long-term patients, though judging from the lack of ambient lampent light, they were empty. She went down the stairs, peeking around the corner with each step so she didn't run into anyone.

One level above her father's chamber was a branch with a room with the faint light of an inactive lampent. Occupied, though whoever was inside was likely asleep. Below, a constable paced the length of the bough leading to her father's door. If anyone came from the inside or if the constable happened to look up, she was done for.

Moving slowly, she eased one foot in front of the other until she was past the constable's line of sight, her father's chambers blocking her from his view. A shuffling sound from the room directly in front of her. She froze, waiting for someone to come out and catch her.

When no one did, she breathed out in relief, slipped over the banister, and braced her foot on a thinner branch. She inspected the roof below her. There, one of the smaller panels was a touch lighter than the others, just as Enderlee had said.

Keeping her movements smooth and quiet, she tied the line to some of the railing's supporting branches. The sound of steps came from the room in front of her. A man in the muted green tunic of a servant stepped out. She flattened herself against the outside of the banister and held perfectly still.

He paused just beside her. His brow furrowed as his quill scratched across the paper. *Don't look left. Don't look left. Don't look left.*

Again, her father's words came back to her, this time to a new guardsman. "Steady. Steady on."

She evened out her breaths and tried to calm her racing heart. After what felt like forever, the man finished writing and moved on. As soon as he was out of sight, Eiryss prayed to the light for silence and eased the rope into her father's room. She wrapped the rope around her foot and shimmied down until she reached the roof supports.

Rope in her mouth and feet braced on the frame, she climbed the domed roof on her hands and feet until she reached the darker panel. Standing with one leg on each side, she peered in.

Her father was alone. Bandages wrapped his middle. His skin was pale and drenched in sweat. But he was alive. Praise the light, he was alive.

She dropped the rope. Hands braced on either side, Eiryss lowered herself carefully and then fell, landing in a crouch. She hurried to his side and knelt. Beautifully done weaves of magic lay against his skin. Those weaves kept his sigils open even while he slept, coaxing them to release some of their numbing sap. Other weaves gleamed beneath his bandage, weaves that had knit his flesh together more neatly than any healer and kept his wound cool.

She couldn't help the tears that welled in her eyes as she took his hand in hers and kissed it.

"Father, oh, Father," she whispered.

He shifted in his sleep and then his eyes opened. His bewildered gaze shifted from her to the rope that dangled from the panel. Horror dawned on his face. "You have to go back the way you came," he whispered. "Now."

She shook her head. "Tell me what really happened. Who forced you to do this? I'll go to the king. We'll get you free."

He gripped her hand so hard it hurt. "Eiryss, go. Before it's too late."

How could he say that? "I know you could never betray us. Not willingly. You can't be helping the Alamantians."

Undrad stared at her as if he'd never see her again. "I did exactly what they said I did," his voice broke.

She shook her head over and over again. "No. No, you wouldn't."

He took both her hands in his. "I attacked the king. Killed the princess. I am a traitor and a liar. Do you understand?"

She looked into his eyes and saw the sorrow and fear and above all the *earnestness*. He... he had done this. No one had forced him. He had killed Ahlyn and nearly Hagath. He had tried to stab the king. He had betrayed them all.

"Why?" she said in a strangled voice.

He released her. "Because the Alamantians are right. Everyone should have access to magic, Eiryss. Not just the nobility."

She reached for him and then stopped. "What?" Even as the words left her lips, her mind spun through all the debates her father and the king had had over the poor. Her father's philosophy books. His lectures on serving those beneath her. *Please. Tell me my entire life hasn't been a lie.*

He turned away, shame clouding his eyes. The man who had single-handedly rescued an entire company of soldiers from an Alamantian raid; the man who had dressed her skinned knees; the man who had stood on the right hand of the king. Her father—her hero—was a liar. A traitor. Deep within Eiryss, something shattered, the jagged pieces tearing her apart from the inside out. She looked up at him from the bloody ruin that was her heart, her eyes pleading.

Her father's voice caught in a sob. "Forgive me, Eiryss. Please forgive me."

At that moment, four notes played and the doorpane shifted from silver to clear. The same servant in dull green stepped in, an enchantress behind him. They balked at the sight of her, eyes wide.

"Constable!" the enchantress cried.

Eiryss didn't try to run. To fight. She just sat on the floor. Even as stunned as she was, she understood it was all over. Her life was over.

"I'm sorry, Eiryss," her father whispered. "Light, I'm so sorry."

The constable and servant dragged her from the room. She hung limp between them. They dropped her in an empty room on the same branch as her father's. The enchantress sealed it in silver.

Eiryss lay on her side where she'd been dropped. Her arm went to sleep. Her hip ached. The pain was distant. Unimportant. The barrier kept out the sound, so she had no idea what was going on. She could only detect the subtle change of light as morning came. It was the longest night of her life.

Finally, the doorpane shifted to clear. From her position on the floor, she could only see the branches beyond. The king stepped inside. His eyes were bloodshot and ringed with shadows, his face unshaven. And the way he looked at her... as if he'd never seen her before. "Light, Eiryss. Do you know what you've done?"

She pushed herself up to her knees and prostrated herself before him. "Forgive me, Majesty. I had to see my father. To hear from his own lips what happened that night."

"And what did he tell you?" the king said, his voice dropped on her like a stone.

She blinked hard, hot tears falling from her eyes. Her leg and arm burned as feeling returned. "Please, Your Majesty. He's my father." She couldn't speak the words. Couldn't betray him.

"Tell me!" he roared.

She flinched and dropped her head. "He said he is a traitor." The words felt like poison in her mouth.

"Light, Eiryss. I warned you. Why didn't you listen?"

"I only wanted—"

"Undrad was kept in isolation in part to see if anyone tried to contact him."

And she had. Suddenly, she understood. She could die for this. All the blood drained from her face. "But I'm not a traitor," she said weakly.

He crouched before her and placed two fingers under her chin, lifting her face and waited until she met his gaze. "I know, child."

"What's going to happen to me? To my father?"

"I will do what I must to protect you."

All the breath left her in a rush, relief flowing through her. "Thank you."

He pulled her to her feet. "It doesn't feel this way right now, but someday you will recover from this."

She wouldn't, but it felt ungrateful to say it. "I'm sorry," she sniffed. "I'm so sorry. I should have listened to you."

"You'll have to stay in here. But I'll send your brother to fetch you home in a little while."

At her nod, he released her, stepped back through the doorpane. From her position, she could see Jala on the other side.

"Seal her in," King Zannok said.

Her back to Eiryss, Jala lifted the flute to her lips. Zannok moved back toward her father's room. She stepped to the doorway and saw a full view of what lay beyond. Silent and still, all the senior members of the council waited on the other side—close enough to have heard her every word. Her cousin, Vicil, was among them. Her father knelt before his room. He wore no shirt or shoes. Only his trousers and bandages thick around his middle. He swayed like a tree in a storm.

She moved without knowing exactly why. Only that the dark premonition rising inside her forced her to slide out of the room seconds before the doorpane went silver. Jala was so busy watching the proceedings she didn't even notice.

Her father didn't look up. Didn't notice her. "I confess before these witnesses that I did attempt to slay the king. I murdered Princess Ahlyn. I did this in league with the Alamantians, who wish to overthrow our kingdom."

No. No. No. Her father could not confess to such things. Nothing could save him if he did. She started running. Past the enchantress. Past the guards. A man stepped forward, his face covered in black. He lifted his ax. Above her father's neck.

She'd nearly reached her father. Only a few more steps. The king caught her about the middle. She screamed. The ax fell. Blood. So much blood. Her father's body slumped to the ground. His head rolled and came to a stop against the banister. His eyes, light, his eyes fixed on her. His expression was so broken and horrified. Then the pupil widened.

"I told you to seal her off!" The king screamed at Jala.

Her father—the one sure thing in her life—was dead. "Why didn't you stop them!" she screamed.

"It was you or him," the king murmured against her hair. "Light, Eiryss. I had to give them one of you."

The king had said he could keep her father alive if he didn't confess. But he had. To her. And she'd told the king. Her shredded heart was poison now. The poison spread through her. She was dying right along with her father. She screamed again and tried to wrench free.

Vicil came to the king's aid. They hauled her between watching councilors. Jala played her song like a heavy current, pulling at Eiryss, trying to force her to sleep. But this was no ordinary enchantress. This was the king's personal enchantress and an emotive at that. Eiryss fought it with everything she had.

And she lost.

CHAPTER

UNDRAD

Eiryss came to on her back on a hard bed. Her brother sat dejectedly in a chair, his elbows braced against his thighs. For a moment, she didn't know where she was or how she'd arrived here. Until she saw the thick silver barrier and recognized the inside of a healer room.

It all came crashing back. The blood. Light, the blood. Her father's expression as his gaze had locked on her. He would never again ruffle her hair or kiss her hand or grumble when she got into trouble. He would never lecture her or make her repeat his quotes.

The pain in her heart—how had it not killed her?

No. This couldn't be happening. This couldn't be real.

She shoved out of the bed, crossed the room in a bound, and banged her fists on the doorpane. "Father! Father!"

"Stop it," Ture said in disgust.

She welcomed the pain in her fists. It was such a relief from the pain inside her. "They killed him! They beheaded him!"

"I know."

"They can't do that! He's our father."

"It's done. He's gone."

Breathless, she rested her forehead against the cool barrier. Details she hadn't even recognized before came back with crystal clarity. Her father's hair was tied up and out of the way. The bruises on his side. The fact that he'd looked at her with horror. The meaty sound of the sword. The way his blood had spurted and his body had slumped. He'd been reduced to an animal to be slaughtered.

His eyes. I will never stop seeing his eyes.

She turned her back to the panel and slid down. Her shredded heart continued to beat in her chest. Light, how could it keep beating amid so much pain? She wished it would stop, wished more than anything for the pain to stop.

She didn't know how much time had passed. Days? Weeks? Centuries?

She did not die, but when she lifted her face, she felt like an old woman. "He betrayed us. For them. For the rabble."

Ture rubbed his face—he looked like he hadn't slept in days. "That's what he said." Ture said it like she was stupid.

Dray's smiling face. His arms around her. The note sliding into her palm. She would kill him for this. "It will destroy Mother—knowing he willingly betrayed us." She was not well. She wouldn't survive.

"Which is why we're not telling her."

She met her brother's gaze for the first time. He wore that glare—the one right before he dove into a lecture, a glare he'd inherited from their father. And suddenly, she was glad for it. Glad to have a little piece of her father in her brother—even if it was directed at her.

"Promise me, Eiryss. Promise you won't tell Mother."

Mother had been homebound for years, but family and friends still came to visit. "We can't keep it from her indefinitely, and she has a right to know."

"Eiryss," he said warningly.

She turned away from him, studying the subtle shifting of the panels—like light on water. When she had her sigils, she would be able to see the weave that made them. "Why did he confess? He knew they would kill him for it."

Her brother shook his head in disgust. "To save your life, you idiot. He confessed in exchange for keeping you out of it."

His words sliced her to ribbons. "What? How—"

"One of the maids found the letter King Dray wrote to you, asking for a meeting. She gave it to a constable. King Zannok managed to convince the council not to have you arrested. But when you showed up in Father's room last night…"

That was why the maids had quit. Why Vicil and her brother had been given jobs while she'd been given constables to follow her. She covered her mouth with her hands. "That letter was for Father."

"Then why was it in your room?"

"King Dray told me to give to Father!" He hadn't wanted the king to know about it. And now she knew why—her father was a traitor. "I never even read it! Surely it was addressed to Father."

Ture shook his head. "Then why was it opened? Why was it hidden?"

"Ramass opened it! He helped me hide it before the constables came." She held her head in her hands. Her father was dead, but her life was just as surely over. The nobility would shun her. Her sweet future turned to bitterness and dross. "Why didn't you warn me?"

"Only the king, the Arbor, and a select few constables even knew."

"It was you or him," the king had murmured against her hair. *"Light, Eiryss. I had to give them one of you."*

The king had tried to warn her. She hadn't listened. She never did. Zannok had been forced to give her father a choice. Accept sole responsibility and a treasonous death, or risk Eiryss facing the same charges of treason.

Her father's expression—the horror as he realized his head had parted from his body, that his daughter had seen it. She would live with the weight of that expression for the rest of her life.

"It was my fault." The fight left her, and she curled around the ruin of her heart, sobbing.

Ture pushed to his feet and glared down at her. "You don't get to cry. You know why? Because we still have to tell our mother her husband is dead."

My fault. My fault. Each beat of her heart felt like a betrayal. Like a death. And she, the living dead. "I am so sorry. Please, Ture, forgive me."

"Not everything is about you!"

She choked on a sob. "Do you really hate me so much?"

He crouched before her. "Our family will be fined. They'll likely take everything we have. Our father is dead. Our reputation is ruined. All because you couldn't do what you were told. For once, why couldn't you do as you were told?"

The panel behind her suddenly dissipated. She went sprawling.

Arbor Enderlee looked down at her. "Ture, a moment in private with your sister."

Ture's jaw tightened before he gave a curt bow and stormed out. The Arbor was powerful enough she only needed to play a couple of notes and the dome shifted back to impenetrable.

Picking herself up, Eiryss rocked back and forth to keep from falling apart again. "Why didn't you warn me what would happen if I was caught?"

Enderlee watched her, expression unreadable. "It's not just Hanama that could fall, Eiryss." Despite her hardened exterior, her voice was impossibly gentle. "The magic is weakened. The war has just begun, and already we are not faring well. I must know if your father said anything. Did he do something to the Silver Tree?"

Eiryss had forgotten to even ask, but she couldn't admit that to the Arbor. Not after all her other failings. *Could Father have sabotaged the magic? Exactly how far did his treachery run?* "Only that he was guilty. That's all there was time for before I was caught."

Enderlee let out a growl of frustration. "Eiryss, I have to suspend you from the academy."

Eiryss stiffened, and she realized again just how much she had stood to lose—the possibility of ever having magic. *Light, how lofty I was—to still be falling.* "I'm not a traitor, Arbor Enderlee. You of all people know that." After all, the Arbor had sent Eiryss to her father's room.

"But your father is." Enderlee folded her arms. "A year suspension. It will give the nobility time to forgive your family."

"You expect me to keep quiet about your involvement in all this?"

Enderlee's mouth thinned in displeasure. "If not for the king and me fighting for you, the suspension would be permanent. We have agreed that your possession of the letter will never go public. Is that not enough?"

Eiryss's eyes fluttered closed. "That letter was never meant for me. I never even read it. Ask Ramass—he'll tell you it was sealed when he opened it."

"The council believes Ramass is simply covering for you—everyone knows how close you two are."

Eiryss pressed the heel of her hand against her forehead. King Dray had coerced her father into betraying his people. Had given that letter to her—and so sealed their fates. He was the one who had single-handedly destroyed her family. He and his wretched Alamantians.

"Light, I will make the Alamantians pay!"

Enderlee's eyebrows lifted in surprise. "You're a healer, Eiryss."

"Not anymore!" The grief, confusion, fear, shame, horror—it all shifted. Anger flared white hot in her chest—sealing over the cracks in her ruined heart. That anger allowed her to uncurl. Rise up. She fisted her hands at her side. "I will become a warrior enchantress. Let me graduate early—let me have my thorns, and I will see that King Dray and his people pay for what they have done to my family. To my people."

Enderlee lifted her flute. "I'm sorry, Eiryss. I've already done all I can."

"Liar," Eiryss snarled.

Turning away, Enderlee shifted the doorpane and stepped through without looking back.

Ture waited for Eiryss on the other side. The constables were nowhere in sight. Ture turned without a word. Head down, Eiryss stormed after her brother. They reached the bridge. She'd taken a dozen steps before she recognized the slush at her feet. The darkness. She turned her head up to the sky, a fat flake landing in her eye. She blinked painfully.

All around her, the hometrees' glossy, fat leaves were curled up, dead. The lampents were black and soggy. The vibrant colors were gone. Snow drifted, lining the trees.

Snow.

In Valynthia.

CHAPTER 9

MEMORIES AND MAGIC

The next day, Eiryss stood with her family in the half-frozen dreck of their estate's peasant graveyard. Three dozen aunts, uncles, and cousins spread out around them. Trees grew in perfect rows, one over each grave, a name and date carved into the bark. Some of the trees were old, the scarred names black and unreadable. Deep below, the roots curled around and fed off the bodies. It was the closest the poor would ever come to a proper burial in the Silver Tree.

Instead of her father's memories and magic melding back to the light, he would be covered with mud. The roots would twist around his body and, over time, tear apart his bones. An igno-minious burial. The burial of a traitor. The burial he deserved.

How had it come to this? Her father had always taken such pride in his kingdom and especially his command. The king was like a brother. Eiryss ground her teeth as the snow gathered on her shoulders. Lightning crackled across the angry sky.

At her side, her mother sagged. Eiryss's grip was the only thing keeping her upright. The servants shoveled the first dirt onto her father's linen-wrapped body. Mother keened, a sharp, bone wrenching cry that tore at Eiryss's very soul.

An enchantress from Eiryss's family played the dirge, the notes hollow and aching. Eiryss looked up and caught Ramass watching her. They held gazes over the open grave, her hair blowing across her face. Hair she couldn't bother to shift away. His father had not come. Eiryss didn't blame him.

The last notes trailed to silence. The service was over.

"Eiryss, I can taste it." Mother's gaze was desperate. Afraid. The look she had whenever a fit built inside her.

"Ture," Eiryss cried.

Mother's eyes rolled up and she sagged between them, her body convulsing. Then came the sharp scent of urine. Eiryss had barely slept in days. Her head pounded. She was hungry yet too nauseous to eat. And the idea of bathing her mother one more time... She bit back the scream building inside her.

Ture carried her away from the funeral-goers—their family didn't need any more spectacle—and beneath a tree. Ramass was already there, laying his coat over the snow. They eased Mother down as she flailed, inhuman sounds forced from her lungs. The three of them arranged themselves around her to block the view of those filing toward the waiting horses.

This was the closest Eiryss had come to Ture since Father's death. He seemed to realize it at the same time she did, for he switched places with Ramass. Ramass looked between them, one brow raised in question, clearly wanting to know what they were fighting about at a time like this.

She couldn't tell him her father's death was her fault. She could never say those words aloud. A whole-body shudder swallowed Eiryss, and she looked away. Ramass's eyes narrowed, but he let it slide.

Mother's wild movement slowly stilled, and she lay panting. Ture knelt and wrapped her up, carrying her toward their carriage while the rest of their family watched with pity. Tears started building again. Eiryss dug her thumb into her bruise, as she'd done so many times before.

Ramass suddenly grabbed her hand—she'd bled through the bandage. He unwrapped it and hissed through his teeth at the wicked bruise. "Eiryss... what have you done?"

Murdered my father. She jerked free. "I'm all right."

"You're not."

She wasn't.

"Let's take you to the healers."

"I don't want them."

He watched her helplessly. "Remember when we were younger? We used to go climbing. See how high we could get." He tried for a grin that didn't quite stick. "You always won."

She sniffed. "Of course I did. I'm a better aim with the grappling hook."

He gave her a sardonic look. "Because you're lighter."

"You can't prove that." Their banter felt so good. Soothing to the bone-deep hurt.

He rolled his eyes, but this time one corner of his smile stuck. "Our parents used to scold us because of how high we were. And the risk of falling—" He reached out, his fingers gripped hers. "But we never did. We never fell. And I won't let you fall now."

The wind picked up, snow drifting from the tree beside them. Glittery beams of light speared down, so bright it hurt Eiryss's eyes. In that moment, next to her father's grave, she believed him.

"Ramass," Ture called from beside their horses. "I need you."

The enchantment was broken. Ramass hurried toward their horses.

"How is Hagath?" Eiryss hustled to catch up.

"She's still very sick."

Eiryss dug her thumb into her bruise. Remembering Ramass's gentle fingers, she stopped herself. "And the vault?"

Ramass frowned. "Arbor Enderlee believes the Alamantians somehow poisoned the tree."

She'd heard all this from Enderlee. "How could they do something so evil?"

"She thinks the sacred tree will recover. Eventually."

They reached her brother. Ramass held Mother while Ture climbed onto his horse. Ramass passed her up. Atop her own mare, Missy, Eiryss looked back at the copse. Her family's fieldworkers scraped mud into her father's grave. She would never see him again. Never read in his library while he pored over his papers. Never watch him train soldiers, his body as lean and honed as their own. They would never spear fish in the lake or dance at a gala.

He was gone. Forever. And now every single one of those once beautiful memories would pain her for the rest of her life. "I hate him."

"Eiryss," Ramass said gently. He had pulled back to wait while her brother rode on. He'd stood by them when most had not. Even on the night of Ahlyn's death and Hagath's sickness.

"Thank you, Ramass." He tipped his head to the side in question. He hadn't shaved in a while. His scruff glowed golden and russet in the sliver of light. Something in her softened. "For everything."

He ducked his head. "Don't thank me, Eiryss."

CHAPTER 10

DEBT

E iryss, Ramass, Ture, and Mother left the horses at her family's land estate. Eiryss cast a longing look back at their second home—memories of their summers racing their horses through the meadows swirling through her. As sure as a door slamming in her face, she knew those days were over. They belonged to a different girl who'd led a different life. Then, she'd been the girl who'd gently swept up all the ants in Marinda's kitchen and ferried them outside to keep them from being killed.

Now, she was the girl who would bide her time until she could find a way to make King Dray and his Alamantians pay for what they had done. Even if that meant she had to wait a full two years to do it. Was it wrong to hope the war lasted long enough for her to seek her revenge?

She turned her back on her old home. Her family took to a small boat and set the sail. The trip across the lake was silent and aching. When they reached their hometree, over a dozen men wearing the official mantle of the treasury and twice as many servants waited for them on the wide, flat root of their dock.

They couldn't do this another day? Eiryss thought bitterly.

Belgrave stood at the end of the dock as they eased in. "Lady, I tried to send them away." His eyes were red-rimmed; clearly, he'd been crying.

Eiryss climbed out of the boat. "It's all right, Belgrave."

Ramass passed Mother up to Ture. She struggled to wake up before losing the battle, her head lolling against Ture's chest. In the end, Eiryss hadn't been able to lie to her mother. When her mother asked for the truth, Eiryss gave it to her. Including her father's betrayal. Mother hadn't taken any of it well. She hadn't cried or screamed or cursed. Instead, she'd gone silent and still. She'd barely ate or drank, and her body had grown hollow and... empty.

Eiryss would have far preferred screaming.

"I'm taking her up. You deal with this." Ture gestured toward the treasurers and marched off. "Belgrave, send Marinda up."

Belgrave shot a worried look at Eiryss before moving to obey.

"What are you two fighting over?" Ramass asked under his breath as he tied down the boat.

"We're not fighting."

He huffed. "I've known you two for as long as I can remember. I know when you're fighting. Curse me, he wouldn't even stand by you after the funeral."

Eiryss wouldn't meet his gaze. He sighed and strode down the dock to a portly, balding man and drew to his full height. "Can't this wait?"

"The money will go to a good cause: financing the war." The portly man stepped past Ramass and addressed Eiryss. "My name is Treasurer Govin, lady. I've brought a team to assess the worth of your valuables and exact payment."

Eiryss rubbed at the headache pounding against her skull. When was the last time she'd slept more than a couple hours? "How much?"

"The council has ordered twenty thousand gold pieces."

"Twenty thousand!" Eiryss gasped.

"That's absurd!" Ramass said.

If they sold everything they had, Eiryss doubted they could get half that much. "When is it due?"

"We'll take what we can now. The council has generously granted you a year to pay off the rest."

"Generously?" Mother couldn't work. Now Eiryss was suspended, it would be two years before she could graduate. Ture's wages certainly wouldn't cover it. By the light, she'd lost everything in the space of a week.

"If you would take me to your father's safe," Govin said.

Numb, she floated up the stairs to her father's library. She stood before the doorpane, suddenly unable to step inside. To smell her father and know he had chosen to betray them. To see his books and know he would never touch them again. And most of all to again see the desecration the constables had left behind.

"Eiryss?" Ramass said gently.

She steeled herself. Letting her eyes go unfocused, she walked inside. The clean lines and lack of clutter drew her up short. Everything was in neat orderliness as always.

Belgrave. She imagined his gnarled hands and shuffling steps. How many hours had the man spent on this? Tears of gratitude filled her eyes. She took the key from its hidden cache in her father's desk. Kneeling before the safe, she inserted the key and twisted. The door creaked open, revealing fat gold coins as well as their finer pieces of jewelry.

She stepped aside as one of the treasurers emptied everything out of the safe, including the deed to their estate outside the city, while another man counted each coin. Govin sat at her father's desk as if he had any right. More men tallied the books, furniture, and jewelry, bringing their numbers to Govin for approval.

Ramass stood beside her as a man took the jewelry her family had inherited from her grandmother—including her favorite emerald ring. The broach her mother had given Eiryss for her first gala. The earrings—each featuring a different colored stone—that her father had given her for each of her birthdays. And last, a velvet wrap containing a flute carved from the branches of the Silver Tree. Lovely thorns and ahlea flowers graced the sides. The same flute she'd been admiring for months.

"How could he do this to us?" she whispered. Ramass handed her a handkerchief, his expression questioning. She wiped her cheeks bitterly. "He bought it for my embedding ceremony." She was sure of it. "And because of him, I was suspended for an entire year."

Ramass's mouth tightened. "You don't have to finish this. I'll take care of it."

If by "take care of it," he meant "intimidate the treasurer" She sniffed. "I don't trust you not to get in a fight."

Ramass had the gall to look offended.

"Where would you have me go?"

"Why don't you and your mother stay with your family—one of your aunts or cousins—or come stay with me?"

"We're nearly finished." Govin started on the documents that tallied their horses and tack, the land, the buildings, and the farming equipment.

Gifts, artwork, precious family heirlooms—the tangible proof of their family's history—all of it gone in a single day.

Outside, Ture yelled, "These are my mother's things brought in from her own estate upon her marriage. They have nothing to do with my father."

He kept yelling, so she assumed it wasn't doing any good. She looked up at the people carrying things from her own chambers. Her fine gowns were draped in a half dozen women's arms.

Two more carried her boxes of ribbons. Three others carried pieces of her bed frame.

Everything they owned streamed toward the bridge in the hands of people she did not know. The deeds were neatly filed away in folders. All the summers she'd spent in the meadows and forests with her family. The picnics and fishing. The climbing. Her gray mare, Missy. All of it was gone.

Govin pushed back from the desk. "As I said before, you have a year to come up with the ten thousand remaining gold pieces."

"A year?" she echoed.

Govin didn't seem to hear. "Though you cannot legally sell your hometree, you could rent it out and make headway."

And go where? They'd already lost their land estate. All her family had left was their social standing. If they slunk out of the city now, they'd never gain it back.

"We're staying." She said it as much for Ramass's benefit as Govin's.

Govin shrugged and pushed past her.

At the archway that led from their hometree, Ture was still yelling at workers as they carted off their belongings. Belgrave paced behind him and made calming gestures.

Ramass's mouth formed a thin line. "I better go make sure he doesn't hit someone." He hurried out.

Stepping out, Eiryss sealed off the door to the library—there was no point in going in there ever again. Without her father's things, it was just an empty room.

Confident Ramass could handle her brother, she went to check on Mother. But as she climbed through her home, it didn't look like home anymore. Where furniture had been there were only faded marks and uniform scratches across the gray wood floor. Without their things, it was just so... empty.

Her mother sat in a barren room on a single chair, her canes in hand and a blanket wrapped around her legs. They hadn't even left her bed.

Beside her, Marinda looked up as Eiryss came in. "I thought to fetch some tea?"

Eiryss nodded her permission. Head down, the woman hurried from the room.

Eiryss stared at her folded hands. "Mother, it's my fault everything is gone. If I hadn't gone to see Father…"

"It's the council's fault. Even if your father did all the things they said, we had the right to see him. At the very least, we had the right to say goodbye. And they had no right to take the things I brought into our marriage."

The way Father had looked at her. With such horror. And the things he'd said. Again, she saw him die. She pressed her eyes shut, trying to force the memory back. "I never thought him capable of any of this."

"The man I know and love would never have murdered anyone in cold blood. But perhaps we never truly know a person."

Eiryss sent her mother a pleading expression. "What happens now?"

"You finish your schooling."

Eiryss closed her eyes. "I've been suspended for a year."

"Bring me my writing board and—" Mother glanced around helplessly. Even her writing board was gone. "Send Marinda to our families. This will not stand."

Eiryss flinched. How had they fallen so far as to beg for charity? "Marinda and Belgrave—how will we pay them?"

Mother began to cry. Eiryss held her and together they grieved. When her mother was calm, Eiryss kissed her cheek. "I'll go." Begging for the money to pay their debts was less humiliating than being forced to sleep on the cold floor.

She stepped outside and came face-to-face with Belgrave and Marinda carrying the lunch trays filled with spicy green soup and potters—fried pastry dough filled with vegetables and pork.

"I made your favorite," Marinda said with too much brightness.

"Help Mother eat, will you?" Eiryss slipped past them.

Marinda blocked her. "You've hardly eaten, lady. You're starting to look too thin."

Eiryss barked out a laugh. "We have much further to go for that to happen." She made to step around her. Marinda blocked her again. She hadn't dared confront Eiryss since she was a child. "I'll eat later."

"It's not right!" Marinda burst into tears. "You were only doing what any devoted daughter would!"

"No. I should have never gone against the king." She swallowed against the lump in her throat. "You know I won't be able to pay you."

Belgrave straightened his shoulders. "I'll stay on regardless, lady. I've served your family all my life. No need to go anywhere now."

Marinda looked miserable. She had a family to provide for.

"Loyalty wouldn't feed either of you," Eiryss said gently. "Marinda, if you haven't already had a dozen offers, I'd be shocked." Other nobles had been trying to steal their cook for years.

"I'll not leave you on the day your father is buried." She stormed past Eiryss and into her mother's room.

Belgrave straightened his shoulders. "I began my work fishing, gathering lake greens, and tending to the tree. I can do so again."

Not with his arthritic joints. "Belgrave, I can find you a good place."

Tears filled his watery blue eyes. "No, lady. You did not abandon me when I became too old to be of much use. I won't abandon you now. You're my family too."

She could barely speak through the thickness in her throat. "I'm honored, Belgrave."

He bowed. "I'll speak with the Mistress."

He shuffled past her. Love for the old man swelled inside her. Would she be so loyal under such circumstances? She honestly wasn't sure. A new voice began shouting from the main level. She knew that voice. She took off at a run.

The platform before the archway was clogged with columns of their belongings. A long line of servants either waiting for their turn to be loaded or were already carting things away. Amid it all was the king, her brother beside him.

"I don't care what the council authorized!" Zannok roared. "You will not strip everything from one of the highest noble families in Valynthia."

"It was not simply Eiryss's disobedience, Sire." Govin trailed behind him. "The council ruled reparations must be made for the damages caused by Undrad's actions. Twenty thousand gold pieces is not too much when you consider the cost of the war and—"

Zannok rounded on him. "The council is made up of a bunch of nobles far more interested in seeing a rival family fall from grace than they are in justice." He gazed at the crates and furniture. "Return it."

Govin straightened his shoulders, though his hands trembled. "Everything in Undrad's estate is worth less than they owe, Sire. Exactly what would you have me put back?"

Zannok rounded on the man. "You will not steal the very beds from under them. Give them back their furniture, bedding, and clothing." He lifted a wooden bowl from a crate. "Light, man, have you taken their spoons too!"

"They're silver!" Govin sputtered. He grabbed Eiryss's navy gown and held it up. "Some of the girl's gowns are worth—"

"Gowns I gave her!" The king snatched an armful of her dresses along with a box of ribbons from atop a precarious pile. He shook the box at the man. "Now I'm taking them back."

Love for Zannok swelled within her.

Govin pulled out his ledger and scanned it, his lips moving. "And what would you have us do with the additional money their things would have brought?"

Zannok threw the box of ribbons at him. "I'll pay it myself."

Govin yelped as the box connected, ribbons scattering everywhere. "I shall inform the council." He beat a hasty retreat, only remembering to bow at the last moment. "You heard His Majesty. Put back the furniture, housewares, and clothing. The rest will continue on."

Heart overflowing with gratitude, Eiryss strode toward the king. Ture blocked her. "Don't."

Hurt turned to anger. "I only wanted to thank him."

Breathing hard, Zannok leaned against the doorframe to the house. "I wish none of this had ever happened. But it did and there's no going back." Head bowed, he strode down the bridge.

Eiryss glared at her brother. "I only meant to thank him."

He pulled his hands through his hair. "Light, Eiryss. You're such a fool."

Clearly, he didn't think her worthy to even approach the king. He was back to blaming her for her father's death again. And this time, everyone was watching. A sick feeling made her gut ache.

Ramass stepped between them. "That's enough, Ture."

Ture's hands fisted at his side. "It doesn't matter anymore anyway. I'm leaving. Tomorrow. My army has been called to defend the city of Lias Lamoren."

Four days ago, the Alamantians had attacked three of Valynthia's border cities—though they'd only received word of it yesterday. Now Ture was going to defend one of them. What if he never came home again? Eiryss took a step toward him, reached for him. He turned away from her.

Rejected and humiliated, she stopped, arms curling around herself. "Ture…"

He looked at her. A blank look. The look of a stranger. Then he turned and walked away. She stared after him. Ramass took her arm and pulled her away from the eyes that had seen and the mouths who would repeat all of what had transpired.

At the colonnade, he pulled her into his arms. "He's just hurt and lashing out."

It was more than that. She'd seen the accusation in his eyes. Their father would still be alive if not for her. Again, she saw the blood. Her father's head fall. His eyes going black, the pupil swallowing up the iris.

"Eiryss?" Ramass asked.

She turned away, thumb digging back into her bruise. "I'm fine."

He gently pulled her hands apart, his fingers smoothing over the hurt. "Light, I would take this from you if I could."

She breathed in the smell of him, and for the briefest moment, peace stole over her. "It's enough you're here."

His whole body sagged. His gaze troubled, he looked to the north, and she knew.

"When?" she choked.

"My army marches for Trapendale tomorrow." Trapendale was the largest and most well-defended border city. If the Alamantians could conquer it, they'd have an impenetrable base of operations with which to attack Eiryss's people. And now Ramass would be defending it.

She wanted to pinch her bruise, but he was still holding her hand. "If I hadn't been suspended, I'd be joining you in a few months." Probably with her own command.

"I can't say I'm sorry to see you stay out of this."

She gritted her teeth. "I swore I'd make King Dray pay."

"Your mother needs you."

She brushed the damp off her cheeks.

Ramass studied the layers of bruises with infinite sadness. "Why do you do that?"

"Because I have to."

He kissed the back of her hand, the merest brush of his lips and the roughness of his scruff against her skin. All the breath left her. Unexpected warmth spread up her arm.

"When I come back, I don't want to see any more bruises."

Her lips parted. Lost in the grey of his eyes, she forgot to answer.

"Will you write to me?"

She nodded.

"Marshal Ramass!" A servant hurried down the bridge toward them.

"I have to go." He released her hand. "Come on. I want to say goodbye to your mother."

He started toward Mother's rooms. She watched him. Knowing something had shifted between them. Wondering if he felt it too.

He glanced back. "Coming?"

At that moment, she would follow him anywhere.

CHAPTER 11

ALL THAT DIES

Three Months Later

Bracing her feet on the gunwales, Eiryss reached into the freezing water to grip the line. Hand over hand, she hauled up the woven fish trap. Her blisters had long since healed, leaving tough callouses behind. She shook dead, slimy lake-greens from her fingers.

Empty.

Baiting the trap with a fish head, she rowed a little farther out. The boat bumped into the rotting carcasses of fish dead of cold, the movement making the stench worse. Even after a month of this, she gagged as she tossed the trap back into the water.

At the next trap, she snagged three fish she would have thrown out two months ago. Now, she eagerly strung a line through their gills. Five more traps and she managed seven fish. Not bad.

Back at the dock, she tied off the boat and climbed the steps to the kitchen. From his chair by the stove, Belgrave snored loudly. He'd started a batch of tea for Mother's cough. It had boiled too long; the leaves settled in the bottom giving off a burnt smell. Three months ago, she would have chided Marinda and demanded more tea. Now, they had to ration every serving.

The rationing, along with the hard work she did every day, had changed her. Her clothes hung off her body. Muscle corded her arms and legs. She'd sold all the dresses the king had given her—none of them would fit anymore anyway.

Moving quietly, Eiryss washed the slime of the dying lake off her hands and arms, strained the tea, and set it aside to cool. After filleting the fish, she set the meat on the stove to cook, washed her knife, sharpened it, and set it back in its place. She plated the fish with some rolls she'd managed to burn only a little this morning. She wished they had some greens—she craved them more every day, but everything green had died the day her father had.

She set a plate before Belgrave and gently shook him awake. He came around, his expression a haze of pain. As soon as he focused on her, his expression fell. "I burned the tea." Tears filled his eyes. "Oh, lady, I'm sorry."

She pushed the cup into his hands. "It should still help with the pain." He drank it down fast enough to burn his tongue—a testament to how much he must be hurting.

"I caught plenty of fish today."

He started to push up from the table. "I'll wash up, lady. You tend to your mother."

She pressed him into the chair. "Eat first. Then take a real nap." She'd lugged his bed down to the kitchen two months ago. Since the cold had come, he simply couldn't manage the stairs anymore. He sighed and tore into the bread. Burned on the outside and doughy in the middle. Gah! She could never get the oven's temperature right.

Belgrave swallowed and tried not to make a face. "Your cooking has improved so much, lady."

She loved him for the lie.

She loaded a tray with food and medicine. She'd just started up when Ramass's servant called for entrance from the archway. The woman would have a letter from Ramass or Hagath. The latter had been moved to some famous healer in Trapendale and seemed to be nearly recovered. Eiryss had come to treasure each letter, keeping them in one of her now-empty ribbon boxes.

Eiryss called out her permission and met the servant in the common room. Setting the tray down on the table, she ignored the woman's nose wrinkling in disgust. Any time spent near the lake left Eiryss stinking. What did she care what a servant thought of her?

Eiryss took the letter. The woman beat a hasty retreat. She read Ramass's lovely script. Heart skipping, Eiryss carefully pried open the seal so the paper didn't tear. She scanned the letter. Winter had grown bitter enough to halt the war entirely. Ture and Ramass were headed back to Hanama on an errand from the King. Hagath would be coming with them.

Trapendale was less than three days away—if you took the river down. Six if you had to use the roads the entire way. Maybe nine in this weather. Mail was unreliable at best. Sometimes she even received his letters out of order. Ture had departed nearly a week ago. He could arrive in Hanama any day. Ramass and Hagath shortly thereafter. She squealed, trying to guess when they would arrive.

She climbed to her mother's wing. The war had churned through three cities and hundreds of Enchantresses. She'd heard from one of her aunts that the enchantresses were growing desperate for reinforcements. They would have to reinstate Eiryss before long—a few weeks perhaps.

She'd never stopped studying, reading books on war weavings and battle strategy long into the night. When she was reinstated at the academy, she'd test out of her classes and have her embedding ceremony. Six months at most, and she would have her revenge.

She could hear Mother's wheezing long before she entered her room. Mother tossed in the bed, face flushed with fever. The pot of herbs Eiryss kept over the brazier had boiled down to sludge.

"Oh, Mother, why didn't you ring?" But Eiryss already knew the answer. With Belgrave unable to manage the stairs and Eiryss out, there'd been no one to call.

"Ramass and Ture are coming home!" Eiryss said. "They could be here any day!"

Mother didn't stir. She needed to drink her tea and eat something. "Mother?" She shook her awake.

She looked at Eiryss with fever-filled eyes. "I had the dream again."

Eiryss hid her wince as she set the food beside her bed. Ever since Princess Ahlyn had been interred in the sacred tree, her mother hadn't gone a night without seeing the girl's death. Her health had been failing ever since.

Her mother's gaze was distant, as if she were still dreaming. Sighing, Eiryss filled a pitcher in the bathroom and poured it into the spare pan. She scattered in more herbs and set it over the brazier. She settled on the side of the bed and caught sight of the worn papers beside her mother.

Even with all the carefully worded sentiments about the might and righteousness of the Valynthian army, the council couldn't hide that three of their cities had already fallen. That Valynthia not only faced the unmatched power of a king, but also his successor, whose magic nearly rivaled his own. That refugees had flooded the rest of Valynthia with nothing more than the clothes on their backs. The kingdom was strained to its breaking point trying to keep them all from starving. Even the nobles were going without, though their family still sent what they could spare.

Most of the enchantress healers had been dispatched to the armies—the lives of the soldiers were accounted as more valuable than any others. Those who remained were overwhelmed with wounded—the healer tree was overflowing for the first time in Eiryss's memory.

Still, Eiryss had been training as a healer for years. All she lacked was magic. So she had managed to care for her mother even without a true healer.

"We're safe in Hanama," Eiryss said for them both, though she didn't think her mother could hear her.

She didn't really believe it. The enchantresses had managed to raise vaults over other cities, but not over Valynthia itself. If the Alamantians breached their defenses...

Shaking off the dark thought, Eiryss took out the jar of salve and undid the buttons on her mother's nightgown. She rubbed her chest with a sharp-smelling ointment. She remembered how strong her mother used to be. How capable.

Now that strong, capable woman was trapped in a broken body.

Her mother coughed, her body locking around her lungs as if to protect them. Eiryss shifted behind her and pounded her back to help her get the phlegm out.

"The darkness is real," her mother murmured.

More fever-dreams. "There is no darkness, Mother."

Her face went pale. So pale. "Shadow comes."

Eiryss leaned over her and rested the inside of her wrist against her mother's brow. Heat radiated off her. "I'll get you some windwallow tea." It was hard on her mother's stomach, but it would bring her fever down.

Her mother snatched Eiryss's hand with surprising strength. Eiryss started and looked at her mother. As she watched, the center of one of her flower sigils on her arm started to glow. That glow spread, washing her in silver. For a moment it held, before retracting, gathering the magic from Mother's many sigils into the one above her wrist. A sigil that began to move under her mother's skin.

Eiryss watched with dawning horror. "Belgrave! I need help!"

"The darkness is real," Mother wheezed. "It's inside and it's spreading."

Her speaker sigil pulsed and grew bright enough Eiryss had to squint. Dark foreboding choked her. Eiryss knew what this was, even as her mind fought against it. "Mother, please don't go. Don't leave me."

She tried to pull away. Mother gripped Eiryss's hand even harder. She was all heat and light and strain. Her sigils writhed beneath Eiryss's palm. Mother screamed, but she did not let go. Between their hands, blood welled. Something formed.

"No, Mother! Don't!" Eiryss tried to pull away.

Her mother gripped her harder. "You must see."

The sigil growing between them pierced Eiryss's skin. She screamed even as the room burned away like fire through moth-eaten cloth. Through the gaps, Eiryss found herself in someone else's chambers. She recognized them: Ahlyn's receiving room, which she saw through Ahlyn's eyes—the musical equipment that took up an entire half of the room and the books that filled every other available space.

She could sense Ahlyn's emotions, feel her thoughts, until it was hard to understand where Ahlyn began and Eiryss ended. She knew that Ahlyn kept rearranging everything—though she'd lived in these chambers for a year, they still didn't feel like home. But that was a distant feeling. There were closer ones.

Feelings of fear and resolve and even a little excitement. And then Eiryss lost herself completely to Princess Ahlyn.

Voices made her look up. On the other side of the doorpane, the shapes of her guards, Vicil and Ture, shifted. They spoke low.

Ahlyn couldn't make their words out until Hagath's voice rose in surprise, "I was informed she was ill."

Vicil made a sound low in his throat. "But the king said no visitors."

"We're the princess's guards, not the king's," Ture responded. "Besides, it's just Haggy."

"Don't call me that," Hagath shot back.

"Are we still meeting up tomorrow?" Ahlyn could hear the grin in Ture's words.

"Depends on if you call me Haggy again." Hagath pushed through the magical barrier into Ahlyn's antechambers.

Instantly, Ahlyn felt she could breathe again, that perhaps this burden wouldn't smother her to death.

Hagath's gaze assessed Ahlyn for obvious signs of injury. She set down her medicinal bag, one hand on the flute hanging from her neck. "Ahlyn? What is it? What's wrong?"

Ahlyn looked up at Hagath. "Put the pipes away, enchantress. That's not the kind of healing I need."

Hagath blinked. "But you called for a healer."

"Oh, I need one." Ahlyn reached across the table and held up a bottle of wine. "Just not for the typical services."

Hagath folded her arms. "You pretended to be sick? Ahlyn, you of all people should understand how important my work is. Have you been taking your herbs?"

Ahlyn avoided her friend's gaze. She'd been diagnosed with acute melancholy, which always felt like she was drowning in darkness. But there were times when she felt unstoppable. At those times, the herbs interfered with her brilliance. There was a part of her that always hoped that brilliance wouldn't fade again. That she could manage without her herbs. She'd felt clev-

er and clean for days, but now ... the darkness lingered along the periphery. A darkness that was closing in.

Ahlyn was an expert at hiding the darkness.

"I was with Sevy," Hagath went on. "She could pass at any time."

Guilt chipped away at Ahlyn's perfect mask. "I'm sure the enchantresses sent someone else. Sevy has her family. I've only you."

"You have your sisters. Your mother. Even Ramass." The last came out awkwardly. Hagath clearly wasn't yet comfortable with her brother and her best friend in a relationship.

The darkness gathered, swirling. Light, Ahlyn didn't know if she could survive another bout of it. She pouted. "Haggy, what I need right now is a friend. You were working, so I had no choice but to request you."

Hagath turned away. "Don't call me Haggy."

Ahlyn rolled the bottle between her hands, the silence stretching between them. The darkness sharpened. Ahlyn had already begun to bleed around the edges. "I've decided to marry King Dray."

All Hagath's anger melted to disbelief. She sat beside her friend. "What? But you already told him no!"

A single, bitter laugh escaped Ahlyn's mouth. "Twice. The last time rather emphatically." She sighed. "But I've been thinking about it for hours. He's right. Our kingdoms are never going to stop going to war against each other. Not unless we're joined as one."

"What does my father say?" Hagath murmured.

"He's determined that no one bully Valynthia, or me."

"He's right," Hagath said. "You can't marry Dray. King or not, he's a monster."

Ahlyn popped to her feet and started pacing. "Don't you start on me too. If I don't marry him, it's war. A war we cannot win."

"We could win in a few months!"

Ahlyn huffed. "The Alamantians' new laws granting every-one access to the conduit thorn have produced record numbers of enchanters and soldiers. Their enchanters outnumber us two to one! We don't stand a chance."

Hagath clearly didn't believe it. Valynthians were cocky to a fault. "But to marry an Alamantian..."

Ahlyn wrapped her arms around her waist. "I know. Light help me, I know. But I am not helpless, Hagath. He can't touch me, not with how strong my magic is. Nor do I disagree with everything he's said."

"What?" Hagath asked in surprise.

"Why should only the nobility have the magic? It wasn't always that way. The Silver Tree used to decide who it would grace with power and who it would not. What's wrong with go-ing back to the old ways?"

"You want everyone to have magic? The woman who scrapes bird droppings off your chambers? The man who emp-ties your urine barrels? By the light, what would the masses do with that kind of power? Not to mention the nobility would rebel. And we're the ones with all the magic, and therefore, all the power."

Ahlyn spread her hands. "Why not? I won't be his subordi-nate but his equal. I can change things for both our people. I can change everything."

Hagath pursed her lips. "Ahlyn, do you want to do this?"

The adoring way Ramass looked at her and the feel of his arms around her... How could she give that up? "Do I want to marry Dray? Raise his wild sons? No." But then she thought of him swathed in power on the battlefield. Of her brothers and cousins and friends fighting and killing and dying.

She took a deep breath. "But I'm going to do it all the same.

"And what about my brother?"

Ramass will understand. He's a king's son. He knows the people come first."

Tears welled in Hagath's eyes. "Will we even see each other anymore?"

Ahlyn reached for a couple of glasses and a tray of cheese and crackers. "We'll split our time between Hanama and Ember." She popped the cork and filled two fat glasses to the rim. One overfilled, red wine spilling over the table to drip into a red pool at their feet. Ahlyn ignored it.

Hagath's eyes widened. "Are you planning to get drunk?"

"Smashingly drunk." Ahlyn swirled the wine and inhaled deeply. "Ah, Dray sent this bottle just for me. It's over five hundred years old."

Hagath sniffed hers with a curled lip. She'd never really liked the taste of alcohol. She nibbled on some of the cheese instead. "What will you tell Ramass?"

Ahlyn abandoned sipping for gulping. She wiped her mouth daintily with her napkin. "I sent him a letter."

"A letter?" Hagath exclaimed.

"Same time as I called for you." Ahlyn drained her glass and poured another. "There was nothing formal between us, Hagath. Only kisses snatched in corridors and late-night strolls beneath the stars. All very romantic, but then I've never been a romantic." She swiped at the single tear that escaped down her cheek.

Hagath's gentle gaze said she knew that wasn't true.

"I'm not getting drunk alone." Ahlyn downed her second glass. "You have catching up to do." She nodded to Hagath's glass.

Hagath grimaced and took a swallow of wine. She never could handle more than a few sips. "Are you sure, Ahlyn?"

Ahlyn could feel her mask slipping. She braced herself, forcing the tears to stay behind her eyes where they belonged. "No, but if marrying Dray will prevent a war, then so be it." At

Hagath's worried expression, she waved her friend's concern away. "Bah, I'll bring him to heel. You'll see."

She kept drinking while Hagath sipped. It wasn't long before the two of them were shrieking with laughter over insults to Dray's appendage. Shouts sounded outside. Ahlyn and Hagath exchanged bewildered glances. They both stood, Hagath a good deal steadier than her friend.

"Come on, man," Vicil said from the other side of the door. "She's the princess. You can't just barge in there."

"I can and I will!" Ramass cried. "Ahlyn, let me in!"

"I think he got your letter," Hagath mumbled.

Ahlyn had hoped he wouldn't open it until late the next morning. Apparently, he'd stayed up as late as she had. Ahlyn splayed a hand across her suddenly queasy stomach. Her head had begun to ache as well. She'd clearly had too much wine.

She staggered to the dome and banished the pane. Vicil and Ture each had a hand on Ramass's shoulder, holding him back.

"Let him in," Ahlyn sighed.

"Are you sure, Princess?" Ture asked.

"Stop acting like a pompous idiot," Ramass snapped at his friend. "I'm the one who got you this job!"

"One I take seriously!" Ture shot back.

"Ramass," Vicil said. "We're all friends here. Calm down."

Ahlyn threw her hands in the air. "Oh, you may as well. My floaty happiness has dissolved anyway."

Ramass stormed into the room and shot a betrayed glance at Hagath. She sipped her wine and pretended not to notice. He held up a letter with an official seal dangling like a drop of blood. "I don't accept this!"

Feeling a little green around the edges, Ahlyn flopped in her chair before she fell. "You don't have a choice."

He crumpled it in his fist. "There's always a choice."

She glared at him over her rising nausea. Light, I've had way too much to drink. *"You want to go to war?"*

"The Alamant has no right to tell us how to live! We are a free and independent—"

Ahlyn wiped the sweat off her flushed forehead. "I do this, and we remain free. I don't, and they will conquer us. This way, I retain all my titles as queen and can affect—"

Gripping her arms, Ramass hauled her out of the chair. "Tell me you don't love me. Tell me you want Dray."

The opposite words were there, on the edge of her tongue. One deep breath and they'd tumble out. And then what? Loving Ramass didn't change the fact that she was still going to marry Dray. She shrugged helplessly. "We'd only begun to explore what was between us, Ramass." At his crestfallen look, she added, "I'm sorry."

"How can you say that?"

In answer, Ahlyn vomited all over his feet. He went from trying to shake answers out of her to holding her up. "How much have you had to drink?"

Light, she'd never felt this humiliated in all her life. And the smell... She gagged.

"Not that much." Hagath hurried to fetch a chamber pot.

Ahlyn promptly emptied her stomach into it. Hagath helped her sit down and felt her forehead. Her skin felt hot and cold at once, sweat rolled down her temples, which throbbed to the beat of her frantic heart.

"Ahlyn? What's wrong?"

Ahlyn felt sicker by the moment, her guts twisting into knots. She tried to stand, but her legs wouldn't support her. "Hurts."

"Where?" Hagath asked.

"My stomach." At least, that was the worst of it, but Ahlyn was finding it harder and harder to speak past the pain that walled her in.

Brow furrowed, Hagath dipped a rag in a basin and tried to wipe the sick from Ahlyn's face. Hagath grew pale, her hands shaking. She swallowed hard. Ahlyn's whole stomach cramped. When she vomited again, Hagath joined her.

Ramass swore. "What's wrong with you two?"

Hagath lifted a shaking hand to her forehead and met Ahlyn's gaze. As one, they looked at the empty bottles of wine sent specially from King Dray.

"I think we have been poisoned," Hagath said.

Dray—she hadn't just told him no. She'd demanded that his delegation leave Hanama at once. He must have been planning this all along if she didn't agree. He left before she could tell him she'd changed her mind.

For a beat, there was silence. A beat in which Ahlyn wondered if they were both going to die. Then Ramass was shouting. "Vicil, fetch a healer. Ture, sound the alarm. Run!"

Hagath leaned over the basin. "Force your fingers down your throat. Make yourself throw it all up."

"I already did," Ahlyn panted, her stomach tying itself in knots around her intestines.

"Do it again!" Hagath commanded.

Together, they gagged themselves, Ahlyn getting up blood-tinted bile. Her heart fluttered frantically in her chest. The darkness that always haunted her closed in. Her head rolled back, her awareness fading. Ramass's arms around her were all that kept her from sliding to the floor.

"Get her in the bed," Hagath said to Ramass.

He lifted her trembling body into his arms and looked back at his sister. "What about you?"

"I only had a glass. She had three or four."

"Where are the damn healers!" Ramass shouted, desperation tinging his voice as he pushed through the barrier into Ahlyn's room.

The alarm bells started ringing throughout the city, calling soldiers and enchantresses to arms. Ramass laid her on her bed. The blackness eased just enough that she could make out his expression. She wanted to tell him she was sorry. That she did have feelings for him. Feelings she'd buried deep. But she couldn't seem to catch her breath.

Vicil appeared above her with a half-filled, cloudy glass. "Hagath said she should drink this."

Why hadn't Hagath brought it herself?

Ramass mouth tightened as if he knew the answer. He took the glass. "Bring in my sister."

He lifted Ahlyn onto his lap and pressed the cup to her lips, but she recognized the darkness. It had been hounding her since she was a child. She could feel it seeping into her now—her body and mind disconnecting one fiber at a time, like a fraying rope.

She was dying. No medicine would save her.

Vicil brought in Hagath and laid her on the bed beside Ahlyn. Over the covers, their hands sought each other out and held on.

"Give it to Hagath." Ahlyn couldn't spare another breath. Instead, she stared at Ramass, willing him to understand.

Ramass shifted so he could look down at her. "You're not going to die. Either of you. I promise."

He thought he had control over death. That if he willed it— that if she just fought harder, she would live. She had believed that once too. But death was not something she could fight. It commanded, and she had no choice but to obey. "You can't save me."

Those words cost her. The blackness edged in closer.

Hagath gripped her hand tighter, their heartbeats crashing through their joined palms. Ahlyn managed to turn her head just enough to meet her friend's eyes, which were full of sorrow and understanding. Hagath had seen death. She understood that Ahlyn had gone past the point of no return.

"Tell... my... family," Ahlyn forced out.

Hagath nodded. "I will."

The blackness spiraled in, tighter and tighter with each rotation. She looked up at Ramass and put as much tenderness as she had into her expression. No more masks. No more duties. Just her and the boy who would never know that she loved him too. So much.

For a moment, she could see the life they could have had together—her as queen and him as her consort. They would have had children with his red hair and her blue eyes, freckles splayed like stars across their skin.

She wanted to tell all her loved ones not to grieve her too long. To find happiness. To live. But the blackness was all there was now. There was only her heartbeat.

"Breathe, Ahlyn," Ramass begged. "Breathe."

And then there was nothing.

Eiryss came back into her body with a gasp. It took her a moment to realize she was no longer in Ahlyn's bed, dying right along with her. She was in her own body, which was strong and whole and hale.

Her mother's was not. Her hand was already going limp, the death amulet slipping from Eiryss's skin to the sheets between them. She'd used up the last of her strength to show Eiryss the memory of Ahlyn's death.

It was not a memory she wanted.

"Choose light." Mother's eyes rolled up, and she collapsed. Her wheeze was gone. Her chest lay still.

Eiryss shook her shoulders. "Mother?" Tears streamed down her cheeks. "Mother, please." Resounding silence. She rested her ear over her mother's heart, and that silence became deafening.

Between one breath and the next, her mother was gone. Some sense that Eiryss hadn't known she possessed told her that the soul of the woman she'd known her entire life was no longer there. Eiryss ached for the lack. For the emptiness where before had been warmth and light.

She reached for the bloody amulet in the shape of the Silver Tree, what remained of her mother's magic now trapped inside. She held it to her chest as she keened.

CHAPTER 12

DEATH PORTAL

Lying on a wooden litter at the base of the Silver Tree,
Mother's skin was pale as the snow beneath her. The cutting wind tugged her hair free, brushing it across her still
face. Eiryss knelt beside her, tears blurred her vision as she gently tucked her hair back into place. Choking on a sob, Eiryss
drew the shroud hood over her frozen expression. Her stiff fingers refused to tie the knot under her mother's chin.

She blew warmth into her cupped hands. Heavy flakes of
snow landed on her head, seeping through her hair to run in
freezing streaks down her scalp. She felt the crowd watching her,
pitying gazes and awkward shuffling feet. Someone cleared their
throat.

Her brother knelt across from her, impatiently tugging the
half-tied knot from her fingers. "Of all the days to forget your
gloves," he grumbled under his breath.

Three months of war had changed Rature. She'd thought
him a man before he'd left, but war had chiseled away the last

vestiges of childhood she hadn't realized were there, leaving him harder. Angrier. From the terse way he'd treated her, he still blamed her for Father's death.

He'd returned with the bodies of the nobility who'd been lost in the fall of Lias Lamoren. Bodies lined up all the way to the docks of the Silver Tree. No matter their father's crimes, Mother was the highest-ranking nobleman among them. She went first.

Ture managed the knot, hiding their mother's face in the sewn-together leaves of their hometree. And just like that, Eiryss would never see Mother again.

She hadn't thought she had any more tears to shed. She'd been wrong. The urge to hurt herself to relieve the pain swarmed her. But her mother wouldn't like that. And she'd promised Ramass.

Eiryss wore the amulet her mother had made with the last of her magic. An amulet she was required by law to turn in to the enchantresses. Instead, she'd pried an old amulet from above one of the panels in an empty room of their hometree to give to the constables who came for it. She'd tied a knot in a leather cord and hung her mother's amulet around her neck. She pressed that amulet against her chest until it left an indentation. She found comfort in that. Comfort in her mother's magic leaving a physical impression on her.

When a person died, their magic surged within them. Most made something useful—the ahlea flowers in their chambers weren't just for decoration. They contained the magic that made the panels. Eiryss sensed her mother's magic had made something far different. Something that had allowed her to use her mother's speaker for the dead gift, if only for a moment.

Her mother had used that moment to show her Ahlyn's death. Why? She had to have known the memory would haunt Eiryss for the rest of her life. Did Mother know how much Eiryss had resented Ahlyn's seeming perfection? Eiryss now knew that perfection was a mask. Darkness haunted the girl's life.

Eiryss's jealousy had been petty and childish.

She pressed her handkerchief into her swollen, tender eyes and cried with them, these women who wept for their dead. A part of her also cried for herself, for the life that was dead and gone as surely as her parents.

A gentle hand helped her to her feet. Vicil's other arm was tied in a sling—a wound he'd received in battle. "All will be well."

Her mother was dead. How could anything be well? Nor had she forgotten that Vicil had been the one to tattle on her father. If he had kept his mouth shut... then all of Valynthia might have fallen.

Eiryss accepted Vicil's arm.

"Ture," Vicil gave a pointed look at the next group waiting to bury their dead. Ture nodded. The two of them placed Mother's stiff corpse against the hollow of the tree and pulled apart the wooden litter.

The bare wood was darker there, nearly black. For a moment, nothing happened. Then vines rustled, curling around Mother, tugging her into the heart of the tree. Into the depths like a night sky filled with stars, shadows shifting like clouds beneath.

Eiryss never got used to this part. The part where vines obscured all but the feet, the point of the nose, leaving only a vague shape of a person. That shape sank with a creaking, hollow sound.

And then she was gone. The vines shifted away.

The Silver Tree demanded little in exchange for his magic—the memories of the dead were one of them. Eiryss made a small sound of protest, the urge to touch her mother one last time overwhelming her.

Vicil held her back. "All her memories, everything about her that ever was, is now held in the Sacred Tree. And when you die, you'll be with her again. Forever."

But not with her father. He hadn't been granted access to the Silver Tree's embrace.

The next dead person was already in place—a girl this time, barely older than Eiryss. Her entire face was purple and swollen, mouth gaping crookedly likely a broken jaw and sunken eyes wide with horror. None of that stopped Eiryss from recognizing her. Shelin. She'd graduated from the enchantress academy only a couple years before. And worse still...

Eiryss spun, searching the faces of those who had gathered and caught sight of Kit, here to bury his sister. His eyes were blank, his expression haggard. A bloody bandage circled his head.

"Wait," she said to Vicil as she slipped out from under his arm. She stood before Kit, not sure whether to touch him—not many people wanted her anywhere near them anymore. After what seemed an eternity, he looked up. At first, he didn't seem to recognize her. Then his eyes widened. He took her in his arms, holding her tight.

"I'm sorry," she whispered.

He sobbed once. "She died holding the vault so the people might escape."

"Then she is a hero," Eiryss whispered against his neck.

"Eiryss," Ture called. There wasn't enough room for all the people who wanted to say goodbye to their dead. They needed to leave.

"Will you come see me after?" she asked.

"I can't. I'm to report to the king in Trapendale. I leave in a few hours." Kit pressed his lips to her forehead. "Next time, I promise."

A hand on her elbow. Ture stood behind her, his expression tight. "Other people need to be here."

125

Stifling a sob, she stretched up and kissed Kit's cold cheek. "I miss you."

Their eyes stayed locked together as Ture tugged her off the platform. As Eiryss made her way down the packed stairs of the dead and those left behind, she couldn't help but remember that Ahlyn had predicted this destruction before her death. Had been willing to marry an Alamantian to stop it. How would things have played out differently if she'd lived? If Father hadn't killed her?

"Your mother isn't suffering anymore, Eiryss," Vicil said from behind her. "She's at peace now."

She wished he would stop trying to comfort her.

At the docks at the base of the Silver Tree, they said their goodbyes to their cousins, aunts, and uncles. Vicil gripped Ture's shoulders and said something too low for Eiryss to make out. They embraced in the pounding hug that men did before Ture turned to untie their boat.

Eiryss endured Vicil's hug and hurried after her brother. Ture barely waited for her before pushing off. They rowed across the flat, ink-black waters to their hometree.

"Did Mother leave a death amulet?" Ture asked.

Eiryss nearly touched the magic below her throat. She should declare it—death amulets were meant for the good of Valynthia. Especially unique ones like her mother had made. But she couldn't shake the feeling her mother had made this amulet specifically for her.

"A regular ahlea," she lied.

He gave a curt nod, his mouth thinned in disappointment. When they reached their hometree, he tied off at their dock, and they climbed the stairs that wound around the trunk until they reached the warmth of the kitchen. Their family had filled the iron braziers while they'd been away. A pot of soup bubbled at the back of the stove. Small kindnesses. There wasn't time or resources for a larger one—even for a family such as hers.

Belgrave moved toward her, arms upraised for an embrace, before his eyes fell to Ture. He stepped back and bowed deferentially. "Will the lord and lady eat in the kitchens or the common room?"

Eiryss longed for that hug. For some kind of comfort. Instead, she had her brother's anger. "The kitchens," Eiryss said. "The common room is cold." It probably wasn't, but Belgrave wouldn't reach it, especially not carrying trays of food.

Ture sat with his bowl of soup while Eiryss held her red, chapped hands over the stove, moaning a little at the heat. How spoiled she'd been before—to only know the bite of winter when she chose it. Like the times they'd gone to their summer estate for a few weeks to play in the snow, always knowing that the warmth of Hanama was only a short ride away.

When her fingers had lost some of their stiffness, she removed her coat, setting it on a chair near the stove to dry. "Do you ever remember a time when it has been so cold?" She tried for lightness but feared she came off as gloomy.

"Belgrave, if you'll excuse us?" Ture asked. Belgrave bowed and left. "Why is his bed in our kitchen?"

Eiryss slumped into a chair. "He's gotten worse since you left."

"The man should spend out the rest of his days with his family. Not struggling to serve you."

Her cheeks heated at the implication. "He chose to stay." And she had been the one serving him. She couldn't say that of course. Belgrave was a servant. Her brother would be appalled.

"Out of loyalty. I've already written to his sister's family. I'm sure they'll take him in."

The ache in her heart expanded until she thought it would choke her. Belgrave had been a staple in her life for as long as she could remember. But more than that, in these last few months, he'd also become a dear friend. And she had precious few of those left.

"Will you tell him, or should I?" Ture asked.

Eiryss owed the man at least that much. "I will."

"Now is better than later. The auctioneer is coming tomorrow. After we're through with Belgrave, go through your things and decide what to keep."

"Auctioneer?"

Ture's mouth thinned. "I've only three days to get everything settled, Eiryss, so I'm going to be blunt. Our hometree is dead."

The hometree had lost its leaves weeks ago, along with all the other trees in Hanama. But she'd held on to hope that it would survive until spring. Her spoon fell from limp fingers, splashing soup down her front. "It can't. It's not that old and—"

"Frost reached the heartwood."

The Arbor's men would cut it down piece by piece rather than risk it falling.

She was homeless.

She remembered the countless times she, Ture, Hagath, and Ramass had swum in the lake while Marinda had cooked and their parents had played card games. When it was just Eiryss and Ture, they'd played in the upper boughs for hours with their cat, Jipson—long dead now. Just like her father. And her mother.

She leaned back in her chair, too numb to feel much of anything. "Where will I go?"

"Vicil will take you in."

"And when his arm heals, and he goes back to war?"

"We'll sell what's left of the furniture. Unfortunately, our hometree isn't the only one to fall so the market is flooded. I'll beg some money off our relatives. Enough for a decent dowry. That plus your title will allow you to marry into one of the powerful lines."

She'd just lost her mother forever, and Ture wanted to speak of marriage? "I'm not marrying anyone."

"What about Kit? I saw you talking to him today. You two had some sort of... relationship."

Not that long ago, Kit had been so far beneath her station as to be laughable. Now, he was her brother's first choice. She cared about Kit. Perhaps there could be something more. "I don't want to marry."

He rubbed his head in frustration. "What else is there for a noblewoman in your situation? You can't go back to the Enchantress Academy."

"The kingdom needs enchantresses, Ture. They'll call me up before long."

He met her gaze evenly. "They won't."

"What?"

"People are dead, Eiryss. And not just peasants—the nobility. *Our* people are hungry and cold. Father's not around to receive their ire, so as his accomplice, they're directing all that anger at you."

Eiryss had never been her father's accomplice. It wasn't fair, but Eiryss was learning more and more that for the powerless, nothing was fair. A lesson that was reinforced whenever she ventured beyond her hometree and had to face the muttered insults and dark looks.

"Even if they hate me, Vicil will be absent. If he were to appoint me to temporarily take his place in the council, I could work myself into the good graces of the other members." It might take a bit longer for her embedding ceremony, but she could do it.

"The council would never accept you—titles or no. Your only other option is to become a tradeswoman and lose your title altogether."

Once her title was lost, it would be lost forever. There would be no more future kings and queens in her line. No more magic. She could never own land. And upon her death, she would be buried in filth like her father instead of being embraced by the Silver Tree and joining her mother.

No. She wouldn't accept this. She couldn't. Still, she'd felt the nobility's growing hatred. So many times—in the glares and snubs and muttered insults. Never anything more. She was still under the king's protection. Enderlee had spoken up for her too; if the woman thought that meant Eiryss had forgiven her, she was gravely mistaken.

They would help her. She knew they would.

Eiryss braced herself against the table. "I was meant to be an enchantress. It was what I was always meant to be."

"Not anymore." Was she mistaking the compassion in his voice?

"You can't know they won't call me up. Not for certain."

He gazed out the window toward the Silver Tree. "Take the night. Think about it."

She pushed the despair down, down, down. She would not break in front of her brother. She would find a way. The king would not desert her. Enderlee owed her. There had to be a way.

"And our debt?" she whispered.

"The king paid it with the understanding that I'll pay him back as I can."

She didn't like her brother taking over the debt completely, but she wasn't in a position to pay any of it. She could barely keep them fed.

They found Belgrave in the next room over, the supply room, which wasn't even heated. It took both Ture and Eiryss to get him back to the warm kitchen. They settled him in a chair by the fire, and for once he didn't protest and demand to start cleaning up their lunch.

Maybe Ture was right. Maybe this was the best thing for Belgrave. She told him as gently as she could, though it was impossible not to keep the wobble from her voice. Belgrave gazed at her, his expression pleading and helpless as a child's.

Unable to bear it, she turned to Ture. "Surely Vicil could use a loyal servant."

Ture sighed and said to Belgrave, "If you don't mind sharing a room with one of the other servants, I imagine we could arrange it." Belgrave blanched. "I can't give you a stipend as I would like. But I will arrange for your travel to your sister in Oramen. Or if not there, I know you have brothers."

Belgrave bowed his head. "I would like to stay with my sister, lord."

Ture pulled documents from his jacket, travel arrangements and the like. "I thought you might. I've already arranged everything. You'll leave tomorrow morning."

Belgrave stared at the papers in his hands. "Very good, Lord Rature."

Ture rose. "I'll go up to your room and gather your things. You can decide what to take with you."

Belgrave nodded.

When her brother was gone, Eiryss knelt before Belgrave and rested her hands on his arms. "You don't have to go. You could come to Vicil's."

Belgrave looked at her. "I doubt they will let me live in their kitchen." She opened her mouth to protest, but he held out a hand. "No, I've not seen my family in years. It will be good to be with them again."

She wanted to wrap her arms around him. But didn't dare with her brother in the hometree. She settled for squeezing his arms. "I'll miss you. And thank you."

He bowed. "It has been an honor, lady."

CHAPTER 13

THORN

Eiryss was up well before dawn the next day to send a missive to King Zannok and Arbor Enderlee, demanding acceptance into the academy. She returned to find Belgrave waiting for her under their hometree's bridge alcove and Ture pacing its length. Eiryss hugged Belgrave tight, not caring if her brother saw. She stepped back.

Tears streamed down his stoic face as he climbed into the rickshaw. It started away. She watched as he grew smaller and smaller. He looked back only once, a hand raised in farewell. Eiryss lifted her own hand, suddenly wishing she could go with him.

Ture came to stand beside her. "It's for the best, Eiryss. You're in no position to take care of him."

She turned away so her brother wouldn't see the tears building in her eyes. How their roles had changed. Now he was the bold one and she the reticent. She rubbed at the soreness deep in her throat, hoping it was just irritation from the cold air and not something worse.

Hugging her coat to her chest, she climbed to her room. At the doorway, she paused at the sight of auctioneers evaluating her furniture. Vicil's servants carefully packed her clothing and books for the trip to her cousin's tree in the next sector.

It's just until I go back to the academy, she assured herself. *Then I can start rebuilding all we have lost.*

Taking a fortifying breath, she went to supervise.

It was dark by the time they were finally done. Everything in her hometree had been carefully cataloged with elegantly written price tags dangling like dead moths from a spider's string.

In the common room, she and Ture shared a soup Marinda had sent along with Vicil's servants. The heat and salt soothed Eiryss's throat, which had grown steadily worse as the day had passed.

"One last night," Ture said softly.

The thought of strangers perusing her family heirlooms made her shudder. Resentment hung between them, but so did their childhood, their shared memories. Eiryss feared bridging the gap—what if Ture hadn't forgiven her? What if he never did? "When do you leave?"

"As soon as everything is settled. We need to begin campaigning to take our cities back."

"And will you?" He shot her a questioning look. "Take them back," she clarified.

"Yes."

No hesitation, and yet he wouldn't meet her eyes. "What makes you so sure?"

He shifted uncomfortably and didn't answer.

"Eiryss," said a new voice. She turned before the sound had finished leaving his lips and was in Ramass's arms before he'd even stepped into the room.

He lifted her off her feet and squeezed the breath from her. "I've missed you!"

She inhaled the smell of him—snow and fire and something distinctly *him*. His arms were strong, his body warm and lean against her softness. She didn't want to let go. She never wanted to let go. The realization shocked her out of his arms, head down to hide the blush spread across her cheeks.

"Ramass!" Ture cried.

Ramass shifted past her, hopefully too preoccupied with her brother to notice. They shared a pounding hug before breaking apart.

"I'm so sorry I missed the funeral," Ramass said to them both.

Body and soul, she had ached for missing him. And her burgeoning feelings for him had only grown with his absence. But if she revealed those feelings and he didn't reciprocate, it could poison their friendship. And now that she'd been in Ahlyn's mind, she knew the connection between them hadn't been some passing fancy.

They'd been in love.

Desperate to hide her turmoil, she searched for some excuse to turn away from him. She fiddled with the tags on the chairs, turning them face out.

Ramass stepped closer to her. "Oh, lady, is it that bad?"

The gentleness in his voice undid her. "It's all gone," she whispered. She did not want her brother to hear. "Father and Mother... Our home. It's my fault."

"No, Eiryss," Ramass said. "Never yours."

"Isn't it?" Ture said, voice hard. "Father would still be alive if not for her. Maybe Mother too."

The words were like a blade to her stomach. How had so much joy turned to rot so fast? Rot like her father rotting in the ground, his head separated from his shoulders. And his emptying eyes... She staggered back, a sob rising in her throat.

"You've made her believe this was her fault?" Ramass asked, his body lethally still.

"It is!"

Ramass shoved her brother. "As if you would have done any differently."

Ture stumbled but caught himself before he fell. "I would have—"

"You wouldn't, and you know it!" Ramass shouted. "We should have watched her closer—we both know how she is." The two stared each other down, seconds from coming to blows.

"He isn't wrong," Eiryss said. "Father wouldn't have confessed if I hadn't come."

Ramass gaped at her. "Undrad's death is not your fault. Do you understand me?" She couldn't answer. He pointed accusingly at Ture. "Put the blame where it rightfully lays, Ture. And it isn't with Eiryss."

"If she would have stayed away from Father," Ture shouted, "none of this would have ever happened."

Ramass gripped his tunic in his fists. "That's a lie, and you know it!"

Eiryss tried to insert herself between them—of the two, Ramass was the better strategist and Ture the better fighter—when she saw movement at the doorway. A servant in the grey-green livery of the enchantresses stood just inside the doorpane, her eyes wide and her mouth ajar. She met Eiryss's gaze and immediately dropped it.

"I'm sorry, lords and lady. I'll just—"

The missive Eiryss had been waiting for. "No!" Eiryss finally managed to shove the two apart. She took the letter from the girl, who instantly fled. Eiryss tore open the seal and scanned the page. With every word she read, the resonant hollow in her grew until it vibrated with sound. Her fingers lost their strength. The letter slipped from her deadened fingers.

Ramass was speaking to Eiryss. Asking her a question. She couldn't hear him over the scream building inside her. He picked the letter up, scanned it. His stunned eyes met hers.

Her suspension had been shifted to expulsion without the option of reentry.

In the months since her father's death, the knowledge that this nightmare would end—that she would have her sigils soon enough—had kept her going. Now that hope shattered beneath her, leaving her floundering in icy waves of despair.

Her purpose was gone.

Eiryss fled. Up the stairs. Past her room. Past the servants' empty quarters. Up, up, up. Beyond the last path and into the high branches that dipped and swayed beneath her weight.

She found herself out in the cold among the remnants of the platforms she and Ramass had spent hours building as children. In the nook of one of the branches was a copperbill nest. Amid the bright orange eggshells were faded ribbons—copperbills were always stealing things that didn't belong to them. She turned away when a flash of purple caught her eye.

Eiryss bent down and caught sight of one of her amethyst earrings. She hadn't even known it was missing. She reached into the nest, past feathers and faded ribbons, to the spark of color. She held the earring in her hand. Her parents had given them to her—a pair of earrings for each of her birthdays. She couldn't remember exactly which birthday this had been—her eighth, maybe—but she remembered the dress her mother had ordered to match. The ribbons the king had brought. She remembered Ture sneaking a bite of her melon sculpture, so the fish had been missing a fin when she went to carve for everyone.

Her father had made him write a report on fair trade agreements and spent an extra two hours running.

She almost threw the earring into the water, but her mother had given it to her every bit as much as her father. She slipped it in her ear and looked once more at the remnants left behind from her and Ramass's escapades. If she tried hard enough, she could smell the sweet cakes she and Ramass stole from Marinda, who always pretended not to notice. Feel the rush of wind as they'd swung out over open air on a rope, a fall certain to kill them, before crashing back on a platform that would tremble beneath their weight. They would lie on their backs and laugh until their sides ached.

Until Ture and Hagath had tattled on them—Ture had always preferred writing songs with Hagath to playing. Their parents had been furious at the reckless danger. All the platforms had been taken down and the lines cut. Eiryss and Ramass had been confined to their rooms for a month. But for one winter, only the knots they'd tied had kept them from falling.

Exposed to years of sun and rain, what little remained was rotted and gaping. And soon, even that would be gone. Like the meadows of the estate Eiryss's family no longer owned. Like the hometree cut down because the heartwood had perished.

Eiryss stood at the edge of her past, looking down, down, down to the depths below. What if she swung out without a rope to catch her? She would never have to relive the light fading from her father's eyes. The blood pulsing hot between her and her mother's palms. She wouldn't have to live with the crushing guilt. She could rest—light, when was the last time she'd slept without nightmares forcing her awake?

Her heart quickened and she stepped to the edge of the branch and looked down, down, down.

"Eiryss?" She glanced back to find Ramass watching her. He looked down the drop then back at her. "What are you doing?" He must have seen some kind of answer in her eyes because he stepped forward and took tight hold of her hand. He led her back to the center of the tree, away from the outskirts, pulled her down beside him, and wrapped his arms around her.

Around them, the dead, clinging leaves of her hometree rustled and wept in the unforgiving wind. The water far below reflected the moonlight, flat and black. The lake had frozen. Her breath came out in a huff of white. Tears slipped down her face, freezing against her cheeks.

"I'm so tired, Ramass."

"Things are going to get better. I promise."

Would it? She couldn't see past the darkness choking her to know. She understood Ahlyn better now that the girl was dead than she ever had when she was alive. She would have laughed at the irony, but she wasn't sure she would ever laugh again.

She shivered. "I watch him die. Over and over again. I don't think I can watch it again. Especially not when I know it's my fault."

He pulled off his gloves and wrapped her freezing hands in his warm ones. His thumbs passed over the scar on the back of her hand. She was inordinately proud of that scar. It represented all the turmoil she'd been brave enough to face instead of escaping into the pain.

"Your brother is an idiot." He took off his coat and settled it around her shoulders. She pushed her freezing arms inside the warm wool. "I already told you—it's not your fault."

She sniffed and wiped her eyes with her wrists—warmth and then even colder than before. "If it's not my fault, who's is it?"

"The man who started this war."

King Dray. The broken pieces in her shifted, hardened into an edge sharp enough to cut. Her brown eyes met his dark grey ones. "I was born to be an enchantress. I won't settle for marrying some lord."

He chuckled without humor. "Is that what Ture wants to do with you?"

"I won't," she said, the words a puff of white. She pressed the amulet into her skin. The past was gone. And what lay before her... It was not the life of power and privilege she'd been raised to. The life that was meant to be hers. "I was meant for more,

Ramass. I know it in my bones." And just as deep, she knew she was supposed to be an enchantress. That she would never find peace if she didn't make the Alamantians suffer as they'd made her people suffer.

He gazed toward the south, toward the Alamant. Something hardened in his gaze—a decision had been made. "My father sent me back to Valynthia to create an enchantress unit under my command."

That was impossible. Men couldn't run women's magic. How could they, when they didn't even comprehend how to use it? "Enderlee would never allow it."

"She doesn't need to. The council has already sided with my father."

Two against one. Hope a green shoot inside her, Eiryss eased closer to him. "I could become an enchantress under you?"

His brows drew together in thought. "We'd have to find a way for the council to approve it."

The hope springing to life inside her threatened to wither and die. She pressed the amulet into her skin, the words of her prayer slipping silently between her lips. "Mother, I would live a life of meaning rather than one of rote. There has to be a way...."

Her mother's voice echoed through her. "Choose light."

When Eiryss looked up, moonlight lit the way across the frozen water, where it met the shining silver leaves of their sacred tree under the protection of a dome. The light beckoned her, called to her. The path to freedom and power—enough power to become the enchantress she was meant to be. If only she were brave enough to take it.

"What if I already had the thorns?" she blurted.

He followed her gaze, his head coming up with understanding. "Even the enchantress can't countermand the will of a sacred tree. But if you're caught... I can't go up against the council and win."

Sprigs of hope caught life inside her again, growing like seeds too long denied the sun. "So I won't be caught."

One side of his mouth quirked up. "Light, I've missed you."

A lock of red hair strayed across Ramass's face. Everything inside Eiryss stilled. Life moved fast. Too fast for fear. He would go back to the war. She could lose him as quickly as she'd lost her parents. She reached out, the pads of her fingers scraping across the stubble on his jaw and her gaze fixed on his mouth. He froze, brow drawn in confusion. She leaned forward. Her lips met his, a gentle press soft as morning light. But it filled her. Every particle of her.

He didn't kiss her back, but neither did he pull away. She broke contact, refusing to look at his face for fear of what she'd find there. She'd kissed other men. Many of them. But this may as well have been her first for the tenderness swelling inside her.

She smiled a shy smile, the feel of it foreign and welcome on her cheeks. "I've missed you too."

"Eiryss, I—" He pulled his hand through his hair. "Ahlyn has only been gone for three months. Even if she didn't love me—"

"She loved you," Eiryss said fiercely. She felt strangely protective of Ahlyn. In a way, Eiryss knew her more intimately than anyone else. Sharing the girl's death had done that.

He shot her a confused look.

Eiryss held out her mother's death amulet. "My mother was a speaker for the dead. As she lay dying, she shared her gift with me—I'm not sure how. But I experienced Ahlyn's memory of the night she died. More than that, I died along with her. I felt the darkness she always struggled to keep at bay close in. Her last thoughts were of you, of her family. She wanted you to know she loved you. She didn't say it before because loving you didn't change what she had to do—the sacrifice she had to make for Valynthia. She regretted it in the end."

Ramass rubbed at the tears spilling from his eyes. "You couldn't possibly have seen all that." The hope in his voice belied his words.

Eiryss looked at him. "Ahlyn knew she was dying. That's why she told you to give the medicine to Hagath. 'Tell my family' were the last words she ever spoke. She wanted her family to know she loved them. She wanted them to find an end to their grief and be happy." Eiryss had written a letter to Ahlyn's family in her mother's handwriting to tell them of the memory. It was the most she could offer the girl who should have been Eiryss's friend in truth.

Eiryss's voice softened. "She wanted you to be happy."

Sobbing, he gripped her hand. Silence stretched between them.

She still couldn't risk looking at him. "I don't want you as my friend, Ramass. I want something more than that. I know you lost Ahlyn not long ago. You don't have to return my feelings. But it's too late to go back. At least for me."

"I don't know what to say."

She hadn't expected any other answer from him. And right now, the joy from kissing him still suffused her. She didn't want to lose it to worry. "I'm not sorry," she said in a whisper. Kissing Ramass had been the happiest she'd been in months.

He finally released her hand. "Go," he breathed. "Take what's yours."

Her thorns. This time, he wouldn't be leaving without her. For now, that was enough. She shifted past him, scurrying down with a speed even he couldn't match. When she finally reached the stairs, she broke into a silent run, her eyes scanning for any sign of Ture. The lights were on in his wing.

Relieved, she made her way to the supply room, donned her winter clothing, and took the grappling hook and rope. Her single vessel lay still next to the docks. She knelt in the small boat, the movement cracking the thin layer of ice surrounding it. She chopped her oar through and rowed. As she picked up speed, her prow managed to break through, though the ice slowed her.

Her sore throat burned in earnest and her arms ached by the time she reached the Silver Tree. It gleamed like the moon, the once colorful lambent flowers shriveled and black from frost. She avoided the docks and its guards. Instead, she paddled to the buttressed roots on the far side of the tree. The trunk rose before her, the rough bark her only handholds.

Shivering and sweating, she tied up her small craft, wrapped the ropes around her shoulders, and climbed. The going was easy at first. The tree was wider at the base, so she was scrambling as much as climbing. About the time her hands went numb, the way went straight up.

Halfway up, she climbed onto the winding staircases. It would be so much easier if she could just take them the rest of the way. But she couldn't risk being seen by the guards. Hands tucked under her arms for warmth, she gritted her teeth to keep from chattering and looked down. A fall from this high might not kill her. But it would wound her. And the cold of it... She shivered.

I'm a good climber. I'll be all right.

Hands a little warmer, she pulled out the grappling hook and hesitated. She was about to profane something sacrosanct. She rested her forehead against the smooth bark of the tree. She thought of all the pain and suffering and loss she'd experienced. Her desire to make it right, no matter the cost.

Something shifted deep within, as if the tree understood. "Sometimes wrong is right," she whispered.

Bracing herself, she threw with a practiced hand. The hook dug into the joint between trunk and tree. She tugged to test the hold and climbed, pulling with her arms and bracing with her legs. She was breathing hard and the pain in her throat sharpened.

She finally reached her hook. She straddled the bough and tried, unsuccessfully, to work up a little moisture to soothe her raw throat. When she could manage, she worked the hook free, wincing at the damage she'd done. Deep gouges leaked sap. Knowing the healing properties, she swiped some onto her bare finger and licked it off. The rawness in her throat eased.

By the light, the Arbor would likely throw her in prison for this. But she would not stop now. She threw the rope and repeated the process. She had nearly reached the canopy when her feet skidded on some loose bark, which forced her arms to take all her weight. Her numb hands refused to grip. She slid. Falling faster and faster. A small branch scraped the side of her head. Abruptly, her feet came up against something solid.

Heart pounding in her ears, she found a small branch beneath her feet. Exhaling in relief, she curled inward, huddled around the scant warmth of her core, and shivered as much from fear as from the cold. Her ear stung. She reached out and felt damp on her fingers. A smear of blood. And the earring she'd only just found, gone. Torn out when she'd slipped.

She felt suddenly bereft. Adrift. Her hands cramped as she peered into the tree, at the swirling shapes there, and swore she saw her mother's face looking back at her.

"Choose light," echoed in her head. Just as quickly, it was gone.

When the cramps had eased, she ascended again, slower and more carefully this time. She reached the canopy and climbed from branch to branch, only using her hook if she had to. When she reached the top of the natural platform, she peeked over. On the opposite side, a sentinel in his pure silver armor stood under the archway built over the stairs, his back to her.

For a moment, she could see how it should have been. A procession of boats bedecked with flowers and ribbons would have taken her to the Silver Tree. She would have climbed the steps barefoot with her parents on either side of her. She would crest those stairs wearing the most beautiful dress—one the king would have given her. She would walk through her gathered friends and family, who would shower her with gifts and praise. She would pass those gifts back to the unruly children who followed her, planning to open them later. At the base of the tree, the Arbor would be waiting.

Her parents would present her with the flute made by a master craftsman—the flute she'd found in her father's safe. The same flute the treasurers had taken to pay her family's debts. Her mother would lay her mantle across her shoulders—the healer insignia on the back, her family's crest on the front.

Atop the dais, Arbor Enderlee would be waiting. Eiryss would step onto the dais for the first time. Enderlee would dip the chalice into the sap that filled the font and hold the dripping cup out to Eiryss.

Eiryss gasped out the breath she'd been holding as what should have been fell away, leaving only what was. A girl who'd lost everything.

No. Not everything. She was still here. Still fighting.

Crouching low, she climbed up and over. Her goal was a third of the way back from the archway. Atop the dais, the pedestal twisting branches and wicked thorns glistening razor sharp. She crawled on her belly to the stairs that led to the font, careful to keep it between her and the sentinel. She rose, mindful of the hundreds of thorns growing from the greenery that surrounded the bowl. Without the chalice, she drank the slightly sticky sap straight from her cupped hands. It was cool and soothing down her throat. Within moments, she felt warm—the sap's numbing properties already taking effect.

Much larger than all the others, the conduit thorn was on the opposite side. She would have to step into the sentinel's line of sight to access it. Thankfully, the man still had his back to her.

Sap dripping from her fingers, she kept her gaze fixed on him as she eased around. Some of the thorns tore her coat. Thick as her wrist at the base, the conduit thorn tapering to a wicked point at the tip. It gleamed the brightest silver, light glittering across the surface.

Normally, Eiryss would be given time for the sap to work as Arbor Enderlee listed off her accomplishments. There wasn't time for that now.

Eiryss pressed her palm into the thorn. Sharp pain radiated up her arm and neck. Her blood welled, swirling through the thorn's hollow core like a drop of milk in water. It danced through the font and spun through one thorn and then another before settling in a handful, which sparked ruby red.

Cool spread up her arm as the tree's heartblood mixed with hers. Dizzy, she pulled back from the conduit thorn. Her hand ached, blood and sap spilling from her fingertips to drip onto the tree. She stared at the nearest red thorn. A companion she would bear for the rest of her life. Its magic would finally make her an enchantress. Her fingers closed around it—it was the size of a fat needle. It broke off with a clean snap—the sound loud in the stillness.

She whipped around. The sentinel turned, his eyes going wide with disbelief. "Breach!" He ran toward her.

No time for hesitation. The cool vibrating under her skin coalesced in the center of her chest—the tree leading her to the proper placement. Laying the thorn flush against the cool spot, she pinched the skin beneath it and pushed. Burning, glittering pain. Breath left her in a gasp. Footsteps sounded behind her. Gritting her teeth, she forced it all the way in.

Only one thorn of the eight she was meant to have. Better than nothing.

He gripped her arm, jerking her back from the font. "Fool girl. They'll only rip it out of you," he said, not unkindly.

She gritted her teeth against the burning throb and tried to wrench free. "They wouldn't dare go against the Silver Tree's will. It chose me!"

He took hold of her other arm. "Not Undrad's daughter. Not after what your father did. What you did."

She reeled, fear coating her mouth.

Footsteps pounded, and another three guards appeared under the archway at the top of the stairs.

The man holding her leveled her with a look. "Fighting will only make it worse." But she was well and truly trapped and she knew it. She sagged and nodded.

He released one arm. "Take her to the Arbor."

Flanking her on every side, they escorted her down the long, winding steps.

CHAPTER

ARBOR

"**D**o you have any idea what you've done?"

Eiryss woke to Ture standing over her. She coughed, her throat raw and weeping. The wound at her chest pulsed with pain. Ture thrust a cup into her hands. She managed to stop coughing long enough to sip, the tea spreading coolness down her throat. Her lower back ached with fever that left her cold and hot at once.

This was her second day in the novice room surrounded by a silver, impenetrable dome. Covered by a thick wool blanket, she lay on a cot. As it always did in the Enchantress Academy, music lifted all around her, the sounds breathy and light as the brush of a bird's wings. Her hand went to the thorn at her breast. She jerked back with a hiss that belied the relief spreading through her. It was still alive inside her. Her body hadn't rejected it. Nor had it been removed. Yet.

If it caught sometime in the next two weeks, the thorn would soften and spread, forming sigils, from which she would draw magic. Her curiosity flared. The chest was an unusual spot for a sigil—most ended up on the arms. She wondered what this would be.

Surely Enderlee won't remove it. She knows I'm no traitor.

But at the thought of the Arbor, a hazy memory drifted into focus. During one of her fever dreams, Enderlee had come. "We'll have to wait until she's well enough to remove it."

To remove it was to kill it and to profane something sacrosanct, just as Eiryss had when she'd taken the thorn in the first place. Yet Eiryss was to be punished for the act, while the arbor would demand it as a right. The rest of the memory drifted away, but those words rang through Eiryss, snuffing out any remaining hope as the strains of music trembled to a silence.

"Is this the same illness Mother caught?" Ture asked, hopelessness creeping into his voice.

Eiryss nodded. She wasn't surprised by the worry and blame warring for dominance inside Ture. Her brother had always been a study in contradictions. As a child, it had been clear he would be a brilliant swordsman, as good as their father one day. Yet in the dark of night, Eiryss had often heard her brother crying. When the other boys were chasing serving maids or drinking too much wine, Ture had preferred playing cards or board games with Hagath. If he wasn't doing that, he was reading books or writing songs, which were actually quite good. Eiryss knew because she'd jiggled the lock on the chest he kept them hidden in, found the most embarrassing love ballad she could, and tacked it up all over the island where the men had their sword training.

For a while, everyone burst into song whenever Ture appeared. Father had banished her to her room for an entire week in punishment. It had been worth it. And Ture had recovered fairly quickly, especially when one of the court singers had performed his song at the king's gala.

Ture might blame her for all their troubles, but he worried for her too.

"Are they treating you for it?"

"The one good thing about being held by enchantresses," she rasped. "How did you find out?" She'd hoped to be taken to Arbor Enderlee before her brother discovered what she'd done. Then it would be decided one way or the other—hopefully in her favor—and she wouldn't have to endure his lecture.

That would never happen now. The only option left to her was marriage. The high nobility wouldn't have any need of her status. But some of the minor lords with money of their own wouldn't mind grafting her pedigree with theirs.

Ture threw his hands out. "All the men in the barracks are talking about it—sentinels never could keep their mouths shut. The names they're calling you..."

Eiryss winced. "And men call women gossips."

"You think this is funny?"

No. No, she did not. "Where's Ramass?"

Ture growled. "You aren't a child anymore, Eiryss! And he should have talked you out of this."

"Stop pretending you're perfect!" This brought on another round of coughing that left her breathless and trembling.

His gaze locked on to her neck. She suddenly felt the amulet there, shaken out of her clothes by her coughing.

He reached out to grasp it and withdrew with a wince. Blood welled where one of the sharp-edged branches had pierced him. "You lied to me."

She pressed it against her skin. "She made it for me, Ture. With her last breath."

Tears slipped from his eyes. "And you didn't tell me."

So she told him: mother's warning about the darkness and the light, and about her vision of Ahlyn's death. "Mother told me to choose light. It's what I'm trying to do. Why I stole a thorn. I want to fight."

Ture suddenly looked so much older than his nineteen years. "War is all about cold and heat, blood and kill or be killed. Half the time you don't know the difference between a king and a murderer. It's no life for someone like you."

She bristled. "Like me?"

"By the light, Eiryss. You cried every time we knocked over a bird's nest. You've trained for years to become a healer."

She could still see the bald, pink, hideously ugly bodies being eaten by fish as the mother birds cried and circled above them. "That was before they used our father. I have just as much right to fight as you and Ramass!"

They glared at each other, breaths coming hard. Finally, Ture shook his head. "If you want to condemn yourself, so be it." He turned his back on her. As he always did.

She could have told him that Enderlee would take her thorn and save her from the war. Could have set him at ease. *Let him suffer. Let him worry. It's the least he deserves.*

"Is Ramass coming?" She couldn't help the catch in her voice. Ramass had always, always been there for her. Now he wasn't. Did that have something to do with her kissing him?

Ture paused, clearly debating what to tell her.

"If I don't survive, I need to know." It was a dirty trick, but a necessary one.

Ture's shoulders fell. "He has to keep his distance until the right time." She supposed that made sense. He looked back at her. "Get better."

She nodded. He passed beyond the panel, which shifted to an impenetrable silver. She pulled her knees to her chest. The music started up again. The notes danced on the edge of a precipice before tumbling into the shadows.

Eiryss's fever soared and her throat became a swollen, raw wound. Too ill to do more than choke down the medicines the healer gave her, she spent five days in the opaque room. Five days of waking nightmares. Five days of reliving the deaths of everyone she ever loved. Five days of faceless people who tore the clothes from her body and the thorn from her chest, leaving a raw, gaping wound where her heart should have been.

The only thing that made any of it bearable was the enchantress's healing music.

On the sixth day, her fever broke. On the seventh morning, she was able to choke down a thin broth.

The healer spread a pungent-smelling ointment on Eiryss's chest, the woman's sigils gleaming faintly in the morning light. Eiryss sipped the tea, marveling that she could draw breath without pain. From below came the strains of an advanced class practicing warrior enchantments. The layers of shrill notes reminded Eiryss of birds protecting their nest from a predator.

"How is your melancholy?" the young woman's musical voice asked. Eiryss had been treated for melancholy, just as Ahlyn had, ever since she'd arrived. And once again, Eiryss realized how deeply she'd wronged the princess.

"Better." She missed her parents. She missed Belgrave. And she missed Ramass and Hagath. She even missed Ture. But she no longer fought the darkness that had seeped into her mind with every breath. More and more, she understood the princess. More and more, she grieved her.

The woman nodded. "It will get worse again if you stop taking the herbs I gave you. You may have to hire a healer to play for you—the music helps as much as the herbs."

Eiryss's hand strayed to the swollen knot on her chest. "Will the Arbor really take it from me?"

The woman's expression tightened—the music's enchantment had faded enough for her to remember who Eiryss was. "I have dozens more patients to tend. Some aren't as lucky as you."

"Lucky?" Eiryss scoffed. "My father was executed as a traitor. My mother is dead. I have lost my home and everything in it. If not for the charity of a cousin, I would have nowhere to go. Everywhere, people look at me the way you're looking at me right now. And that's not the worst of it. I will go my entire life without the buzz of magic beneath my skin. Without ever weaving an enchantment with my flute."

"At least you're alive," the woman said bitterly.

Eiryss would rather die. She didn't say it. Clearly, this woman would never take pity on a traitor.

The woman paused before leaving. "They'll come for you tomorrow."

Eiryss closed her eyes against the fear. They would try to take her thorn. She would fight them. Useless as it may be, she would fight until her last breath. Trying to calm her thundering heart, she listened to the music. Her fingers traced the pattern across an imaginary flute—all noble girls learned to play the instruments of the enchantresses.

Just before noon of the eighth day, a girl in the bland blue novice robes came for Eiryss.

She fought to keep from rolling her eyes at the thought of a twelve-year-old minder. "I can find it on my own."

"Mistress Tria says I'm to see you all the way there."

Mistress Tria had a habit of picking the most stringent girls for her assistants. The kind of girl Eiryss always took great pains to avoid. It was almost as if they thought she'd run.

If there was any chance she might escape the city, she would have. But she had nowhere to go. They must have known that too, for there were no guards. No one watching her.

The girl led the way from the high branches to the ornate carriage like a delicately wrought birdcage. It carried people up and down the tree using an intricate system of pullies and counterweights. The grouping of trees, called the Enchantress Copse, was the most elaborate in all Valynthia, but the center tree also held more platforms than most, so the effect was a bit gaudy.

She found her steps falling into rhythm with the relentless beat of the war songs coming from below. Appropriate, since she was headed to battle for herself. She searched the assembled boats for any sign of Ramass's, heart falling when she found none. Had he too abandoned her?

Once the carriage had stopped, the novice set a quick pace. It no longer hurt to breathe, and Eiryss's nose remained only a little stuffy. Still, her strength was no longer what it had been.

She fell behind as she took in the rooms she might never see again. The main platform had been turned into a library—the largest gathering of tomes in the known world. Carvings flowed along the curving panes, all of them featuring an amulet made from the last surge of enchantress magic.

Beyond that was the music room. An enchantress stood before the students, her sigils alight. They played their instruments, weaving the different colors of the woman's magic into complex enchantments. The instruments themselves were as varied as the girls playing them—though all involved the movement of air through the sacred wood of the Silver Tree. Some girls had more than one instrument. Some were so large they had to rest on a girl's shoulders. Some were steadied against their waists with wooden braces. Some were smaller than Eiryss's littlest finger.

And yet they all played in harmony. The enchantresses woke the living magic inside her; the song told that magic what to do.

Eiryss didn't realize how much she'd missed her time at the academy. She swallowed hard against the thickness in her throat.

One of the younger girls, who played a tavit—little more than a whistle, really—glanced up, her gaze locking with Eiryss's. Her mouth went slack around her mouthpiece. She looked quickly away and nudged her companion. More and more of the acolytes noticed Eiryss.

The enchantment, a battle shield, began to unravel, the weave fraying. "Girls." The enchantress rapped her baton on her music stand. The girl's focus snapped back into place, though the weave was disfigured.

Head down, Eiryss hurried away. Hip cocked impatiently, the novice waited for Eiryss to catch up before turning down an enormous branch toward the Mistress Wing. They bypassed Tria's office and continued to Arbor Enderlee's. How many times had Eiryss climbed these steps, an angry teacher marching beside her? How many times had her father been waiting beyond those panels?

His expression was always the same, disappointed. But beneath that disappointment lurked a smile. He would lecture her. Tell her he knew she was better than this. And when he thought she couldn't hear him, he had chuckled.

Was it wrong that after all he'd done, she still loved him so much it hurt?

Muted, heated voices came from the other side—a man and a woman. The novice folded her hands and waited patiently until the voices ceased before knocking on the frame.

Eiryss found her head too heavy to lift.

"Come!" Mistress Tria barked, and Eiryss most certainly did not want to obey. Out of sight beyond the cloudy barrier, she stared at the ornate frame, the ahlea flowers down the sides and in the center.

You are descended from a line of queens. Her mother's words rang through her.

Eiryss clenched her fists at her side and gritted her teeth. They hadn't taken her thorn. Not yet. And while she still had her thorn, she still had hope.

"Well, are you going or not?" the novice pressed.

Eiryss lifted her head high and pushed through. Centered before long columns of books, Arbor Enderlee and Mistress Tria stood behind a table and perused documents. Instead of her father, Ramass waited for her. His back to her, he looked out a window toward the Silver Tree. He wore leather studded armor and a cloak, hood drawn.

He had come. Relief shuddered through her along with the memory of their kiss. And though embarrassment chased closely behind, she couldn't find it in herself to regret her actions.

Ramass turned and took a step toward her before remembering himself. He passed a hand over his chapped face; his expression shifting to unreadable. His left hand grasped his right wrist, freckles dotting his fingers.

Hair tied into a neat braid, Arbor Enderlee glanced up, dark eyes hardening, before she went back to the papers before her. "And you think to make her your first rogue enchantress?" She was clearly speaking to Ramass.

Excitement bolted through Eiryss. Maybe she would keep her thorn after all.

Ramass merely watched the Arbor.

"You can't do this." Mistress Tria snapped her fingers, her jowls trembling as she ground her teeth.

"I can," Ramass said evenly. "The council and King have already approved it. Eiryss will be my first recruit."

"This insult will not stand," Enderlee said, her rich voice slung low and dangerous. "The Enchantresses are *mine*. I command them. Not the king. Not the council. Certainly not you."

Eiryss blinked in shock. The Marshal commanded the enchanters. The Arbor commanded the enchantresses. It had always been this way. That the king and council had ripped away Enderlee's command revealed just how dire the situation at the border really was.

"We need more enchantresses," Ramass said. "You've refused to send them."

Enderlee leaned forward, pale fingers splayed across the table. "Do you have any idea how many of my enchantresses I have already laid to rest?"

Ramass frowned. "Your job isn't to keep them alive."

"I will not serve half-trained girls up to your foolish war!" She paced, the stones on her mantle swinging with movement.

Foolish? How was defending their lands and people from invasion foolish?

"Enderlee..." He pinched the bridge of his nose in frustration.

"I told you to allow me to train lower-caste girls," Enderlee said.

Mud lords was what she meant—the nobility who didn't have the honor of living in the sacred city, but instead had to eke a living out of the dirt.

"Which will not pass the council or the king," Ramass said. "Even if you could have them trained by spring."

Tria shook the papers at Ramass. "The girl climbed the Silver Tree, damaging it in the process, and embedded herself. Not to mention the amulet she didn't report. She must be held accountable!"

Eiryss had hoped the healers hadn't noticed her amulet. "You know I'm not a traitor, Enderlee. You sent me to my father's room all those months ago, knowing that if I were caught, I would be accused of treason. That only my father's death would spare me."

Enderlee drew up to her full height. "I would never do such a thing."

Lies. Eiryss's hands fisted with fury. She imagined them smashing into the Arbor's lovely face. "And when I demanded my thorns, you expelled me from the academy."

Tria's imploring gaze landed on Eiryss. "There are things you don't understand, child." She opened her mouth to say more.

Eiryss cut her off. "You condemn me with your right hand while your left does far worse!"

Enderlee rested a restraining hand on Tria's arm. The older woman gritted her teeth and shot a bitter look Ramass's way. "Leave her be, Marshal."

Eiryss kept waiting for Ramass's famous temper to reveal itself, but he remained remarkably calm. "As she is now under my command, I will see she is punished accordingly."

Tria huffed in disgust and shot a pleading look Eiryss's way. "Child, do you have any idea what you will face?"

Eiryss was taken aback by the concern on the older woman's face. Why would the women who'd betrayed her and denied her from ever having magic—the same women who'd threatened to rip that magic out—care what happened to her?

Shelin's dead face flashed in Eiryss's mind. "I saw the dead from the battle of Lias Lamoren."

"Then why do you want this so badly?" Tria asked.

Heat flushed through Eiryss's body. "The Alamantians corrupted my father. They destroyed my entire family. I will see justice done."

"You're just one girl," Enderlee said.

Eiryss tried to put into words what she knew deep inside. "I may be only one girl. But given the chance, one girl can change everything."

Enderlee tucked the papers into the leather folder, wound a string around the button, and tossed them at Ramass's feet. "Get out."

He picked up the folder. "My men will bring the enchantresses to the border, Enderlee. You will remain here with the children." He strode to the door, tugging on his gloves as he went. Just like Ture, the war had changed Ramass. His famous temper was nowhere in sight. Instead, calm emanated from him.

"Wait," Enderlee called.

Ramass paused but didn't turn back to her.

"Tria will go in my stead and take command of the Enchantresses."

157

He half-turned back to her. "If she is willing to work under my command."

Tria glared daggers at him. "Very well. I have things to see to here. I will meet you in Trapendale."

He gave a curt nod. "Come on, Eiryss."

Mouth dry, she followed. Ramass stepped beyond the panel.

"Eiryss," Mistress Tria whispered and hurried around the table. "You don't understand who you're getting involved with. Do not go with him."

She shook her head in disbelief, her anger palpable. "So I should stay here so you can rip out my thorn and banish me?"

"No," Enderlee said from her place behind the table.

"Enderlee," Tria said, warning in her tone.

Enderlee held out her hand palm out. "They're taking all the girls in your class and the year younger. I've tried to delay you. Keep you safe. I may still be able to. You may keep your thorn. You may even stay in one of the rooms above the academy. Only don't go with him."

If Enderlee was unwilling to do whatever it took to defend her people, she didn't deserve her command. Still, Eiryss's gaze narrowed. Something was going on here. Something she didn't understand.

Eiryss hesitated a moment before shaking her head. "I will not abandon my kingdom as you have."

"He'll get you killed," Tria said.

"Please. Trust us," Enderlee said. "We can help you."

Eiryss's burning gaze shifted to the Arbor. "The same way you helped me with my father?"

Enderlee frowned. "Give me the amulet."

"But—" Eiryss began.

"Do you think your friend can override this too?" The Arbor held out her hand.

Eiryss swallowed back tears. "My mother made it specifically for me." When Enderlee didn't relent, she pulled the amulet over her head and dropped it into the woman's waiting palm.

Enderlee played her flute. A tongue of her silver magic licked over the amulet. She trilled an enchantment, but the amulet didn't respond. She tried another. And another. Finally, she pressed it into Tria's hand. "See if you can make something out of it."

Tria worked one enchantment after another before looking at Eiryss with a touch of pity. Clearly, neither of them knew that for this particular amulet to work, it had to pierce the skin. How rare was such a thing that they didn't even consider it?

"Sometimes the magic doesn't take." Tria held it out for Eiryss.

Eiryss pressed the edge of the sharp branch into her thumb until it dented her skin. Felt the power thrumming in the amulet. But she wasn't about to tell them that. She hastily slipped the amulet over her head and hurried after Ramass. Soft steps sounded behind her.

"Let her go, Tria," Enderlee murmured. "We have more than one girl to think of."

CHAPTER

RAMASS

As soon as Eiryss passed through the barrier, she bent over, hands braced against her knees. She had won. She would keep her thorn. If it took, she would have magic. She wanted to laugh or cry or both.

Before she could do either, Ramass hauled her into his arms and squeezed so hard she couldn't breathe. Not caring, she squeezed him back.

"After all we have been through," he said, "the thought that I might lose you to the same sickness that took your mother…"

Light, she missed her mother. "How did you manage to sway the council?"

He released her abruptly and glanced about as if worried about being overheard. "Your family still has allies, and Vicil fought hard for you. He convinced them it would be foolish to waste a nearly trained enchantress—especially one who already has her thorns." He started down the steps at a trot.

She hurried to catch up. "Slow down," she panted.

"Do you have any idea how worried I was about you?"

"Then why didn't you visit?" She tried to moderate her voice to mask her hurt and feared she failed miserably.

"I needed it to look professional. Not personal."

That wasn't all this was. He wasn't slowing down, and she was falling farther and farther behind. "Why are you in such a hurry?"

"I'm not."

She broke into a cough. If he wasn't in a hurry, then… "Why are you running from me?"

He eased up but wouldn't look at her. "I don't—I don't know what to say to you."

She froze. This was about the kiss. *Tell me you love me too,* she thought. She felt very small and frail. Like the slightest breeze might blow her away. "You clearly don't feel the same about me."

He tugged his hand through his hair. "You've always been *Eiryss.* Not a woman." At her withering look, he held out his hands. "I mean, I know you're a woman. But I've never seen you that way." He groaned. "I'm making a mess of this." He really was. "Can we just—can we pretend it didn't happen? Give me some time to figure things out?"

He'd had a week. How much more time did he need? Mute, she nodded.

He sighed in relief. Together, they made their way to the carriage and rode silently down. He opened the gate and gestured to her amulet. "They let you keep it?"

She nodded—apparently it was the only form of communication she could manage at present. They stepped onto the busy dock.

Very carefully, Eiryss shuttered away her feelings for Ramass as well as his less-than-enthusiastic reaction. She had her thorn. For now, that was enough. "You've made an enemy of Enderlee," she said.

He grimaced. "She's going to make me pay for it too."

Down one of the piers, a group of his soldiers waited for them. Ramass said something to one of his men. He motioned to the enchanters, who took off toward the main tree at a jog. To gather girls to take to the front.

The idea sat uneasily with Eiryss. But she had no doubt such a decision was necessary for taking back their captured cities come spring.

Ramass hopped into one of the small enchantress boats.

She settled into the bow. "Why are we stealing an enchantress boat?"

"Because we can," he said with a smirk that quickly faded. "And because I can't give you the embedding ceremony you deserve, but I can at least keep it private."

She gasped in delight. "I'm to have more thorns? Today?"

He nodded.

She pressed the amulet to her heart and above the thorn between her breasts, glad she had at least this part of her mother to take with her. Oar in hand, she glanced up and caught Enderlee watching them from her office. Eiryss quickly looked away and forced herself to remain silent until they were clear of the trees and any listening ears.

She rounded on Ramass. "And after my embedding?"

"I leave tomorrow with the first wave. You'll be among them."

Tomorrow. She would be leaving her old life in Hanama tomorrow. Her role in her father's death haunted her. It would for the rest of her life. But if she fought well, she could restore honor to her family. Perhaps then she'd be able to live with herself.

Ramass steered them to the Silver Tree. They tied off at the dock, climbed the steps, and crossed beneath the archway. The sentinels standing on either side-eyed them but made no move to interfere as they made their way up the winding stairs.

"I thought only the king and the Arbor had unlimited access?" Eiryss asked when they were out of earshot.

He cast her a sly smile. "During times of war, so does the Marshal."

Her fingers trailed along the smooth bark. Shapes always moved within the depths of the semi-transparent Silver Tree. But now, those shapes were darker. Shadows paused when her eyes fell on them. And they... turned toward her. Looked at her. Lunged. Eiryss stumbled back as they slammed into the exterior of the tree, spreading like writhing ink stains.

A shape of torn shadows loomed over her. Malevolent and furious and...

Ramass gripped her shoulders and turned her away. "Best not to look too closely." But he was looking, his expression fierce and angry.

"What was that?"

"Enderlee believes the Alamantians poisoned the tree, damaging the enchantresses' ability to raise the vault. I call it the shadow."

"By the light," she breathed.

Ramass released her. "Come on."

She sneaked a look back. The shadow was gone. She scrambled up the stairs and to the main platform. Ramass went to the font and filled the ornate chalice. He drank the silvery liquid that filled the bowl in a single gulp.

"What are you doing?" Wasn't she supposed to be the one getting thorns? Ramass already had his.

He looked back at her. "If we don't change the way we fight this war, we're going to lose it."

In only three months, they'd already lost four cities to the Alamantian advance. Only six more and their enemies would reach Hanama. And with the vault still not working...

"Surely it isn't that bad?"

"Don't believe the propaganda. We're losing. Badly." Ahlyn had seen this coming. Ramass set down the cup. "You still have your thorn?"

She resisted the urge to touch it. "Yes."

"Let's hope it takes or Enderlee is going to be too smug to stomach."

He pressed a scarred palm into the conduit thorn. At first nothing happened, and then his teeth clenched and his skin flushed. His blood spilled through the font, red dancing with the silver before settling in a thorn. He took it, sliding it into an arm already covered with sigils.

"Why do you need more?" she asked.

"As if you can ever have enough magic." Finished, he pressed a handkerchief to the wound and turned toward her. "I have something for you."

He reached into his coat and pulled out a velvet wrapped package. She instantly recognized the shape of it. The weight and feel in her hand only confirmed it.

Eyes misty, she unwrapped it to find the flute her father had bought for her. The one the treasurer had taken away. "How did you find it?"

He chuckled. "I dug through boxes at the auction and then wrestled it from a noble intent on buying it for herself."

It must have cost him a small fortune. She sniffed. "Do you think my father bought it before or after he plotted to betray us?"

"I think he bought it for his daughter, whom he loved very much. And who loved him back. Loves him still. As any good daughter would."

She fisted the flute to her chest and against the amulet. Now, she had something from them both to see her through. She gave him a soft smile. "I'm ready."

He dipped the chalice back into the font and held it, dripping, to her. She drank; the sap was sweet and thick. Wiping the back of her hand across her mouth, she paced around the font and studied the glittering thorns as she waited for the sap to numb her body.

When she felt warm and floaty, she stopped before the conduit thorn and pressed her hand in. She gasped as her blood swirled through the font, slipping in and out of glittering thorns.

Including the one she had, her total would be eight thorns: build and break, seek and repel, seal and loose, light and dark. The weaving of the magic from those sigils created the larger enchantments. That is, if all her sigils took.

"You haven't rejected your first thorn?" Ramass asked, his voice sounded strange.

She wondered what that thorn would do. "No. Why?"

Ramass pointed. "Because you've darkened eight of them."

Eyes wide, she counted again. He was right. "Eight?" she gasped. That would mean she would have an additional thorn for a total of nine.

Ramass's gaze narrowed on her. "Perhaps you'll be a speaker for the dead like your mother."

She shuddered. "Light, I hope not."

Floating and dazed and more than a little dizzy, she made to pull back. Ramass stepped up behind her, holding her hand in place. "The unit under my command will have an extra thorn."

The heat from his body crossed the space between them, sending gooseflesh up and down her arms. "But I already have an extra—"

"One in addition to that."

She was to have ten thorns? "But—the Silver Tree didn't light up an additional one."

"The tree will fight you. It won't want to give up its thorns. You have to make it."

"Make it?" The Silver Tree was to be worshiped, not forced into anything. They didn't take thorns from him. He gave them freely. "I didn't have to make it before."

He stepped even closer, his words stirring the fine hairs at the nape of her neck. "It's just a tree."

Everything in her rebelled. "This is blasphemy."

"One girl can make a difference, remember?" His grey eyes met hers. "I'm giving you that chance."

So it came to this. Desecrate the sacred for a chance at saving her people and bringing justice to her family. Or go back to... what? Try to snag a husband who would always hold power over her? Give up her title for the life of a commoner?

Her life was her own, to live as she saw fit. She would give it in the defense of her kingdom. And if that meant she had to violate something sacred...

"We do what we must," Ramass said.

"Sometimes wrong is right." Hadn't she said that to the tree before? *I'm sorry,* she thought. *But I cannot falter. I cannot back down.*

"How?" she asked.

"Your blood is mixing with the tree's—your consciousness is mixing. Make it do what you want it to."

Give me another thorn.

The cold ache spread up her arm, settling in a frozen knot in her chest. Her veins vibrated. The tree didn't want this. Resisted it.

No.

This was what she was meant to do.

Nothing—not even a sacred tree—would stop her.

"Demand the weapons of a warrior enchantress," Ramass said.

I will become a warrior for my people. She pushed—her will against the tree's. The magic resisted. Foreign emotions—betrayal and hurt—flashed through her. Gritting her teeth, she forced her way through it, shattering it.

The blood settled in another thorn. She stumbled back, her thumb digging into the wound in her palm. Ramass handed her a cloth, which she pressed against the wound. Ramass went to each of the thorns, plucking them with an efficient flick. She studied him—this man she'd known for as long as she could remember. And the familiar feeling of waiting to be caught after they'd done something wrong washed over her.

"What does your extra thorn do?" she asked.

"That will only be revealed to those whose thorns form sigils." He held up the first, long and needle-thin. "Where?"

The cold gathered, thickened onto her upper, left arm. She turned away as Ramass lined a thorn up vertically and pushed it into her skin. A sharp ache. He wiped the blood with his handkerchief. Though she shivered with cold, sweat broke out on her brow. Nine times he pierced her with thorns—the right side of her body throbbed with the potential for positive magic, the left for negative. She now had thorns in her upper arms, forearms, thighs, and calves. The ninth he slid in above her navel.

She swayed and stumbled into him. He held her, his chest solid and unmovable beneath her. Frozen from the inside-out, she didn't notice other girls arriving until Ramass motioned to them.

Red hair cut severely short and her body frightfully thin, Hagath hurried up to them. Eiryss nearly cried out in relief at the sight of her friend.

Hagath, however, took one look at Eiryss and rounded on her brother. "Ramass, you selfish idiot, we agreed to keep her out of this." She still sounded sick, her voice thin and raspy.

"You didn't see her," he said, his voice wavering with emotion.

A weighted look passed between the siblings. Eiryss knew them both well enough to read it. Something bad had happened. Ramass would tell Hagath about it later—*it* being that Eiryss had considered throwing herself from her tree.

Shame washed over her in a sick wave. Eiryss frowned at them. "Keep me out of what?"

"The war," Hagath replied.

Eiryss bristled. Hagath was always trying to mother her. "I decide what to do with my own life."

"You're doing a lovely job so far." Hagath pressed her wrist to Eiryss's forehead. "She's freezing! Why didn't you wait for me?"

Eiryss jerked out of her touch.

"Because you would have tried to stop her." He looked worried.

"She's going into shock," Hagath said. "She'll be fine if I can keep her warm."

Eiryss had hoped she'd be one of the few girls strong enough not to experience shock. Though the wounds were small, the thorns had their own kind of consciousness. The foreignness, the otherness, was hard for a body to accept at first.

Ramass nodded curtly and looked over the three dozen or so women. "This is all you brought?"

Hagath shot him a poisonous look as she helped Eiryss over to a large brazier.

"Hagath told you the risks?" Ramass said to the newcomers. He must have received the answer he was looking for. "Then step forward."

Eiryss would have pulled out of Hagath's grip were she not afraid her knees would buckle. "Stop fussing."

Hagath's mouth tightened in a thin line. "One of us should come out of this alive and untainted, Eiryss."

"What's that supposed to mean?" she asked.

Hagath eased Eiryss to the ground and propped her feet up. She called to one of the enchanters who'd accompanied them and ordered him to remove his coat.

She spread the coat over Eiryss. "We'll talk about it later."

Eiryss caught Hagath's hand. "I'm so glad you're all right."

Shadows darkened Hagath's gaze. "I see you couldn't stay out of trouble while I was gone."

Before Eiryss could protest, Hagath tugged out her pan-pipes. She didn't use her sigils, instead relying on the magic of her instrument made of the sacred wood. The melody recalled a meadow Eiryss had visited as a child.

Hands linked, she, Ture, Hagath, and Ramass had whirled. Faster and faster. Until they had spun apart to land in the tall grass. The world still twirling around her, Eiryss inhaled the intoxicating scent of crushed plants and hot soil as yellow flowers with black heads bobbed in the hot breeze. Sunlight so bright her eyes watered. In the distance, her mother had called them in to lunch.

In that moment, Eiryss had felt whole, complete in a way she rarely had before or after.

One after another, the shivering, pale girls were brought to the fire for Hagath to dress their wounds, which mirrored Eiryss's. A gaggle of haggard, frazzled women of all ages came next. Even more shocking than those with gray hair receiving new thorns was that they came from outside Hanama, as evidenced by the mud on their shoes and the hems of their clothes.

They were all mud lords—people who had nobility in their lines, but far enough back as to be ridiculous.

An old woman and a younger girl—perhaps fourteen—were the last of this group. Judging by their similar looks, they were related. The whole group huddled together in near silence. From their haunted expressions, they were from the cities that had fallen.

But the last two of the thirty or so who were led to the brazier made her teeth ache with the need to bite something. Wyndyn and Iritraya. The one bright spot in Eiryss's suspension was these girls would be gone by the time Eiryss returned to the academy. And now here they were.

Shivering and pale, Iritraya glared daggers and said just loud enough for Eiryss to hear, "Will we never be rid of her?"

"This is my unit to command," Wyndyn ground out. "Not hers."

Eiryss huffed. "Not your unit. Ramass's."

"Men don't command enchantresses, idiot," Iritraya chattered.

"Nor do enchantresses graduate two years early." Everything was changing. These girls would figure it out eventually. "So you see, you command no one."

Iritraya huffed. "We're to lead groups of mud nobles."

Seventeen-year-old girls? Girls as spoiled as Eiryss had been. "That's ridiculous."

"If it's so ridiculous, why are you here?"

Because I didn't have a choice. But you did. Eiryss pointedly turned away. Servants brought more braziers. Ramass gave an order Eiryss was only slightly aware of. Hagath kept playing. The songs niggled inside Eiryss, coming up against a hard, cold knot.

Joy, Eiryss realized. *She's playing joy.*

The cold abated to a chill, then nothing at all. Eiryss took her first free breath, her body heavy and exhausted. The other girls seemed to be coming out of it as well.

Ramass stood over Hagath and motioned to the font. "Your turn."

Eiryss didn't understand. Hagath already had all her thorns—unless she too needed a ninth thorn.

Hagath gritted her teeth. "No."

"Someone has to train them. Better you than *her*."

Who was "her"? Surely not Wyndyn—Ramass knew how despicable she was.

"No," Hagath said again. Eiryss didn't understand the look that passed between them. The silent debate.

"Her who?" Eiryss asked.

"Sir," Wyndyn interjected. "I was told the highest-ranking nobles would have their own commands."

Ramass shot her a flat look. "Your unit leader will be announced tomorrow. If she shows up," he muttered the last bit. "She will report to Mistress Tria, who will report to me. Those of you from the Enchantress Academy will help teach the other nobles."

The girls exchanged wide-eyed glances. Enchantresses reporting to enchanters was unheard of.

Ramass pulled Hagath aside, and they spoke in heated tones.

"How can the marshal supersede the sacred tree's appointed Arbor?" someone whispered. Eiryss didn't see who.

"Enderlee refuses to send replacements to the front," Eiryss said. "What choice does Ramass have?"

"Well, I'm not following a healer's orders into battle," Wyndyn said with a disgusted look in Hagath's direction. Despite her bravado, Wyndyn didn't speak loudly enough for Ramass to hear her.

Regardless of how much Eiryss loathed the girl, she didn't exactly disagree. Hagath had never excelled in military training. She was a healer. Wyndyn and Iritraya, however, had been trained as warrior enchantresses.

Iritraya huffed. "Any healer worth her pipes would have saved the princess instead of herself."

"How was she supposed to know the wine had been poisoned?" Eiryss snapped. "And what do you know about countering unknown poisons?" All Eiryss's research had suggested such a thing was nigh impossible.

Ramass glanced their way and Hagath stiffened. Eiryss had been too loud. Arms folded and back stiff, Hagath left without looking back.

Wyndyn's eyes narrowed in on Eiryss. "Says the traitor girl who stole a thorn."

"Child, you should hush," one of the older women said. She had tired brown eyes and long gray hair that had slipped out of its bun.

Wyndyn sent the woman a scathing look. "Learn to recognize your betters and keep your mouth shut."

Ramass strode toward them. "Balendora is right. You should hush." He gave a nod of approval to the older woman. "As far as the enchantresses are concerned, you've all stolen thorns." He stared at Wyndyn and Iritraya until they dropped his gaze. "My men will see you to the barracks."

He crouched beside Eiryss and dropped his voice to a whisper. "You could stay with Hagath and me."

Ignoring the little thrill that went through her, she shook her head. She'd suffered enough hatred at the hands of those who resented her for the privilege she'd been born to. She had no desire to earn their contempt. "I better stay with my unit."

He shot a meaningful look at Wyndyn and Iritraya. "Let me know if you change your mind."

Eiryss watched him go and rubbed at the ghost of the knot in her chest.

CHAPTER 16

HAGATH

Long before dawn the next day, twenty-seven testy women lined the barrack docks. They all moved with careful stiffness. Judging by all the shifting and muttering going on last night, they hadn't slept any better than Eiryss—ten hot, throbbing thorns all over her body had made finding a comfortable position impossible.

Instead of enchantress blue, their unit wore charcoal grey—matching tunics, trousers, and boots as well as heavy coats, gloves, and hats—just like the enchanters wore. For weapons, they'd been supplied a dagger and knife in addition to their wind instruments—all of them individually made by a master. Besides her flute, Eiryss also had a panpipe—plain military issue. Over all of this, she wore the soft leather mantle with the enchantress crest, toggles latching it over the right shoulder.

Tucking her head into her collar to filter out some of the rotten smell of the lake, Eiryss waited in line to receive her food rations. At a table set out for them, she wrapped up travel bread, smoked fish, fruit, and nuts. Everything was a bit soggy from the fog—she could only hope it didn't absorb any of the stink of dead fish.

Above the shuffling of numerous feet came two pairs of purposeful strides. Wyndyn and Iritraya took up positions on both sides of Eiryss, making her stiffen.

"What are you doing here?" Wyndyn said through gritted teeth.

"What are *you* doing here?" Eiryss shot back. "You only had six months until graduation."

Iritraya's eyes narrowed. "The war will be over before then. As will any chance of glory."

Had the girl not seen the lines of dead? "What glory?"

Wyndyn stepped closer. "This was supposed to be my command."

Eiryss stowed the food in her satchel. "That was never going to happen."

She made to push past Wyndyn, but the girl grabbed her arm. "I refuse to play second to some traitor's daughter."

Eiryss opened her mouth for a sharp retort, but a whispery rasp spoke up from behind them. "Don't you both have older brothers stationed in Oramen?" Hagath calmly tied the toggles on her satchel.

Iritraya's eyes narrowed.

"Why?" Wyndyn asked.

Hagath blinked innocently. "Sometimes I advise my brother on which brave men he should send to the front." Hagath could be vicious when she was angry.

Both girls stared at their hands. Wyndyn's fists twisted around her satchel strap with helpless fury.

"Well," Hagath prodded. "Are they brave or aren't they?"

"They are very… happy, serving where they are," Wyndyn said through gritted teeth. Iritraya mumbled her assent.

"Ah. Well, you inform me if that changes." She gripped Eiryss's arm and pushed past them. "Why am I always getting you out of trouble?" Hagath muttered when they were out of earshot.

Eiryss jerked free. "As if I sought that out."

"You're welcome." Hagath huffed.

Eiryss rounded on her. "Stop treating me like a child."

"When you stop getting into trouble like one—"

"When you stop acting like a bully!"

Hagath made an exasperated sound. "I'm not—"

"I don't see you for months. I worry myself sick over you. Then the moment I see you, you deride and humiliate me." Eiryss stormed down the empty pier, her steps satisfyingly clipped and loud. Hagath hurried to catch up.

"Stop being stubborn." When Eiryss didn't slow, Hagath sighed. "I'm sorry, all right?"

Eiryss walked faster.

Hagath caught her arm again. "Burn it, Eiryss. I'm trying to explain."

Eiryss rounded on her. "I don't want to fight!" She sagged, all the tension draining out of her. "I've lost too many people to fight with the ones who are left."

Hagath leaned over, panting. "It's not you I'm angry with. I'm just—I've lost people too. And the thought of you being in the middle of this." She made to tug her hair and then seemed to remember it was short. "I thought at least one person was safe."

Eiryss looked her up and down. She was thin and pale and trembling. "Are you still sick?"

"My healer said it could take me a year or more to fully recover—or at least recover as much as I'm going to. My voice will likely never be the same."

Hagath swayed, her face going terribly pale. Eiryss grabbed her arm to steady her and felt thick, knotted lumps on the other girl's forearm. She blinked, too shocked to understand what she was feeling.

She jerked back Hagath's sleeve, revealing twisted, purple scars where beautiful sigils should have been. "You've been excised?" Sometime in the last three months, she'd been exiled from the enchantresses, her sigils forcibly removed.

Hagath wrenched her arm free and cradled it against her body. "Don't," she begged.

Perfect, rule-following Hagath would never do anything to risk excision. "What did you do?"

"Nothing."

"The enchantresses don't excise for nothing." Except, they'd nearly excised her.

Hagath's eyes flashed. "You don't want to fight? This is one topic we don't discuss."

Ramass clearly knew—that's why he'd tried to talk her into taking thorns the night before. *I'll force answers from him later.* She folded her arms. "Fine."

The other girls had started to catch up with them. They shot curious looks at Hagath, who hastily turned her back to hide her shattered expression.

Eiryss knew what her friend had suffered. Had felt the pounding of her heartbeat through Ahlyn's palm. Hagath had watched her dear friend die and then been on the brink of death for months afterward. She didn't need the others seeing her like this.

Eiryss gently pulled her hood over her face. "Come with me."

She led Hagath to the furthest boat of the half dozen or so boats and pulled her down on the seat facing the prow. Their backs were now to everyone, their faces toward the open water, mist curling around them and water lapping gently on the sides of the boat.

Hagath struggled to put herself back together one piece at a time—she took a deep breath, rubbed her face, let that breath out, and opened her eyes. "How long has it smelled this bad?"

"Too long," Eiryss answered.

By the time the boats had all been loaded, Hagath's haunted look was gone, replaced with a confidence Eiryss now knew was a mask, and a tenuous one at that. It could easily be shattered by the wrong questions.

The last to arrive, Ramass hopped into their boat and stood at the bow. He looked at each of Eiryss's thorns, before shooting her a questioning glance.

She mouthed, "I'm fine."

That questioning gaze shifted to Hagath, and his brows drew together with worry. He glanced into the lifting fog and back to the tree in exasperation. He was clearly waiting for someone. Knowing he was trying to appear professional with her, Eiryss didn't bother to ask.

Minutes later, Jala sauntered down the dock, paused beside their boat, and held her hand to Ramass. "Marshal."

What is she *doing here?*

His face shifting to unreadable, he helped her aboard. "You're late."

She flashed him her venomous smile. "How can I possibly be late to my own command?"

Command? *Light. They'd chosen* Jala *to command?* And why under the light had she been demoted from the king's enchantress to a unit commander? She shot Ramass a "what were you thinking" look. He shot her back a "save me" look. Eiryss huffed. He could very well save himself.

Hagath followed the silent conversation and leaned in to whisper in Eiryss's ear, "She's the only experienced enchantress Father could find who'd take the command. She said she was bored."

She stifled a groan. "I think I prefer Wyndyn."

Ramass gave the order to move out. Well accustomed to rowing, Eiryss hauled out her oars and paddled through heavy slush. After days of inactivity and sickness, she welcomed the strain on her back and arms as well as a slight sheen of sweat under her clothes.

Still, the movement made her thorns pulse, especially if she inadvertently brushed against them. Her chest thorn was particularly bad; it throbbed with each beat of her heart. Sweat dripped down her forehead and temples—she was not as strong as she'd been a mere ten days ago, and she'd lost even more weight. It took everything she had to school the pain from her features.

"Here, chew on these," Hagath said from beside her.

Apparently, everything she had wasn't enough. Eiryss took the nemroot and used her teeth to loosen the woody, irregular fibers, which she sucked on.

"Can we have some too?" Balendora said from behind them.

Hagath opened a sack beside her. It was full of nemroot. Apparently, she'd come prepared. The spindly root was passed around the boat amid murmurs of gratitude.

"I'm Balendora," the old woman said. "And this is my granddaughter, Namishka."

The girl beside her couldn't be older than fourteen. Far too young to be headed for the front lines. Her hair was cut short and blunt, like it had been sheared off by a knife. Her dark eyes wouldn't meet Eiryss's.

"Where are you from?" Hagath asked.

"Lias Lamoren," Balendora said, the pain obvious in her eyes.

The first city that had fallen. Eiryss wanted to ask for details, but the way Namishka wouldn't look at anything or anyone... Grandmother and granddaughter were present, but no daughter.

She looked at Namishka. "I lost my mother three months ago."

Namishka looked at her for the first time. "She was at Lias Lamoren too?"

"No," Eiryss said. "She died of fever."

"Many people have died from it," Balendora said. "I myself was very sick."

"As was I," Eiryss said.

Balendora held Eiryss's gaze and nodded once. So much was communicated in such a single gesture. Understanding. Solidarity. Eiryss thought of how the high nobility shunned the mud lords, just as they shunned her.

Who'd have ever thought Eiryss would have more in common with a mud lady than her high nobility?

As they neared the river head, Eiryss looked back at the sacred city. In the predawn light, she couldn't make out the Silver Tree's faint sheen. Movement caught her attention. With a great rending sound, one of the distant treetops shuddered and disappeared from view.

"Another dead hometree," Hagath said from beside her.

My hometree, Eiryss realized. Her mother was dead. Her father. And now, the place that had held all her memories was gone. She had gone from powerful and loved to a homeless orphan. She was glad she wasn't there to witness it. Glad she wasn't forced to watch the end. A wave approached them, surging them into the river, pushing her from one life into the next.

The boat caught the river current, so they didn't have to paddle anymore. Eiryss slumped in relief—she was already exhausted. Neither she nor Hagath had their strength back. They passed treehomes built into smaller trees that didn't grow out of the lake, as well as manor houses lording over the snowy fields. Smoke rose from the large buildings where the servants lived on the top floor, with grain storage on the bottom. They would be busy threshing and winnowing, repairing equipment, sorting seeds, weaving, and tending the children.

Ramass signaled the other boats, which maneuvered to float beside them.

Jala stood at the helm and called out to all the people in the boats. "Not all your sigils will take, and you will be naturally stronger in some than others."

"And the ninth sigil?" Balendora asked.

"You'll find out if it takes," Jala said dryly.

"Why all the secrecy?" Eiryss whispered to Hagath, who merely shrugged.

Jala examined her long nails. "We will begin with the most basic of enchantments: building magical armor around the people you are to protect. After that, we will move on to creating shields."

"As if we don't already know the songs for those," Wyndyn grumbled to Iritraya.

Jala's gaze zeroed in on her. "Problem, ugly girl?"

Unfortunately, Wyndyn wasn't ugly. Jala was just being mean.

"My name is Wyndyn," the girl said through gritted teeth. "My problem is we already know all the songs. Have for years. And you would do well to remember my *father* is on the council."

"I like ugly girl," Jala said, clearly not intimidated in the least.

Eiryss felt sorry for Wyndyn. A little. Very, very little.

Jala gave a long-suffering sigh. "Mud nobles don't usually receive thorns and so haven't received the training you do, whatever-your-name-is."

"Wyndyn," the girl said through clenched teeth.

Jala waved her name away, as if she couldn't be bothered.

What training, exactly, did they have? "How can you send them to war if they don't know the basics?" Eiryss found herself saying.

Jala's gaze narrowed in on her, and her mouth opened for a retort.

"They'll have the winter to catch up," Ramass answered. He gave Jala a withering look. "Jala, remember when we talked about dealing with people?"

She touched his arm, lightly. "Very well. I shall behave for you, Ramass." She actually purred his name.

He stiffened under her touch. Eiryss felt the hair on the back of her neck stand up and her fists clench. She forced her hands to open, her jaw to unclench. Ramass was not hers. She had no right to be jealous.

Jala sighed and clapped her hands. "Instruments out!"

Rustling sounded as women retrieved their instruments. Luckily for Eiryss, her flute and pipes were small. She tugged them out of their carved cases and slipped the cords for each around her neck, being careful not to let them tap against the thorn between her breasts.

Jala waited until they were all ready. Then she moved, her sinuous body swaying. The music moved with her. It started low, a hum that rose to a palpable vibration before bursting to life like a newborn mountain rising from the plains. One after another burst until it seemed an entire range of craggy, uncrossable mountains encircled them.

Had their thorns been sigils, a dome would have formed around them.

Eiryss was surprised at the mud nobles' skill. They may not have been given magic, but they had been taught to play. And play they did; all through the morning, only pausing at midday for a meal. Until Eiryss's mouth was so tired she could barely keep her jaw shut. Her tongue ached, and her lips were numb.

Jala finally called for them to stop, but not so they could rest. The river had widened and slowed enough that they had to paddle. Eiryss was still weak from her long illness and the toll of her thorns. Her body grew weary, and that she longed for a place to lie down.

They reached Mendolin at nightfall. Though the enormous hometrees were larger than the rest of the forest, they were not nearly as large as the ones in Hanama. They had a wild, untamed look about them, unlike the elegance of the trees and carvings of her home city.

As they came closer, Eiryss noted their rough bark. How dirty and... brown it was instead of silvery. The farther they went from the sacred city, the more the trees became... well, just trees. Like the magic of the Silver Tree faded with time and distance.

She touched her thorns, glad to have a piece of the tree within her. Even if the one in her chest burned like an ember. They tied the boats to the docks and clambered up. Eiryss paused before stepping onto the snow-covered ground. The last time she'd touched earth had been the day she'd buried her father.

She couldn't shake the feeling that if she stepped down onto the filth, something even worse would happen. She was being irrational; she knew it, and yet that didn't stop her heart from skipping a beat. Teeth gritted, she stepped down.

Nothing happened, but that didn't mean it wouldn't. Sometimes evil just bided its time.

While the others loaded their supplies from the boats into a wagon, she staggered into the forest until she reached untouched snow. A hard throb forced her to lean against one of the wide roots for support. She clawed up a handful of snow and pressed it against the pain of her first thorn.

Eiryss wasn't aware Hagath had followed until she stood before her. "By the light, you're transitioning early." She pulled out a decorative canister, unscrewed the metal lid, and held it to

Eiryss's lips. "One swallow. Only one! Any more and I'll have to drag you back by your ankles."

The stuff was bitter and awful. The moment it hit her stomach, her body wanted to reject it. Hagath swore, dug in her satchel, and came up with some hard cheese. "Here, nibble on this." Eiryss pushed it away. "It will help with the nausea."

Relenting, Eiryss crumbled some in her mouth and swallowed. When she didn't immediately vomit it back up, she nibbled some more. After a few minutes, something clicked, and she found she didn't care about the pain as much. Or about anything, really. Back against a tree, she slid down on her haunches in relief.

Hagath let out a shaky breath. "Has it taken the edge off yet?"

"A little." Her skin flushed with heat and her head spun.

"Which sigil?"

Eiryss nearly pointed to her chest sigil, but the thorn at her breast throbbed in time to her heartbeat, a warning growing cold in her breast. Like a seedling inserted in her skin, the thorn was alive and possessed a will of its own. And it didn't want to be known. Which was silly. Tria, Enderlee, Ramass, and who knew how many healers knew about it. What was wrong with Hagath seeing it?

She wished she could communicate with it, ask why. But trees were so foreign to people that communication wasn't usually possible. Not outside feelings and visions given to speakers of the dead or seers, and sometimes the Arbor.

Eiryss would have liked to explain that Hagath was someone to trust. But perhaps it wasn't about trust. Perhaps it was something else altogether unknowable to a woman. Eiryss tapped her right forearm.

"Build." Hagath nodded. "Focus on the pain instead of trying to ignore it." Eiryss shot her an incredulous look. Hagath returned it with a level one of her own. "Just do it."

Eyes closed, she slid her right hand inside her coat, fingertips resting lighting over her chest sigil. Another throb, but with the medicine numbing the pain, she could feel the sigil growing beneath her fingertips; roots and branches stretching. Her mouth fell open in wonder. It wasn't a thorn anymore. It had grown to a sigil.

"I'm an enchantress," she breathed.

"Only if you can access the magic," Hagath said.

"How?"

"Some say it feels like opening a door. For me, it was like turning my face to the sun."

Warmth started on the top of Eiryss's head and spread down her whole body. She breathed deeply, freely, for the first time in so long.

Hagath choked back a sob, pushed to her feet, and staggered a few steps. Eiryss looked up at her in bewilderment. "Hagath?"

Expression pained, Hagath wrapped her hands around her forearms. Over the scars where her sigils used to be.

And here Eiryss had been rejoicing over hers. Pushing herself up, she stepped closer to her friend and rested a hand on her shoulder. Her body had become so sharp—all hard edges, skin draped over bone.

What happened to you? she wondered. She hadn't had any time alone with Ramass to ask him.

"Ramass said you could have them back," she said gently.

"No!" Hagath's shout sounded hollowed out. "I don't want them."

Eiryss shook her head in bewilderment. "But, Hagath, you always wanted to become a healer. More than anything." How could that have changed?

"I'm still a healer. Just not one with magic."

So that was why she was here—as their unit's surgeon. Such a lowly station—all their healing was done with sharp knives, herbs, and the healing music played through the sacred pipes. "What happened to you?"

Hagath turned away. "This war."

"I don't understand."

Hagath sighed. "Sometimes something happens that changes who we are. We are altered and no longer fit into the mold we once knew."

Eiryss desperately wanted to know what happened. But Hagath would only refuse to tell her and then they'd be fighting again. She sighed in resignation. "Let's get back."

They returned to the group to find the wagons already loaded and awaiting their journey in the morning. Intent on interrogating Ramass, she looked for him to no avail. Blast it.

An older servant bowed, motioned for their group to follow him, and shuffled ahead. "As the enchantress copse is full, the mayor has offered to host you all in his own hometree."

The old man reminded her of Belgrave. The first time he'd hugged her had been when he'd found her sobbing in her father's library. He'd pulled her into his arms and let her soak his tunic, which had smelled of camphor. Light, she missed the old man. Missing him made her miss her parents. Emotions swamped her. Ones she barely managed to choke down.

They passed through a working-class neighborhood, people who lived in stone cottages with split shingle roofs. Their clothing was well made and sturdy, if not fine. And they seemed healthy and well-fed. The farther Eiryss went into the city, the less true any of that became. The houses were wood, gaps visible between the shrunken boards. Those gaps had been stuffed with mud. A young woman was shoveling snow up against the house. She paused to look at the group of enchantresses as they reached the stairs that would take them into the canopy.

She wore no expression, but her eyes followed their every movement. Eiryss stopped walking to watch her. The girl's gaze met hers. Eiryss looked away first. She followed Hagath into the canopy—the circuits around the tree much shorter as it was half the size of the Hanama hometrees. Here was all beauty and light. Each platform had been painstakingly carved. The peaked roofs bore motifs of the Silver Tree or Ahlea Flower or a family crest.

The mayor's tree was the largest in the city. Eiryss stepped through the archway and along the bridge that led to the main platform. Each step brought her closer and closer to a wonderful, savory smell. Past the doorpane of the main platform, she found a steaming meal laid out on a single table.

It was nothing special. Some roasted fish and root vegetables, but it set her mouth watering more than any delicate feast ever had.

Sitting beside Hagath, Eiryss ate fish and wonderfully chewy bread. After, Eiryss slipped away from her friend to go looking for Ramass, intent on asking him about Hagath's excision, but she couldn't find him. She even went so far as to ask the mayor if he'd seen the red-headed Marshal.

The man bowed to her, his eyes skimming her family crest before they widened with recognition. "Your name?"

She stiffened, knowing what was coming. "Lady Eiryss."

His lips tightened in disapproval. "A marshal is never without missives to send and read, lady. He and Jala have already retired to their rooms."

Hagath stepped up beside her. "I'm looking for him too."

Eiryss stifled her sigh. She needed a moment alone with him to drag Hagath's secret out of him.

The lord bowed deeply. "Lady Hagath, I have prepared a room for you and Ladies Wyndyn and Iritraya. If you will follow me."

Hagath's eyes widened. "And Lady Eiryss, surely."

His false smile slipped a fraction. "I'm afraid there aren't enough rooms for everyone, my lady."

The man was nothing more than a mud lord. He was a nobody. His opinions were as irrelevant as he was. But no matter how many times Eiryss told herself these kinds of slights didn't matter, they still hurt.

Hagath stiffened. "Lord Yonald, is it?"

He nodded eagerly.

Her lip curled in disgust. "A name I will forever associate with boorish hospitality and the kind of vastly inferior breeding that even a mud lord should be ashamed of." His eyes widened with panic and outrage. Hagath looped her arm around Eiryss's, snatched a couple of blankets from a passing servant, and turned on her heel.

"My lady." Lord Yonald gripped Hagath's arm.

She pierced him with a stare. "You dare touch a high lady without her permission?"

He recoiled. "Of course Lady Eiryss is welcome—"

She lifted a hand and he fell silent. "Frankly, your hospitality is beneath me. I'll sleep in the common room." She turned her back on him and took hold of Eiryss's arm. The two of them marched through their unit, who stared with wide eyes.

"That man will find himself a pariah of the nobles," Hagath whispered. "I'll make sure of it."

Eiryss felt a little sorry for him. "I don't really blame him. He believes I'm a traitor."

"Well, now any mud lords will think twice before insulting you."

Eiryss squeezed her friend's hand. "Light, I've missed you."

Hagath laid her blanket out before the brazier and sank regally onto it. With a sigh, Eiryss motioned for Balendora and Namishka to join them, and she lay down next to Hagath.

It wasn't long before Namishka muttered in her sleep and Balendora snored. Eiryss couldn't stop thinking about how wretched Hagath had seemed that afternoon. Eiryss glanced over to see Hagath staring at the enchanted barrier ceiling above them, the bare branches like spears of dark frost against the starstrewn sky. Her eyes were haunted and lost.

The look Hagath and Ahlyn had shared over a basin of their own vomit. Both of them understood at once that they had been poisoned. That they could both die.

"When my mother died," Eiryss began, "she somehow shared a vision with me. I died along with Ahlyn."

Hagath gasped in a breath but wouldn't meet her gaze. "Then you know I drank the medicine meant for her." She held up her hand, the bones and veins as delicate as a songbird's. "I lived. And she did not."

"She was too far gone for the medicine to save her, and she knew it."

"I know." The despondency in her eyes said she didn't believe it.

Eiryss stared at her own healthy hands. "Her last thoughts were that she didn't want anyone she loved to grieve her too long. She wanted you to be happy."

Tears slipped from Hagath's temples into her hair. "We're going to the front lines, Eiryss, and I'm scared. I don't really want to live, but I'm afraid to die."

"You just don't want to hurt anymore." Eiryss knew that feeling all too well.

Hagath scrubbed her eyes. "Why are *you* here, Eiryss? You shouldn't be."

Eiryss took a deep breath to calm her rising anger. "You're not my mother, Hagath."

"I just want you to be safe."

"But *I* don't want to be safe."

Hagath turned away. They were silent for a time, and Eiryss thought Hagath had fallen asleep when she suddenly said, "I'm going to look after you. Whether you like it or not."

Two could play that game. "And I you."

"Forever."

CHAPTER 17

WEAVER

Long before dawn, they left the city to trek across the frozen landscape. Between the haphazard messiness of the wild forest and the adjustment of re-orientating to being trapped on one plane—with sideways, forward, and back the only available directions—Eiryss felt a bit dizzy. The mud didn't help. One minute she was on firm, frozen ground, the next her left food was sliding out from under her.

She snatched onto Hagath's arm to keep her balance. Her feet were wet and her hem muddy. She was freezing. "This is undignified."

"Life on the ground is so filthy," Hagath agreed.

Eiryss rubbed her sore hip from sleeping on the hard floor. "Why anyone would choose it is beyond me."

Hagath gave her a tight look.

"What did I say?"

Hagath looked away. "Nothing."

Not wanting another argument, Eiryss let it drop. The two of them shifted to the edge of the road—the snow was cleaner there.

The morning sun hadn't even risen when Ramass rode up beside them on a strange horse. Framed by the deep green of wild evergreens, he looked handsome, with his hair neatly tied back and his face shaved clean. From behind, Jala called for him to wait. Ramass shot a pleading look at Eiryss. She crooked an amused grin. He rolled his eyes. Then his gaze shifted to Hagath, and he winced at the glare she pinned him with.

He scanned the gathered enchantresses. "Do as Jala says when she says, and you stand a higher chance of surviving." He nudged his horse to a trot, eager to escape Hagath or Jala or both.

"And where are you off to?" Jala called to him, hip cocked to show off her curves.

"We meet up with a company of soldiers tonight. I'm going on ahead to speak with their commander." Ramass rode on, leaving them in the tender care of Jala, who watched him with narrowed eyes.

"And with that rousing rally, we go to war," Hagath said under her breath. Eiryss snorted despite herself. She'd missed Hagath's wry humor.

"He's very handsome," Namishka whispered to her grandmother.

If you can get past the temper and the indecisiveness, Eiryss thought bitterly. They started up a rise. The wind picked up and she shivered inside her coat.

"You realize he's my brother," Hagath said dryly. Namishka's jaw snapped shut. "At any rate, better stay far away from any man Jala has her eye on." Hagath grinned wickedly—like only a sister could at her brother's expense.

"Poor, poor Ramass," Eiryss mocked.

"He deserves it," Hagath said darkly.

Ramass and Hagath bickered just as badly as she and Ture. She considered asking what they were fighting about and decided she'd rather not know.

Jala reluctantly shifted her gaze from Ramass's backside to them. "As enchantresses, our duty is in the creation of barriers, which we form into armor, domes, and vaults. We are the shield that protects our people from harm.

"Your fledgling sigils are too new to draw from," Jala went on, "So you will memorize which command goes with which sigil. Positive powers like *build, seek, seal,* and *light* with their negative twins like *break, repel, loose,* and *darken.*"

"And the ninth thorn?" Eiryss asked.

Jala's expression darkened. "None of you are to draw from that one. Don't even open it."

"And why is that?" Balendora asked.

Jala's blank expression settled on the older woman. "Try it if you dare. But you won't like the results."

Eiryss's hand splayed across her navel. More secrets. She'd come of age among the high nobility, where secrets had grown like tangled briars all around her. She'd once thought herself above the snare of their sharp embrace. What a fool she'd been.

With no more arguments, they marched and practiced through wild forests intermingled with snow-covered fields. Up and down hills until Eiryss's legs ached. By midafternoon, the day warmed enough for her to undo her coat. But that warmth came at a high price. She was coated in mud from her thighs down, and her feet squished in her soggy boots.

At dusk, they approached an empty field. Atop a small rise, a single tent had been set up. Around it, dozens of men milled about small fires. They were heavily armed, though they wore no uniform.

A sentry pointed to the south, to a bare spot near the forest. "The trees there will block most of the wind. Stay out of the main camp."

Hagath and Eiryss exchanged confused looks. Eiryss shivered—the warmth of midafternoon had added to the humidity, which cut through her worse than this morning's cold. A fire out of the wind sounded wonderful. Skirting the edge of the camp, they started to the south.

Eiryss and Hagath had been assigned to set up their only tent—Jala's.

Eiryss nodded toward the encampment. "Who do you think they are?"

Hagath glanced up from where she was pounding down a stake. "Probably one of the council members."

"Why so many guards?"

Hagath pointed to the rise. "And why does Ramass want to meet with them?"

His features barely discernable, Ramass stood outside the tent, seemingly observing them, before disappearing inside again.

"What I want to know is why he didn't bring us a horse," Eiryss muttered.

She and Hagath finished with the tent. Scowling at the idea of sleeping out in the open, Eiryss sat beside Hagath on a log around one of the fires and settled into her dinner of dried meat and fruit. The silence between them was like a wound—raw and tender, but perhaps healing.

Eiryss took off her boots, propped them open with forked sticks, and set them before the fire. Within a minute, they were steaming as much as her trousers. Namishka and Balendora eased down beside them and ate their own food. When the mud had dried sufficiently, Balendora passed around a horsehair brush to scrub the mud from their trousers and boots.

One eye on the tent Ramass had disappeared inside, Hagath quizzed the four of them on the sigils until they could name them without thinking. As Eiryss concentrated on the sigil in her right arm, a painful buzz built. She paused, lifting her sleeves to reveal the sigil lit up like a tiny, raised star beneath her skin. Just like the stars under her mother's skin.

"See if you can light the rest," Hagath said.

She concentrated on each in turn. They hurt, like a strong current battering through too small an opening. She pulled up her sleeves and trousers, her skin pebbling with cold. But her sigils shone on her body—eight little stars gleaming white. Tears of joy traced Eiryss's cheeks. They'd all taken. She breathed out in relief—not realizing the worry she had been carrying that her thorns would die until that worry was gone. Still, they didn't hurt as much as they first had.

Namishka's brow furrowed as she stared at a lump on her arm. She huffed. "Why aren't mine working yet?"

Hagath laughed as she pulled back. "Two days is sooner than most."

"It's sooner than anyone." They turned to find Jala behind them, arms crossed and gaze narrowed. Kneeling, Jala pulled back Eiryss's sleeves. Her hot palms rested against Eiryss's chilled skin. The woman pressed too hard—the dull ache shifted to a sharpness that made Eiryss draw a startled breath.

"Good." Jala glanced up at the sky, the stars starting to come out in earnest. She made a sharp, sweeping gesture toward the other girls. "To bed." Shooting a dark glare at the tent Ramass had disappeared into, she pulled open her own tent flap and slipped inside.

Everyone let out a collective sigh of relief. Eiryss's fingertips rested lightly at the sigil on her chest. It ached fiercely, though she was still chewing nemroot, even if it stuck in her teeth and made her tongue feel raw with splinters.

They cut down pine boughs and spread their blankets on top of them. Balendora and Namishka lay on the other side of the fire. Side by side, Hagath and Eiryss curled under a single blanket for warmth. The boughs poked Eiryss in a dozen different places. She could already feel the sticky sap seeping through the blanket to gum up her clothes and hair. But if she closed her eyes and listened to the wind through the boughs of the trees, she could almost pretend she was lying in her own bed.

"Light all of them but the navel," Hagath said.

Instantly, the memory was gone and she was freezing and sticky and an orphan. She fought back tears even as her chest sigil beat out a warning. Why was the sigil so reluctant to draw attention to itself? Hagath was her friend. But just the thought of telling her sent a thrum of panic through Eiryss.

Pulling out her pipes, she opened the sigils on her limbs and played. The music communicated with the living sigils inside her. Her magic gleamed into view, fluid and lovely like liquid moonlight of slightly different shades. They hovered, waiting for her next command.

How many times had she watched with a mixture of longing and awe as other enchantresses had done this very thing? How many times had she gritted her teeth and promised herself that her time would come? And despite all the odds against it, she had magic. "It's mine." Hers in a way that nothing else was. Even her own body would betray her eventually—she'd watched it happen to her own mother—but the magic never would.

"Weave, build, repel, and a tiny bit of light," Hagath said.

"A dome enchantment," Eiryss said.

Hagath nodded.

Eiryss played and the magic responded to the flute's commands; the sigils wove together to create a small sphere before her. Some of the threads were a bit wobbly. Some were already fraying before unraveling to smoke. The dome's shape was misshapen, lumpy, and bulging on one side. But it was an enchantment. Her first.

What she would have given for her mother to see her like this.

"Tie it off," Hagath whispered.

Eiryss hurriedly played *seal*. "It's a mess," she said as she brushed her fingertips lovingly over it.

Hagath chuckled. "Your sigils are young yet. The more you train them, the more they will learn." She lay back on her blankets. "Less *build* and *repel*, and a little different order of weave, and you have armor. Add the magic you've taken from the enchanter's weapons sigils, and you can create a vault."

Eiryss reached out, her fingers resting across the rapidly dissipating surface. It felt like starlight—hard and misty, cold and hot. She had the overwhelming sense that the magic was aware of her touch. Acting on pure instinct, she rested her hands over two fraying ends and smoothed them together. The magic moved, the frayed ends sealing. Breath in her throat, she gaped at what she'd done.

Hagath sat up and leaned forward. "Do that again. Without touching it."

Eiryss pulled her hands back. She found another frayed weave and gestured. The magic moved, as if it were part of her. As if it innately knew what she wanted it to do.

Hagath gasped. "Eiryss, you're a weaver."

Only the strongest enchantresses were weavers. People like Tria, the king, or Jala. Eiryss held her flute close, pressing it against her amulet. She wished her parents were here. Wished they could see her weave. Her father would have nodded as if he'd known it all along, then drawn her in, his forehead pressed against hers. "That's my daughter." Her mother would have laughed and clapped for joy and called for Marinda to cook all their favorite dishes and send a servant to call the king and his family to join them. They would have had a lovely dinner with Ramass's family.

"Light," Eiryss whispered. "I miss them so much."

"Remember when we stumbled upon that sleeping nest of gilgads?" Hagath asked gently.

They'd jumped off a boulder and found themselves smack in the center of a hot spring. Giant lizard gilgads were hibernating in a huddled mass at the base. "We were too scared to move."

"Your mother found us," Hagath said.

"She formed a dome around us and went for Father."

"We had gilgad for dinner."

Eiryss grinned. "It was delicious."

They giggled. Someone hushed them. It felt so like when they were little and had spent the night at each other's houses. They were only missing their annoying brothers. They lay back, looking at the stars.

"Why so many secrets behind the other sigil?" Eiryss touched her navel. "What does it do?"

Hagath's expression shuttered. "I don't know." She scooted down in her blankets and turned her back to Eiryss. "We should get some sleep."

She was clearly lying. Eiryss considered pushing it, but the truce between them was still so fragile—almost as fragile as Hagath seemed.

Tossing another log in the fire, she settled down in her own blankets, the smell of pine sap growing sharper each time she wiggled. She reached under her blankets to shift some of the branches that were poking her back. "What's going on between you and Ramass?"

Hagath let out a long breath. "Ahlyn's death changed him."

Ahlyn's death had changed everything, Eiryss thought bitterly. "And it didn't change you?"

Hagath was silent so long Eiryss thought she wouldn't answer. "Maybe it destroyed us both."

CHAPTER 18

ATTACK

A *boat filled with soldiers dressed in their finest rega-
lia rowed toward Eiryss's hometree. They carried a
single, intricate lantern. She refused to go down the
steps to meet the soldiers. Didn't want to know the message they
carried. But she couldn't stop watching as they docked and filed
out.*

*Two men laid her father's bloodstained, broken armor on
the ground at Mother's feet. "Emlon, we honor you."*

*Her mother fell to her knees as the man lifted the lantern,
opened its ornate door.*

And blew it out.

Eiryss sat bolt upright in her bedroll. Beneath her skin, her
chest sigil flared with cold. It was the deepest part of night, when
the stars shone brightest. Everyone seemed dead asleep. An undercurrent of music thrummed in the air, making Eiryss's chest
sigil pulse with dread—the same dark dread that had flooded her
as she'd dreamed of her father's death the way it should have

been. With his soldiers bringing his lantern and armor to her family. The kind of tribute he would have received had his death been honorable.

A deep heaviness and confusion tried to press Eiryss down into her bedroll. It promised peace and comfort and oblivion. She struggled against it, her sigil flaring colder still.

The banked firelight bathed a man in red as he left the tree cover and snaked toward the main tent. He'd probably just relieved himself in the forest. Perhaps come in from his shift of sentry duty.

And yet.

Something about the way he moved and the darkness that hung over her, heavy as a grave... From all around the encampment, more men left the cover of trees. At least a half dozen of them. All picking their way up their hill toward the command tent.

Eiryss's group of Valynthians were well within their own territory. A guard rotation had been set.

And yet.

She suddenly understood. Her sigil was trying to warn her. The heaviness was dark enchantment—more specifically, an emotive who used magic to control emotions—to make people too exhausted to even raise their heads. And those men sneaking through the bedrolls toward Ramass's command tent—they weren't men. They were women.

"Alamantians!" she cried.

Her voice seemed to break the spell. Her confusion banished. The Alamantians broke into a run toward the command tent. Barefoot, her fellow Valynthians sprang from their bedrolls, swords and shields forming in their hands. Silver met gold in arcing streaks of light. Two dozen more soldiers burst from the trees, the light from their magical weapons casting an eerie glow that revealed female Alamantian soldiers in their mottled green clothing.

For a moment, Eiryss was transfixed by the sight—she'd never seen a real battle before. Then a woman stepped from the distant command tent and fell screaming, an arrow in her side. Ramass was in that tent. Eiryss jerked back to the reality of the danger. Panic flooded her.

Jala burst from her tent. She played her instrument, her sigils shining through her clothes. Shimmering silver threads slipped from her body to form a silver sphere. Jala shifted her song and that sphere sped through fighters, up the hill, to hover over the command tent. Her song shifted, and the sphere expanded, passing harmlessly over Valynthians as it recognized their familiar sigils. It forced Alamantians back from the now collapsed tent.

With a shout, soldiers split away from the main group of Alamantians and headed toward Jala.

Hagath gave Eiryss a shove. "Jala is vulnerable. You have to help her!"

All Jala's magic was wrapped up protecting the command tent, leaving her exposed. Hurrying to the woman's side, Eiryss tugged her flute free.

"Build and repel," Hagath instructed. "A little light so you can see what you're doing."

Eiryss woke her sigils and played, the melody bold and steadfast and woven with intimidation to make the Alamantians falter and look elsewhere. The silver streamers from her sigils wove into a small, misshapen sphere that wavered before her eyes. The other enchantresses clustered around her. Soldiers bore down on them, close enough the dome reflected in their eyes.

Eiryss fingers flew over the sphere, trying to fix its flaws.

"There isn't time," Hagath cried.

Eiryss threw the sphere; it rose and swelled into a dome that surrounded her fellow enchantresses. Barely. The soldiers reached them and slashed their weapons across her magic. Eiryss gasped in pain.

"You forgot to tie it off," Hagath cried.

Eiryss opened *seal* and played a different song, weaving a loose net. Sweat slid down her temples at the sensation of her magic shredding beneath sharp blades.

"Merrek, get this blasted dome down!" an Alamantian shouted. Her mantle declared her their unit commander.

Eiryss's gaze flicked to the man the woman shouted at. Partially hidden in the deep shadows of the treeline, an enchanter had molded his magic into a battering ram that pounded relentlessly against Jala's distant barrier, sending a dull shock wave that made Eiryss's own dome shudder with each impact. Now, he turned that battering ram toward her.

"*Seal*, Eiryss!" Hagath cried. "Seal it now!"

Eiryss finished the weave and tossed the magic. Before it touched her dome, the enchanter struck. She woke up on the ground. Far above, the stars and nearly full moon glittered against the cold. The sound was gone. Her magic thrummed with aftershocks. Then the pain came, forcing the breath from her lungs. She couldn't inhale.

Hagath knelt before her. Her lips moved, but it took Eiryss a long time to understand the words. "*Seal*! Seal it off before he kills you!"

Another percussion slammed into Eiryss. Her scream was drowned out by the resinous gong going off in her skull.

Hagath shook her. Her lips repeating the same word over and over and over. Though Eiryss couldn't hear, she understood what her friend was saying. "*Seal! Seal! Seal!*"

Only the knowledge that another attack was coming forced Eiryss to stagger to her feet with Hagath's help. She grabbed the unraveling net and tossed it upward. It melded with the dome, which shifted colors slightly.

Her dome shuddered with impact, but the pain was a distant echo now.

"You did it," Hagath said in a shaky voice.

Eiryss tasted blood and wiped her nose with the back of her hand. More trickled from her ears. Without her power to continually feed it, the dome dented under his strikes.

"Break, loose, and *light,"* Hagath said desperately. "Use the song to form your own battering ram and take down his dome!"

Generally, the larger the sigil, the older and more in tune it was with its enchanter or enchantress. Eiryss's had only manifested that night. Only the barest dregs of her magic remained, the rest was tied up in the dying dome.

Still, she had to try. She played the song for a web. Her magic formed an invisible, low-lying mist that rolled forward and sent back sensations and smells—broken earth, wood, blood, leather. The enchantment edged against the enchanter's dome and rolled over it like smoke. To her newly awakened magic, his armor felt like glass, but where her magic was cool, his was warm, as well as tough and flexible.

But she found a weakness. A spot where the threads frayed. She gathered up the dregs of her magic, weaving it to a needle-like point, her song urging her magic to arrow into his. It bounced harmlessly off. Seconds later, his magic hit hers. She felt her own dome shudder, a phantom ache. Cracks split from the dent. One more hit—two at the most—and her dome would crumble.

Eiryss's magic hit his again. Again, it bounced harmlessly off. Eiryss waited for the next hit, but it didn't come.

One of the female soldiers held up her fist, and the enchanter had paused. "I am Commander Habbia." Her mantle affirmed her words. "Surrender before your dome falls and you will live. Continue fighting, and we will kill you all."

Hagath steadied Eiryss, who felt achy and hollow. Blood still ran from her nose down her throat. She spat and wiped her nose again.

Ringing silence echoed through the clearing. Jala looked over the terrified girls huddled around her. "You're better off dead than what they will do to you in their prison camps."

"I swear you will be treated well," Habbia said.

In answer, Jala played. A tiny sphere formed before her. It grew until it barely encompassed her form. Only an enchantress as strong as Jala could form two domes, weak and wavering as the second was.

Habbia dropped her hand. The enchanter struck. Eiryss's dome chimed, pieces of it flaking off. The girls screamed.

Eiryss gripped Hagath. "What do we do? What do we do?"

Hagath shoved her off, drew her dagger and knife, and assumed a fighting stance.

What good were a knife and dagger against magic-forged blades? Still, Eiryss pulled her own weapons. Some of the girls pounded against Jala's dome, begging her to save them. To take them with her. Encased in magic, she ignored them as she passed through Eiryss's dome and into the waiting Alamantians. They struck her dome, which rippled violently, but did not break.

Face screwed up in concentration, she passed through the heart of them, heading uphill toward the command tent one hundred yards away. It was still safely locked behind her first dome. She was abandoning her enchantresses to protect the men. Why?

"She left us," Namishka whispered.

"Left us to die," Wyndyn said.

Balendora shoved a few of the girls, shouting at them to draw their weapons. Wyndyn and Iritraya obeyed. Namishka and most of the others cowered.

Ramass cupped his hands around his mouth and shouted. "Jala! You can't abandon them."

Twenty yards away, Jala's dome pulsed and warped with impact. "I can't protect you both, Marshal!"

Motioning to his men, Ramass and a half dozen others abandoned the protection of Jala's dome and charged down the hill toward the trapped enchantresses. He was immediately blocked by the dozen Alamantians who'd stayed behind to surround the command tent.

Ramass's ax cleaved the man before him, spraying blood. "Through them," he shouted to his men, but they were already fighting as hard as they could.

Another impact and Eiryss's dome shattered, fading bits of light that crumpled to dissipating ash. Eiryss braced for attack even as her magic came rushing back to her. But the Alamantians didn't attack. Eiryss flared her newborn sigils, but she knew if she so much as lifted her pipes to her lips, she would die.

The Alamantians, women who had trained their entire lives to fight, hesitated. "Will you surrender?" Habbia's gaze was fixed on Hagath. Did the woman recognize Hagath as the daughter of the king? Or did she simply note her leadership?

"I'd rather die fast than surrender to murderers," Balendora murmured to Hagath.

But the Alamantians weren't murdering them, though clearly they could have. Instead, they'd given them two chances to surrender. Namishka whimpered. Some of the girls drew their dagger and knife. Some dropped to their knees.

Habbia cocked her head in question at Hagath, who wet her lips and glanced at Eiryss, who shot Hagath a pleading look— better to be captured than slaughtered. Then they at least stood a chance of escape.

Slowly, so slowly, Hagath tossed her blades to the ground and eased to her knees. Terrified she was about to die, Eiryss followed suit. Balendora let out a string of profanities before grudgingly dropping her weapons. Wyndyn, Iritraya, and the few others still holding out gave in.

Habbia nodded in relief. "Bind them."

Eiryss gasped in relief—the Alamantians really didn't mean to execute them. Halfway to the command tent, Jala cried out and staggered. Her dome vibrated, pieces of it flaking off. Even from this distance, Eiryss could see the woman's tendons standing out on her neck as she struggled to keep moving through the soldiers slicing and the enchanter ramming her shield. Despite their efforts, Jala stood a chance of reaching safety before they broke her armor.

"Bring her down!" Habbia motioned to another woman who lifted a gleaming white bow, flecks of color dancing inside. The woman sighted down the arrow and released. It flew true—an arrow formed of the sacred wood of the Alamantian White Tree.

It hit Jala's armor in tandem with another magical strike. The arrow slammed into Jala's back. She pitched forward and did not move. The dome over the command tent shattered into increasingly smaller pieces until all that remained was silver dust drifting over the dead grass and snow.

Inside the distant dome were a dozen Valynthian soldiers. Why hadn't they come to help instead of hiding behind a dome like cowards? They were warriors! Soldiers of Valynthia.

With a barked command, Habbia left behind five soldiers to guard Eiryss and her fellow enchantresses. With a shout, she charged up the rise, the rest of the women right behind her. They slammed into Ramass's men, forcing them back. Ramass bellowed a rallying cry, but his men were outnumbered two to one, most of them still barefoot. Valynthians were cut down. Men with wives and children, parents, siblings.

Eiryss waited for the dozen soldiers who'd been inside the shattered dome to charge to their fellows' aid. Instead, they retreated. Abandoning Ramass and the handful of men who still fought with him. Abandoning Eiryss and her fellow fledgling enchantresses.

How could they do it?

Habbia's group pushed past Ramass and his men, forcing the retreating Valynthians to face them.

"Anyone moves, and I will kill you," one of their captors said. She watched carefully as she gathered their knives and daggers, throwing them out of reach. Another woman tied Namishka's hands behind her back with swift, efficient movements.

If that woman bound Eiryss's hands, her magic would be useless. This might be her only chance to escape. Yet she could not make herself move. The woman had meant what she'd said. She would kill her. Eiryss knew it down to her marrow.

And then the man guarding Ramass's back collapsed. From behind, an Alamantian's shield slammed into Ramass's side. He fell to all fours, one hand gripping his ribs. The other men were disarmed or disabled, Alamantians standing over them.

Fury in his gaze, Ramass glared up at the woman.

"Surrender or die," she said simply.

He spat at her.

"So be it." The woman drew her sword back for the killing stroke.

Eiryss's magic wasn't strong enough. Not yet. But then, she had two other sigils, neither of which were known. Warnings never to draw from her navel sigil pounded through her as she lit all ten of her sigils at once.

Torrents of magic and shadow tore through her. Hands shaking, she pressed her mouth to her flute and played a single note, but it was as if the magic knew what to do. Armor sprang around Ramass, coating his skin in shining silver. The Valynthian's sword bounced off Ramass's head as though he were encased in steel. The woman's magical sword winked out.

"No!" Hagath cried.

Eiryss whipped around as Hagath lunged, tackling an Alamantian who had been charging Eiryss. They rolled, the Alamantian ended up on top, her knives gleaming to life.

No.

Flute still in her mouth, Eiryss gasped, the note shrieking from her flute. She placed her fingers over the holes. The guards converged, swords poised to strike. Magic rushed from Eiryss's chest sigil, yanking magic from her other sigils so hard it hurt. A boom deafened and flattened her.

CHAPTER 19

CHAOS

Eiryss blinked up at the perfect dome gleaming above her. She sat up. The five guards had been thrown nearly to the trees. They struggled to their feet.

Hagath gasped and pushed to all fours. "How-how did you do that?"

Everyone, including the Alamantians, gaped at Eiryss. At the magic she'd displayed. Even as the darkness swarmed inside her navel sigil and its cold spread, she had no answer.

"Leave them," Habbia called from the top of the hill, where her soldiers gathered their injured from among the dead. "We have what we came for." As if to punctuate her words, a burly woman hoisted a man dressed in the manner of the Alamantians over her shoulder. Between the dark and the distance, Eiryss couldn't make out his face.

They were kidnapping him. Who was he? Why was he so important that the Alamantians had risked invading Valynthia in the dead of night and attacked an encampment?

The guards backed away from Eiryss as if afraid. One by one, they hustled to the main group, which limped into the forest.

Ramass. Eiryss had forgotten about Ramass. She pushed to her feet and came to the edge of her barrier. There. The faint sheen of magical armor. He lay unmoving among the rest. Light, had she been too late to save him?

Hagath stood silently beside Eiryss. Both aching to go to him, both afraid the Alamantian retreat was some kind of ruse.

"Tie it off," Hagath said.

Eiryss sealed the dome with a handful of notes but didn't release her magic—she might need it again.

Hagath looked back at the other women. "Stay here." Namishka started sobbing. "Keep her quiet." Softer to Eiryss, "Stay with them."

Knowing she was planning to go out there by herself, Eiryss charged out without waiting for Hagath to argue.

"Stubborn, foolish..." Hagath's insults trailed off as they passed the first dead man. The Alamantian lay partially on top of a Valynthian, as if the woman had killed him even as he stood over her to strike the final blow. He'd collapsed on top of her, and they had died together. Their position was intimate, a lover's embrace instead of a dying one.

There were more. Bodies strewn at unnatural, broken angles. One of them moved, making Eiryss jump. She tensed, ready to run back to the safety of the dome. But it was one of their own. He looked around, as if judging if it were really safe. Others joined him—all clearly too injured to continue fighting and had been playing dead.

Convinced there wasn't an ambush lying in wait for them, Eiryss broke into a trot—she dared not go faster as the shadows cast by the fire were deep and long, hiding weapons and worse things—things like the fingers she accidentally stepped on. Hagath reached Ramass first. When Eiryss caught up, he was moaning and blinking hard. She staggered to a stop in relief, her hand automatically going to her heart. The side of his head was swollen and bleeding. She took the last few steps and knelt beside him.

"Alamantians. Sword." He broke down into unintelligible mutterings. His sword and shield flickered to life, nearly taking Eiryss in the side. She gripped his arm, shocked at how easy it was to restrain him.

Hagath pinned his shoulders down. "Easy. Take it easy."

His magic sputtered and then went out. "A'right," he managed. She tentatively released him, and his fingers touched a wicked knot on the side of his head.

"The armor didn't work," Eiryss said in horror.

He flinched and then looked up at her with squinting, watering eyes. "That was you?" He started to sit up. "Gah! Head. Hurts." He hunched over his drawn knees and waved off her hands. "No, the armor worked—saved my life."

"The composition was a little off," Hagath said not unkindly. "It was too flexible."

"It saved my life," Ramass repeated, his words growing stronger, clearer.

Hagath embraced him. He yelped in pain and she jerked back. He held his ribs.

"Broken?" Hagath asked.

He tried an experimental breath. "Bruised, I think."

"Eiryss," Hagath ordered. "Weave him a compress."

"But I haven't ever actually done one before," Eiryss said.

"You've practiced plenty," Hagath said.

"Without magic," Eiryss said.

"Come, it's an easy enchantment."

Eiryss played a song with the cool pressure of deep water. Magic poured from her sigils and wrapped around Ramass's ribs as easily as if she'd been doing it her whole life. She would have been proud, but the more magic she used, the more the clammy, oily feeling seeped from her navel sigil.

Shivering, she tied the enchantment off.

Ramass breathed out in relief. "Thank you."

"Nicely done," Hagath said.

Ramass assessed the situation. "Eiryss, drop the dome and armor those who are left. Hagath, get those girls looking after my men."

Shivering, Eiryss managed to do as he said. It should have taken her decades to train her magic so well, not to mention use it so deftly. That it came so easily left her caught between worry and gratitude.

If Hagath or Ramass noticed, neither said anything.

"Look after the enchanters!" Hagath called to the enchant-resses.

Helping her granddaughter up, Balendora barked, "Build up the fires and get the medical equipment out of the wagon! Help those men!"

The women jumped to obey. The fires flared, adding light to the dark night. Women hurried among the injured, helping those they could.

Ramass glanced around. "Where's Father?"

Father? "The king?" Eiryss gasped.

Hagath shook her head. "They took him."

"Why was he here?"

"He was headed back to Hanama," Ramass said.

All the pieces suddenly fell into place. The unconscious man the Alamantians had taken had been the king. No wonder the Alamantians had risked moving far behind enemy lines to attack. That also meant the woman who'd come out of the command tent moments after Eiryss had shouted a warning had been his personal enchantress, a woman Eiryss knew from the nobili-ty. She'd been shot down first, leaving Jala alone with the ability to protect him. Which explained why she had abandoned her unit, and why the soldiers inside the dome hadn't come to their enchantress's aid. They were the king's personal guard. Their only priority had been his safety.

Now they were all dead or incapacitated. Zannok was at the Alamantian's mercy. What would they do to him? A sick feeling started in Eiryss's gut. "We have to save him!"

"What—" Ramass jumped to his feet and swayed, the heel of his hand pressing on his temple. "Which way?"

Hagath and Eiryss reached out to steady him. Hagath pointed to where the Alamantians had disappeared.

He followed her gesture. "How fast were they moving?"

"Not fast," Hagath said. "They had injured."

"Emers?" Ramass twisted around, his face hardening when he saw his dead and dying men. "Emers, where are you?" He started turning over bodies as if looking for someone.

Hagath knelt next to one man after another, searching for signs of life.

Intent on helping her, Eiryss released her sigils. Only, the navel sigil didn't close. Instead, a cold shadow continued to slither wider and wider. So much so that made her teeth chatter. She tried again to release it, but it only continued to spread. She tried a third time, but... it didn't want to be shut down.

Something was wrong.

Fear coated her mouth. "Hagath."

Hagath must have sensed something off in her voice, for she whipped around, her quick gaze locking on Eiryss's, who'd hunched over her middle. "You used the sigil."

"I can't close it."

Blood on her fingers, Hagath yanked up her flute. "Follow my lead."

"There are shadows in the sigil." Eiryss said it in a whisper, an irrational part of her worried the sigil could hear her. "They're spreading. They don't want to stop."

Hagath played a shaky note that eventually strengthened. Following her lead, Eiryss played of long summer days of laughter and sticky melons and sunburns. The cool of her other sigils spread, pushing the shadows back. Deeper. Until they sucked back into her navel sigil, which finally, finally closed. She released her magic and sagged, body aching with cold.

"Hagath." Ramass had found the man he'd been looking for and rolled him to his side. The two of them hurried to stand next to him. The man was clearly dead. Ramass closed the man's eyes before tugging off his satchel and rummaging through it. He tipped the contents of a vial—pain medicine—into his mouth, made a face, and threw it, glass shattering.

He handed the satchel to Hagath. "He was our surgeon. There should be things in there you can use."

Hagath took the satchel, her gaze already assessing the injured men. "What do you mean to do?"

"Go after them." He winced as he rose to his feet.

"You're what?" Eiryss cried.

Hagath moved to intercept him. "You're not going anywhere." He pushed past her. Hagath tugged the satchel's strap over her head and hurried after him. "In the shape you're in, you're no good to anyone in a fight."

"That's where the pain medicine comes in." He grimaced. "Are any of you up for a fight?" he called to his remaining men.

"No, sir," came the chorus of answers.

"Kit?" Ramass called as he circled. "Where's Kit?"

Eiryss stopped in her tracks. Kit? Kit was here? She hadn't seen him since her mother's funeral. Not since he'd kissed her goodbye. She hadn't known he'd joined the king's guard. She spun, looking for him.

A hand raised. Ramass hustled to his side, Eiryss a half dozen steps behind. She stepped past Ramass, who was blocking her view, and froze, gaping at all the blood. Kit's coat and tunic were soaked with it, as was the snow beneath him. His dark skin was ashen, his breaths shallow.

"Kit," she whispered in horror.

"Too much of a coward to come with me?" Ramass's gentle voice belied his words.

Coming up last, Hagath's eyes widened. She knelt beside him and gently tugged at his coat.

Kit's back arched, his face lined with agony. "I need a break from all your whining," he panted.

Hagath's gaze was hard with determination. She looked up at Eiryss. "Hold him."

You've seen blood before. Just because it's from a friend doesn't change anything. Forcing herself forward, Eiryss knelt beside him.

"Use your magic—all but that one." Hagath touched her near her navel sigil. "Bind him up."

Such delicate work was far beyond Eiryss's skill, but there was no one else. She opened nine of her sigils and played, the song coaxing numbing sap from Kit's sigils. There wasn't time for it to take full effect. She switched songs, to a complex, probing song like the mating dance of two fala birds. Her *seek* explored torn flesh, pulsing veins, punctured liver. All the while, Kit writhed at her intrusion.

Light, his injury was just like her father's. She could taste his blood in her mouth, feel the warm, torn fibers of his flesh all around her. And at the apex, a sharp point. The tip of a sword had broken off in his back rib. Her magic trembled, threatening to fall apart.

Kit screamed. Pain she was causing him with her clumsiness. She pushed away all thought. She played a song like the clack of the loom, the rhythm of the treadle, the shush of the fibers. *Repel* drew the sword tip as well as torn fibers of shirt up through his flesh. *Build* and *seal* bound flesh and stopped up bleeding.

When she had finished, she tied off the enchantment. As long as she lived, it would hold. She had a moment of intense satisfaction. She'd done it—her first time. She'd finally been able to use the skills she'd worked all her life to master.

Light, her sigils were brilliant. It was like they'd already been trained. And what she had done... it felt *right*. Like she'd fit neatly into a slot that had been made for her. With that belonging came a beat of loss. She was a warrior enchantress now. *There will be time for healing after the war.*

She opened her eyes as Hagath wiped the blood and sword tip from his now-closed flesh, the sheen of her magic visible over the angry red wound. Kit's lips were powdered with white residue; Hagath must have given him pain medicine too. Even with it, his whole body was tight with agony.

"You did beautifully," Hagath whispered.

"Will it be enough?" Eiryss whispered back.

Hagath's expression said that she didn't know.

Ramass squeezed Kit's shoulder and then spoke to Hagath. "Bandage him up. Get the wounded on the supply wagon and head northeast to Trapendale. Kit knows the way. We'll catch up when we can. Come on, Eiryss."

Eiryss paused in the middle of mixing the powder with water. "You want me to come with you?" A helpless, waiting-to-die feeling welled up, paralyzing her.

"Isn't this what you wanted?"

It had been. But after having lived through the horrors of battle...

Hagath glared up at her brother. "Eiryss isn't going anywhere." She was clearly furious that she couldn't leave Kit to come strangle her brother. "She's the closest thing we have to a healer. We need her."

"We have to go after the king," Ramass said. "The Alamantians left twenty or so minutes ago. With their wounded, I doubt they could have made it much farther than a couple of miles."

Hagath's hands tightened to fists, but she didn't argue further.

Ramass seemed to peer inside Eiryss. His pupils were huge, devouring the blue of his eyes—the medicine was working. "I need you."

Something in her shifted from panic to protectiveness. She pushed to her feet and followed him toward the opposite side of the clearing.

"Anything happens to her," Hagath called after them, "and you'll be running from me instead of Alamantians."

Ramass didn't bother to answer.

Just before they entered the trees, Eiryss stepped over the body of the king's enchantress—the same one she'd seen taken down in the first moments of battle. Her mantle marked her as the king's personal enchantress—eight stars spaced evenly over a dome that surrounded the king's silverfish symbol. The poor woman had only had her post a few weeks.

Knowing the woman would be an asset to their bedraggled group, Eiryss knelt next to her and rolled her over to check for breath. The Alamantians had been thorough—nearly a dozen stab wounds pierced her torso. Eiryss winced at the face—familiar, and yet not. Death had changed her into something other, her face purple, jaw slack, pupils solid black.

Eiryss answered Ramass's questioning look with a shake of her head.

His mouth tightened. "Use *light* for a small sphere. We're going to have to run."

With the light it cast, they found a game path through the trees. Within a half-mile, Eiryss's throat was raw from the winter air and her legs burned—another reminder her body had yet to recover from her illness. They reached the bottom of a hill and started up, Ramass leading the way, her light before him. Her lips and hands tingled, and she stumbled more than she'd ever willingly admitted.

When they reached a rocky clearing at the top of the hill, Ramass's face was white, his freckles standing out starkly in the moonlight reflecting off the bright snow. He staggered and caught himself against a tree, one hand around his ribs. That run had taken more out of him than he'd let on too.

He pointed south. "They're down there. Somewhere. Use *seek*. Find them."

Letting the sphere fade, she woke up *seek*, the buzz building from the small point of light gleaming beneath her skin. Her fingers shifted over the holes. She softly played a wandering, sweeping song—so gentle she could feel the slight buzz of the residual magic inherent to the sacred wood, which gleamed softly.

Her magic niggled along, bringing back scents of pine, visions of squirrels tucked deep into the canopy, the mineral and silt taste of a river. Wider she spread until her magic dissipated like tendrils of smoke on the wind.

She didn't realize her eyes were closed until then. "I can't go any farther."

"An enchantress who can make armor that strong that fast can easily reach over three miles. There's no way they've gone farther. Yet."

"I can't." She dared not open her eyes for fear of losing her connection.

"What did you do before?" He'd come close enough she could feel the warm puff of his breath against her chilled cheek.

She'd lit all her sigils. But perhaps it wasn't her navel sigil that had made her so strong. Perhaps it was the one on her chest. Carefully, she eased it open. Yes. There was cold and shadow, but not like with the navel sigil. She could bear it.

Her magic surged, allowing *seek* to speed along, sorting through images, scents, smells, tastes, textures. Until she encountered soft murmuring vibrations and heavy footfalls, felt gasping breaths.

She played again, snapped her broad net into a steady stream, and shot forward. A beat later, she felt the heat coming off the Alamantians. Smelled the sharp scent of their fear. She found the king. Running, his hands tied in such a way he couldn't call forth his sword without slicing his own arms open.

"I've found them," she murmured.

"Good. Build armor around my father."

She played and armor sprang up around the king. She was shocked at how easy it was. Hadn't Hagath told her it would take years to train her magic this well?

"Is it done?"

She nodded.

"Now, use *break*, *darken*, *loose*, and this." His fingertips rested lightly above her navel sigil.

"Light, no! Not again!"

"Eiryss, if you don't do this, they will have our king. We will lose this war."

This was why she had come all this way. To make a difference. To save those she could. But it frightened her in ways nothing else ever had. The shadows felt—evil. But she'd stopped them before.

She shifted uneasily. "What will that do?"

"It will stop them."

Light, she didn't have a choice. Opening her chest sigil, she used *darken*, *break*, *loose*, and the new sigil. The shadow inside Eiryss reared up, quivering with pleasure, and shot out from her body into the stream of magic. Between one blink and the next, it reached the distant Alamantians, coiling around their legs.

"Habbia!" their enchanter shouted in alarm. He played a couple of notes, his magic flared, heat to her cold. He managed to form armor around himself. Tried to armor the women.

It was too late.

The shadow struck, writhing and twisting, plunging down the throats of the Alamantians. They fell to their knees, hands around their throats as they choked, coughed, and gagged. Zannok stumbled back from the sight around him. He turned and ran. No one tried to stop him. Not even Merrek, who played harder, his magic nothing more than a nudge against hers.

The fight left the Alamantians' bodies as quickly as it had come on. As if moving to a beat she couldn't hear, they rose smoothly to their feet, heads down.

Merrek stopped playing. For a moment, there was no sound. No movement, save the shifting of a stray lock of hair or the hem of a cloak. Their silence was eerie, as was their blank expressions. What were they seeing?

Maybe the shadows only disabled them. Eiryss thought *Maybe they will leave the Alamantians as quickly as they came.*

Merrek reached for the nearest woman and touched her shoulder. "Are you all right? What happened?"

Merrek jumped as swords and shields suddenly formed in the Alamantians' hands, their swords and shields the only light within the dark. Face expressionless, a woman with a port-wine stain drew back her sword and thrust it at him. It clanged off his magical armor.

He staggered back, shock on his face. "What are you doing?"

She drew back to stab him again. From behind, an older woman slammed her shield into the port-wine stained woman's face. Her jaw hung crookedly, clearly broken. Instead of screaming in pain, she charged the older woman. The two hit the ground, rolling, clawing, punching for dominance. Neither of them made a sound.

The woman with the broken jaw drew a dagger and shoved it into the older woman's side. She didn't so much as grunt in pain. Their expressions never changed. And the same silent, eerie battle played out with each of the enchantresses in the company.

Merrek swore and played, his armor wrapping around the women to keep them from killing each other.

Ramass was speaking to Eiryss. She couldn't hear him over her bitter horror.

Eiryss cut off her navel sigil and played again, trying to call the shadows back. Tried to suck them back to whatever hell they'd emerged from. But they would not obey.

"How do I draw them back?" she asked, panic edging her voice.

"Where's my father? Can you find him?"

A sob built in Eiryss's faraway chest. "What have I done?"

Ramass gripped her forearms and pinned them against his chest. "Find Zannok, Eiryss. Find him."

Fighting back the sob, she again shifted her attention to her magic. The king was running. On his way back to them. The women fought with strength and majesty. It was beautiful and terrible. "He's escaped."

Merrek's magic was spread thin. The women were breaking down his armor as fast as he could rebuild it. The older woman had managed to slit the throat of the woman with the broken jaw. Blood gushing down her front, she fought on until her legs suddenly gave out from under her.

The older woman turned on Habbia, who was already fighting off a woman much larger.

Merrek snuck up behind the older woman and struck her in the back of the head with the butt of his dagger. The older woman staggered, sword and shield winking out. Face devoid of expression, Habbia raised her sword for the killing stroke. Merrek darted in front of Habbia and blocked her with the dagger, one startlingly similar to Eiryss's blade.

"Habbia, don't. You'll never forgive—"

Her magical blade cut through his dagger and slammed into his chest. He head-butted her. The two of them dropped to their knees. The sword inside Merrek faded to nothing. He looked down at the blood gushing from his middle in surprise. One hand pressed against his wound. The other reached out, tracing Habbia's face as she moaned and held her head. "It wasn't your fault. It was mine. I should have protected you better. I promised your mother that—"

He fell to his side, choking on his own blood. All his sigils flared; his magic hot against Eiryss's, driving her back. Instinctively, she dug in. For a moment, the magics were equal, neither giving way. Then his receded. Eiryss drove forward until she realized he was no longer fighting her.

Blood stained his lips and teeth. He looked about—he could sense her magic, even if he couldn't see her. "All magic is light," he repeated the enchantment mantra. "If that light be darkened, shadow and punishment come."

Eiryss had brought that shadow and punishment. She had done this to the Alamantians. "I have to stop it!" she cried to Ramass. "Please."

But the shadows were already dissipating. The women shook their heads, staggered back from each other, and clutched freshly bloodied wounds.

"Where, where are the monsters?" one woman asked.

"Where's my baby?" another cried. "That thing was eating my baby!"

There were no babies. No monsters. Eiryss had made them see things that weren't there.

"Merrek." Flat on her back, Habbia tried to stand and fell back to her knees. "Get a dome around us before that enchantress attacks again."

When he didn't answer, Habbia glanced around, caught sight of him, and stared as if not understanding. "Merrek, get—" She saw the blood. Horror dawned on her face. "Merrek—Father—no!" Crawling to his side, she shook him, trying to rouse him. It was far too late for that.

Eiryss recoiled. "I killed him." Her voice sounded so very far away.

"Killed who?" Ramass's words echoed.

Eiryss remembered her body. The one she no longer felt connected to. Realized it had collapsed. That Ramass cradled her in his arms. "I killed their enchanter."

"Focus, Eiryss. Where's the king?"

The Alamantians were already rallying to go after him. "He escaped."

"You have to incapacitate them before they recapture him." Ramass voice was so full of guilt. He'd known this would happen. Known she would unleash this. From the very moment he'd pushed the navel sigil into her skin. And now he wanted her to use that enchantment again.

She released her magic altogether, came back to herself in the near dark of the clearing. Ramass loomed over her. She slapped him. "You tricked me!" She launched herself at him, kicking and hitting.

He pinned her against his chest. "If Zannok falls into enemy hands, the war ends. We lose. Alamantians will flood our lands. We will be utterly at their mercy."

A sob pounded through Eiryss. "Do you understand what you've made me do? I forced a daughter to kill her own father!" She'd done to another what had been done to her. Wrecked the life of another as her life had been wrecked. In her mind, she watched her father die over and over and over.

"This is war!"

Her brother's warning came back to her. "War is all about cold and heat, blood and kill or be killed. Half the time you don't even know what the difference is between a soldier and a murderer."

But she knew where she stood. She was a murderer. The worst kind of murderer. All the fight left her. He rolled out from under her. She let him go.

"You have to finish them," he said gently.

She glared at him. The navel sigil pulsed greedily, as if it hungered for another opportunity to be unleashed. "What is this sigil? What could make them see something that isn't there?" She held her hand over her navel as a sudden memory overcame her.

It had been her seventh birthday. Her lips had been stained red from sugar berries, the aftertaste sweet and sour on her tongue. A man had bent down and opened his hand. Inside, the lampent trembled, transforming into a bird that shook out wings lined with pulsing rainbows and flew away.

Eiryss had known it wasn't real—she could see a shadow of the flower beneath the bird, but it hadn't stopped her from clapping her hands with glee. Her father had hired a dreamer for her party. The strongest dreamer in all of Valynthia. The man gave Father long blue hair, her mother a crown of fire, and Eiryss a dress made of a thousand delicate silver moths, their wings leaving brushstrokes of gold on her skin.

His final bit of magic had been to dump two fighting fish into the same bowl. They became fiery dragons battling in the clouds. By the end of the party, the man's eyes were tired and he kept rubbing his sigils as if they pained him. After the man had left, Eiryss had overheard the king tell her father what a waste of magic dreamer was.

"Nothing more than cheap tricks," her father had replied.

What if he'd been wrong?

"Is this sigil some kind of dream?" After all, it had made the Alamantians see things that weren't there.

"What dreamer could possibly be that powerful?" Ramass scoffed.

He was right. Of course he was right. Why now? Why this horror of a sigil?

"Eiryss, if you don't stop them, they'll rally and come after us. This time, they won't take prisoners."

She pulled herself together enough to stand. By the light of her sigils, she could make out his expression. He was sorry. So sorry. She could see it and she didn't care. "That is not an honorable way to die. Or to fight."

"No," he agreed. "But it is the way to win. Now do it, or every one of us is going to die this night."

The Alamantians hadn't slaughtered Eiryss and her enchantresses. They'd offered them surrender not once, but twice. Clearly, they were more honorable. She gritted her teeth. She would not do what he'd asked of her. She would never do what he'd asked.

But he was not wrong.

She could see only one way through. Shutting Ramass out, she played and pulled from *darken* and her chest sigil. Her music called forth the gentle dark of soft breezes and sleep. She was no emotive, but her magic was unexpectedly strong. Would it be strong enough?

One way to find out.

Full of dreams and soft sleep, her magic stroked against the Alamantians. They staggered.

"How?" Habbia moaned. "How is she this strong?" But they were already falling into dreamless sleep. Eiryss used her seal sigil, hoping it would keep them asleep for hours yet. Then her magic fled. Back in her own body, her flute dropped from her lips. She collapsed to her knees and vomited.

"The king?" Ramass demanded.

She pointed in the direction she'd felt him running.

"Get back to the others," Ramass said. Before she'd finished spitting the last of it out, he had already disappeared into the night.

TORN SHADOWS

Eiryss played to herself for a full five minutes before the shadow was safely contained. She pushed the horror of what she'd done to Habbia and the others down deep, knowing she would have to deal with them at some point. She followed the sounds of shouting back to the clearing. Who was shouting and why? She'd just left the cover of trees when something whizzed past her. An arrow impaled in the dirt just behind her. She jumped belatedly. Her lighted sphere snapped out of existence.

A soldier rode toward her, his bow in hand. "Announce yourself!" he chided her. "I could have killed you." He pointed to the arrow, clearly wanting it back.

She could have died. She wouldn't have even seen it coming. She deserved it and more. Shaking, she pulled it from the dirt and handed it back to him. He rode off, cursing her as he went.

The clearing was awash with campfire light. Bloody bandages wrapping various appendages, seven enchanters were already astride their horses, strung bows in hand as they surveyed the perimeter. Enchantresses milled about, packing their supplies into the wagon.

"Give me the powder!" Jala screamed from beside one of the fires.

"You're only making the pain worse." Hagath tied off the bandage pinning the woman's arm to her side and headed off.

Jala bit off a string of insults.

Eiryss had seen the arrow strike Jala down. How had she survived? "Hagath!"

Hagath whipped around and hurried toward her. "Where's Ramass?"

Trying to hold back the rush of anger at the mention of his name, Eiryss met her halfway. She noted the blood staining her friend's clothes. "He went after your father." Jala still slung insults. "She's alive?"

"Broke her shoulder blade and maybe a few ribs. She'll live." She headed back the way she'd been going. "Eleven of the forty men survived." Eiryss shuddered to think of so many dead. "Four are being loaded in the wagon. The others are fit to ride."

"Should they really—" Eiryss began.

"They insisted." Hagath knelt next to Kit—they hadn't moved him from where he'd fallen, instead building a fire next to him. He was so, so ashen. At the sight, unease stirred in Eiryss's belly.

Hagath gently woke him. "You're the last one, just like you demanded." She tipped the last of the powder into the wooden cup, added water, and stirred.

He held out a forestalling hand. "Give it to Jala."

Just like Kit, to offer it to someone else. Eiryss knelt on his other side—her knees immediately soaked through with slushy, bloody snow—and smoothed the hair from his face. "Kit…"

"This is all that's left," Hagath said gently.

"I know," Kit said.

Hagath's lips thinned. "You think it hurts now, wait until the wagon starts jostling you."

"He said to give it to me!" Jala cried. One of the other girls was helping her shuffle past them toward the wagon. "If he wants to be noble, let him!"

Hagath glared up at her. "Clamp it before you bring an Alamantian patrol down on our heads!"

Eiryss didn't mention Hagath's shouting had an equal chance of that.

Hagath tipped the cup toward Kit's lips.

"It doesn't hurt," Kit said. "Not anymore. Give it to her."

Something Hagath saw in his steady gaze must have convinced her, for she turned away without another word and shoved the cup into Jala's hand. The woman tipped her head back with a whimper and drained every drop.

Hagath knelt in front of Kit. "At least we won't have to listen to her whine anymore."

Eiryss eyed his blood-soaked coat. Had her healing not gone well? "Why did you refuse the medicine?"

Before he could respond, the men on horseback sounded the alarm, bows rising.

"Don't impale me, you great idiots," Ramass called from out of sight.

"By all means," Eiryss ground out. "Impale him."

Hagath winced, and Eiryss's eyes narrowed. Did her friend know what Ramass had forced on them? Is that why she'd refused thorns? Been so angry when she'd seen Eiryss at the embedding ceremony? She almost demanded an answer. But one look at the bloody, wounded men and the frightened women stayed her tongue. Questions could wait. For now.

Unfortunately, Ramass emerged unscathed from the tree line with King Zannok's arm draped over his shoulder. Blood painted the king's right leg, and his face was pale.

Ramass helped his father into the wagon and surveyed the five men already inside. "Where's—" Ramass caught sight of Kit, still lying where he'd fallen. He hustled toward them. Eiryss tensed with each step.

"Why isn't he in the wagon?" Ramass said. "We need to move."

"He won't go," Hagath said softly.

"Kit." Ramass's voice gentled. "Let's move. That's an order."

Kit smiled. "I'm afraid you're going to have to arrest me for insubordination."

Ramass bent down, shouldered Hagath out of the way, and made to lift him.

Kit held out a forestalling hand. "I'm dying, Ramass."

No. Not Kit. Eiryss lit *seek.* Her magic seeped through his skin. He cried out in pain. She felt it immediately. A small section of his bowels was limp and lifeless. This was one of the rare times when they needed the expertise of a surgeon healer— someone who could use a knife and magic. Someone who could cut out the dead and piece him back together. If not, this was a death sentence. Her magic recoiled, the light snuffing out.

"Part of his bowel is dead. Can you cut it out?" Eiryss asked.

Hagath shook her head. "Only one or two women in all of Valynthia could."

She held her head in her hands. "Light, it's my fault." She'd killed him. How many was that now? After tonight, likely more than a dozen.

"No," Hagath said, voice shaky. "It was done before you ever healed him—when the sword severed the blood supply. We just didn't know."

"Know what?" Ramass demanded.

Hagath's mouth thinned. "Kit is right. He's not going to make it."

She felt Kit's chilled fingers on her forearm. "It would have taken the best healers and surgeons in all of Valynthia, Eiryss."

It was the truth, but it didn't *feel* like the truth.

He tugged at her arm. "Look at me." Taking a deep breath, she did. "You'll tell my mother and my father and sisters that my last thoughts were of them? That I wouldn't have left them if I'd had a choice."

Ahlyn's thoughts had been much the same. Mother's and Father's too, she suspected. In the end, perhaps everyone thought of their families. And now, she had another person to miss. Another person whose lack would leave a cold hollow where before there had always been warmth.

Hot tears spilled down her cheeks as she nodded.

His eyes slipped closed in relief.

Hagath wept. Ramass stared stonily at the ground and rubbed at his eyes. Kit was their friend too, Ramass especially. He, Ramass, and Ture had terrorized the Enchanter Academy for years.

Ramass's head fell in defeat. "Have everyone move out."

Hagath nodded. "Kit…"

"I know, Haggy," Kit said.

For once, Hagath didn't complain about her nickname. Tears welled in her eyes. "Eiryss, come on."

"I need Eiryss to stay behind and ride with me," Ramass said.

Eiryss shook her head. She was done with Ramass.

"Out of all of us," Hagath said softly.

"I know," he returned just as softly.

Eiryss didn't know what they were talking about. Didn't care. Hagath rushed away without looking back.

"Ramass," Kit said softly.

Ramass stormed a half dozen steps away and then came back to crouch beside the man. "I'm so sorry, Kit."

"I was a good son and a good man and a good soldier. I don't fear dying. Not much, anyway. Just sad at all the things I never got to do."

His eyes fell on her, his expression soft. She remembered his cold lips pressed against her forehead the day her mother and his sister were given to the tree. The warmth of his arms around her. He hadn't turned his back on her. Not when so many others had.

For a moment, the possibility of their lives entwining had been ripe and full. And now it was dying as surely as Kit was. She grieved the life they might have lived.

Ramass choked. "This shouldn't be happening."

Kit's eyes were clear. "I know you think you failed somehow—" Ramass tried to pull away, but Kit balled his sleeve into his fist. "No, you listen to me." Ramass stilled. "I know what haunts you. But the sum of a man defines him. Not his worst moment. Do you understand?"

Kit's words could just have easily been directed at her. She should have trusted the king to take care of her father. Instead, she'd been so full of herself. So sure her rank would save her.

"What if it's the sum that falls short?" Ramass choked.

Kit gripped Ramass's hand. "I know more than you think, Ramass. This isn't your fault. I tried to help you. I failed." Something passed between the two that Eiryss didn't understand.

"Light, Kit," Ramass said, his head down.

"Know more about what?" Eiryss asked.

"Look after her," Kit said with a pointed look at Eiryss.

Eiryss wanted to argue that she could take care of herself. Now was not the time.

"I will see you in the afterlife, brother." Kit released him. "Now go, or you'll be joining me before your time." He looked at Eiryss, one side of his mouth turned up. "I'll miss our dances."

Why had she ever thought herself above such a good man? "Me too."

Ramass rose from his friend and strode toward where one of his soldiers had hung back with a horse.

She hurried to catch up. "We can't just leave him to die alone. He'll be frozen to death by morning."

"It's what he wants."

She looked back as Kit lifted a hand in farewell. She would never see him again. Ramass rode up behind her and held out a hand. "Come on, Eiryss. He gets to choose how he dies."

She thought of Ahlyn. Her father. Her mother. *No,* she wanted to say. *Death chooses how we die and when. All we choose is how we live.* She let him haul her up behind him. He pushed the horse into a lope. She buried her face in his back and cried for her father and mother. For Kit. For herself and all she had lost. For a princess who died before her time and for a woman she had only met on the field of battle. A woman who had spared her life. In exchange, Eiryss had made her take her father's.

"Come on, Eiryss. We can't stay here. Who knows what else is waiting for us in these woods."

She couldn't breathe, and the shadows prowling at the edge of the navel thorn... "I want it out."

His hold tightened. "Any weapons we have at our disposal, I will use. And I will not apologize. Do you understand me?" He softened. "I've already lost so much, Eiryss. I can't lose you too."

"I turned them into monsters! I made her kill her own father! Her own father!" Eiryss had hated the Alamantians for using her father. But he'd made his own choices. He chose to become a traitor to their people. To his family. To her.

Merrek had only been trying to prevent his daughter from killing one of her women.

In the end, Eiryss wasn't any better than the Alamantians.

"Sometimes killing is protecting. By stopping those Alamantians, you may have saved us all."

Because the Alamantian couldn't attack them if they were dead. But she hadn't killed them. Only put them to sleep. Light. In sparing those Alamantians, had she doomed them? "At least tell me the name of the sigil that unleashed the shadow."

He held out a hand to her. "It's a new sigil. We call it chaos."

CHAPTER 21

SECRETS

The moonlight reflected off the snow and gave everything a blue tinge. Eiryss sat behind Ramass's saddle, her arms wrapped around him as much to keep from falling off as a protection from the cold. The wind as they rode cut through her gloves and sleeves. Her knees were damp from kneeling in the snow, and her skin was still a bit sweaty from her run through the forest.

She couldn't remember ever being so cold.

Had she not still been furious with him, she would have felt sorry for Ramass taking the brunt of the wind. So she ducked her head behind his back, shifting every so often so a different part of her scalp was protected from the cold coming over his shoulder.

They made good time, as the mud had frozen in the night. With any luck, they'd reach Trapendale by morning. Ramass slowed his horse from a lope to a trot as they came up at the back of their unit. The enchantresses rode the horses left behind by the king's guard—they must have been corralled on the other side of the clearing, as Eiryss hadn't seen them until after the battle.

Ramass eyed the horses the girls rode. "Wyndyn, Eiryss will take your horse. You ride with someone else."

Rippled muscles and a proud bearing, the animal looked fast. Glad to be free of Ramass, Eiryss slid off the saddle into a hard crust of snow. The landing jarred her cold feet and ankles. Arms folded protectively over her core, she walked stiffly over to Wyndyn, who dismounted and shot Eiryss a look that would have pierced her to the quick had she cared what the girl thought.

Their little spats seemed so childish and pointless after everything she'd been through.

"Ramass and Hagath won't always be around," Wyndyn said and sidled over to Iritraya, who scooted back, and swung up in front of her.

Ignoring her, Eiryss hauled herself into the still-warm saddle, glad the stirrups were about the right length.

Hagath stood in the wagon, leaned over, and braced herself against Ramass's saddle. The two exchanged whispers that fell silent when Eiryss rode up. Ramass handed her a blanket, which she gratefully tucked around her legs. Sometime between being attacked and entering the forest, Eiryss had lost her hat. Her ears burned—she wondered if she'd still have them come morning.

In the wagon, King Zannok pushed himself up. His leg was wrapped in bandages, which were dark with what had to be blood. "Am I to understand you were the reason I was able to flee the Alamantians?"

An evil that reared out of the shadows and down the throats of the Alamantians. She hung her head, unable to answer.

"So strong so soon after her imbedding," Zannok said proudly. "And she has already saved her king."

The remaining soldiers and some of her fellow enchantresses watched her with something close to admiration. After so long with their hatred, she wished she could welcome it. Yes, she had saved the king, but at what cost? She ran her tongue nervously over her crooked teeth.

"You're with me," Ramass said to Eiryss as he reined his horse around.

"Shouldn't I heal them?"

"You have more important things to do." He nudged his horse into a lope.

What was more important than healing? Relieved to be free of scrutiny, she directed her horse to follow him, the hard crust of snow crunching under the animal's hooves. Thankfully, the mud had frozen and the snow wasn't deeper than the animals' fetlocks, so it was easy going. Unfortunately, that meant they might freeze to death before they reached their destination.

Ramass sent the man riding point back to the wagons and slowed his horse to a swift walk.

Eiryss glanced back at the wagons, which creaked and groaned, sounding overloud in the stillness of the night. Were the Alamantians she'd enchanted awake? Were they coming for them? If so, they only needed to follow the sound of that blasted wagon.

She took off her glove and held her warm palm against her ear. "What were you and Hagath talking about?" she whispered.

Ramass waited until the soldier was out of earshot. "Spread out a web."

He hadn't answered her question, but now wasn't the time to argue. She flared her sigils and cast her magic in a web around them. There was an undeniable rhythm to the forest: a pattern of life that went uninterrupted as far as she could reach with her regular sigils. No sign of Alamantian magic.

Her ear buzzed more painfully as the feeling came into it. "I don't sense anything out of place."

He let out a breath, which formed a cold mist before him. "Let me know if that changes."

His horse had a faster pace than hers. She had to continually nudge him to a trot to catch up. She shivered and drew her coat tight at the throat. Light, she needed sleep and warmth. She tried to guess how many hours until morning and if the sky was any lighter than it had been before. Would this night never end?

"Do all the girls in our unit have *chaos*?"

He was silent a moment. "Eiryss, I can't divulge kingdom secrets."

"There are lines you don't cross, even in war. There is evil in that sigil, Ramass."

"Enchantresses have always used their sigils as weapons."

Her fingers were freezing. She sat on them in turn to warm them up. "It's not the same thing and you know it."

"You all agreed to fight for your kingdom, did you not?" said a familiar voice from behind.

She turned to find the king riding up behind them, his bandage darker than it had been before. She quickly pulled her fingers out from under her and tugged on her glove. "You should be resting in the wagon," she said, adding a belated, "sire" after she realized her error.

"Sire, she—" Ramass began.

King Zannok held out his gloved hand as he came up to ride beside her. "She already knows more than she should. At this point, she needs to understand how important her silence is to Valynthia."

She had let the Alamantians who attacked them live. The secret wouldn't remain a secret for long. "Why, sire?" she asked.

"There isn't time to debate the ethicality of *chaos* with the council and Arbor. The Alamantian magic wielders outnumber us two, perhaps three, to one. They slowly wear down the vault around our cities and overrun them. Three of our cities have already fallen into enemy hands. If Trapendale falls, they'll have a clear path to Hanama, where we still can't raise a vault. By summer, all of Valynthia will have fallen to the Alamantians."

She looked to Ramass. "Surely it isn't that bad?"

"If we continue on the way we are," Ramass shook his head, "we will lose." There was little he hated more than losing.

"That's where *chaos* comes in," Zannok said.

"But the *chaos* sigil is... evil." How was it even possible for something evil to come from the Sacred Tree? But she couldn't deny the echo of churning, torn shadows eating her from the inside out.

Zannok's searching gaze bore into her. "More evil than allowing ourselves to be ruled by the kind of people who would poison our tree and kill our princess?"

Her horse stumbled and righted itself. "Hasn't my father done worse? Haven't I?" She saw her own father's empty eyes. The shadows that had made monsters of the Valynthians.

"No," Ramass said firmly. "You were trying to save people. Not destroy them."

"Was the end result not the same?" she said.

"Do you know what they do to any citizens they capture, Eiryss?" King Zannok asked.

She shook her head.

The king shuddered. "Torture—even the children. They hang their bodies from thorn trees like rotten fruit."

Bile rose in her throat. She covered her mouth with her hand to keep it down. "But to fight evil with evil... Will we even be worth saving in the end?"

King Zannok looked at her with such immense sadness. "There is no other way."

She looked to Ramass for confirmation, but he only stared at his clenched fists, his sigils' light flaring in the space between his gloves and coat. The things he must have seen in battle... The bodies of children hanging from trees. Even now his expression was haggard with remembering.

In using *chaos*, she had done a terrible thing. An unforgivable thing. Was the king right? Was there no other way? But then she saw Ramass's haunted expression. "You were in Oramen when the city fell?"

His haunted expression confirmed it. What atrocities had he seen? "I didn't know," she whispered.

"No. You don't," Ramass said, not unkindly. "And I can't-I can't tell you." A tear streaked down his cheek.

Pity took the edge off her anger.

"Ramass," his father chided.

Zannok had never liked it when Ramass cried. He didn't think it manly. Eiryss wanted to rebuke Zannok, but he was her king. And Ramass wouldn't welcome her interference. She shot her friend a sympathetic look, but Ramass looked away, into the shadows of the forest.

He hadn't meant to trick her. Only to save his kingdom. Her anger softened. She hated it, but... "I understand why you tricked me," she whispered. She wasn't sure whether she agreed with the methods or not, but she hadn't lived through what he had.

He looked at her, his pained expression revealing that he hadn't forgiven himself. That he had so much he wanted to tell her and couldn't. But she saw it in the haunted shadows in his eyes.

"Ramass..." She rested her palm on his shoulder and tried to convey that she understood.

He only looked away.

King Zannok let out a long sigh. "I knew you would understand; the daughter of Undrad and Emlon could do nothing less than forgive me."

She choked at the mere mention of her parent's names.

King Zannok bowed his head. "I miss them too."

Instead of giving in to the urge to damage herself to distract from the turmoil, she fisted her flute and pressed the amulet against her skin. The flute's carvings marked her palm, the amulet her chest. And for a moment, she could pretend her parents were with her still.

"What will happen to us?" she asked.

Zannok cleared his throat. "I have your word this will remain a secret?" She nodded. "Girls are being gathered from the lower nobility and some of the more powerful families." More mud nobles. "Over the remainder of winter, you will be trained in secret. And when spring comes, you will win this war for us.

"I have high hopes for you," the king went on. "That you managed any defense against those Alamantians, untrained as you are, is miraculous. You shall be the strongest enchantress in a decade, perhaps more." He leaned closer and said in a conspiratorial whisper, "Just wait until the people hear a fledgling enchantress saved the king's life! You'll be the darling of the social scene!"

Despite everything, warmth spread from her core. It had been so long since anyone had believed anything good about her.

The king shifted his attention to Ramass. "I told you Jala would make an excellent teacher."

"Jala deserted them," Ramass said coldly.

"She was only trying to save her king." Zannok clapped his gloved hands. "We shall spread the news of Eiryss's heroism with an announcement that we're lowering the standards of those who can join—say ten generations back and up to four times removed from the monarchy?"

Were such people even nobility at all?

"Isn't that one of the reasons we're in this war?" Ramass said bitterly. "To prevent magic from spreading through the masses?"

"Isn't that what Enderlee wanted to do?" Eiryss asked.

"Enderlee wants them to have the full gamut of sigils," the king said. "I only plan to give them chaos."

Eiryss's mouth fell open. "You aren't making them en-chantresses. You're making them weapons." In her horror, she'd forgotten she was speaking to the king.

"Now you sound like Enderlee," Zannok said, a note of warning in his voice.

"She's not going to be happy," Ramass said.

Zannok huffed. "Let her bluster. She knows moving against me will spark a civil war. One Valynthia can ill afford.

"Your Majesty." Eiryss forced herself to be polite. "Aren't we just using them?"

"Giving them the power to defend themselves isn't using them," Zannok said tightly.

"Will they see it that way?" Ramass asked.

"Public favor is on our side. Propaganda, son, wins a war every bit as much as battles." Zannok shot them both a look that said the matter was closed.

Ramass passed a gloved hand over his face, his expression saying he'd heard this lecture dozens of times and only hated it more each retelling.

What if Zannok was wrong?

Eiryss closed that line of thinking down hard. Her father had thought the same, and it had cost them everything. Zannok was her king. Chosen by the Silver Tree and far more experi-enced in matters of state. She needed to defer to him.

"It would be safer back at the wagon," Ramass said, just short of a demand.

"The Alamantians risked sneaking far behind enemy lines. How did they know I would be on the road to Hanama tonight?" The king had clearly chosen to ignore Ramass's near-order. An order—near or not—that he had no right to even hint at. Eiryss's mouth thinned in disapproval.

"No," Ramass replied.

"They were sent," the king went on. "There is a traitor among us. And when I find out who…" His fists clenched around his reins.

A traitor who had caused Kit's death. She could feel the ghost of his lips against her forehead. His arms at her waist as they'd danced. Kisses stolen in the moonlight. She'd never let herself love him—he was never an option. But he could have been. She wept again, this time for the loss of something that would never be.

"What is it, child?" the king asked.

"Kit…" She couldn't finish.

Zannok's expression softened. "I'm so sorry, Eiryss."

Ramass turned away, eyes glinting with anger. "Don't." He tugged his collar up against the cold. "Now, Your Majesty, I must insist you go back to the safety of the wagon."

Why was Ramass being so harsh with his father? None of this was his fault.

The king made a sound of displeasure low in his throat. "Very well, Ramass. I know you have nothing but my best interests at heart." He held his horse up, leaving them alone once more.

"Eiryss, your web?" Ramass reminded her.

Blast. She'd completely forgotten. Again. She spread her senses back with her magic. She wasn't sure how long she was caught up in the magic when Ramass's voice startled her.

"There," he said.

They'd crested a rise. Under the charcoal sky, the glow of hundreds of lampents gilded the trees over three miles away. The sky seemed a bit lighter than before. Morning was coming. Safety was near. This night and its horrors were nearly over.

They started down the hill, losing sight of the city as they came upon a wide, shallow river. Eiryss's horse balked. She squeezed with her legs, but the animal only lowered its head to the water and blew hard. She drove her heels into the animal's sides. His back hunched, a threat to buck.

Ramass booted his horse, which plunged into the water. Her horse finally followed. The freezing water grew deeper, creeping over her feet, her shins, her knees.

Ramass motioned the wagon forward. It was halfway across when the wheels mired in the mud. Suddenly, the images and sensations coming from Eiryss's magic-sense clashed with those coming from her physical senses and she grew dizzy.

Closing her eyes, she dove back into her magical sense. Something shifted against the web she'd cast. Probably another herd of animals. She zeroed in on it, and her magic recoiled.

As if it had been repelled.

CHAPTER 22

TO SAVE A KING

Eiryss's eyes snapped open. "Alamantians to the south-east."

Ramass stiffened beside her. "How far?"

The magic-sense was so new to her. She wasn't sure how distance converted. "Not far." At least, it didn't feel far. "They're armored and headed straight for us."

Head swiveling, Ramass's sigils flared to life, but he didn't use them. Not yet. "Get that wagon moving," he whispered harshly.

In the driver's seat, a woman slapped the reins across the oxen's backs. The creatures strained against the harness, the wheels churning mud. The seven mounted soldiers formed a circle around the wagon, bows out. With their injuries, they wouldn't be able to fight in hand-to-hand combat.

The king dropped from his horse into chest-deep water, pressed his shoulder against the wheel, and drove forward. Enchantresses dropped from the saddle to help. Ramass's horse danced sideways, splashing water. "Drop *seek*. Armor yourself and the king."

"Shouldn't I make a dome?"

"Not until we clear the river."

Eiryss flared her chest sigil, gritting her teeth at the trace of chilly shadows, and armored everyone. The cold added to the bitterness of the river sluicing around her legs from the knees down. The wagon reached the center of the river as two dozen figures detached from the shadows under the trees and blocked the road ahead. Ramass's sword and shield flared to life, the soldiers behind him lifting their bows. The horse sidestepped nervously beneath Eiryss. She glanced back and swore under her breath. The road behind them was blocked by another dozen soldiers.

Her sigils flared, and she lifted her flute to her lips.

"Wait," Ramass murmured. "They haven't attacked yet. Let's see what they want."

"Surrender," one of them said. "You know you are defeated." Eiryss's head whipped up in recognition. Habbia. Somehow, she'd found more soldiers and another three enchanters. The woman watched her, fury dancing in her eyes. She knew. Knew what Eiryss had done. And still, she gave them the opportunity to surrender instead of slaughtering them.

She was a better woman than Eiryss. Shame left her wanting to sink into the river. Disappear forever.

"Curse it, Eiryss. I told you to end her," Ramass said under his breath.

She flinched.

"I will never surrender!" King Zannok cried from behind the wagon, his sword raised as if his entire company wasn't practically helpless and severely outmanned.

The woman bowed her head. "So be it."

"Now!" Ramass cried to Eiryss.

Eiryss managed to play two notes for the dome before something sprang up from the river to their left and grabbed her arm. She scrabbled for the saddle horn and gripped it with her legs. The horse shied, jumping sideways. Whoever held Eiryss didn't let go. She couldn't hold on. She hit the water, the sound of the river rushing in her ears. The cold assaulted her, forcing the breath from her lungs. Something sharp hit her ribs and skittered, tearing flesh.

Eiryss gasped in a lungful of water. She struggled to find footing and fend off her attacker as they writhed in the depths. Suddenly, the attacker was gone. Eiryss didn't know which way was up. Water sloshed in her lungs. Something tore at her magic, cutting it with swift, precise strokes.

Her vision faded, her limbs going limp. Arms gripped her, hauling her out of the water. She latched on, coughing up river water and gasping in sips of air. Someone was shouting, but she couldn't make sense of it. The hands dragged her back. Her heels scrabbled over soft mud. Her vision came back as she was hauled between two horses. She struggled, terrified of going under again. Terrified of being taken.

More shouting. Suddenly, the words made sense. "Get under the wagon." Zannok. The person dragging her was Zannok. He wanted Eiryss under the wagon, which was now in the shallows. Alamantians and Valynthians fought on the embankment. The horses on either side of her were Ramass's and Zannok's. A lumpy pile of clothes floated away from them. A body.

Eiryss stopped fighting. Tried to stand. Fell. Hagath took over, practically dragging Eiryss under the wagon, only her head and shoulders above the frigid water.

The king climbed in his saddle. His soaked clothes clung to him as he pushed his wet hair from his face. His leg was bleeding. The king had killed her attacker. Had saved her. He and Hagath.

Golden and silver swords arced above her. Two Alamantians attacked the king on the right and Ramass on the left, leaving an opening for the third to lunge for Eiryss and Hagath. Her ax raised, gaze fixed.

Ramass gave a great shout and stabbed the Alamantian in the back. She fell, screaming. The Alamantian on his other side slashed at Ramass. Ghostly silver light rippled across his body, the magical blade sending splinters through Eiryss's magic that made her cry out.

The pain—it was from attacks on her magical armor. Idiot, she'd never tied it off. But she hadn't dropped it either. Which explained the pain in her side and also the lack of blood. Relief washed through her.

Hagath tried and failed to haul her deeper under the wagon already crammed with twenty-seven other women. "Get a dome around us!" Hagath reached down the collar of Eiryss's coat and hauled out her flute.

"Someone get Jala fighting!" the king cried.

"She's unconscious, sire," one of the injured soldiers in the wagon said.

"Rouse her!" he shouted back.

Eiryss would have to take the armor down—she wasn't strong enough to armor everyone and maintain a dome. She let the enchantment fade, the magic rushing back into her.

Eiryss was shaking too hard to hold the flute. Hagath crawled behind her and worked the finger holes while Eiryss blew. Using *build* and *repel*, Eiryss played, her body going rigid with the shadow that flooded her chest sigil. The heat of the Alamantian's magic battered against her, the aftershocks rattling Eiryss deep in her bones.

So small it could fit in her palm, the dome steadied and grew thicker, passing harmlessly over the sister sigils of their fellow Valynthians while forcing their enemy back one step at a time. The dome was misshapen and pitted, but it would keep them safe until she could manage one better.

The Alamantians prowled the edge of the barrier, their swords scratching at the surface and making ripples of light and dark. Eiryss was shivering so hard now she could barely hold her flute.

"Tie it off," Hagath said gently. What if the enchanters overpowered it? Hagath must have seen the panic in Eiryss's gaze. "It will hold a little while at least."

"No," Ramass said. "We need to get out of the river first. Add light to the enchantment and follow me."

To shift the dome, Eiryss would have to play while she moved. She wasn't even sure she could stand.

"Light would only be a beacon to every other Alamantian out there," the king said.

"And our own army," Ramass said. The army was stationed three miles away in Trapendale.

"She can't hold it, Ramass," Hagath said.

"She will." Ramass held her gaze with unshakable faith. She gave a curt nod. She would hold it.

Eiryss added *light* to the enchantment. The barrier glowed bright silver—a beacon to the city a few miles away. Balendora climbed into the wagon seat, pushed over the body of the girl who'd sat there—a girl who must have died in the moments between when her armor had gone down and the dome had gone up—and clucked to the oxen, which strained at their harnesses. The other girls braced their shoulders against the wheel and pushed. The wagon came free of the mud it had settled in with a jerk.

Steadied on either side by an enchantress, Eiryss moved slowly, steadily. The three enchanters tore down her shield as fast as she could build it up. And the cold—she was shivering badly now.

They took her to the edge of the barrier. She leaned against it for support. They stepped back as she smoothed over the weave, inserting a strand of *build* where she'd missed it before.

Something made her look up. Standing in the river a half dozen paces away, Habbia pulled out an arrow that shimmered with inner colors—an arrow made from the sacred wood of the White Tree—and aimed for Eiryss.

She froze, unable to look away from the woman she'd forced to kill her own father.

Ramass's horse suddenly lurched between Eiryss and the dome, knocking her onto her bottom. The animal reared over backward and thrashed on the ground, screaming. Feet digging in the snow, Eiryss scrambled back from the dangerous hooves.

"Ramass!" she screamed.

Before she could push herself up to help, Habbia leaped over the fallen horse. How had she managed to get past the barrier? There wasn't time to consider, as Habbia's shield slammed into Eiryss, knocking her flat on her stomach. Habbia grabbed her by the hair, wrenching her head back. Her blade was razor sharp and a finger's width from her skin.

"Anyone moves and she dies!" Habbia dragged them until the barrier was at her back. Ramass hauled himself out from under his struggling horse, a sacred arrow in the animal's neck.

Habbia had sent the arrow through, which tore a hole in the weak dome, and used her blade to widen the hole just enough to fit through. Valynthian soldiers charged the gap and shoved one of their shields in place to keep the Alamantians from breaking through. Four of them braced themselves against it.

"What did you do to me?" Habbia hissed.

"I didn't mean to. I didn't know—"

Habbia jerked her hair. "Do it again. Only this time, do it to your people."

Shadows would crawl over them, claw down their throats. Ramass, Hagath, Zannok, they would all turn on each other. Destroy each other.

Not even limping, Ramass snatched a bow and lifted it, aiming for Habbia, who wrenched Eiryss higher and ducked behind her. Ramass hesitated, the bow shaking in his grip. A soldier beside him shot Ramass a disgusted look and lifted his own bow and drew back.

"No!" Ramass rammed his shoulder into the man, his shot swinging wide.

"Do it," Habbia hissed in Eiryss's ear.

"I won't," Eiryss said.

Ramass's gaze flicked to Eiryss and then at the woman behind her. "Let her go, and I'll let you live."

"I was dead the moment I came in this dome," Habbia said. "And if it stops monsters like you, it will be worth it."

"Us, monsters? You string our children from the trees!" Eiryss cried.

Habbia stiffened. "We would never harm children."

"Liar!"

Habbia licked her lips. "Just yourself, then. Do it to just yourself."

Eiryss's mouth went dry. The shadows plunging down her own throat. What demons would it show her?

The blade touched her skin, which peeled back. "Do it or die."

"Eiryss," Ramass said, his gaze pleading. What did he want her to do? What did he think she could do? There was only one answer—hadn't she thought that she deserved death and more for what she'd done?

Eiryss shut off her brain and opened her sigil. The shadows swirled around her and Habbia. Eiryss considered siccing the shadows on Habbia too, but the woman would kill her for that. And even after all she'd done, Eiryss did not want to die.

She released the shadows on herself.

Shadows tore through her throat—shadows that tasted of ice and rot. Habbia released her as she dropped, gagging, choking, her body desperate to expel the bitter cold presence invading her body down to her bones.

Without her guidance, a dome formed around herself and Habbia, forcing Ramass back. He pounded on it, screaming her name. All she could see were shadows that surrounded her like sheets of smoke with a dark, evil purpose.

And suddenly, she wasn't freezing inside a dome but kneeling beside her father's body. It flickered to her mother's. Then her father's again. His neck bled, soaking through the leaves she'd so carefully sewn. His hand shot out, catching her wrist.

"I asked you to run," Father's dead lips said. "And now I'm dead. It's your fault."

Eiryss shook her head and stumbled back, straight into her family table. Confused, she whirled around the kitchen of her hometree. She watched her father take down a powder from a shelf and mix enough medicine to kill himself before tipping the cup to his lips.

"Father! No!" She rushed toward him.

Ture jerked her back. She was suddenly at her mother's funeral again. Now Ture held her wrist, pinning her in place. "I won't have you humiliating me at Father's funeral the way you did at Mother's."

She gaped at her father's body, laid out beside them in his shroud. "No," Eiryss cried. "No, this can't be. I was just with him. I—"

"All you had to do was stay away from him! You let him die!"

The sigil at her chest flared so cold she staggered, her hand over it. Like it was trying to tell her something. She shook her head. This wasn't right. This wasn't how it had happened. "Father didn't kill himself. He was executed."

Ture slapped her. She fell, landing on top of the body. But it wasn't her mother's body. It was the man she'd killed—Merrek. She stared into his sunken eyes, the chew marks on his skin where an animal had gotten to him. Eiryss screamed and scrambled back, trying to scrub the feel of death off her skin.

Habbia stood at her father's feet. Her eyes were sunken into her skull like her father's. "Murderer," she hissed.

But Habbia wasn't dead. "I'm sorry!" Eiryss cried. "I didn't know what that sigil would do! I was only trying to save my king!"

"I tried to warn you," Ture said from behind her, his breath hot against her neck. "But you wouldn't listen."

Habbia stepped toward her, pinning Eiryss against her brother's unforgiving chest. "You murdered my father."

"You murdered our father," Ture added.

They closed in on her. Trapping her. There was no escape.

"Better to die by your own hand than cause anyone else any more pain." Ture maneuvered her hand to the dagger at her waist. She choked on a sob as he guided her to draw it from its sheath. It came free with a soft scraping sound. The tip pressed against the softness beneath her sternum. "Up and in. Twist. It will all be over. You'll be with Mother and Father."

She tried to pull the knife away, but his grip was iron. The cold at her chest pounded, reminding her this wasn't real. "I was trying to save him, Ture."

"You killed my father!" Habbia pushed the knife so the tip cut through the folds of her coat. "You have to pay for what you've done."

"I was only trying to save the king!" Eiryss said.

"Murderer," Habbia whispered.

Eiryss shoved her, but she didn't budge. "Stop!"

Ture and Habbia stepped in closer until she couldn't move for the press of bodies. The knife parted her skin, blood seeping into her clothing. She was helpless. As helpless as she'd always been. Heat and light flashed from somewhere far away.

No.

She was not helpless anymore.

Not anymore.

It was *chaos*. Making Eiryss see things that weren't real. Weren't true. She reached for her own magic—the same way a drowning man reaches for air. Magic flooded her. Cold bloomed sharply in her chest, spreading through her like starlight. The magic struck against something foreign and cold and wrong inside her.

Never again.

She flared *repel*. Her brother and Habbia were suddenly gone. The real Habbia stood in front of her. Eiryss held a knife to the tender skin beneath her ribs. She fisted her hand around the hilt and punched the other woman hard. Habbia fell into her own barrier, slid down the edge, and plopped onto her backside. She struggled to stay conscious.

Eiryss stood over her. But she hesitated. She wasn't a killer.

All she had to do was let the dome down. Ramass would rush in and kill Habbia. She would be dead. Dead like the baby birds who'd fallen from the nest, the fish dragging them from light and warmth into the cold depths to be devoured. Dead like the panthyrn that had killed her inverns. Dead like Eiryss's father.

"You're not made for killing." Was it Ture who'd told her that? She was honestly too tired to remember.

Eiryss wove, forming a third sphere, stronger than the first. She expanded it. It pushed Habbia back. She blinked up in disbelief at Eiryss. Their eyes locked. Then Eiryss turned away. She expanded the dome over the misshapen one, which she then banished along with the smaller dome that had trapped her in with Habbia.

Ramass rushed forward, just in time to catch her as she collapsed.

Hagath hurried to her side and pressed a hand to her forehead. "She's freezing. Start a fire and bring me some bedding."

Ramass lifted her higher in his arms. "Bring me a horse! We have to get on the hill where our armies can see the light."

"Ramass," Hagath said uncertainly. "She needs to seal off the dome before she passes out."

"She can make it." He met her gaze, his commander glare firmly in place.

"I can make it," Eiryss managed.

CHAPTER

TRAPENDALE

Zannok handed Eiryss up to Ramass, who settled her on the saddle in front of him, opened his coat, and wrapped her up in it. She pushed her hands under his tunic, burrowing into his warmth.

He flinched. "Light, you're freezing."

Battered and shivering, the whole group moved out. Alamantians prowled the dome for weaknesses. They wouldn't find any.

From somewhere, Hagath was playing, the song bringing back golden memories, all of which featured Ramass. Her family. Memories tainted by shadow. She was trying to shut down Eiryss's *chaos*.

"You never answered me," she murmured. "I kissed you and told you how I felt, and your answer was to pretend it didn't happen."

"You want to talk about this now?"

She scoffed. "We could have spoken about it before. You were too busy avoiding me."

"I wasn't avoiding you. I was saving you!"

She shifted her hands to a warmer spot, which made him cringe and grunt. "Is that what you were doing?"

"Yes!" He growled in frustration. "Eiryss, I don't want to lose you."

She flinched. "I don't want to be your friend anymore." She wanted so much more than that. They reached the top of the hill. She pulled away from his warmth. He caught her.

"Eiryss…"

She refused to look at him. "You have to let me go." It seemed all the things she thought would last forever were gone.

When he didn't let go, she let her weight drop. She slipped through his fingers, her knees buckling when she hit the snow-packed road.

"Get fires going!" Hagath called as she hurried over.

Ramass dismounted and reached for her. She recoiled from his touch. He looked hurt. "What's wrong with her?"

"She's sopping wet," Hagath bit out.

"We're all sopping wet." Ramass trailed after them.

Hagath didn't bother answering as she half-dragged, half-guided Eiryss to where enchantresses stacked wood. "Seal it off," she murmured to Eiryss.

"Too cold to play," Eiryss chattered.

"Weave it," Hagath said.

Eiryss lit her sigils and drew light from them. She wove the light into the *seal* pattern and released her magic. She nearly gasped in relief when the shadow stopped assaulting her. Still, the aftereffects lingered.

"She's a weaver?" Ramass asked, something like dread in his voice.

Hagath played, her song holding the shadow at bay, and didn't answer.

"Get the fire going!" he snapped.

"We're working on it," Wyndyn snapped back.

"Fetch the bedding from the wagon," Hagath said to someone Eiryss couldn't see. She started stripping Eiryss's coat.

"Sir," one of the enchanters approached. "We have lost two more men. Your horse has taken an arrow wound. It needs to be put down."

Ramass growled something under his breath. "Let me know what she needs," he said to Hagath as he stormed away.

Hagath was too busy hauling off Eiryss's tunic to answer. She paused, staring at her chest sigil, which mostly looked like a mess of intersecting lines at this stage. Her secret sigil bared for her friend to see. With a start, Hagath hurriedly wrapped her in blankets and set her by a roaring fire. Within minutes, her skin was baking, but the cold went far deeper; so deep she wasn't sure she would ever feel warmth again.

She shivered uncontrollably. "What's happening to me?"

Hagath stripped out of her own clothes. "We'll figure it out."

The group ended up splitting in half, men on one side and women on the other.

Hagath settled down next to Eiryss. "The sigil at your chest—does cold or shadows come from it?"

"Some," Eiryss admitted. "Not as bad as *chaos*."

Hagath shook her head. "Eiryss, the things you've done with your magic this night—it shouldn't be possible. What's happening to you?"

Eiryss buried her head in her hands. "I don't know."

Eiryss woke when the constant barrage of attacks on her dome suddenly ceased. Alamantians faded into the tree line. Keeping tight hold of the blankets, she rose and peered into the distance. A long snaking column of soldiers came toward them, all of them in Valynthian gray.

She sat up and wept in relief. When the soldiers were nearly upon them, Hagath held the blanket as Eiryss dressed in damp clothes that reeked so badly of smoke they made her eyes water. Then Eiryss did the same for her friend. They climbed on horses or back into the wagon and headed out to meet them.

Ramass wouldn't let her take down her dome until the two groups merged. She sagged in relief when her magic—and its tracery of shadows—came back into her and disappeared within the sigil.

The army swallowed them, pushing them into the center. Ramass and the king immediately disappeared in the sea of gray—this was Ramass's personal army, after all. He had been stationed at Trapendale at the outset of the war.

Eiryss kept nodding off, only to wake with a jerk. It was midmorning when they reached the city of Trapendale. In the distance, the white wall of trees grew with towers and fighting platforms spaced between. The vault was visible along the edges of the city. Eiryss had never been so happy to see treehomes and enchanted panels and braziers.

But even though Trapendale had managed to raise the vault, it lacked its normal luster. She flared her magic, which allowed her to see the weave. There was something... off about it. Not in the weave's construction, but the magic itself. It seemed... thin. An effect of the poison King Dray had dealt the tree?

The city gates parted, and Eiryss slipped into the safety of the city, dead leaves slushing around her horse's hooves. The temperature didn't warm. Not as it should have. The trees had suffered as well, bare of leaves and dusted with snow. No wonder three cities had fallen so quickly.

"But the vault is up..." Eiryss murmured.

"Up, but weakened," Hagath said darkly. "So far, it has repelled the Alamantian attacks, but not the cold."

What did that mean, that the vault worked here, but not in Hanama? "The weave must be thinner." Large enough to keep attacks out, but not the heat in.

"Yes," Hagath said.

They started down a road. The lower caste watched them curiously from within their small, dark homes. Before, Eiryss would have paid them no mind. But after three months of struggling to survive and of growing closer to Belgrave, Eiryss couldn't help but notice them. One boy glared up at her from beneath a ragged blanket, his toes peeping out of his too small shoes. Toes that were black from cold.

The soldiers started breaking apart, companies moving toward their own barracks. "Durbin will take you both to my tree until other accommodations can be made." Ramass called to her from across dozens of soldier's heads.

"Why aren't we going to the enchantress barracks?" Eiryss called after him.

"The king insisted," Ramass hollered back. He kicked his horse into a gallop.

"Where is he going?" Eiryss asked.

Hagath rubbed bloodshot eyes—she was practically sagging in the saddle. "What I want to know is how he's still moving."

After thoroughly rejecting me, he's lucky I didn't abandon him in those woods, Eiryss thought bitterly. She searched for the boy, thinking perhaps she could look at his feet, but he was already gone.

They rode a carriage worked by an intricate pulley system up the tree—Eiryss didn't think she could have climbed it otherwise—and hailed a rickshaw driver. The soldier told the man to take them to a large tree a mile or so from the vault. Eiryss blessed the rickshaw that carried them effortlessly across the bridges made of woven boughs. It came to a stop at the opulent, arched entrance of a platform. The guard who opened the gate wrinkled his nose at the sight of them—or maybe it was the smell?—before his face shifted back to unreadable.

Eiryss passed through the metallic wash of the barrier and into warmth that made her fingers tingle hard. She followed Hagath to the heart of the tree and the largest platform—a common room with a large table, bookshelves at the joints between magical panels, a large sofa, and stuffed chairs set before the biggest brazier Eiryss had ever seen.

Valllay, the king's long-time servant, hurried to meet them. The woman had an enormous head and a tiny chin, making her look rather like an upside-down vase. "Ladies, we were not expecting you. If you like, I can have the cook prepare a meal?"

"Just whatever she can manage quickly," Hagath said. "Eiryss and I haven't slept yet."

Vallay nodded and her gaze shifted to Eiryss. "Lady, I would be remiss if I didn't express my condolences on the passing of your parents."

Eiryss rubbed her face. The servant meant well but reminding her of her loss only filled her head with nightmare images—some real, and some brought to life by Habbia.

"Sleep, eat, or bathe?" Hagath asked.

Before Eiryss had lost all their staff, she would have said sleep. But she knew how impossible it would be to get the smoke and grime from the sheets. Thinking of washing sheets made her think of Belgrave. What was he doing now? Was he safe, warm? Was his sister taking good care of him?

Eiryss had to clear the emotion from her throat before she said, "Bathe then sleep."

"I'll see you when we wake." She started up the stairs.

Vallay motioned to a doorpane that led to a colonnade. "The spare room is through here. Would the lady like a maidservant sent in?"

"No." Eiryss wouldn't even know what to do with a maidservant anymore. "I'll manage on my own."

The colonnade led along a wide branch, at the end of which was a platform. The bed was huge, with ornately carved posts and a gauzy curtain all around. There was also an armoire, a small dining table, a desk, and a cheery brazier. A short colonnade led to another platform that housed the bathroom. Above the spigot were two copper tubs of rainwater—one with a roaring brazier underneath to heat the water.

Too tired to wait for the water to fully heat, Eiryss stripped off her clothing, adjusted the temperature, and stepped into the stream with a gasp. *I don't think I'll ever be warm again.* She shut off the water, soaped up, then rinsed. Finished, she shut the vents in the brazier and toweled off. After she'd cleaned her teeth, she collapsed onto the woven horsehair bed and fell instantly asleep.

CHAPTER 24

KING'S ENCHANTRESS

Eiryss flinched as sunlight streamed into her room. She worked her pasty tongue over the roof of her mouth. Her body was layers of pain—bruises, cuts, and sigils. Always her sigils. The worst was still the chest sigil.

Wincing, she pushed up on aching arms to find three maid-servants moving about her room. One shifted the panels to transparent; another filled the brazier. Vallay stood before Eiryss with her hands folded before her. Light, she had an enormous head. Trying not to stare, Eiryss sat up.

The woman's pleasant smile didn't shift even when her gaze lingered on Eiryss's bruises. "Lady, do you need a healer?"

"No."

The woman nodded. "The gala is in an hour. We must ready you."

Eiryss blinked. "Gala?"

The woman's vase-face remained blandly pleasant. "The gala in your honor, lady. For saving the king's life."

If he wanted to honor her, he could let her sleep more. Eiryss passed her hand up and down her face and debated on whether she could demand a few more minutes when she smelled sausage. A servant laid a steaming breakfast on the table. Scones with clotted cream and jam. Fat links of juicy sausage. Eggs. Hot chocolate.

Eiryss swung her legs out of the bed. They protested as she put weight on them, but she ignored the pain and limped across the room to sit in a padded chair. She'd taken a dozen bites before she noticed the maid laying out a beautiful enchantress uniform on the bed. Tears filled Eiryss's eyes. The king had remembered their tradition. But instead of an extravagant dress, he'd ordered a new uniform.

She cleared her throat. "Who's coming to this gala?"

The woman smoothed the finely woven fabric. "All the high-ranking nobles in the city."

Eiryss sipped her hot chocolate, which suddenly tasted too sweet. She enjoyed the galas—dancing with men she'd known for years and spending time with her friends. What she hated was large groups of people she either didn't know or didn't want to know. And worse, being the center of attention. Which she would be if the gala was held in her honor.

She finished the rest of her meal with less gusto, but she finished it. Who knew when the next meal would be? Or if it would be travel bread and dried meat? The maidservant took the breakfast tray away. Her bed had already been made, her dirty, torn uniform gone. She wasn't used to being spoiled anymore. And for reasons she couldn't pinpoint, all the pampering made her uncomfortable.

Which was ridiculous.

"The water in the bathroom is hot," Vallay said. "An array of scented oils has been laid out for your use."

Eiryss wanted to protest the servant's attentions. But why? All those things had always been at her beck and call. "I bathed last night."

"You still have soap in your hair, lady," Vallay said.

Eiryss touched her hair to find it grimy with soap. There were still dirty spots where she hadn't scrubbed off all the pine sap too. She sighed and made her way to the bathroom.

After she'd stripped, she stood naked before the mirror, her eyes skimming down her body. Bruises, cuts, abrasions, and knots covered her body—most from her fight with Habbia. The sigils were starting to show the beginnings of patterns—right now it was impossible to tell what they would be. But when they were finished, they would be beautiful.

She looked beneath the wounds and sigils and tried to see herself as Ramass would. Narrow through the shoulders and chest, her hips flared and her backside plumped out. Her breasts were medium-sized and shaped like bells. Discounting the silver already threading through her hair, she wasn't bad looking. Until she smiled and revealed her snaggled teeth.

Her looks had never really been an issue before. Not much anyway. What did a few physical flaws matter when she was a high lady from one of the most powerful families in the kingdom?

But she had never been higher than Ramass. And now? Now she was much lower. Did he care about such things? She'd never thought he had. Perhaps she'd been wrong. She flared her sigils, watching the lovely lines gleam a faint silver beneath her skin.

What did beauty matter when she had the power to forge her own path?

Turning her back on her imperfections, she stepped into the shower. The water stung at first. She washed herself—the dirty sap spots took quite a bit of scrubbing—and then simply enjoyed the soothing heat as it eased the soreness deep inside her muscles.

The boy with the frozen toes flared in her mind. He didn't have hot water. Nor sausages and chocolate. Why did she deserve to be pampered while his toes froze black? She made a note to see what was being done for him and people like him.

"Everyone should have access to magic, Eiryss. Not just the nobility." Some of the last words her father had said to her. The words that had condemned him.

What if he'd been right?

She shut down her treasonous thoughts and shut off the water. She toweled dry and rubbed her favorite scent over her skin and through her hair. Finished, she stepped into her uniform.

In the bedroom, the three maids were waiting by the vanity. This was one part Eiryss had never missed. She sat on the chair. "Just a simple braid."

"The king has required more, lady," Vallay said.

The servants were clearly the king's and not Eiryss's. Still, the women were gentle and efficient. They twisted Eiryss's long blonde hair into elaborate coils shot through with star-shaped flowers. One of the blooms fell on Eiryss's lap. She picked it up, wondering at the extravagance of an ornamental hothouse when food grew scarce.

With heavy hands, she tucked it behind her ear. "Where's my mantle?"

"The king insisted it be cleaned, lady." Vallay motioned to the other girls and followed them out.

Eiryss opened her mouth to ask where they were going but stopped when she saw Hagath waiting by the doorway. Her friend was still too thin, but she was clean and dressed in a lovely gown. Every bit the daughter of a king. Only the vivid bruise on her cheek said otherwise.

Eiryss closed her eyes as memories of the night before washed over her. *Light, the things chaos made me see.* And what of the things Eiryss had made Habbia see, to make her kill her own father?

Eiryss tried to get herself under control.

"Whatever you witnessed under chaos," Hagath said gently, "it wasn't real, and it wasn't true."

"I know the horror of what they saw—what my magic made them see." Eiryss rubbed at the shiver that had sunk into her bones. "How it finds your worst fears and turns them against you. I did that to them, Hagath."

Eiryss sniffed and wiped her nose with a delicate handkerchief. "The enchanter tried to save a woman—his daughter. She killed him." Eiryss couldn't meet her friend's gaze. "She killed her own father. Because of me. And after they offered us surrender. Twice. Is this how we fight?"

Slowly, Hagath crossed the room and lifted the hem sleeves to reveal scars crawling up and down her skin where her sigils used to be. Only her right arm remained untouched, the sigil for light, lovely and unique.

Hagath traced the raised, scrolling lines of her remaining sigil. "I kept light because it could never be used to harm."

Kept? But how could Hagath have kept any of her sigils if the enchantresses excised her? Unless... "You did this to yourself?"

Hagath methodically rearranged her sleeves. "As soon as I was well enough to hold a knife. I had planned to stitch myself up, but I passed out. Father found me. He ordered me under constant guard and shipped me here, to Trapendale. To a healer by the name of Illin."

A cold wash of horror doused Eiryss from head to foot. Her hands protectively covered her own sigils, the lines just starting to show; the skin above them numb and cooler than the rest. "The chaos sigil—I could understand cutting that out. But the rest of them?"

"I will not be used," Hagath said it like an oath.

Used? "Who would ever dare use the daughter of the king?" Hagath's fervent gaze fixed on her. "Everyone."

Hagath... Watching Ahlyn die and nearly dying herself... It had broken her friend. Eiryss closed her eyes as a wave of guilt washed over her. "I'm sorry I was so angry with you."

Hagath turned away. "You don't see it yet. You will."

See what? Before Eiryss could ask, Vallay stepped into the room. "Ladies, it's time."

Eiryss let it go. Hagath would be all right. She just needed time. When she was ready, she would take new sigils. To do anything else would mean a life almost devoid of magic. Who could possibly choose that?

Vallay led them into the long, clear-paneled colonnade. The public platforms above and below were packed with people and ringed with tables of food. Scattered throughout were platforms with empty space where the dancing would occur. Though they weren't performing yet, acrobats hanging from sheets of silk or wire contraptions took up three whole levels. Another featured seats facing a stage where none other than the legendary Badubay himself waited to sing—he was Ture's favorite singer. He'd hoped to write songs for the man someday.

But now, silence reigned. Every single pair of eyes watched Eiryss in complete silence.

She inched a little closer to Hagath. "What is this?"

"You're the guest of honor."

Eiryss swore under her breath. "He could have just sent jewelry. Some new dresses."

"You know how Father loves a good party," Hagath said bitterly.

Again, Eiryss thought of that little boy and his blackened feet.

They reached the wide platform above the common room. Set before the massive trunk, King Zannok sat on his throne carved like a miniature of the Silver Tree. Behind and to the side, Ramass stood proud as the dawn.

Vallay stepped aside. Eiryss and Hagath crossed the door-pane. A hush fell, and people parted neatly before her, their heads bowed. The same people—many of them council members—who at best wouldn't have met her gaze a week ago. At worst, they would have spit in her direction to ward off evil. The same people who had celebrated her father's fall from grace. The people she had once respected.

Anger vibrated through her. She wished she could look to Ramass for reassurance, but she was every bit as angry with him for rejecting her earlier. To keep from glaring at every traitorous face, she locked her gaze on the king. The one person who had never rejected her.

As Eiryss took her first step into the room, an orator began telling a story. A story of a daring girl determined to take hold of the life always meant for her. A story that began with the theft of her first thorn.

Eiryss's steps faltered. Her story. Only without the fear and doubt and trouble. The orator made her sound far more beautiful and far braver than she had ever truly been. By the time she'd reached the dais, the man had reached a crescendo. Eiryss could almost see a more beautiful, powerful version of herself tear bravely through the woods with nothing but her fledgling sigils to save a king. And then, as the Alamantian horde had descended upon them as they'd crossed a freezing river, she'd saved him again.

His ringing voice, filled with triumph, faded. Into that silence, the king rose to his feet, his black velvet cape rustling as it settled around him.

He reached down and pulled her onto the dais beside him— a great honor. "Eiryss, First Granddaughter of Queen Brenna, you saved my life, not once, but twice in a single night. But more than anything, you've taught me that one girl—one woman—can change everything."

Her words—the words she'd spoken to Ramass not many nights past. Her friend's proud bearing dominated the right side of her field of vision.

King Zannok looked out over the crowd. "The girl the enchantresses expelled. The girl who lost everything but her title. She didn't give up. She found a way. So must we." He took Eiryss's hand. "Arbor Enderlee will not send us more enchantresses. She will not allow us to experiment with new sigils. And so we will raise up enchantresses of our own—women eager to prove themselves. Women who are not entrenched in the follies of the past."

Mud lords. The crowd grumbled—part of the reason the war had been fought was to keep the magic among the privileged few. By keeping it among themselves, they guaranteed themselves power and unimaginable wealth, which was provided by the very poor Eiryss had seen on her entrance to the city.

Her father was right. *You could have gone about making this another way,* she silently pleaded with him. *Could have lobbied the king and council. Why did you choose instead to betray us?*

King Zannok held out his hand. "Once this war is won, things will go back to the way they were. Better, even. For instead of one sacred tree, we shall have two. Plenty of room for the lower nobles."

The grumbling shifted into murmurs of speculation. For this was no longer simply a war to defend themselves. Now it was a war of subjugation and gain. Eiryss couldn't help thinking of Habbia. Of how honorable she'd been. For the first time, she realized the Alamantians didn't all deserve to be punished. Just their king. King Dray.

"We win this war against the evils of the Alamant, our holdings will increase twofold."

Murmurs of speculation shifted to cries of approval. An approval fueled by righteous indignation and more than a little greed.

Amid the building energy, Zannok turned to Eiryss. "Kneel."

She hesitated only a moment before dropping to one knee, her head bowed dutifully.

"Eiryss, you have proven your loyalty, courage, and tenacity. For that, I bestow on you the title of King's Enchantress."

His former enchantress had been killed the night of the attack. And before that... Eiryss still didn't know why Jala had been demoted—though, from the woman's predatory ways with men, Eiryss could guess.

The job was a great honor. But it was a job for a woman who loved following the king to his parties and ceremonies and leisure. It was not the life of a girl desperate to make a difference.

Zannok settled a new mantle over her shoulders. From the front and back hung sapphires the size of her fist. Onyx adorned the shoulders. The supple, royal-black leather had been tooled with an artistic representation of the Silver Tree.

Eiryss resisted the urge to wipe at the sweat breaking out over her skin. As the king's personal enchantress, she would be responsible for the king's armor and dome. Only her chest sigil was strong enough for that. And this wouldn't be a desperate, last-ditch resource. She would always be required to use it.

Somehow, she knew that the shadow in her sigil—though weaker than that of *chaos*—would build over time. It would kill her.

CHAPTER 25

DANCE

E iryss's desperate gaze found Hagath's. Her friend glared
at her father. Eiryss noticed a tug on her hand and belatedly realized the king was trying to pull her to her feet. She
rose, her head spinning. She took a wide stance to keep from
falling over. Cheers rose from the crowd. Her desperate gaze
fluttered over them, unable to focus on anyone.

"You certainly know how to work a crowd." Ramass directed the comment at his father, though he was close enough
that she could feel the stirring of his breath against her hair.

Ignoring his son, Zannok smiled at her. The king was clearly pleased with himself. "I knew I'd find a way to restore to you
everything that was lost."

Everything except her family. She plastered on a hard smile
and bowed before her sovereign. "Thank you, my king."

"Ramass, come here," Zannok said. Eiryss didn't meet his
gaze as he stepped up beside her. "Escort Eiryss through the fes-
tivities. This is her night."

She ground her teeth. *What else could go wrong?* But there was no denying the king. Not without revealing her reasons for being angry with Ramass—his rejection and trickery—which was out of the question. She bowed, and the king sat on his throne, effectively dismissing them.

Hagath immediately stepped up beside them.

"Did you know he meant to do this?" Eiryss whispered.

Hagath faced her father. "Let me finish her training before she takes up all her responsibilities."

Zannok lifted an eyebrow. "Clearly, she's trained enough."

Hagath's fists clenched. "I won't risk her."

He blanched and rubbed his mouth. "Very well."

Hagath gave a stiff bow, turned on her heel, and marched through the crowd.

Dodging well-wishers, Eiryss caught her arm. "Hagath?"

Her friend turned enough to reveal her stricken profile. "I'm going to find someone who can help you."

"Are you all right?"

She tugged a shaking hand through her hair. "Light, Eiryss, these people have no idea what's happening. And I can't..." She choked. "I have to go." She turned and fled.

Eiryss watched her leave. Hagath had always been the most grounded of the two of them. The one who made Eiryss do her assignments and kept her out of trouble, as much as anyone could keep her out of trouble. Seeing her so unhinged left Eiryss feeling adrift.

She tried to rub some warmth into her arms and felt Ramass's presence behind her. "It was bad, wasn't it," she whispered. "When she cut them out?" Before he could answer, she turned to him. "Why didn't you tell me?"

"I was commanded not to."

She stiffened in surprise. "Surely the king knows I'm trustworthy?"

"My father trusts no one." He looked around the room, at the people held back only out of respect for Ramass's status. "Which platform?"

"Could I just go back to my room?" she whispered.

"Not if you want to seal your return to favor."

She didn't, but protecting her family name was a habit too ingrained to shake. "Dancing it is." That way she'd only have to deal with one councilman at a time. At least there weren't as many of them. Only a dozen or so had come with the king. That way they could keep an eye on him. Make sure their interests were served.

Ramass nodded and lead the way through the crowd and up the stairs to the second largest platform. The band in the center already played a merry tune.

"I can't keep them off much longer. Not unless you want to dance?" He held out his hand to her.

She'd rather dance with the council. "A drink?"

He frowned and slipped into the crowd.

The instant he was gone, Councilman Lonrick stepped before her and bowed. "A dance, lady?" The man had an enormous mustache waxed to a point sharp enough to stab his collarbone every time his mouth twitched.

She nodded and they started around the dance floor. "Eiryss, lovely to see you back in favor again. I always knew you had nothing to do with any sort of betrayal."

Coming from Lonrick, she believed it. She smiled and squeezed his frail hand—a hand that reminded her with a pang of Belgrave. She wished he was waiting in his rooms for her. It would be lovely to speak with him again. Maybe, with her new stipend, she could hire him just to sit in a chair by the fire and drink tea.

They shuffled across the floor, councilmembers watching. A few had remained secretly loyal—people who had fought for her family when they could. Most had not. Over the three months of her fall from grace, Eiryss had made mental notes of each, promising to never forget who their true friends were.

The song ended. Ramass was waiting for her with a glass of wine. She forced herself to sip instead of gulping the whole thing down. Her cheeks were starting to hurt from smiling so much when she caught sight of Vicil working his way toward her.

"Cousin!" He kissed both her cheeks. His arm was still in a sling.

As always, she tried to push away the betrayal she felt at his revealing her father poisoned the princess's wine. He was handsome, this cousin of hers. On him, the gray wisps looked distinguished and contrasted wonderfully with his youthful, dimpled cheeks and pale blue eyes. Luckily for him, he hadn't inherited their grandmother's crooked teeth.

He took the wine from her and pushed it into Ramass's hand. "I'm sorry, fellow council members, but I simply must dance with my cousin."

He whisked her through the crowd, Ramass watching sullenly. Probably angry she was snubbing him. What did he expect? Things to go back to how they were—her waiting for him to have time for her?

"What are you doing here?" she whispered.

He leaned in. "They cut down my hometree."

She inhaled sharply. "Oh, Vicil, I'm so sorry."

He shrugged as if it didn't matter, but the sadness around his eyes said differently. "Not to worry. If the king has any say about it, I'll have a new hometree in the Alamant soon enough."

She thought of Habbia pressing her hands into her father's chest to stem the bleeding and her unease grew.

Vicil studied her with a hint of worry, and she realized she'd missed her cue to say something patriotic. "That doesn't explain why you're in Trapendale."

He raised an eyebrow. "I'm one of the councilors driving the king mad with my interferences, at least until my arm heals."

How had she failed to realize that? "Eiryss, you're not the only one who's been fighting to retain our family's rank. The king has given you the opening you need to become a key player. Don't let our family down."

As if she didn't have enough to worry about. "What do you expect me to do? I can't fix everything that's gone wrong."

"Neither one of us can afford a misstep, Eiryss."

She narrowed her eyes in question.

He leaned in. "What do you think will happen to me if I fall out of favor with the council?"

Or if she failed to protect the king.

Or if her brother lost his city.

Her shoulders curved under the weight that settled on them. It was an old burden. Without its constant weight, she'd forgotten how oppressive it was. Vicil nodded in satisfaction at her expression, and she realized this had never been a social visit. He was here as the new head of their family. To make sure she remembered her duty. Family and kingdom, in that order.

He gazed at something behind her. "You know what would really solidify our ranking?"

She followed his gaze to Ramass, who moodily drained her glass of wine before settling it beside his own empty glass. She huffed. "No."

He raised an eyebrow and half shrugged. "Falls to me, then. Have you seen a certain king's daughter?"

Eiryss nearly missed the next step. "Hagath is not well, Vicil. Ahlyn's death... She's not well."

"I don't need her to be well." Vicil nodded to other young men about the room. "There are lots of choices, Eiryss." He steered them to the outside of the dancing and bowed. "Start flirting."

He was gone before she could protest. Almost immediately, she turned and nearly ran smack into one of the younger lords, Hark of King Domni's line.

"Would you honor me with a dance, lady?"

She could not refuse without insulting his entire family, something Vicil had clearly said she could not do. Nor could she turn down the next lord. Nor the next. And when they hinted at an alliance between their families, she offered her best closed-lipped smile to cover her grandmother's crooked teeth.

She'd danced with a dozen and received half as many offers when Lord Darten stepped into place. "Lady Eiryss, care for a dance?" He was a skinny man who still looked too much like a boy, though he apparently already had three illegitimate children. Also, she probably outweighed him.

Even worse, he was one of Iritraya's cousins. Marry him, and Eiryss would have the privilege of spending feast days at Iritraya's table. "A drink first, I think."

He took her arm to lay claim to her and motioned to a servant. "Red or white?"

As if she needed wine stains on her teeth to emphasize their crookedness. "White."

She guzzled it nearly as fast as Ramass had earlier.

The moment she set the empty glass down, Lord Darten spun her around the floor. "My family is most pleased to have yours back in power, lady."

A flaming lie. "Is it?"

His brow furrowed at her tone. "Certainly. Our families have a long history of working together."

Is that what he called their decades-old feud?

He huffed at the look on her face. "Fine. Let's be blunt." He looked her over as a buyer might a horse. "Perhaps a match between us could smooth over any bumps between our families."

"And your dalliances?" If he could be blunt, so could she.

He shrugged. "Honestly, I like my women on the delicate side." They were the only women smaller than him. "I'll keep it to the serving girls, if that helps."

She appreciated his honesty. "Not really."

He growled low in his throat. "Fine. A mistress or two."

She had not drunk enough wine for this. "I would keep you locked in a dome for the entire marriage."

His face hardened with anger. Blast. Vicil would be furious. She choked down her pride. "If only to keep you for myself." He brightened considerably. She bowed to hide her disgust. "I will consider your generous offer."

He spent the rest of the dance on one of his favorite topics: translating ancient texts from fallen civilizations. Only half listening, she was relieved when the music finally ended. She made some excuse about needing to speak with her cousin and fled.

Light, the next idiotic offer I have is going to end in broken teeth. Someone called her name, voice dripping with false sweetness. Another bachelor moved toward her. Pretending not to hear, she kept her head down to prevent eye contact and bolted for the stairs that led to the women's bathroom platform.

Dodging conversations, she reached the covered stairs with relief. She hurried to one of the small receptacles, used the toilet, and splashed cool water from the spigot on her face. Back in the stifling colonnade, the panels seemed to close in on her, and her head spun from the wine. She swung her legs over the banister and diverted up a branch, climbing out from the dome into cold, clean air.

She basked in the stillness. Until a familiar voice broke the quiet. "You're sure you saw her come up here?" Wyndyn asked.

"Right after she spoke with Darten," Iritraya answered. Eiryss slipped silently down and watched as the two girls disappeared behind the obscured panels before coming out again.

Eiryss eyes narrowed. She was in no mood for this.

"If she thinks anyone in my family will welcome her..." Iritraya's tone turned bitter.

"She steals her thorns, and they reward her by making her one of the most powerful enchantresses in the kingdom,"

Wyndyn said. "Now all the men are after her again. And she soaks up the attention like she wasn't a pariah hours before."

Eiryss face heated and her fists clenched.

Wyndyn threw up her hands in defeat. "How did she get past us?"

Iritraya blew a lock of hair out of her face. "Poor, poor Darten. Stuck with a girl who looks like an overstuffed gilgad."

"Those teeth!" Iritraya howled in laughter.

"And her oversized rear!"

"Her hair is already gray!"

Eiryss's sigils ached with power that begged to be let loose. She stepped into view. "Looking for me?"

Instantly, Iritraya and Wyndyn's sigils lit.

Eiryss wanted to laugh as her own sigil's flared. "You really think the two of you are a match for me?"

"What you *supposedly* did isn't possible," Wyndyn said. "You're cheating, and we're going to find out how."

Iritraya nodded in agreement.

Eiryss huffed. "We're at war. People are dying. Grow up." She maneuvered over the banister. She only managed a step toward the dancing platform when Wyndyn blocked her.

"It has to do with the thorn you stole. I know it does."

Eiryss fought hard to keep her expression blank.

Wyndyn wet her lips. "There's only one explanation for what you did. You're a dark enchantress."

Eiryss stiffened. Dark enchantresses were what mothers threatened naughty children with. Such evil people didn't exist. At least not for long. Not without a sacred tree warning someone. Wyndyn thought Eiryss one perhaps because of what she'd seen unleashed when Habbia captured her. She didn't yet know she too possessed the chaos sigil. The darkness she would unleash in the name of her kingdom... Eiryss's anger shifted to pity. She pushed past the girl and started down.

Wyndyn grabbed her arm. "You may have fooled the king. You may have tricked all of them into accepting you, but I know the truth."

Eiryss glanced at the other girl's hand on her arm and realized something profound: she didn't care what Wyndyn thought. She didn't care what Iritraya thought. Something in her jerked free—the tether that had kept her bound to these two girls and their hatred.

"Why are we enemies?" she asked. "We'd make far better allies."

Wyndyn looked stunned.

Wyndyn carried dark magic in the chaos sigil and didn't even know it. Eiryss leaned closer and whispered, "I'm not the only one to receive a new kind of sigil." She looked pointedly at Wyndyn's navel.

"What are you implying?" Wyndyn breathed, her hand splayed over the sigil.

She'd promised the king secrecy, but these girls never should have been given dark magic without their knowledge. "That if there is dark magic, you have it too." She tried to pull away.

Wyndyn's fingers dug deep enough to bruise. "You're a liar and a thief and your traitorous alliance with the Alamantians will be the downfall of us all."

"Threaten me again, and you'll regret it," Eiryss said softly. And she meant it. She was more powerful than Wyndyn in every way. And she was done.

As if responding to an invisible signal, Iritraya and Wyndyn pulled out their flutes and played.

They thought the two of them could overpower her.

They were wrong.

Eiryss flared her sigils, knocked the instrument from Wyndyn's hands, and snatched the threads of her magic. A dome formed around both girls—a minor variation in the weave made it impenetrable to anyone. She sealed it off.

Face twisted with rage, Wyndyn motioned to Iritraya. They fought her; their magic niggled against Eiryss as the shadow bled through her chest sigil. Cold bloomed, jagged frost flowers spearing through her.

Knowing she couldn't let the other two see, she hurried out of sight, flared her light sigil, and played her flute, the carvings smooth under her fingers. It took a long time to coax the shadow back into the sigil. Longer still to feel warm again. The shadows—the evil—in her chest sigil were growing stronger. Why? Why only in her chest and navel sigils and not her others? Why was the navel sigil so much worse?

She suspected Hagath knew. She had to find her. Had to know for herself what this was. She left the covered walkway and stepped onto the dancing platform. She turned toward the exit and ran smack into something solid and warm.

Ramass looked down at her. "Eiryss? What's wrong? Why were you gone so long?"

"*Chaos* is dark enchantment, isn't it?" she blurted.

He glanced around and pulled her closer. "What? Of course not."

"Curse you, Ramass, if you don't tell me the truth right now."

"I am telling you the truth. Eiryss, there's no such thing as dark magic."

"But the shadow—"

"A result of the Alamantians poisoning the tree."

"Then why don't all the sigils have it?"

"We don't know the answer to that any more than we know why we can't raise the vault over Valynthia." His gaze narrowed as he studied her. "What's this all about?"

She wrapped her arms around herself. "Wyndyn and Iritraya accused me of being a dark enchantress. They attacked me."

His jaw tightened. "Where are they now?"

"Sealed in a dome."

"Can you keep them there?"

"Indefinitely."

He motioned to a servant. "Bring me a pair of guards. And send a message to the enchantress who has temporarily taken over Jala's unit that two of those under her command need discipline."

The servant bowed and hurried away.

"Eiryss, you know those two are trouble."

Not to mention how much they hated Eiryss. She rubbed her arm, trying to combat the chill that had seeped into her. She knew she couldn't trust the pair. Just like she knew she *could* trust Ramass. Even if he was a bone-headed idiot.

And yet, *chaos* felt like dark enchantment. Maybe Ramass wasn't lying. Maybe he was simply *wrong.*

I must get rid of this thing, she thought.

She took a wine glass from a passing servant and downed it. "Escort me to my room. I'm done for the night."

"You can't be the first one to leave your own party."

"Watch me."

"Eiryss—"

"The only reason I'm anywhere near you is to keep the vultures off me until I'm safely locked away. So shut it and walk."

For three wonderful steps, he was silent. And then suddenly, he took hold of her arm and pulled her toward the dance floor.

She stumbled after him. "What are you doing?"

He pulled her into his arms. "I didn't like it."

She arched away from him and forced every shred of her patience to hold. "Like what?"

"You dancing with those fools. All the men watching you and scheming."

Eiryss eyed him suspiciously. "Are you drunk?"

"No."

"Then what exactly are you doing?"

His eyes closed briefly. "Trying something new." He tried to lead her. She resisted. "Please, Eiryss. Dance with me."

Her traitor heart fisted with hope that wouldn't relax no matter how much she willed it. "How is dancing with me trying something new?" They'd danced dozens, perhaps hundreds of times.

He tugged her closer, her body bumping against his. She hated the blush that stained her cheeks. "Don't," she warned.

He leaned forward and breathed in deeply. "You smell nice."

"Ramass…" How could she tell him how terrifying it was to open herself up again? To loosen the hold on the anger that kept her safe?

"One dance, Eiryss. Just one."

Could she risk being hurt one more time? But this was Ramass. How could she resist? As if he sensed her softening, he pulled her in even tighter. His body flush against hers sent a thrill of heat through her core. He moved. Their bodies found a rhythm—the same rhythm they'd always had. The kind of rhythm from knowing what a person was going to do before they did it. Of communicating a whole plan with a single look or a loaded word.

The song ended, and she found herself breathless. Ramass snatched them both a glass of wine from a passing servant. When the band took up another song, she didn't resist. There was more dancing and more wine until everything softened. The gold and silver of the setting sun set the whole room ablaze in gilded copper.

When the orchestra paused, and the room emptied to go to Badubay's performance, Eiryss rested her head against Ramass's chest. Though they were motionless, she felt like she was still spinning. The jewels bedecking the women still glittered behind her closed eyelids.

"Do you want to hear his performance?"

"I'm tired." She giggled. "And I think I've had a bit too much wine."

"That makes two of us." He took her hand and led her through the crowd. They slipped past a guard and into the colonnade that led to her quarters. Eiryss sighed in relief to have finally escaped the throng.

"Remember that time we sneaked a gilgad egg into the chicken coop?" she asked.

Ramass laughed. "That chicken never did get over a gilgad hatching with the rest of her clutch."

Eiryss laughed at the memory of all the chickens panicking over the little lizard—a lizard that would one day grow larger than a man. She shook her head ruefully. "I still think we would have been able to tame it if Hagath and Ture hadn't tattled to your father."

"It bit me!"

She snickered. "You slept for two whole days!"

"I was not asleep. I was paralyzed. And I've never been so sore in my entire life."

By then she was giggling uncontrollably. They reached her chambers first. They ducked inside to avoid Vallay coming down the corridor. The room was dark, the first stars beginning to appear above.

"Why are we hiding?" he whispered.

Eiryss pressed her fingers to his lips, his breath hot against them. "She'll report to your father that we're drunk."

From somewhere above, Badubay sang, the ballad sweet and sultry.

"Are we drunk?" he asked.

She grinned up at him. The intensity of his gaze utterly stilled her. "Ramass?"

He leaned forward and kissed her. He tasted of sweet wine and *him*. Her hand scraped against his rough stubble before sinking into his curly hair. Her other hand splayed across his broad chest, the muscle hard beneath.

The back of his fingers traced down her neck. His hand rotated, the tips of his fingers tracing along her collarbone. He traced his nose across her jawline, and the quivering inside her grew hot and shivery.

He cupped the side of her face, tipped her head back, and deepened the kiss. All at once, heat licked up her spine and chased down her legs. She tugged the tunic over his head and admired his body, the way the moonlight shone on the soft curls of hair on his chest.

Light, he was beautiful.

She pulled off her own shirt.

He stared at her every bit as much as she stared at him. "We shouldn't do this," he whispered.

"When has that ever stopped us?" she whispered back.

CHAPTER

PROPOSAL

A rms snaked around Eiryss, pulling her in close. Confused, she opened her eyes to find herself in bed with Ramass's arms banded around her from behind. He planted a kiss on her bare shoulder. She peeked under the blankets. Every bit of her was bare. She studied the hands cinched around her waist. Dry knuckles dusted with freckles. Arms covered in red and golden hair.

"Ramass?" she said cautiously.

"Mm?" he murmured against her unbound hair.

"We're not drunk anymore."

"As my head keeps reminding me." The bed shifted as he rolled away from her. "Gah, I need some pain powder. You?"

She watched him move away from her, marveling at the pale, baby soft skin of his backside. He poured two cups of water and rummaged around the vanity.

She clutched the blankets to her as he offered her one. She took it, staring into the swirling, chalky liquid. "What happens now?"

He drained his cup. "First, bathroom. Then we need to try that again."

She blushed hard. "You know what I mean."

He sat in front of her. She stared. She couldn't help it. Light, he was beautiful. The sunlight streaming from the panels gilded him in red and gold.

"Once I make up my mind about something, I don't go back."

She forced herself to meet his gaze. "But is this what you want?" *Me, Ramass? Do you want me? Because I've already fallen in love with you, and I can't go back.*

He leaned forward and kissed her. "You have fifteen seconds before I take over the bathroom."

"Ramass, we need to talk about his."

He quirked an eyebrow. "Thirteen."

"I've never done this before."

"Neither have I. But I plan to do it again. Very soon."

"But—"

He started toward the bathroom. "Five."

Squealing, she bolted past him. He swatted her bottom. She pushed the door shut and leaned against it, her heart pounding in her temples.

"Ah, such a glorious backside," he muttered to himself from the other side.

A grin exploded across her mouth.

Much later, when they were both dressed, Ramass rang the bell for breakfast.

Eiryss gaped at him. "We can't let the maids see us together like this."

"Why?"

"Because then everyone will know."

"Let them."

"Ramass! You can't!"

"Why?"

"Because… Because men have dalliances and women are trollops."

He nodded sagely. "My father is sure to find out."

"Exactly!" She peered out the doorpane, but there were servants up and about all over the tree. Someone was bound to see him leave. "You'll have to risk it."

He plopped down in the chair. "My father will be furious."

She waved him toward the doorpane. "Hurry."

"Probably insist I marry you."

"Ramass, stop teasing me!"

He looked up at her. "Sooner rather than later."

She stomped her foot. "Ramass!"

He strode across the room. But instead of leaving, he took her face in his hands and kissed her again. Even frustrated with him, she couldn't help but kiss him back. "Why are you doing this?"

"I told you," he said between kisses. "Once I decide, I don't go back. If we're caught together, we won't have to wait for months for a fancy wedding at the Silver Tree. We'll be married soon. Within the week."

Her mouth fell open. "But—a week!"

He eyed her. "We have been together our whole lives, Eiryss. That's long enough."

Her breath caught. "What changed?"

"Seeing you with all those other men. Realizing I didn't want to share you. With anyone. Ever." He made a sound low in his throat. "If I had to watch one more man touch you, I was going to break some teeth." But he'd watched other men dance with her for years.

A knock sounded at the side of the doorpane. "Breakfast, lady."

"What say you, Eiryss? Will you marry me?"

She bit her lip and glanced toward the door and back up at him. Something in her eyes gave her answer, for he grinned. "Come in!"

He bent down and kissed her again as the door opened behind him. Eiryss tried to break away, but Ramass held fast. Vallay paused at the sight of them in each other's arms—Ramass still in his clothes from last night. Her gaze flicked to the disaster of a bed. Her expression still didn't shift.

She laid the tray on the table. "I'm afraid I did not bring enough for two. I will be right back with your tray, lord."

Ramass pulled Eiryss down onto the chair beside his. "Will you pack us a lunch as well, Vallay? I'd like to take Eiryss on a picnic."

Vallay arranged the tray. "I will see it done, lord."

The woman turned to go. Eiryss cleared her throat and made a study of the sliced fruit. "Vallay, bring some maidweed tea." She willed her face not to heat, which only seemed to make it worse.

"I would like some tea as well," Ramass said. "Madrick gray would be lovely. There's also something in my room I'd like fetched." He took a pen and pot of ink, scribbled something down on a scrap of paper, and handed it to the servant. The woman inclined her head and left.

Ramass stole Eiryss's sausage. "You should see your face right now."

She kicked him under the table. "You're the reason I had to ask."

He'd eaten most of her breakfast when Vallay returned with an entire jar of maidweed leaves and a pot of hot water. She handed Ramass a heavy book, which he set beside him on the table.

Vallay spooned leaves into the infuser. "Two spoonfuls. Let it steep for five minutes."

Ramass took the tea tray from her. "Here. I'll do it."

Vallay folded her hands before her. "Would you like the basket now, lord?"

He nodded, and the woman left. Ramass prepared their tea while Eiryss dug in.

She was nearly finished when a familiar voice called, "Eiryss?"

The spoon slipped from her fingers to clattered against the plate. She shot a desperate look at Ramass. He grew very still. His expression disappeared.

"Ramass?" she said worriedly.

"I'll be all right, lady," Ramass said. "Come in, Father."

Zannok stepped into the room, his gaze going from one of them to the other. "So it's true then?" In answer, Ramass wrapped his arms around Eiryss and kissed her neck.

Zannok sighed in apparent relief. "It's about time. Though I can't say I'm happy about the circumstances. You were supposed to escort her. Not take her to bed." He sat at the table. "The wedding will have to be soon, but I suppose you know that already, since you clearly let Vallay find you."

Ramass shrugged. The king palmed a handful of berries. He noticed the tea steeping, and his eyes narrowed. "Good. I just appointed you my enchantress. I'd not want to lose you so soon to motherhood. And I'm too young to be a grandfather."

Light. Eiryss wished she could climb beneath the table and hide.

"No," Ramass said softly. "We wouldn't want that."

Zannok patted her hand, his eyes moist. "I'm pleased to give you a family, Eiryss. So very pleased."

A pang of longing shot through her. Her parents would have been thrilled. And Ture... She wasn't sure how he would react. "I suppose I should write my brother."

"I'll do it," Ramass said.

She nodded gratefully.

Zannok groaned in mock exasperation as he pushed to his feet. "I shall have to throw another gala! And so soon after the first. This will empty my wine cellar!"

"Vallay," the king called toward the doorpane. She immediately stepped into view. "Call in the twins. We have a wedding to plan."

She bowed and backed from the room.

Eiryss stifled a groan. Meyo and Trevo were the royal gala planners. They had designed her dress the night the Alamantian Delegation had destroyed Eiryss's entire world. The twins lived for parties. The bigger and more elaborate, the better. "Sire, could we not have a simple wedding? Something under the stars?"

The king wagged a finger at her. "You know better than to ask." He started for the door. "Come, Ramass. There's still a war on, in case you've forgotten."

"Father, I wanted to take Eiryss on a picnic."

The king eyed them. "It'll have to be tonight. We're already late for our meeting with the war council."

Ramass sighed. "In a moment."

The king nodded. "And only a moment." He left them alone.

Ramass strained the leaves and handed her the tea. She stared dubiously into its brown depths before taking a sip. "Not as bad as I've heard." Though it tasted like hay.

Ramass sipped his own tea. "Tonight then?"

"What am I supposed to do for the rest of the day?"

"Have you forgotten Meyo and Trevo?"

She groaned.

"I have a gift for you." He held out the book he'd had Vallay fetch. She took the tome. It was small but well read; the corners bent and worn from use. *Wicked King Ramadal.* It smelled musty.

"A book?"

"As the king's enchantress, you're going to be spending a lot of time bored out of your mind."

She flipped through the first few brittle pages. "And you thought a dry history would remedy that?"

He laughed. "Give it a chance. You might learn something new."

She came to a drawing of a man with a high forehead, round face, and an enormous nose. "I'm not familiar with this king."

"That's because he was not ours."

"An Alamantian, then?"

"No."

Brow furrowed in confusion, she found a drawing of a sacred tree near the back. But she didn't recognize it, for it was black with sparks of light like a star-strewn night. "There have been other trees besides the Silver and White?"

"I believe there were many."

"How is such a thing not common knowledge?"

"If my calculations are correct, the last one fell nearly four hundred years ago. It's a long time to forget. Especially when the only records remaining are in my father's library."

Already engrossed in the first page, she sipped her tea.

"I wouldn't mind starting a family right away."

She sputtered, tea going down wrong. She coughed violently and wiped her eyes. "You can't be serious?"

His expression didn't shift.

Light. He was. "Not with the war on. And I'm only seventeen."

"You'll be eighteen in a month."

He was not yet twenty. "I'm not ready."

He stood, leaned over, and kissed her brow. "Are you happy, Eiryss?"

For the first time in a long, long time. "As long as you don't bring up children again for another five years, at minimum."

He chuckled and pulled away from her. She missed his warmth immediately. "I'll see you tonight."

"What about Hagath?" she called after him.

He half-turned. "I'll tell her."

"Will you have her come see me?"

He nodded. "I'll send her."

CHAPTER 27

ESCAPE

Eiryss grew impatient waiting for Hagath. She left her chambers, obtained directions from a servant, and found her friend's room herself.

"Hagath?"

No answer, she stepped closer, tipping her head to catch the rustling sounds on the other side of the doorpane. "Haggy?"

"What?" came the muffled reply.

Eiryss pushed through the panel. On the other side, Hagath wore a plain brown tunic and trousers. Her hair was tied back in a simple braid, none of the noble lady of last night apparent. Without looking up, she stuffed bread and fruit into a satchel.

"What are you doing?" Eiryss asked.

"Going to the hospital," Hagath replied. "The healer I told you about—Illin—thinks she can help you."

Light, she could get *chaos* out of her.

"I'll get my coat." Eiryss turned to go.

"You have a wedding to plan and fittings to attend."

Eiryss planted her fists on her hips. "I need this bloody thorn out first."

"I'm going to try to arrange for her to come here."

Images of shadows and blood and twisted faces flashed in her head. "Hagath, I think I might have made a mistake when I chose to become a warrior enchantress. I was meant to be a healer."

Hagath slung the bag over her shoulder. "You'll have to take it up with Father."

The king wouldn't budge. He never did. Not that it had ever stopped Eiryss before. She followed Hagath out. "I don't have to assume any duties until after I've had more training. Let's just sneak—"

"Lady Eiryss," Vallay called from outside the doorpane.

Eiryss jumped and made a strangled sound. "Vallay!" What had the woman heard? Had she been listening on the other side?

"Meyo and Trevo are waiting for you in your rooms, lady," Vallay said.

"Tell them to do whatever they want. I'm going with Hagath to the hospital."

"The king insists, lady," Vallay said.

Eiryss growled low in her throat. Hagath shot her a pitying look over her shoulder. "Where is this hospital?" Eiryss called after her.

"On the ground. You'll never find it." Which was as good as a challenge for Eiryss, and Hagath knew it. Her friend waved without looking back, deserting Eiryss to this expressionless woman.

The ground? Then it must be a hospital for the poor. Eiryss considered a half dozen plans for escape before giving up. She was not a child anymore. And responsibility meant dealing with things she didn't want to.

Meyo stood in the center of her room, foot tapping impatiently. She zeroed in on Eiryss the moment she saw her. "A whole wardrobe and now a wedding dress. Does the king think I'm a seamstress or a miracle worker?"

"Probably a little of both." Trevo kissed Eiryss's cheek, his thick mustache tickling. He tossed his perfectly styled hair. "You're right. Black isn't her color."

Meyo hadn't said anything about black.

"And yet it's the royal color. We have to use it."

"Silver always looks lovely on her. We'll darken it to charcoal at the base—like moonlight through water."

Meyo's eyes lit up. "Trevo, you're brilliant."

He shrugged. "I know." He snapped his fingers. "Vallay, call in my team. We'll build the gala around the dress."

The two set to work measuring Eiryss. "You've trimmed down a lot since the last dress we designed for you—it will have to be taken in," Meyo said.

"It was sold," Eiryss whispered. "They've all been sold."

The twins flinched as if she'd slapped them. Trevo rested his hand at his chest. "Light, you can't just take a dress made for one woman and put it on someone else! Savages!"

Meyo patted his hand. "We'll make her another."

Trevo's frown was severe. "Do they not understand how blessed are those my hands touch?"

Meyo hummed. "They were last season anyway."

Trevo grumbled.

"Belted at the waist," Meyo murmured. "It will soften her hips and backside."

"Some men like a hearty backside." Trevo waggled his brows suggestively at Eiryss.

She blushed. She always blushed. She wondered what plans they had to hide her teeth. A mask, perhaps? A large, lovely mask.

"Soft lines and flowing, ethereal fabrics," Meyo went on.

"Diamonds," Trevo said.

"No, pearls."

Trevo made a sound of approval. "But the diamonds will make her glitter like stars."

Meyo half shrugged in agreement. "Fine. Diamonds and pearls."

Their team arrived. The design set, the two draped fabric over Eiryss from every angle while calling out directions to a team of men and women who sewed and cut and wrote down notes.

"Now," Meyo pulled out paper and quill. "Tell us about your ideal wedding."

Wedding. Light, Eiryss was getting married. To Ramass! She pressed the heels of her hands into her stomach and tried to even her breathing. Closing her eyes, she imagined her parents behind her. The high boughs of her Silver Tree swaying gently. The moon heavy and full, shining out over the lake. The music drifting, gentle and soft.

Sniffing, she wiped her cheeks. "It can't come true. Not anymore."

Meyo looked uncomfortable. Trevo sympathetic. "Tell me," he said.

With a sigh, she did. "A lovely, comfortable dress. My dearest friends and family. Dancing. A simple dinner and a cake with sugared berries. A dreamer who kept gold-wing moths flitting about all night, their wings dusting me with gold." Just like the dreamer had at her seventh birthday party.

Meyo took notes while Trevo stared out the window, his gaze distant and dreamy. As Eiryss's voice drifted off, Meyo wrote the last line with a flourish. "You're right. It was a dream. But we can at least get the color scheme right—silver and gold."

"The wedding will be at midnight," Trevo said.

"Keep the lampents to a minimum," Meyo added. "We want the stars and the dress to outshine everything." Trevo and Meyo sipped yeasty smelling beer, of all things. Eiryss would have guessed champagne or perhaps wine. "But first, let's start with the buffet tables."

Eiryss rubbed her forehead. "I really—would you two mind just taking care of it?" Menus and color schemes seemed ridiculous in light of everything that was happening.

Meyo sputtered in outrage, but Trevo slowly rose from the table and came to stand before her. "You're a moonlight girl being forced into the sun. I understand." He pivoted with a flourish. "Come, Meyo. We have full reign over the event of the decade!"

Her gaze turned considering. "I suppose you're right." She clapped her hands. "I want orders out for everything we need by tonight."

They gathered up their things and left.

No sooner had they stepped through the door than Vallay appeared again. "And what will the lady be doing with her time now she's sent her wedding planners away?"

Something about the woman made Eiryss decidedly uncomfortable. She lifted the book Ramass had given her. "I plan to read."

Vallay's gaze narrowed in suspicion.

Eiryss had a sudden sense the woman was spying on her. But why?

"I shall bring your lunch."

Eiryss sat and dutifully read the tale of a foreign king as told by the survivors of his fallen kingdom. It was a thoroughly depressing tale of a man who had been born to poverty and abusive parents. In his kingdom, it had been the tradition for each girl and boy to visit the sacred tree to be tested.

Ramadal had been chosen as king. Uneducated, homely, and cursed with a stutter, he had been thrust into the machinations of court alone. Eiryss winced. She had been trained her entire life to survive court. Even her close friendship with the king hadn't been enough to save her.

Why hadn't Ramass given her a nice herbal or tincture guide? She was always collecting those, fascinated by the reaction of one plant with another. And when had he grown fond of ancient histories?

Pitying the boy king, she set the book aside when Vallay brought lunch. She ate quickly, packing the excess away in a satchel as Hagath had done. Ramadal's tale had dampened her spirits. Her thoughts turned to her lost family. To Ture. What would he think of her marrying Ramass? Would he have time to make it to Trapendale before the wedding?

She had to move. Do something before the memories devoured her. Which meant she had to sneak out from Vallay's watchful eye. Luckily for Eiryss, she'd been escaping watchful eyes all her life.

Her travel pack contained a nice sized rope. She used it to slide from her platform toward the ground below. Ramshackle houses had been hastily made of mud and branches huddled at the base of the trees. Most of the occupants disappeared at the sight of her, but a collection of children watched her descent with astonished looks. Probably because of the unused carriage that sat on the other side of the tree.

"Sometimes things need to be done the old-fashioned way. Don't you agree?" When they didn't respond, she smiled brightly. "Which way to the hospital?"

The oldest pointed into the canopy and to the west. An older man appeared, probably their father. He gathered the children and ushered them away.

Eiryss hurried after them, her foot breaking through a thin layer of ice and soaking her boot with freezing, muddy water. "No. The hospital for the poor."

They didn't turn.

She hurried to catch up to them, grabbing the father's sleeve. It fell apart under her hand. She gaped at his bony elbow, visible through the hole. "I'm sorry!"

He motioned his family on and kept his distance, his sunken eyes making her nervous. "We don't want any trouble."

She held out her hands. "I mean you none."

He rubbed his mouth. "It's full of sickness. People of your station don't go there."

She shrugged her coat off her shoulders, revealing her mantle. But instead of reassuring him, it only made him take a step back, his gaze not meeting hers. Had this man been abused by the nobility? Her family had always treated their workers with kindness and respect, but not everyone did.

Moving slowly so as not to frighten him, she held out the coat. "Just point the way."

He lifted a shaking, bony finger to the south but made no move to come closer. She set her coat on the ground, placed her leftover lunch on top of it, and stepped back. "Why are you afraid of me?"

Instead of answering, he took the food, left the coat, and hurried away.

She watched him go through narrowed eyes. "Next time, I'll put on worn brown like Hagath."

Pulling her coat back on, she hurried in the direction he'd indicated, every other step breaking through ice to sink into mud. Word must have spread, for though she felt eyes watching her, she saw no one. Smoke rose from the roofs. The mud hastily stuffed between the boards had grown soggy, dripping away to reveal flashes of light and movement beyond. Eyes peered out at her, but whenever she looked closer, they disappeared in a blink.

No field workers she'd ever seen lived like this. They had had cozy cottages—the managers' nice estates.

The vault grew more distinct with each step, a faint silver glimmered around the edges. Open sewage and rubbish ran in the streets. Her boots would be ruined. She should turn back—this was no place for her. But then she caught the sweet decay of infection. She followed the smell to a large building. The stench of unwashed bodies, infection, and human waste grew stronger with each step. She held her lapel to her mouth and breathed through her nose to keep from vomiting.

She'd found the hospital.

She paused to look the sturdy building up and down. This was where the king had sent his ailing daughter? Why?

Eiryss eased open the door and peered inside. Long rows of beds lined both sides of the room, braziers struggling weakly to keep the cold at bay. Men, women, and children—all of them filthy and starving—stared at her. Most lay on soiled bedding with a thin sprinkling of straw directly on the dirt floor. Even her worst shifts at the hospital hadn't prepared her for this.

"Who's letting in the cold!" A dark-skinned, heavyset woman marched down the row. Gray hair tied back with a scarf, her face and hands shone from multiple washings, though her apron was filthy.

She stopped before Eiryss. She was much shorter, with a turned-up nose and ruddy cheeks. "Who are you and what do you want?"

"I'm here to help," Eiryss said.

"Help?" The woman scoffed. "Gawk, more like. All you enchantresses are the same. The only people you want to help are your wealthy friends."

She tried to shove the door shut. Eiryss blocked it with her foot. "Who are you?"

"Name's Illin. And you can help by getting your rich friends to send us food, water, and clean bedding, for starters. Now get out."

Illin. The woman who'd nursed Hagath back to health. The woman Hagath had claimed could help her. Eiryss tugged out her flute and played a few notes while flaring *build* and *repel*. Her dome formed around her, forcing the older woman back a dozen steps.

Eiryss shut the door firmly behind her. "I came here to protect people. Not sit idly in trees waiting for the Alamantians to attack. Now, what can I do?"

"We're quarantined," Illin said. "You'll not leave now even if you want to."

"She's already had the sickness." Appearing through the doorway, Hagath hurried toward them, her apron as filthy as the older woman's.

"Plague. Call it what it is, girl."

The sickness that had killed her mother, that had laid Eiryss low for a week, they were calling it a plague now? Light, when had that happened?

Illin's shoulder's squared. "Eiryss, is it?"

Eiryss released her dome, her gaze going to Hagath. "You think this woman can help me?"

Illin huffed and strode down the dirt floor. "More than any of those fool enchantresses. Hagath, get back to work."

Hagath obeyed like she hadn't just been ordered about by a peasant. This woman must have impressed her greatly to have earned Hagath's respect like that.

Eiryss grabbed Hagath's arm. "This is where your father sent you? To this horrible place?"

Hagath's shoulder's sagged. "Illin came to me at first. And when I was better, I started coming here to help her."

That made much more sense.

"To work!" Illin snapped. "New girl, come help me."

Hagath motioned for Eiryss to go after the woman. "You better hurry."

Eiryss hustled to catch up to Illin. "How would you know anything about enchantresses?"

Illin knelt next to a woman insensible with fever, her pretty dress soaked with urine. "I know the shadow is destroying you."

Eiryss swayed on her feet. "Hagath told you."

"Don't just stand there!" Illin snapped. "Help me."

Eiryss knelt on the packed earth and helped strip and bathe the woman. "How do I stop the shadow?"

"First you must know how it began."

"The Alamantian king poisoned the Silver Tree." And probably used my father to do it. Eiryss rolled the naked woman to the side as Illin packed straw beneath her.

Illin piled too thin blankets over the woman. "All you enchanters, for all your knowledge, don't really understand the sacred tree at all."

Eiryss stiffened in affront. "As if you do."

Stone-faced, the woman rolled up her sleeves, revealing precise scars marching up and down her forearms.

Eiryss gasped. "You were an enchantress?"

Illin jerked her tunic, revealing a horrible scar on her chest. "Until they excised me."

"But you're a peasant!" She clapped her hand over her mouth when she realized how rude that sounded.

The woman didn't seem offended by Eiryss's outburst. "Arbor Enderlee found me. She said the tree had need of me. My existence was kept secret so as not to anger the nobility, who wouldn't stand for peasants with their sigils."

She moved on to another patient—a child. They gently changed her soiled clothing, urged her to sip feverfew tea, and replaced the rags at her forehead.

"What did you do?" Eiryss whispered.

Illin stroked the girl's hair away from her face. "I imagine it sometimes. The very first sacred tree and the very first person to be pierced. The tree awakening to movement, sound, and sight— an experience so different, so foreign from its own. But man and tree were too different to understand each other. Until... music."

"What does any of this have to do with the shadow?" Eiryss asked.

Illin bent down and whispered something into the girl's ear.

Eiryss swallowed her impatience. "Where's her mother?"

"Died in the fires of Lias Lamoren, along with the rest of her family." Illin rocked the child gently back and forth. "If the tree became angry, furious even, how do you think he would react?"

Eiryss had seen thorns stolen from the tree with no consequence. She bore some of those thorns. "He can't."

Illin made a soft sound of distress. The girl had stopped breathing. Illin held her tight, as her own mother might have. Then she laboriously rose to her feet, carrying the child through the rows of coughing, fevered people.

She paused while Eiryss opened the back door. They spilled into the cold. Illin laid the little girl beside a row of frozen bodies and crossed her arms gently at her breast. She looked so small. So pretty. Especially compared to the frozen rictuses around her.

How could such an ugly thing as death have stolen her away?

A succession of the dead faces marched behind Eiryss's eyes. Her parents and those who'd died when the Alamantians had kidnapped the king. The book Ramass had given her had contained dozens of names—all people long since forgotten.

As she would one day be forgotten.

Illin breathed out, vapor forming around her head. "The *chaos* sigil is infecting your monarch sigil. It's turning you into something... other. You want to survive? Cut out *chaos*."

Eiryss gaped at her. "Monarch sigil?"

Illin looked at her with pity. "The Silver Tree has chosen you as the next queen."

CHAPTER 28

PRINCESS

Eiryss staggered back, her hand going to her breast. To the
sigil there—it couldn't be *rule*. "How could you possibly
know anything about my sigil?"

"Hagath has seen it."

And told Illin. How could she trust the woman so completely? And then tell her without asking permission? "No. It can't
be."

But then, it made sense. The power she'd displayed—it was
beyond anything she should be able to do. But not for a princess.
And the way her sigils seemed to know what to do without even
being trained—the monarch sigil wasn't a new seedling but an
actual grafting from the Silver Tree, coming with hundreds of
years of memories. It wouldn't need to be trained.

"Light, Ahlyn should have been queen. Not me." She didn't
deserve that kind of power and recognition.

"The Silver Tree chose you."

But why? She remembered climbing the tree, placing her hand against the bark. Remembering all her pain and her fierce desire to make it right, no matter the cost. "Sometimes wrong is right," she'd said. She'd sworn the tree had heard her.

She rested her hand on her chest. Could the tree hear her? Could it understand? *I may be the wrong person, but I will make it right. I swear to you.* She felt nothing change, nothing to show her the Silver Tree heard or understood. She hoped it had.

"Be very careful who knows what you are, child. Those behind the princess's death were never found."

Never found. Never found. "My... father killed the princess." Each word felt ponderous in her mouth. She thought of all the people who'd seen her sigil. Enderlee, Tria, a handful of healers. Had any of them suspected that her tenth sigil might be a monarch sigil?

By the way Enderlee and Tria had begged her to stay, she thought they might. But if so, why not just tell her?

Illin shook her head, lips pursed. "Are you sure your father killed her?"

"He admitted it to me."

The woman didn't seem convinced. "I am a seer, Eiryss. The tree shows visions of what is to come."

And she had been excised. Eiryss recoiled in horror. Seers were rare and precious. Only born every few centuries. "Who would have dared excise a seer?"

"Someone who did not want me to see." She rubbed her scars. "They took my sight, but sometimes, when I touch the sigils of others, I can still see a little."

Eiryss would have never believed it possible a few months ago. But then, weren't her own thorns nearly torn out because the enchantresses disagreed with how she acquired them? "Did you see me?"

The woman studied her. "I saw something. I didn't know it was you."

"My father… Have you ever seen anything about him?"

"My visions are never that specific."

Eiryss lifted her sleeves, baring her sigil. Illin hesitated and then gripped Eiryss's arms. "You have to light the sigils."

Eiryss opened them.

Illin closed her eyes, head tipped to the side. "A razorbeak destroys the eggs in a nest and replaces them with its own. The parent birds raise these chicks, never knowing its own offspring has been murdered."

"What does it mean?"

"An imposter, perhaps," Illin mulled. "Treachery yet to be discovered, certainly. Perhaps that we see what we want—or expect—to see?" Illin released her. "The tree doesn't think in words but memories of the dead. Trying to understand the visions means I must think the way the tree does. Which I cannot. You see the problem?"

Eiryss pulled down her shirt, exposing her monarch sigil. Illin hesitated before resting her fingertips atop it. She immediately stiffened.

"What do you see?" Eiryss breathed.

"A cursed brier, trapping and staining all it touches."

"The shadow?"

Illin rested her other palm on Eiryss's chaos sigil. "Yes and no."

"I don't understand."

"Two branches from the same tree—one light, the other dark." She withdrew her hands, folding them across her belly. "So will you allow me to excise *chaos*?"

Eiryss's feet had gone numb with cold. She hugged herself and bounced to get her blood pumping. "How do I know you are what you say? Valynthia hasn't had a seer in over a century."

"I'm not Valynthian."

"Alamantian?"

Illin shook her head. "What's left of my people tend your fields."

Eiryss looked around, at the shacks and shanties around her. "King Ramadal's people?"

Illin looked surprised. Eiryss was too. What were the chances that a rare, ancient book would turn up just when she needed it?

The door opened, and Hagath appeared silhouetted by the low-burning lamps. "Eiryss? We must go before dark."

"You knew," Eiryss whispered accusingly.

"Only a fledgling monarch sigil would have been strong enough to defeat *chaos*," Hagath said softly.

Eiryss rested her fingertips lightly over the aching sigil. The healers who'd treated her in Hanama had seen the sigil, but it was little more than a raised lump then—it wouldn't be recognizable as the monarch sigil until it had formed into a likeness of the Silver tree. And it wasn't uncommon for an extra sigil to form on the torso.

"Who else knows?" Eiryss asked.

"Just the three of us," Hagath answered.

Eiryss breathed out in relief.

"I have patients to tend to," Illin said.

Even if Illin were lying, Eiryss didn't want *chaos*. If that meant angering the king, so be it. And as for the position as his personal enchantress—she didn't want that either. Surely, he would come to understand that. "Cut it out."

Back inside Illin's personal room, the woman brought out a small knife. She spread numbing cream across Eiryss's skin and waited for it to take effect. Eiryss looked away as Illin cut. Even with the cream, the pain made her hiss. Sweat beaded her skin as Illin pulled back the skin to reveal the sigil beneath. Eiryss clenched her teeth and eyes and fists and toes. She forced herself to breathe through it, to accept it. To look.

Through the skin and blood, she saw a silver-white sigil shot through with strange, shadowy markings.

"Light," Eiryss whispered.

"This part is going to hurt," Illin warned as she removed a pair of pincers. Light, worse than what they'd already done? "Hagath, hold her."

Hagath laid over Eiryss's chest and gripped her arms. "The more it hurts, the harder you squeeze."

Sweat trickled from Eiryss's brow into her hair. She was hot and cold and shaking inside and out. Illin moved. It was like the woman was ripping her skin off. Her back arched. She bit back a scream. A tearing sound. Eiryss tried to push Hagath off, but the girl dropped all her weight. With a sucking sound, something popped free. Eiryss collapsed as the pain lessened to a raw ache instead of a stabbing, ripping sensation.

Hagath examined the sigil about the size of a coin. "You're lucky it wasn't fully grown. Try to light it."

Eiryss did, but nothing happened. No cold. No shadows. She breathed out in relief and nodded.

"We got it all, then." Illin stuffed the bloody mess into the brazier and shut the door. "Now to stitch it up."

After Hagath was done, Eiryss flared *rule* and gasped. "There is still a trace of shadow, just like before."

Illin froze.

"What does that mean?" Eiryss asked.

Illin set down the rags. "Nothing good."

"Maybe it's just an echo from *chaos*," Hagath suggested.

"Maybe." Illin didn't sound convinced.

"What do we do?" Eiryss asked.

"Either remove your monarch sigil or wait and see," Illin said.

Eiryss rested her hand protectively over her sigil. It felt... part of her. "We'll wait."

Hagath's eyes slipped closed, and she let out a long breath. "Come on. We need to be back before dark."

Eiryss paused at the woman's doorway. "Have you seen a little boy with ragged shoes and blackened toes?"

"Every time I go outside," Illin said.

Light, how could there be so many? And how had Eiryss not known? Again, she thought of her father. Of his sentiment that everyone deserved a chance at magic. Her heart pained her again for the wrong he'd done trying to make a right.

Illin didn't bother saying goodbye. Eiryss and Hagath slipped out the back. Hagath shut the door behind her. They walked through the rows of frozen dead. Questions burned inside Eiryss, but she found she could not speak them in the presence of the dead. When they reached the end, men with layers of cloth wrapped around their mouths gathered the bodies onto a cart.

"Where will they take them?" Eiryss asked, thinking of the little girl.

"To a mass grave at the edge of the city," Hagath said.

Nothing could hurt the girl now, and yet it pained Eiryss to think of her forgotten and alone. Did she not deserve to have her memories preserved in the tree? Did she not deserve to be grieved? "How long have they been dying like this?"

"Since their cities fell."

The two of them moved through apparently abandoned huts. Appearances could be deceiving. "Why didn't you say anything? About all these people dying? About me being..." *The princess.*

"There are spies everywhere. It was safer to bring you to Illin."

Eiryss thought of Vallay, always hovering. "Light, what am I to do?"

"I don't know."

Eiryss dragged her fingers through her hair and let out a ragged breath. "We have to tell someone."

"No! You mustn't tell anyone! Swear it!"

"I have to. At least the king—"

Hagath slapped her. Eiryss reeled back, palm pressed to her stinging cheek. Hagath's hands flew to her mouth as if the slap had shocked even herself. "Promise me! You can't tell anyone!"

Furious, Eiryss pushed past her.

Hagath hurried after her and grabbed her arm. "I'm sorry, Eiryss. Please, you have to trust me."

"You won't tell me anything, and then have the gall to slap me when I won't do what you want?" Eiryss jerked out of her grip. "Leave me alone, Hagath."

"No, please," Hagath broke down into sobs. "Please, I can't lose you too. I can't. Please."

Hagath had already been through so much; something inside her was broken. *Be patient,* Eiryss reminded herself. Her shoulders sagged. "All right. I promise." It wasn't a promise she could keep. But she would wait as long as she could.

Light, she was the princess. When her magic grew stronger than the king's—anywhere from months to years—she would become queen.

She didn't know how to run a war. But she would start with that sorry excuse for a hospital. Proper bedding and heat and food for a start. Medicine too.

She and Hagath reached the edge of the makeshift town. Eiryss secreted herself behind a tree and watched as people emerged. One little girl had rags wrapped around her feet in place of shoes as she gathered firewood. There was a body outside the hospital with shoes that might fit.

Tears filled Eiryss's eyes. There had to be some good to the monarch sigil. Something besides the shadow. Her fingers against the tree tingled, an answering buzz building in Eiryss's sigil. It grew brighter inside her, a river of light aching to be let free—almost as if the Silver Tree had answered her call.

She opened her magic, the buzz building to an almost painful level as light filled her, flowing from her into the trees. She could feel the connection of roots from one tree to another and realized with a start that there wasn't a single tree, but rather a network of them. Deep within their heartwood, sap moved faster and faster, pulsing through branches.

Life spread outward, warm and sweet and golden. Above the ramshackle village, flowers bloomed and faded, petals dropping like fallen leaves, splashes of color against the dirty snow. Their bases grew fat and full. Fully ripened fruit, thousands of them, dropped from the sky.

One plunked down on top of the little girl. Rubbing her head, she glared up at the trees then down at the fruit. Slowly, she bent down and picked it up. She bit into it, juice dribbling down her chin. Eyes wide, she chewed in wonder.

"Mama!" she cried. "Mama!"

"You should not have done that," Hagath whispered from behind her, but her eyes were shining.

Because what Eiryss had done was not something any sigil other than *rule* could do.

"Come on," Hagath said. "We can't let anyone see us."

This time, Eiryss didn't sneak anywhere. She took the carriage up with Hagath, who had grown very still and somehow smaller.

"Will you be all right?" Eiryss asked at the junction that took them to their separate platforms.

Instead of answering, Hagath said, "Promise?" in a small voice.

A promise Eiryss could never keep. "Promise."

Hagath ducked her head and plodded on. Only Eiryss's training as a healer enchantress sent her to hang her clothing outside, where it would stay, untouched, for days. By then the sunshine would have killed the plague inside. In her bathroom, she scrubbed plague from herself in water that hadn't even been heated yet. She didn't complain. At least she had a place to wash the sickness away.

Her damp hair tied back and wearing her standard issued tunic and trousers, she inquired after servants until she found the king taking his supper with his war council.

He looked up at her with a smile. "Ah, Eiryss, my new personal enchantress, and soon to be my new daughter!"

She willed herself to be patient. "Sir, may I speak with you?"

He followed her to the edge of the room. "Do you know about the appalling conditions in that ground hospital?" Even as she said it, she realized he had to know. His own daughter had been there all day. Addled as Hagath was, Eiryss doubted she went anywhere without the king's knowledge.

Zannok sighed heavily and led Eiryss up one of the corridors. "I'm sorry you had to see such appalling conditions, Eiryss, truly I am. But what would you have me do?"

"Feed them. Send enchantresses down to heal them. Build them better shelters."

He leaned against the banister, the pane outlining him in silver. "And risk exposing my enchantresses to plague? If I divert food away from the nobility, I lose their support. I lose their support, I lose the war."

All the food and wine she'd consumed the night before... "You said yourself propaganda wins a war every bit as much as battles. Make it sound like it's the noble thing to do."

"The nobility care very little for the plight of commoners."

She couldn't argue with that. After all, they hadn't cared for her plight, and she'd been one of them. "Take the food from my wedding gala."

He raised an eyebrow. "Your position back in society isn't as secure as you'd like to think, Eiryss. You need the nobility's support."

If she wasn't careful, they would eat her alive. "Switch the hothouses from flowers over to food. Reduce the excess of the nobility. Create domes for the poor to live in."

"The enchantresses would never allow their amulets to be used in such a way."

"They will if you tell them to."

"Eiryss," he said with forced patience. "I understand you're trying to help, but you know better than most how fickle the nobility is."

"Then replace them," Eiryss said coldly. *The nobility doesn't deserve magic any more than the next man. Not because of a simple accident of birth.* Light, when had she begun to harbor such treasonous thoughts?

But she would not be like her father. She would go about this the right way. And as the princess, she could make some real changes.

His brows rose. "Replace them how? Would you have me murder them in their beds? Take away their titles? How do you think their magical sons and daughters would react?"

It would be a civil war. She began pacing. Queen. Queen in less than a year. What would she do? For starters, she'd stop this blasted war. Perhaps the Alamantians didn't have such a bad idea, giving magic to the masses. And if they had one good idea, perhaps she could convince them to have another, and they could end this.

But only if she could forgive them for what they had done to her family. She shied away from the thought. No. Punishment must still come. King Dray would pay. But all of the Alamant needn't.

She remembered Illin's vision of the bird that forced the eggs out of their nest and replaced it with its own. "How do we know the Valynthians really killed Princess Ahlyn? They've denied it."

"Of course they've denied it."

"It doesn't make sense to kill Ahlyn and then refute the act. Not after they'd already started the war."

"You'd be surprised what a man spurned will do."

Eiryss opened her mouth to argue when Ramass burst into the corridor, looking flushed and pale. "Eiryss!" He glanced nervously from his father back to her. "What are you doing?"

Zannok chuckled, but it was strained. "Eiryss, I must get back to my war council. I promise to find some more supplies for that ground hospital. Yes?" He squeezed his son's arm, a look passing between them she didn't understand before the king moved on.

She started to follow Zannok, but Ramass blocked her. "What about our picnic?" he blurted.

She looked at him curiously. "You're being strange." What was going on between him and his father? They'd always gotten on fairly well before.

He tugged his hand through his hair. "No. I'm not."

"Liar."

He smiled his dazzling smile and moved closer. "Well, if I am strange, can you blame me?"

"Now you're trying to distract me."

He kissed her, and curse him, it worked. "Come on. We need to reach it before nightfall."

"Reach where?" She'd been frozen all day. And after that cold shower... "My hair is still wet."

"It'll be worth it. Promise."

CHAPTER

ARBOR RING

A snowstorm was coming. It did not smell of ice and bitter wind, but of a foreign spice Eiryss could never quite name. Something earthy and full of musk. She and Ramass crossed bridges that connected the trees like webs. He kept talking, trying to distract her from something. What did he think she needed distracting from?

At any rate, it didn't work. She couldn't stop thinking of her father, and the Alamantians who had used him. Of the dead little girl or the living one who could use her shoes. Of the boy with the blackened toes. Of the monarch sigil on her chest.

Had Ramass noticed it in the dark? Even if he had, it wasn't fully formed yet. He might not have known what it was.

Finally, Ramass paused before a carriage.

She raised an eyebrow. "We're going down?" Nobility never went down unless they had to. Or unless they were sneaking after an addled friend who liked to visit plague-riddled hospitals.

He waited, arms crossed. Rolling her eyes, she stepped into the carriage and waited as it made its descent. The temperature had dropped considerably. They stepped onto the forest floor. Their footsteps crunched through snow that had melted and frozen and melted again until it had formed a thin sheet of brittle ice.

He paused, leaning against the trunk of the tree, and watched her expectantly.

She wrapped her arms around herself, breath misting before her. Despite her woven hat, her head was freezing. "I thought we were going somewhere."

"That depends on if you can find it."

She rolled her eyes. "I've never been in Trapendale before."

He moved closer. "Close your eyes and open your magic. Move where it takes you."

She sniffed through her cold nose. "Where my magic takes me?"

"Just try it."

"Which sigil?"

He brushed snowfall off his sleeve. "Your strongest one."

She hesitated, afraid of the shadow. But they had not come when she'd grown the fruit for the poor. Hesitant, she opened *rule*. Only the barest trace of shadows—maybe Hagath was right and it was merely an echo left over from *chaos*. She relaxed and breathed in the scents of the forest—snow and trees and life buried deep. Beneath her feet and high above her head, roots and branches tangled and grew together. One enormous creature, magic coursing all through it. And she was part of it.

"The tree is inside me," she said without opening her eyes.

"Yes."

The magic was strongest to her right. She moved, her body a compass needle pointing toward home. A row of trees appeared to have been built rather than occurred naturally. Their trunks were perfectly uniform and evenly spaced. Their branches formed delicate, repeating arches, their canopies filled with leaves that hadn't succumbed to the bitter cold.

She stepped past them into a clearing. Instantly, the wind stopped. The light changed, becoming softer, silvery. It was like she'd stepped into moonlight. The air smelled of minerals, and she could hear the crystalline tinkle of the sacred leaves.

In the center stood a great old tree. Magic was thick as honey in the air. In response, her sigils chilled under her skin, making her shiver.

"The Silver Tree—it's here."

"After all these centuries, there are things we still don't know about the magic. How it works, exactly. The nature of it.

"The Silver Tree," he went on, "is connected to all the trees in the forest. But in certain places, the magic bubbles up stronger than others—Arbor Circles. Most people never find them—the magic repels them. Others, the magic calls to. Long ago, one of our people found this place and built a city around it."

Eiryss approached the center tree and laid a hand on the thickly textured bark—damp and spongy beneath her fingers. "If the whole city is built around it, doesn't everyone know it's here?"

"They forget—and if you remind them, they promptly forget again. The only ones who come here are the ones the tree calls. Or if they have strong enough magic on their own."

She eyed him. "Which are you?"

He folded his arms and leaned against one of the trees. "I'm the man trying to save Valynthia. And you."

She narrowed her eyes. "Save me? From whom?"

His gaze slipped to the front of her tunic. "What do you know of the sigil on your chest?"

She pressed her hand to it in surprise. "How…" Her breath caught as she remembered being pressed up against him with nothing but the skin she was born in. Suddenly, she couldn't look at him again.

Ramass's cheeks turned as pink as hers felt. "Can I see it?"

Eiryss bit her lip and turned away.

"It wants to remain hidden, doesn't it?" Ramass asked softly.

She forgot her embarrassment and looked at him. "How did you know?"

He took a single step forward. "Eiryss, you've known me your entire life. You can trust me."

An unfamiliar instinct warned against it. But this was Ramass. She unbuttoned her coat and pulled down her tunic, revealing the top half of the sigil. It was still sore and would be until it stopped growing. But for now, a thin line divided her breasts. Above and below were the first signs of branches and roots. When it was finished, it would be a perfect replica of the Silver Tree. And then she would be queen.

"You know what it is, don't you?" he asked.

Snow began to fall, a brush of cold against her exposed skin. She shivered and started to tug her tunic up. His fingers blocked her and rested against her skin. "That's why I wanted you to see this place. Because whoever killed Ahlyn is still out there. If you're ever in need—if you ever need a place to hide—you will find shelter here."

Her father had killed Ahlyn, but he had never been the mastermind of her death. That must be what he meant. She breathed out in relief that she didn't have to hide this from him anymore.

He pulled her into his arms. "Light, Eiryss, I wish I could shelter you from this."

She wasn't meant to be sheltered from it. "Don't you see? Now I can really change things."

"Not until we know where the danger comes from."

"But—"

"You're not strong enough politically. Not yet. Not after…"

After her father's betrayal. "Like it or not, when my magic grows stronger than the king's, I will be queen."

"That could be months away. Years."

He almost sounded hopeful. Did he not believe in her? Or perhaps he wasn't eager for things to change?

He reached into his pocket. "I have something for you. A betrothal gift." He unwrapped a square of fine, purple velvet. In the fading light gleamed an amulet in the shape of a leaf. Someone had made this with their dying magic. Just as the amulet Eiryss wore had been made by her mother.

She ran the pads of her fingers along the leaf's veins. "What is it?"

"It's a dampener." So called because it dampened the effect of invasive magic. They were rare, as only a dying dreamer could make them.

"How did you come by it?" The Arbor strictly controlled all such amulets—most were stored in a vault at the Enchantress Copse, though they might have been lent out to senior enchantresses for the war.

He unclasped the simple cord around her neck and slid the dampener next to the amulet her mother had made for her. He slid it under her hair and let the chain drop out of sight down her tunic. "It's too late for me, but it might still save you."

She shivered at the cold metal between her breasts. "What's that supposed to mean?"

"I've done things, Eiryss..."

The guilt that had haunted him since he'd returned. She carried that same guilt now. "We all have."

He wouldn't meet her gaze. "You don't understand. And I've tried to tell you... in every way I can think of."

Light, war made a ruin of them all.

She reached out and took his hand, willing the touch to comfort him. "And if I'm caught with an unregistered amulet?" She couldn't guess what Enderlee would do to a princess, but then the woman had been an expert at punishing her without punishing her ever since she'd first come to the academy.

"You're good at not being caught."

She pressed her fingertips against it through the cloth. Now she carried a piece of her mother, father, and Ramass with her everywhere she went. "I haven't anything for you."

"I demand a new tunic and breeches, all over embroidered with gold and embellished with diamonds."

"And lace."

"Frothing with lace."

She tipped back her head and laughed. Light, how could she ever survive without him?

He brushed the snow from her hair. "Did you read the book I gave you?"

She made a face. "Horrible history. But I suppose useful." Useful just when she needed it. But Ramass couldn't have known that.

"Who cares about lowly field workers, right?" he said bitterly.

He had seen the suffering juxtaposed with the excess just as she had. Clearly, he didn't like it any more than she did. She murmured low in her throat, thinking again of the dead girl. Of those awful months she'd spent scrambling to survive. Even scrambling, she'd had warmth and shoes.

She used to believe herself above everyone. She huffed. *I've been a fool.*

"What is it?" Ramass asked.

When she didn't answer, he tipped her chin up and kissed her. His lips were soft, gentle. The hands that held her trembled, uncertain. She smiled against his lips, wondering if alcohol had made him brave the night before. His uncertainty made her bold. She explored the planes of his face, the stubble as rough as she'd thought it would be. The strong column of his throat, his broad shoulders, the muscles of his arms.

When she moved her mouth to his throat, he moaned. "Light, Eiryss." The need, the surrender in his voice banished the cold. Warmth blossomed inside her, filled with light and color. His kissed deepened. They stumbled backward, into the shadows of one of the trees. Her back stopped against the rough bark. They fumbled with clothing and then he lifted her. Her legs wrapped around his waist.

She gasped at the pleasure and pain of it. Being with Ramass was its own kind of magic.

Hand in hand, Eiryss and Ramass stepped past the sentries who guarded the entrance to the king's tree. Eiryss tried very hard not to blush as their eyes silently followed them.

When they'd passed them, Ramass chuckled and kissed the back of her hand. "It's a good thing I'm making you a married woman soon. The scandal!"

She bumped him with her shoulder. "And what of your reputation?"

"Me? Men keep clapping me on the shoulder and congratulating me."

She rolled her eyes. "It's not fair."

The branch beneath them trembled. Two guards ran past, a messenger between them. They were headed to the king's private chambers. Eiryss and Ramass exchanged a worried look before their gazes rose to the vault gleaming a faint silver at the edge of the vision. It rippled like stones thrown in water.

They were under attack.

They rushed after the soldiers. The men began calling for the king before they even reached his rooms. He came out in his nightclothes, a magical sword in one hand.

"Sire," the messenger panted. "The Alamantians have attacked the southern defenses."

Zannok swore. "The enchantresses are holding?"

"Yes, sir. Though they are vastly outnumbered."

Zannok swore again.

Ramass marched up. "Order the reserves brought up. Rouse the council and captains."

"Vallay!" the king shouted as he marched back into his room. "Where are my messengers?"

The hometree came alive with running messengers and soldiers.

Ramass grabbed her arm. "Go back to your chambers and stay there."

"What?" she roared in disbelief. "I'm to protect the king." *And you, you big lumbering idiot.*

"You're not ready. And you're too valuable to lose." He gave her a push in the direction of her chambers and took off with one of the soldiers.

"Bumbling, overprotective twit." She'd been working for months to make a difference. She wasn't about to sit at home while everyone else defended the city.

She hurried back to her room and jerked on her coat and knives, laying her mantle overtop. She grabbed her satchel, gloves, and hat. Half out the doorpane, she swung the strap over her head and ran into Vallay. She stumbled back—Vallay was more solid than she looked. The woman didn't even stagger.

"The king has ordered you to remain in your rooms," she said in that emotionless voice of hers.

"I'm his personal enchantress!"

The woman remained silent and unmoving.

Eiryss could certainly handle a servant, but Vallay would call for the guards swarming the tree. Besides, Eiryss still had her rope dangling from her platform.

"Fine." She backed into the room.

Vallay followed her and said in a low voice, "The rope has been cut and your room is being watched. Try to leave and you will find yourself sleeping with guards beside your bed." Vallay eased outside the doorpane, her head bent in mock servility.

Eiryss stared after her long after she'd gone, insults and arguments rising and dying before she'd ever had a chance to voice them. In the distance came a great rending sound. Eiryss had heard it before—when she'd left Valynthia. The sound of a great tree falling.

The rope was easier, faster, and safer. But it was by no means the only way down. She pried up some of the floorboards. The branch beneath housed birds' nests and spiders. Deciding it was best not to look, Eiryss lowered herself.

Cupped in the cradle of the spreading branch, she shimmied down the length and came up against the main trunk. Wedging her hands and feet, she worked her way down from there, her heart sinking every time the vault shuddered.

She hit the forest floor and ran until she slipped and fell hard, bruising her right side and coating her fancy uniform with mud. Blast. If there was one thing it would be hard to hide from tree dwellers, it was mud. They'd know she'd gone to ground level. And they'd wonder why.

Scooping a handful of snow, she tried to clean it off and only ended up smearing it. Giving up, she kept on at a careful pace. When she reached one of the communal trees, she abandoned the mud and ice to spring up the stairs.

At the first intersection, she headed toward the war music, passing couriers and soldiers alike, who all winced at the vault thrumming like a beaten drum above them. The sound filled Eiryss to bursting.

The perimeter trees marked the edge of the city. They grew into a wide wall, the thistlelike bark of one tree blending seamlessly with the next. Their branches tangled in a thick canopy of sharp thorns. Evenly spaced along the exterior were enchantress platforms that bulged outward like the mushrooms along the bark of her hometree.

Her back to the dozens of enchantresses in her unit, the weaver stood on a raised dais, channeling the light streaming to her from the enchantresses. A quarter of a mile distant, the vault glowed with faint light.

She peered over the edge and froze at the sight of Alamantian armies. Tens of thousands of women in leather winter armor milled about. On raised platforms, weavers spun the ghostly light channeled into an orb that crackled with energy.

"Why aren't you with your unit?" Her mantle marking her as a mid-level commander, an enchantress marched toward Eiryss. "We're hard-pressed enough as it is."

Eiryss turned toward her, revealing the markings on her mantle. The woman hastily bowed. "My apologies, enchantress. Are you looking for King Zannok? He's there." She pointed to the tallest perimeter tree above the main city gates.

Eiryss couldn't go to either the king or Ramass. "Jala's unit. Where is it?" The woman hesitated, her eyes lingering on the mud slicking Eiryss's side. "Now!" Eiryss snapped, hoping her shortness would override the woman's suspicion.

She pointed the way she'd come. "Fifth platform down from the king's. Above one of the side-street gates." She bowed and made a hasty retreat.

Eiryss took off in the direction the woman had just come from. At the fifth archway, she stepped onto the flat platform, a half-circle that jutted out from the wall. She recognized Wyndyn and Iritraya before she caught sight of Jala standing before them, facing the enemy army. She gathered the magic of her enchantress unit. Her hand was bound tightly to her chest to protect her broken ribs and shoulder blade.

Eager to see the weave, Eiryss lit her sigils. Her magic connected her to the enchantment around her. At once, the details of the woven magic that made up the vault came into crisp focus. Right in front of Jala's enchantresses, the magic gleamed duller, strands of the magic frayed. A weakness in the weave.

Above the Alamantians, light pulsed, gleaming brighter and larger. All at once, the weaver flung his hands. The orb arched directly toward her. Eiryss dropped, arms crossed over her head as the vault bulged inward, stretching dangerously close before snapping back. The repercussion slammed into her, blowing her hair behind her. A deep-throated roar echoed through her skull. Above her, the vault shuddered and groaned like a wounded thing, arcs of light scattering across its surface.

From the enemy, a cheer arose. Above the enchanter, another orb already formed.

Breathing hard, Eiryss ran from the main bridge to the platform. Jala played, but the pain of her broken shoulder and ribs was clearly too much. The enchanter would send another orb before she ever repaired the damage to the weakened area.

Someone had to do something. Stop her and take over her command.

All at once, Eiryss realized she outranked Jala. By a lot. "Jala!" Eiryss called as she pushed through the enchantresses. "Give way!"

Expression dark and ominous, Jala glared at her, the distant magic lighting the deep shadows under her eyes. Her hair was tied back with a simple cord, strands of it frizzing around her face. Eiryss had never seen the woman without makeup before. She looked older and haggard—like she hadn't slept in days.

"I didn't spend three years playing nursemaid and courier to a king to give up my one true chance of glory!" she shouted to be heard over the groaning of the vault.

Eiryss squared off in front of her. "You are unfit. Give way and fight when you are."

"I have worked too hard. Sacrificed too much to—"

There wasn't time for this. Eiryss lit her sigils and took hold of the magic, cool and slick beneath her fingers. She wove the strands—*build, repel, seal,* touch of *light,* her own sigils feeding into the magic.

Suddenly, a hand planted itself in her back and shoved.

"It's mine!" Jala roared. "I will never—"

Behind the woman, the orb careened toward the weakness. All went white.

CHAPTER

ASSASSIN

E iryss groaned. Above her, stars fell and landed on her like spent ash. A rent tore through the vault from far above and disappeared out of sight beyond the edge of the platform. She brushed ash off her face, her hands coming back coated in black. She sat up to bedlam. Women sobbed and screamed. Blood and silver coated every surface, smearing black when disturbed. And yet for all this, there was no sound but a faint ringing.

Jala lay face down, her forearms crossed under her head as if she were simply napping after eating too much at a picnic. Eiryss rolled her over. Her head didn't turn like it should; it flopped over at a weird angle, her tongue hanging out. Her neck was clearly broken.

Eiryss recoiled as faces of the dead flashed through her mind—Ahlyn, Father, Mother, Shelin, Kit, and a dozen more. People she had barely known or not at all. The whole world was dying—everything she knew being eaten away one person at a time.

Stop, she commanded herself. *Or you'll lose all who are left.* She shoved the horror and panic deep, hauled herself up, reeled, and nearly went down. Fighting dizziness, she leaned over and gripped the raised lip of the platform. The rent in the vault went all the way to the ground. Through the gap and far below, enchantresses poured through ash that fell like snow, leaving a black trail in their wake.

They had to repair the rent or the city would fall. All the poor below—they wouldn't be able to defend themselves. She imagined the boy with the blackened toes hanging by his neck from one of the trees.

Light, she had to stop it.

Eiryss whipped around to assess her unit. Some of the girls staggered to their feet. Others were clearly dead. Some would be soon. Wyndyn cradled Iritraya, who was missing half her head. She was unnaturally still, the rise and fall of her chest absent.

Dead.

Eiryss ran to Wyndyn's side. "Get up! Get the other women up!" She couldn't hear her own words.

Wyndyn shook her head, a lost look on her white face— clearly in shock. Eiryss hauled her up by the front of her coat. "Fight! Fight, blast you!"

Eiryss shook other girls in her unit, pushed their instruments into their hands. But they were only girls. They'd never fought before. Never seen death. Hadn't learned that if they didn't keep moving, it would come for them too. Not that long ago, Eiryss had been just like them. Experience had taught her differently.

Grappling hooks bit into the wood on the platform's lip. Through her feet, she could feel a slight tremor—axes biting into the perimeter trees?

Where are my reinforcements?

It didn't matter. They'd never get here in time. And the girls couldn't fight.

Eiryss could. As if sensing her intention, the monarch sigil recoiled. She had the feeling that it would tear itself from her skin, if it had the ability, rather than reveal itself.

"Power is the blade of change," her father had once said. *"A blade that cuts both ways."*

He had forgotten that in the end, and the blade had cut through their entire family.

I have to do this. Of course, the Silver Tree couldn't understand. It thought in memories, not words. *This is what I'm meant to do.* She imagined all those she had left—Ramass, Hagath, Zannok, her brother, other faces flashing through her mind. The girls from her school. Her extended family. *I have to protect them. Make it so none of my people suffer as I have suffered. So no more daughters are forced to bury their fathers and mothers. No parents their children.*

No response save for a deepening of dread.

She couldn't save everyone, but by the light, she would save those she could.

Alone, she stepped onto the edge of the platform and opened her monarch sigil. A river of light gushed through her, shadows winnowing in the depths. She wove a patch, tugging threads into place and smoothing others. Hands appeared at the top of the balcony. An enemy enchantress hauled herself up, eyes zeroing in on Eiryss.

Eiryss's hands worked faster, desperate and somehow sure.

The woman charged. Her magical sword outlined in golden light reached the apex of her swing. Eiryss shoved the weave outward. It pulsed in a concave arc that slammed into the Alamantian and those climbing up just behind her. They toppled, screaming, off the balcony. The patch settled against the weave, which was still weak and wavering. Eiryss doubted it would hold against a direct hit.

She wove another patch, the magic like malleable glass in her hands. All her sigils worked together, *rule* adding power. Another orb arced toward her. It slammed into the first patch, which bulged inward before shattering in a rain of ash. She enlarged the weave so it covered her unit and braced her feet. The orb slammed against her magic, driving her back. Heat and light crackled along her magic. With a roar, she pulsed, her magic flaring bright. The orb toppled off the balcony.

As if from down a long tunnel, muffled screams echoed from below. Her hearing was coming back just in time to hear the screams of the Alamantians as their own orb crushed and burned them. Light, how many had she just killed?

There wasn't time to find out. She wove a second patch, her hands working frantically, racing to form a patch before the Alamantians finished their orb. She flicked it away. The patch covered the rent just as the orb slammed into it, crackling along the surface. The repair buckled and shattered.

Light, she needed more magic if that patch was going to hold!

As if someone had heard her, music sounded behind her. Eiryss turned to find Wyndyn playing. She nodded at Eiryss, the tears streaking through the ash on her cheeks, her hands red with blood that darkened to black as it mixed with the ash. Other enchantresses formed up beside her, adding their magic to Wyndyn's.

Eiryss opened her sigil, magic gushing through her chest to form the weave. She snatched her unit's magic, added it to hers, and threw the weave, which caught the tattered ends of the vault and bound them. The weave blended seamlessly with the broken vault, so she couldn't tell where the rent had ever been.

This time when the orb struck, the vault bulged as it had before, but it did not break.

Sagging in relief, she shifted to the edge of the platform and peered down. The orb she had pulsed down had struck the center of the breeching Alamantians, taking out half. Valynthian soldiers poured in from behind Eiryss. They loosed arrows, threw rocks, and poured hot water down on the heads of the half that remained.

A man with an impressive beard squared himself in front of her. "Well done, enchantress."

She didn't... didn't know how to react. Yes, she had done well. She had saved the city from falling. But she'd also killed dozens, perhaps hundreds of people. She waited for horror, but it didn't come. She was numb.

Eiryss turned away without a word and took her place on the raised platform. She fed her unit's magic into the vault. It no longer bulged, only rippled under the Alamantian's constant assault. The longer they worked, the stronger the vault became, until it glimmered silver, the arcs of Alamantian magic crackling harmlessly along the exterior.

Hours passed as the Alamantians continued their relentless assault while Eiryss and the other weavers repaired and strengthened the vault. The bodies littered around Eiryss were cleared away, the wounded transported to the healers. Surrounded by her unit, Eiryss sipped water and took a few bites of fruit a servant brought, not caring that her hands were filthy with ash. The section of vault before them shone brighter than the rest and it barely even rippled when struck. Along the whole line, the vault held firmer than it had before.

That was the difference a princess could make.

Dawn of the next day was just starting to light the horizon when their replacements arrived. As the women relieved them, Tria herself stood before Eiryss, her blue eyes searching.

Eiryss had forgotten that the woman was sent to Trapendale. "What are you doing here?"

Tria's already thin mouth thinned even more. "I came for you."

"Came for me?"

"May I see it?"

Eiryss swallowed. She'd known when she'd used *rule* before so many that they would guess what she was. But some foolish part of her had hoped she'd have a little more time.

Knowing there wasn't any point in hiding it, Eiryss undid the toggles of her mantle then the buttons of her coat. Last, she pulled her tunic down, revealing the beginnings of a likeness of the Silver Tree.

Tria dropped to one knee, the rest of her unit following suit. "Princess."

Eiryss's eyes fluttered shut. She took a deep breath and forced herself to face her unit. Namishka and Wyndyn both looked shocked. Balendora was already on one knee and tugging at her granddaughter's hand. Her gaze never leaving Eiryss's face, Wyndyn sank down to both knees and nodded. Eiryss nodded back.

Perhaps the two of them would make allies after all.

Aside from the women already pouring their magic into the weaver who had taken Eiryss's place, every other woman knelt. Near the entrance, Vallay and a pair of king's guards lowered themselves. How long had they been there?

"I don't think I'm the kind of princess who stands much on ceremony," Eiryss said.

They took that as an invitation to stand.

Tria looked about suspiciously and stepped close. "You need to come with me now."

Eiryss noted the two Silver Tree guards behind Tria. "So you can excise me?"

Tria winced. "So we can keep you safe."

"I'm safe enough with the king and Ramass."

Tria stepped closer still, her round belly pressing against Eiryss's side. "Those who plotted the princess's death are still out there. I promise, we'll defend you with everything we have."

Eiryss's father had plotted the princess's death, and he'd paid for his crimes when his head was severed from his shoulders. As for King Dray—he should fear her. Not the other way around. "The Arbor has already broken one promise to me." She pushed past the women.

Tria grabbed her arm. "Don't do this, Eiryss. Don't let our mistake cost your life." She glanced at Vallay. "Let's speak in private."

Eiryss jerked free. "I'm your princess. You don't command me, Tria. You never will again." Eiryss nodded to Vallay as she stepped past her, the king's guards falling in behind her.

Everyone Eiryss passed paused to kneel, murmurs of "Princess," following her like a wave.

Months ago, she would have reveled in this. Now, their obeisance felt hollow. Fake. And she would inherit disaster upon her ascension... if they even survived that long. But despite their perfidy, she felt the weight of the responsibility crushing her already exhausted body.

How was she going to save them?

She was almost relieved when they left the chaos of the front for the relative quiet of the predawn city.

Clearly, Ramass and the king had noted her absence and sent Vallay to fetch her. But surely she wasn't in trouble. The king would be thrilled to discover a new princess—her magic would safeguard the city against any number of Alamantian enchanters. She was marrying his son. The power of their lineage would ripple out for generations.

Still, she had broken her promise to Hagath. Even if it was a promise she never could have kept.

"Is the king at his hometree?" Eiryss asked without turning.

"Yes," Vallay said. "He is waiting for you in his library."

The king's hometree came into detail up ahead. Something seemed off. The sentinels under the archway were gone. She'd learned to be wary over the last few months. Her sigils flared and she wove a quick armor and settled it over herself. She turned. "Where—"

Vallay was right behind her. She thrust, her knife skittering against Eiryss's armor. Eiryss gaped down at the weapon in the woman's hand. A hand that gleamed with sigils.

Servants didn't have sigils.

Before she could process what had just happened, Vallay's magic slammed against Eiryss's. The force of it shattered her hastily constructed armor. Shadows swarmed Eiryss.

Chaos.

Vallay was using chaos. Eiryss had to stop the shadows before they touched her. She flared *rule*, pulling every scrap of magic she could reach. A shield formed in her hand.

Vallay scrambled behind the two guards, who brought up their own magical shields. Eiryss thrust outward, her magic pulsing. It slammed into the two guards and sent them careening through the air. One slammed into Vallay, scattering shadows, dispelling her weave. Arms and legs windmilling for purchase, they toppled over the side of the bridge. The men's bodies thudded as they hit the forest floor far below.

Vallay launched to her feet. She gasped, knife clattering to the bridge. Instead of attacking, she pulled out a canteen and poured water onto a shallow wound at her wrist, blood dripping from her fingers. Tensed for attack, Eiryss gaped at her as the woman staggered a step, her face going deathly pale.

"No," Vallay said, voice emotionless even as foam drew a pale line from the corner of her mouth. The blade—she'd cut herself with her own poisoned blade.

She'd nearly been assassinated. By the king's most trusted servant. Vallay must have been in league with the Alamantians from the start. A traitor, just like Eiryss's father. "Who sent you to kill me?"

Vallay turned wide eyes to Eiryss, as if she didn't understand.

Eiryss gritted her teeth. "Who are you working for? Who was my father working for?"

Vallay's eyes rolled back and she collapsed, her body shaking uncontrollably.

The missing guards. The king—Ramass—they could be in danger. Eiryss sprinted past the unmanned archway, into the tree, across a bridge, and up a level. Shadows moved beyond the library's cracked door. Glass shattered. She forced her tired body to move faster, harder.

"Curse you!" Ramass roared.

"It had to be done," the king said.

Eiryss staggered to a halt and her knees nearly buckled in relief. They were alive. But the danger had not yet passed. She hurried forward stealthier now, eyes wary for danger.

"How could you? She was like a daughter to you," Ramass sobbed.

"I did it for you," the king said smoothly. "So that someday you will be king."

Eiryss's steps faltered. Something about this was wrong. She couldn't think what. Couldn't think. She started shaking, her body hot and cold, fingers freezing.

"I would have married her!" Ramass said. "Why couldn't that have been enough?"

Bile rose in her throat.

Eiryss inched closer, peering through the doorway. The scent of alcohol burned her nostrils and made her eyes water. Shattered glass littered the floor, crunching under Ramass's boots as he paced. His face was flushed, hair a mess of curls. Hagath rocked back and forth before the brazier.

"You said you'd leave her alone if Ramass married her," Hagath accused.

Ramass sank to his knees and clenched handfuls of his hair. "You killed her. How could you?"

Vallay—the king had sent Vallay to kill Eiryss.

Not the Alamantians.

Zannok.

Zannok, who was as dear to her as her own family.

Tears blurred her vision. How could he? *Why?*

The king sat in his chair, his body sagging as if burdened with a weight too heavy to bear. "I will choose my kingdom over a single life every time." His gaze met his son's. "As I did with Ahlyn."

"And Undrad," Hagath said bitterly.

Her father. The king had killed her father. And the princess. It had never been the Alamantians.

The Alamantians hadn't started this war.

Which meant her father hadn't been in league with them. The king had known he had been innocent—that *she* had been innocent—and killed him anyway. Light, Eiryss never thought anything could hurt her as much as watching her father die. But this... this was just as bad.

Zannok had comforted her—hugged her. Bought back their furniture and clothes, things that never should have been taken. Allowed her family, her father, to take the fall for the king's own treasonous murder.

Why?

Light! Why? She wanted to scream it. Charge into the library and kill him. The heat and hot sickness coursing through her begged her to do it. But she was not the impetuous child she'd once been. No, the king had killed that part of her too.

She was no match for him. Not until her magic surpassed his and she became queen. And when she did, she would see justice wrought upon him. Light, for the sake of her father and mother. For Kit. For the little boy with the blackened toes. The dead girl behind the hospital. Even Iritraya.

All dead because of him.

"Eiryss was never a threat to your kingdom!" Ramass cradled his head in his hands. "You swore you wouldn't hurt her. Never her."

Eiryss turned her gaze to the man she loved. The tension between him and his father. All the times Ramass had tried to keep her away from the king. Light, he'd been willing to marry her to keep her safe. But he hadn't been willing to reveal his father's treachery.

And Hagath—no wonder she was broken. The weight of her guilt would have broken anyone.

Eiryss hated them.

"It's done now." The king wiped the tears from his cheeks. "We will grieve, but it will be better in the end."

Eiryss eased back, her mind shutting down. All she knew was she had to run. And she had nowhere to run to.

CHAPTER 31

BETRAYAL

Eiryss's sigils burned with cold that spread through her like frost. Her body took over, mind shutting down. It wasn't safe in the trees. She took a line down, her feet hitting the frozen ground with a shock that reverberated up her ankles and into her knees. From the corner of her eye, she saw the jumbled bodies of the guards she'd killed lying abandoned in the street. The houses looked abandoned—as if the people wanted nothing to do with the dead king's guards.

She took off running, ducking between houses and around trees, not knowing where she was going, just that she had to get away.

When her lungs burned and her lips tingled, she forced herself to stop. To think. All around her, the trees formed a perfect circle, their boughs laced together. She was in the Arbor circle. Where Ramass had told her she would be safe. Where he'd touched her. Made love to her. And he'd *known*. She leaned over and vomited on the ground. It splashed her shoes and the hems of her pants. She wiped her mouth with the back of her hand.

When she straightened up, he was there, just inside the line of trees. His cheeks were red, his breaths coming in puffs.

He braced his hands against his legs. "Light, you're alive. You remembered."

Someone must have found Vallay. Maybe the guards. He'd come for her. Come to finish her off.

How many times had they run from trouble together? How many times had they hidden in the boughs of a tree or in the eroded bank by the creek that cut through her father's estate, their hands over their mouths to smother their giggles? Ramass was never the one she ran from. He was the one she ran beside. Sixteen years of instinct made her want to move to him. Embrace him. Instead, she double-checked her armor and stepped back.

He watched her, his expression shifting from relief to grim realization. "You know."

"That your father murdered the princess and let my father take the blame? Or that you lied to me—all of you lied to me." Ramass, her brother, Hagath. Even Vicil.

She remembered hot summer days swimming in the lake with a spear in hand, fish wriggling on the line tied to her hip.

Ramass flinched as if she'd struck him. "I never had a choice. None of us did."

"Why?" Had the king threatened them?

He shook his head. "It doesn't matter. What matters is that you need to run."

All her life, Ramass had been her safety. Her best friend. What was he now? "Run where?"

Shouting came from the other side of the ring. His head whipped toward the sound and he started toward it. "I'll try to lead them away. Use the Silver Tree. Like you did before."

"Come with me." She didn't mean to say it. But she couldn't imagine losing him. Couldn't imagine losing hot summer days in the lake. Racing down the snowy hill on a sled, the wind stinging her cheeks. Glittering gowns and delicacies as she'd danced in his arms. He was a part of her, and she no more knew how to lose him than to lose a limb.

He froze, his body rigid. "I can't, Eiryss."

"But I love you." Light, she sounded like a desperate child, but she couldn't seem to stop herself.

He wouldn't face her. "I—I never loved you. Not like that. I was only marrying you to try to keep you safe. I'm sorry."

Just like that, the sound of laughter and the dazzling light of adventure snuffed out forever. *Light. Oh, light.*

He took off at a run toward the milling voices, taking all the happiness she'd ever had with him. He looked back only once, when he reached the edge of the trees. "Run, Eiryss."

It was all ash and dust now. Nothing was left.

No. There was something left. Her heart still beat in her chest. And she knew that if she didn't keep moving, she would die. And she couldn't die. Not until she'd saved the boy with the blackened toes and the girl without shoes. She closed her eyes, her breath puffing around her face in a moist cloud. She rested her hand on her monarch sigil. The sigil that had tried to warn her not to reveal that she was a princess.

Where can I go?

She felt a tug back the way she'd come. Away from the voices that were even now moving in the opposite direction. She followed that tug. She paused at the edge of the ring and, seeing no one, darted away. Movement inside one of the houses. She was being watched and had been from the moment she left the trees. And her mantle would make her easy to track. She took it off, abandoning it in the crook of roots, covering it with snow and bits of leaves. She stole a moth-eaten blanket from an empty house, wrapping it around her fine coat.

She pulled her hood over her notable hair and forced herself to keep her head level and move with purpose. To look like a woman who belonged instead of one on the run. She took a step to skirt the king's tree. But the magic tugged her back into the same direction—south. an instinct.

The closer she came to the perimeter, the more the after-shocks from the attacks on the vault drummed against her, so strong it forced sound in her lungs. She began to recognize her surroundings. The melted mud on the huts. The sound of crying children and the smell of death. And she knew where the Silver Tree had led her.

Head down, she hurriedly pushed open the door and stepped into the warmth of the hospital—warmth where the patients' bodies were mottled with cold. Only then did she realize how cold she was. She walked blindly down the rows of sick, their eyes following her silently. She only stopped when hands grasped her arms.

"Eiryss?" Illin placed her wrist on her forehead.

The woman had called her name numerous times, Eiryss realized. She swayed on her feet, unable to think.

"You're in shock." Illin's strong hands wrapped around her shoulders, tugging her to her tiny room with her tiny cot. She wet a cloth and wiped at the soot on Eiryss's face.

Eiryss stared at her blackened hands. Light, she had only left the battle an hour or so ago.

"By the light, what happened to you?"

She'd lost everyone she'd ever loved. She was alone. More alone than she'd ever been. Eiryss opened her mouth, words clogging up and bursting free in an inhuman cry. She collapsed, fingers digging into the packed earth, her eyes squeezed shut. She rocked back and forth as everything shattered.

Illin knelt before her, both hands on her shoulders. "You have to tell me what happened. I can't help you if you don't tell me."

"The king—he tried to kill me!"

"Light save us," Illin gasped. "Are you sure?"

"I heard him admit it." She covered her mouth with her hand. "Hagath," she whispered. "Hagath and Ramass knew."

Illin stiffened and murmured something that might have been a curse or a plea.

Eiryss barely heard them. "They knew the king killed Ahlyn. He knew, and he ordered my father's death anyway. My father must have known. Why didn't he fight—why didn't he tell me the truth? Instead, he lied. Why would—"

She gasped. The king must have threatened their family— threatened *her*. And when Eiryss had shown up in her father's room, she'd given the king the proof he needed to accuse her of treason as well. Unless her father admitted to a crime he hadn't committed.

Her father had died to save her life.

He'd never betrayed anyone. He'd been the honorable, wonderful man she'd always known him to be.

The king had poisoned that too.

"Light, I'm going to see him hang for this. See his body fed to a nest of gilgads."

Illin frowned. "You're not safe here."

A bitter, manic laugh burst from her mouth. "I'm not safe anywhere."

"Go to the enchantresses. They'll protect you."

Tria had offered. Sworn she would see her safe. "She would try. But if the king attacked her, she couldn't keep me safe. And he already turned the nobility against my family once. If he did it again, it would mean a civil war." How many people would die? And in the end, so would she.

Illin was silent a beat. "You're safe with the Alamantians."

Eiryss gaped at her. "They're the enemy."

"Are they?"

"Light. Light!" She pressed the heel of her hand into her forehead, which pounded—she'd fought all through the night, and her body felt the strain. "They were never our enemies, but they are now."

Illin poured headache powder into a cup and handed it to her. "They're Zannok's enemy. Not yours."

She stilled as another thought spun through her head. There had been four people there when Ahlyn was killed. Hagath, Ramass, and... her brother. Vicil too. And they had all testified that her father had attacked the king. Obviously, much more had gone on that night—long after Eiryss's vision of Ahlyn's death had ended.

The world spun around her. Her brother. Her own brother—her father's son—had known the king was the true murderer. And he'd blamed her anyway.

And Hagath—the king had nearly poisoned his own daughter. And yet she'd kept his secrets. They had all lied. Watched as Eiryss and her family had been systematically destroyed. As their kingdom had gone to war. As the dead and displaced had flooded the remaining cities.

"Why?" she cried.

Illin tipped the cup up until Eiryss drank it. As soon as the moisture touched her mouth, she sucked the bitter liquid down—she hadn't realized how thirsty she'd been. Illin tucked warm blankets around her and viciously rubbed her chest. "I know you've had a shock. But they'll be looking for you. You have to go."

Go.

To the Alamantians. Her enemy.

Above, the vault thrummed. "The city is sealed off," Eiryss said.

"Against Alamantians."

Not against Eiryss. The vault would recognize her sigils. It would let her through.

"My own," she faltered and tried again, "my own people would kill me before I ever reached them." And if they didn't, the Alamantians would.

Illin gripped her hands. "You have the magic of the Silver Tree inside you. It would take more than an army to destroy you."

It would take a king.

"There's nowhere you can hide from him," Illin went on. "Not here. This is your only chance."

"How will the Alamantians know who I am? That I don't mean them any harm?"

Illin shook her head. "You don't have a choice."

She's right. Light. Eiryss closed her eyes. She pushed the betrayal down; it cut her, the wound digging deeper, but she did it anyway.

Illin pulled her to her feet. She came back with a steaming mug of watery tea. "Keep your eye on your destination. Don't let anyone stop you."

Eiryss spilled half the cup. She hadn't realized she'd been shaking. She downed the rest. The heat did nothing for the gaping wound inside her, but it warmed her. Illin wrapped a ragged shawl around her head and led her to the side door—the same door the bodies bracketed in two long rows.

They slipped into the dead and cold, pushing through the huts with their heads down and their steps quick. Illin stopped within sight of the perimeter trees and one of the smaller side gates that led out of the city.

Eiryss stared at the gate. "How will I ever get through?"

"All trees obey the Silver Tree."

Eiryss double-checked her armor. She would not risk enclosing herself in a dome, not when the sound of her playing would bring her unwanted gazes. She lit her sigils and wove a small dome, just large enough to hold in her hands. At the first sign of trouble, she would throw it around herself. Running would only draw attention. She eased beyond the last of the huts, into a place that, judging by the still fountain and bare thorns, had once been a garden.

She paused before leaving the protection of the garden. Her gaze never wavering from the gate, she stepped out into the bareness of the empty cobblestones.

When she'd crossed halfway, one of the king's guards stepped out from behind the gatehouse and strode out to intercept her. How had he known where she would go? She turned and took a step back, but soldiers left the cover of trees, blocking her. Trapping her. She tossed up the dome and flared it around her.

She faced the soldier, who had settled before the gates, his silver sword and shield in hand. She tied off her dome and checked her weaves, *rule* pouring rivers of magic into it. She stopped about ten steps from him.

"Let me pass."

"Eiryss," the king called from the walkway above, "daughter of Emlon and Undrad, you are hereby condemned for treason, the murder of my servant and two guards, as well as the attempted murder of your king."

The king was too far away to make out the features of his face. But she knew it. Had known it all her life. Had watched the silver thread through his red hair. The lines bracketing his mouth. Had loved him.

Light save her, she still did.

His magic slammed against her dome. She recognized the taste and touch of his *rule*—the same magic pulsing through her. A magic tainted by shadows.

"Admit your guilt and your death will be swift!" The shadows in his magic crawled over her dome like thorned vines. She recognized *chaos*'s dark influence. He would break down her dome and attack her with shadows. Make her into a monster who would put her own knife in her chest.

At her breast, the silver leaf grew unbearably cold. So cold that ferns of frost spread across her skin. His magic ate at her own like acid—the light and shadows digging at her from all sides confirmed the undeniable truth: the king was stronger.

"You murdered Princess Ahlyn! You framed and murdered my father! As you tried to murder me!"

The soldiers atop the wall shifted, a low throated murmur spreading through them.

"I treated you like my own child. When all along, you conspired against me!" Lies. The king played a few notes and spun his orb, preparing to throw it at her.

His assault on her dome was taking longer than he expected. He was going to kill her outright before she could condemn him further.

Just then, the vault behind him bulged and snapped back. The thrum blasted the soldiers, knocking them against each other. The king stumbled as one bumped into him, his magic spinning out of control and striking to her right.

Eiryss had this one chance. This one opportunity. She unbuttoned her coat, letting it slide down her arms to the ground. She grasped her tunic on either side of the collar and ripped it just enough to bare her breasts and the spreading branches of the Silver Tree.

"I am chosen of the Silver Tree. I condemn you, Zannok, for your crimes against my family and my kingdom. I condemn you for stealing sigils from the Silver Tree." *Rule* pulsed brighter, silver light cutting distinct lines through the ash and dust raised from the king's botched shot. The shadows were stronger than ever, carrying a dark taint she could taste—like rot in her mouth.

And if the Alamantian king hadn't murdered the princess, then... "You poisoned the Silver Tree." He had tainted the magic. Why? It had only weakened him.

The king gathered another orb. She pointed at him. "The poison that has infected the Silver Tree did not come from the Alamantians—but from your own foul deeds!"

The king threw the orb as his guard charged her, his sword raised, his face determined.

The orb struck, enveloping her in light so cold it burned and overwhelmed her magic, eating away the last of her dome. Dying stars fell into silver ash. The guard stabbed at her. His sword skittered off her armor, damaging it. She threw herself to the right, rolling and lunging to her feet. Running, she grasped her magic, started to weave.

She felt his steps behind her. Felt the heat of him. His hands buried in her hair. They fell, rolling and tangling. She tried to remember her father's lessons. Tried to hook her arm around his throat.

He wrenched her to the side and straddled her.

She held out her arms to defend herself. His sword cocked back. And then he paused. She gasped, her eyes going from his sword to his anguished face. His gaze was on her chest. On the sigil there. He reached out, resting a bare hand on the naked skin between her breast. "It's real."

She managed to nod. His head came up. "Then the Silver Tree chose you." He pushed off her and faced the soldiers coming from the trees. "Run, princess!"

"Kill her now!" Zannok screamed from above.

Eiryss didn't know this man, but she didn't question him. She was up and running, her magic bursting to life around her.

"All trees obey the Silver Tree," Illin's words echoed through her head.

Eiryss hastily wove a web enchantment and thrust it forward. It niggled across the closed gates. The tree communicated in memories. So she remembered the gates opening before, when she'd first come to the city. The gates gleamed, silver filigree coming to life on the scrolling panels. They swung apart, revealing the shuddering vault and the dark line of Alamantians beyond.

She passed beneath the gates and came out on the other side. The Alamantian orbs shifted, turning toward her. She slowed enough to weave her dome into place. She thought her magic strong enough to resist them. At least for a time.

Then she was careening forward. She slammed hard into the ice and ash before the gates, her vision dimming before returning with a snap. All around her, she tasted the king's magic—the rot and minerals of the Silver Tree. Recognized his orb's fraying weave. She hadn't had time to tie off her magic from the dome before he'd hit her. She heaved breath into lungs empty of life and managed to roll over as another orb arced toward her.

She didn't have time to weave another dome. Didn't have time to do more than scream.

A second orb slammed into the first, knocking it off course. Earth exploded around her. She curled up, head under her hands, as dirt and rocks pelted her. The world went silent and still.

Far above, the enchantresses on the balconies formed orbs of their own. Tria stood at the head of the one on her right, her hair whipping as she shouted orders to her enchantresses. The walkways were a mass of soldiers. Some fought to break into the enchantresses, who were sealed safely behind their domes.

Safe and trapped.

Twice they had saved her. If she kept running, she would abandon them to the king. No matter how corrupted he'd become, he still held the magic of the Silver Tree. They couldn't stand against him.

Not for long.

Tria waved her onward. "Go, you great idiot!"

Staying wouldn't save them. It would only ensure her death. She scrambled to her feet, weaving her weakened magic into another dome spell, and ran.

CHAPTER

SIEGE

The vault grew closer, the shimmering air shifting silver in her periphery. Eiryss hit it and for a moment hung suspended. It stretched and warped, the tang of crystals sharp on her tongue. The magic reached inside her. Recognized her sigils.

Then she was through.

An Alamantian orb slammed into her dome. Depleted as her magic was, it shuddered and broke, ash crumbling. She ducked behind a tree, gasping. On the wall, Valynthian soldiers and enchantresses turned against each other.

Light. Light, how has it come to this?

Her magic seeped back like a river steadily rising during a rainstorm. Until it returned, she was trapped. She peeked around to see two orbs forming on her right and left. This tree wouldn't shield her from that.

She'd come all this way. Defeated all these obstacles. In the end, she was going to die anyway. She pressed her amulet and flute to her skin. Her father. Her mother. She would be with them soon.

"I'm sorry I believed his lies, Father." She squeezed the amulet and waited to die. One of its branches slid into her skin. Magic rushed into her. Nothing like the magic of *rule*. But certainly more than Eiryss's sigils could manage.

Warm and familiar, the magic flowed through her. Her mother's magic. One hand occupied with holding the amulet, Eiryss played her flute, the dome forming around her seconds before the tree exploded. She ducked reflexively, her arms wrapping around her head as the remnants of an orb crackled around her.

When the destruction stopped, she lay in the center of a crater made of the remains of a shattered tree. The dome gleamed perfectly around her. Her own magic rose in a steady tide. Still gripping the amulet, she wove more magic into the dome and moved forward. Sticks and debris parted before her as she approached the enemy army.

Before her were neatly regimented rows of soldiers in magical armor and riots of color. In the back, enchanters clustered around a raised dais, where weavers channeled the magic into orbs that crackled with energy.

The nearest enchanter group threw another orb. Her mouth went dry as she watched it arc toward her. It exploded across her dome in a crackle of energy that blinded her. Her magic was stronger now and held. After the third one, the attacks stopped coming.

The remnants of her tattered tunic hung around her waist. Knowing the monarch sigil might be the only thing to save her life, she steeled herself and marched toward the Alamantian front line. The enchantresses watched her warily, their swords and shields firmly in place. None moved to attack her. Their enchanters had clearly failed. The soldiers parted before her until an enchantress stood, blocking her path.

Habbia.

Eiryss's stomach did a sick twist, but she forced her expression to remain steady. "You never hung our children from the trees." It wasn't a question.

The woman snorted in derision. "What do you want?"

"I will speak to your king," she said simply.

"You will speak to me." Habbia studied the sigil at her chest in disbelief. "Who are you?"

Eiryss lifted her chin. "I am Princess Eiryss. I've come to negotiate peace with King Dray."

Habbia's head came up. She whispered something to a woman at her side, who shouted an order. The woman mounted a horse and took off toward the back of the encampment, soldiers scattering out of her way.

They waited. Hundreds, perhaps thousands of eyes watched Eiryss. She'd always hated attention. Now, she found herself too wrung out to care.

Finally, a company of horsemen appeared. At their head rode King Dray. He wore his peaked mantle dripping with fire opals. Beneath, the green serpent peeked out from his coat. His long black hair was braided. His piercing eyes fixed on her. Then at her chest. She gripped her ruined clothing to keep from raising her arms to cover herself.

He dropped from his dappled gray stallion. When he reached Habbia's side, she leaned in and spoke low—no doubt informing Dray that Eiryss had killed the woman's father. He spoke back just as low. Her face reddened, and she grew more animated, gesturing wildly to Eiryss.

Dray held out his hand. His own sigils flared, his magic brushing against Eiryss's. She felt the raw power of it, matured and much stronger than hers. Easily the equal to King Zannok's, and therefore, far more powerful than her own. "You're the princess."

"My name is Eiryss."

Dray's head came up. "I remember. Undrad's daughter. The man was not a traitor to your people."

"And you didn't kill our princess. King Zannok did."

He glanced behind her at the chaos going on atop the walls. "Is that why your people have suddenly turned on each other?"

"I have come to negotiate terms."

He raised an eyebrow and glanced behind her. "Not on behalf of your king."

She stiffened. "He's not my king." Not anymore.

Dray nodded slowly. "I'm listening."

She couldn't help the shudder that pulsed through her. She held out her hands. "Cease attacking my people, withdraw into your own lands, and I will be your prisoner."

He stepped as close as her dome allowed. She was the granddaughter of a queen and would be a queen in her own right soon enough. She straightened under his scrutiny and never broke eye contact—even when his gaze lingered on the sigil between her breasts. She wished she could read his intent.

He held out his hand, an open invitation. "Drop your dome, princess. No one here will harm you."

"If that's true, why are your enchanters still trying to break it down?"

"Commander Mav," Dray called without taking his gaze from her. "The rest of you, withdraw your weapons and get back in formation!"

"Your Majesty," Mav said under his breath. He was a handsome man in his mid-fifties with one arm missing. "You don't know what she'll do."

Dray met her gaze. "I can handle her, and she knows it." There was a subtle warning in his words.

Mav barked a command. The attacks against Eiryss's dome halted.

"Cease all attacks and hold a defensive pattern," Dray said.

The command went out. All up and down the line, the magic slowly faded back into those who had created it.

"Just so we're clear," she murmured. "I won't marry you. Ever."

He grunted. "Marrying Ahlyn was never my idea, but our Arbor thought it might stave off war."

Double-checking her armor, Eiryss released her dome. When no one attacked her, she relaxed a fraction.

Dray shrugged of his coat and held it out to her. "I don't need a prisoner, Eiryss. What I need is a warrior."

All at once, Eiryss realized how cold she was. She snatched the coat, suppressing a moan as the borrowed warmth surrounded her. From behind the king, Habbia glared at her.

Eiryss tried to ignore it. "What are you suggesting?"

He followed her gaze, his expression contemplative. "I'm suggesting we press our advantage."

Her shoulders sagged. For so long, she'd thought of the Alamantians as her sworn enemy, the capital city of Umber their lair, and their king the worst kind of monster.

All of that was a lie, but that still didn't make Dray a good man. "You want me to attack my own people?"

"I want you to come to the aid of your enchantresses."

She hesitated.

He pointed to the city. "Your forces are divided. The two of us together are more than a match for Zannok."

She'd failed to attack once, and it had only caused more deaths. "How do I know I can trust you?"

He held out his arms. "Brush your magic against mine."

She did so, his magic warm and steady beneath hers. The magic suddenly went out. He stood before her with no protection. She could kill him before he could so much as raise his armor.

"Some risks are worth taking," he breathed. She thought she sensed the smallest thread of fear in him.

He was asking her to trust him. She would never fully trust again. Ramass's words echoed through her, *"We do what we must."*

She took a steadying breath. "I will fight with you."

He stepped up beside her. "First, you bring down the vault."

He signaled, and the Alamantians lifted their instruments to their mouths and played. Eiryss and Dray wove a dome over their entire company, the combined magic of the Silver and White Trees making it gleam with gold and silver, like the colors of her wedding that would never be.

Someone brought him another coat.

When they reached the vault, Dray simply said, "Take it down."

She reached out with her hand, *rule* flaring. As she had with the city gates, she imagined the vault fading. It flickered to nothing.

"Advance," Dray called.

Under an impenetrable dome of gold and silver magic, the Alamantian soldiers marched to the front of the gate, Eiryss and Dray in the center.

Above them, Tria leaned over the barrier. "I've ordered my enchantresses to stand down. We are at your disposal, Princess."

He glanced up at Tria. "Add your magic to ours, enchantress. We shall create a vault to entrap those who resist."

Face grim, Tria called out the order. On a scale that had not happened in decades, Alamantian and Valynthian magic melded, the vault full of dancing colors and light. It was the most beautiful thing she'd ever seen.

"Now we shrink it," Dray said.

Long minutes passed as they advanced, slowly, steadily— the vault just before them. The Valynthian army was under Ramass's command. But without the enchantresses to protect them, the soldiers could do little better than retreat.

Mav whispered something to Dray. The king turned to her. "Tria wants to meet with you. She has some enchantresses and soldiers with her."

Eiryss nodded.

Tria jogged up, a pair of enchantresses flanking her and a dozen guards at her back. She shot the Alamantians a distrustful look. "You should have your own people with you, Eiryss."

It would certainly help her Valynthians believe she was their princess. "Do you trust them?" Eiryss asked with a meaningful look at the guards and enchantresses Tria had brought.

"They're loyal to the enchantresses," Tria said. "Loyal to you."

Eiryss motioned, and the soldiers took up defensive formations around her. They marched on.

She leaned into Dray. "You did not kill Ahlyn or poison our tree, so why did you strike first?"

Dray stiffened. "War was coming no matter what I did. The chaos of the princess's death gave me a clear advantage. It's one of the reasons I'm winning, so you see it worked."

Habbia approached them. "We have a pocket of Alamantians trapped in one of the trees, sire. They demand to see proof of the princess for themselves."

Of course they would want to know if the Silver Tree really had chosen Eiryss.

Dray shot Eiryss a questioning look.

"Where?" Eiryss asked.

Habbia pointed. Eiryss motioned for her new guards to form up around her and climbed the stairs. Behind her, King Dray played a horn decorated with gold leafing. Almost instantly, layers of armor fell into place around her. His magic felt familiar in a way she didn't understand. Shaking away the feeling, she followed a soldier into a library, where an enchantress had formed a dome around two dozen Alamantians.

Eiryss unbuttoned her borrowed coat so her sigil stood out and related the king's treachery. "Swear allegiance to me and you will not be harmed."

The enchantress's face fell. "It's true what they're saying... Our king killed Princess Ahlyn?" Word must have spread quickly.

Throat thick with emotion, Eiryss could only nod. The woman unraveled her dome. She glanced around nervously before dropping to one knee. One by one they swore their allegiance and took their places among the ranks fighting for Eiryss. All but three.

A father and his sons. "I will not betray my king," the father said.

No one made a move. Dray watched her as if waiting for her to do something.

Mouth drawn in a tight line, she motioned to the enchantress who'd just sworn her allegiance. "Bind them and put them under guard."

She waited to see what the woman would do. If she would pass this test. The woman's face grew pained, but she nodded.

Dray immediately drew Eiryss away. Mav waited for them at the bridge that led toward the heart of the city. "A dozen more pockets of resistance, Sire. All of them demanding to see the truth for themselves."

Eiryss tried to ignore the sound of a struggle coming from behind her. "Tria?" The woman stepped up beside her. "Send in your enchantresses. If they won't believe them, entrap them until we can figure this out."

Tria bowed and hurried away.

"This is going to take forever," Eiryss murmured. Rature had been right. She was not built for war. Perhaps no one was.

Eiryss and Dray moved along the bridges, going to those few who would not trust even the highest-ranking enchantresses.

Those who would not swear allegiance were set upon by Eiryss's enchantresses.

That night, they reached the heart of the city and the king's hometree. Under the banner of a white flag, Eiryss met with representatives of the council—save Vicil, who was missing. Upon seeing her sigil and hearing Tria's account, they threw their lot in with hers. The war was over.

Soldiers charged through the king's hometree.

He and his children were nowhere to be found.

CHAPTER 33

COPPERBILLS

Three Weeks Later

An impenetrable envoy of Alamantians and Valynthians stretched up and down the long road. Nestled deep in furs on a sleigh that cut through the snow, Eiryss watched the capital city of the Alamant, Umber, take shape. Unlike the drab destruction of her own home city, this sacred city shone with colors: the deep green of the trees, the vibrant feathers of the birds, and the luminescent scales of the fish that swam between the buttressed roots.

A paradise. One uncorrupted by the shadow of an evil king.

Tears stung Eiryss's eyes at the destruction this one man had caused. She rubbed at the familiar ache of her sigil. It had grown to cover most of her chest and half her belly. The topmost branches nearly touched her collarbone. When they did, she would be queen. Zannok's magic would fade.

At the shoreline, the sleigh came to a stop.

King Dray waited for her. He held out a hand to assist as she stepped down. "Any word on your brother?"

She shook her head. "But I managed to convince Dystin to swear his army's allegiance." His was the last army besides the remnants of Ramass's army. "Any word on Hanama?"

He frowned. "No change."

King Zannok had fled back to Hanama along with his children. Ture and Vicil had not been found. Eiryss wondered every day if they were dead. Why they had betrayed her. If they were betraying her still.

Hanama was swathed in impenetrable shadow vines—ones Eiryss was sure had been cast by Zannok's *chaos* units, as every single woman with a chaos sigil had disappeared, including Wyndyn, Balendora, and Namishka. The people had taken to calling them copperbills after a bird with a habit of stealing things that didn't belong to it. A fitting insult, as the women with *chaos* had all taken thorns never meant for them.

After her coronation, Eiryss intended to take back what was hers. She intended to rescue all of them from the king's clutches. "Are both our councils and Arbors in agreement?"

Arbor Enderlee had escaped the city with most of its people, having been warned by Tria before Zannok's arrival. Both women were in Umber even now.

"They better be," Dray grumbled. "They've been arguing for weeks." He tucked her hand under the crook of his elbow and led her down a wooden dock and onto a boat.

Working with Dray over the last few days, she'd come to appreciate his dedication to peace at any cost. That determination reminded her of Ramass. Light, she missed him and hated herself for being so weak.

Eiryss pinched herself hard to keep her emotions in check and stepped into the boat waiting for them. Soldiers pushed away from the dock. She and Dray took an oar and rowed against the current.

They approached the vault—golden instead of silver. The perimeter trees rose behind it—looking nearly identical to the ones around Valynthia. Passing through the vault tasted the same. Or nearly so. Instead of an echo of starlight, she swore she could taste sunshine.

Heat instantly baked against her chilled skin. She shed her coat and gloves and turned her face to the sun, soaking in the warmth. A thread of tension she hadn't known she carried eased, and she released a long breath.

This was not home. But it *felt* like it.

When she opened her eyes, Dray was watching her again. He looked quickly away.

She scrutinized the White Tree as it grew larger until it took up most of her field of vision. Opalescence that shifted to gold at the periphery. Like the Silver Tree, shapes moved in the depths. Rainbows danced across the surface like light through water.

No wonder the Alamantians liked their color so much.

The boat turned before it could reach the White Tree and slid into a hometree well-guarded by soldiers in the mottled uniform of the Alamantians. The serpent on their mantles declared them the king's guard.

Dray held out a hand to help her from the boat. "I'm sure you'd like a chance to clean up."

She could already hear the arguing going on above. "I'd rather finish this."

His brows rose. "As you wish."

They rode a carriage to the main level and headed toward the largest platform. Members from both councils as well as the Arbors filled the common room. The Arbors were seated on either side of the dais.

Hands clasped before her, Arbor Enderlee nodded at Eiryss.

Eiryss's mouth tightened. She'd not seen the Arbor since she'd left Valynthia with Ramass at her side. The woman had known something of Zannok's betrayal—her warning not to go with Ramass as well as Tria trying to keep her away from the king were evidence of that. But she clearly hadn't trusted Eiryss. Hadn't trusted anyone close to the king.

Side by side, Eiryss and Dray crossed the room. Voices fell silent as they passed. Eiryss sat on the ornate chairs Dray had procured for them.

"Dray tells me you have reached a consensus," she said.

"Mostly," Enderlee muttered.

A document was brought before her. Eiryss scanned it. It detailed an immediate cessation of hostilities, an expansive trade agreement, even a common currency (her idea). An entire page dealt with the coalition of their two armies to bring Zannok and his copperbills down.

She turned to the last page and saw the final paragraph. Her eyes widened in disbelief. She handed it to Dray. "Did you know about this?" She tried very hard to keep the accusation out of her voice.

"What?" He took the document from her, his eyes widening before locking in on the Alamantian Arbor, a man named Vesos. The man was fat and round—the kind of man who would be easier to jump over than walk around. "I told you to take this out."

Arbor Vesos lifted liver-spotted hands. "And I told you I would think about it."

Eiryss launched to her feet and glared at anyone who dared meet her gaze. "I will marry when and whom I wish."

Enderlee wove her sigils into a silver dome around them. Abruptly, outside sounds were cut off. "Neither council will sign it otherwise." The Arbor jabbed a finger in Vesos's direction. "Most especially him."

Vesos pushed his spectacles higher up on his fat little nose. "If you want our people to start acting as one, they must become one. Ruled by a king and queen who are united in all ways."

"Because that turned out so well the last time," Dray said sarcastically.

Vesos peered at them each in turn. "This peace you two have brokered among your people is more tenuous than you know. A spark in the wrong direction and war will flare all of us to dross."

"Oh, stop being so melodramatic," Dray said.

"You want to subject the next pair of monarchs to this barbaric law?" Eiryss huffed.

Vesos leveled her with an even look. "To prevent a future war, yes."

"She is a woman, not a commodity," Enderlee said.

"She's a queen," Vesos said. "As such, her life belongs to her people."

Eiryss shoved up from her chair and paced before the throne. Eventually, Dray stepped up beside her and said softly, "Eiryss?"

She eyed him. He wasn't a bad-looking man, really. He was just so much older. "I don't love you."

He huffed. "Nor I you."

She remembered the Arbor circle. Ramass walking away from her. "It's over, Eiryss."

She rubbed the chill from her arms. "This is a bad idea."

"It could be a marriage in name only," Dray said.

"Not if you want to show a good example to your people." Vesos stood from his chair. "Your coronation and your wedding on the same day. A celebration of our people coming together as one."

Eiryss had already chosen the man she wished to marry. How much worse could this be? "Fine."

Dray passed a hand over his face and muttered something she didn't want to understand. Enderlee's mouth tightened in disapproval, but she banished the dome, which let in the sound of arguing again.

Eiryss marched over to the table, took the pen in hand, and dipped it in ink. She scrawled her name—her first ever as acting queen—and held out the pen to Dray.

Drawn with worry, he took it from her and signed his own name. "You had better have the needed signatures for that peace treaty, Vesos, or I swear I'll remove you from office myself—White Tree or not." He motioned for Eiryss to follow him out.

As soon as they left the main platform, arguments erupted behind them.

"Light, what did I just do?" Eiryss gasped.

Dray looked back at the chaos behind them. "What we had to."

CHAPTER 34

DUSK

Two Weeks Later

"Good morning, Princess."

Eiryss's eyes shot open to find Dray striding across her room. His gaze traced her form appreciatively under the silk sheets. Even though she was to marry him today, she wasn't yet comfortable with that appreciation. She sat up, pulling the blankets over her shift.

Seeming to sense her unease, Dray sat on the edge of the bed, his hands on his knees. "It's an Alamantian tradition for the groom to offer the bride a gift on her wedding morning."

What more could he possibly give her? She already had armoires full of dresses and fine linen uniforms. New jewels to wear every day for a year. Servants. A new mare in a barn just beyond the lake. As well as the barn. And the mansion uphill from it. But every time she opened her armoire or wore jewels, all she could see was blackened toes and rows of frozen dead.

"I'm trying, Eiryss."

She dredged up a smile for him. Dray was a good man. She thought he would make a good husband.

He sighed—she hadn't fooled him. "Just because the wedding is tonight doesn't mean we have to rush things."

Centering herself, she slid across the bed and kissed him. His lips were soft, patient. There was no fire between them. But she'd had enough of fire. She'd settle for kindness. "What is the point of waiting?"

He rested his hand over hers. "As you say, Princess." He smiled an almost shy smile. He lit his magic. Even last week, this would have set her on guard. Now, she just waited patiently.

"Light a sigil."

"Which one?"

"Any you like."

She chose *light*. He took hold of the threads of her magic—as a monarch, he, too, was a weaver—and combined them with hers. The same, aching familiarity washed over her.

"Do you feel that?"

She nodded. "What does it mean?"

"The Silver and White Trees are mates. The magics recognize each other." He traced his fingers down her cheek. "We're stronger together than apart, Eiryss. And not just us, but our people as well."

"You were right all along."

He cocked a grin. "Don't worry. I won't rub it in." Standing, he retrieved her robe from the back of a chair and held it out. "Come now, your gift is very impatient to see you."

"See me?" She stood and wavered a bit, suddenly dizzy.

"Are you all right?"

"Just stood up too fast, I think." And she was starving. She took her robe and settled them around her shoulders. "Who's here to see me?"

"Come in," Dray called.

Her brother stepped into the room. She took a startled step back. "Ture?" The last time she'd seen him, he hadn't cared if he ever saw her again. And that was before she'd found out he'd betrayed her.

He staggered to a halt beside the table, one hand gripping the chair as if to steady himself. "Thank the light," he murmured as if to himself. "Perhaps it's not too late."

"What is he doing here?" Eiryss voice shook.

"Hear him out," Dray said gently.

Ture lifted his hands. "Zannok said he'd kill you and Mother if I didn't spread his lies, Eiryss."

She shook her head. "You killed our father."

Ture flinched. "No. Zannok did. But I took the fall because I knew it would make our family look inculpable."

She rested her hand on *rule.*

"Tell her what really happened that night," Dray said.

Ture took a shaky breath. "Father realized Zannok poisoned the princess. He tried to arrest the king. The king delivered a mortal blow. He held Ramass and me back with his shield."

Hagath wouldn't have been in any shape to challenge him, and Ahlyn was dead. "Why,"—she broke off, her voice shaking—"Why did you blame me for Father's death? You knew it wasn't my fault."

"I thought I had saved his life—my silence for my family's safety, which included Father's. But when you showed up in his room…"

"The deal was off," Eiryss finished for him. "And it was easier to blame me than yourself." He flinched. The anguish. The weight he so obviously carried. "What happened to you? Where have you been? We couldn't find you after your army surrendered."

"I was taken captive and kept underground," he said.

"How did you escape?" she asked.

"I didn't." He choked. "Hagath let me go."

Not Ramass. Eiryss went to the window and looked out at the White Tree.

Dray came to stand beside him. "Can we trust him?"

"I don't know."

"Are you armored?"

She wasn't. She lit her sigils and wove armor around herself.

Dray looked over his shoulder at her brother. "Do you want me to stay or go?"

She wasn't comfortable with Dray seeing her emotional. Not yet. "I'd like to speak with him alone."

"I'll be just outside the door. Keep your armor up." He gave Ture a hard look and then left.

"I was a fool," Eiryss said. "For not seeing through Zannok's deception. I should have trusted Father." Not Ramass and the treacherous king.

If Ture noted her armor, he said nothing. "There's nothing foolish about trusting someone who had always been trustworthy. Someone you loved."

She closed her eyes as the pain flared all over again. "What about Hagath?"

"The king kept her isolated except for those he trusted most. Even sick as she was, she nearly escaped him to warn the council. He had her moved to Trapendale, where he could control her better." He closed his eyes, hand going through his hair, more silver than blond now. "Only when the king threatened her with my life did she agree to keep his secrets."

They'd been the best of friends since they were children, same as Eiryss and Ramass. "Why didn't any of you tell me?"

"He would have killed you, Eiryss. We tried to keep you out of it. Hagath and I were both furious with Ramass for letting you into his army."

That explained why Hagath had been so angry at Ramass.

"I've done things... Eiryss, I've done horrible things. I didn't feel like I had a choice, but..." He choked and fell silent.

Stupid, hot-headed, unforgivable things. "Do you want my forgiveness?" Could she ever give it to him?

He shook his head. "No."

Eiryss studied her brother. The haggardness and hollow cheeks. The color had been robbed from his skin. "When was the last time you slept or ate?"

He looked at her as if surprised she was there. "Dray has seen to me."

She poured herself a glass of water. She'd been so thirsty lately. She sipped it and ate some bread to soothe her upset stomach.

She didn't know what to do with her hands. She ended up folding them and willed them to be still. "What's happening in Hanama? Did you see anything or hear anything?"

He strode to the liquor cabinet, searched the bottles she hadn't touched, and poured himself a drink. "I was kept underground. Hagath released me outside of the city and told me to run. She seemed afraid."

Eiryss dug her nails into her hands to drive away her unwelcome thoughts. "Why didn't she come with you?"

"I don't know." He drained the glass. "Do you still have Mother's amulet?"

She tugged at the cord, pulled it free of her robes, and held the amulets in her hand.

His hands shook as he laid the glass so carefully down on the cabinet. "Never take either off. Promise me."

"Why are you afraid?" she breathed.

"If you had seen what I have..." He crossed the room to her.

She resisted the urge to back away from him.

Expression dark, he reached for her then seemed to catch himself. Moving slowly, carefully, he lifted Mother's amulet. "I need you to understand the things I'm not saying. The things I can't say."

What was that supposed to mean? "Ture, do you know something? Zannok's plans?"

He rubbed his mouth, callouses scraping across his scruffy cheeks. "The darkness…"

The amulet dropped against her chest with a thump. His face went a vivid shade of red and he choked, as if his air was suddenly gone. She pounded his back. His body locked around a cough, and he gasped in a breath. He panted, sweat sliding down his temples. His gaze went to her before skittering away.

"Are you all right?" He shook his head. She didn't know what to say. What to think. "Can't you just tell me what's wrong?"

He wiped his streaming eyes, gripped her hand, and pulled her after him. "Dray has another surprise."

"What do you mean—"

"Get dressed, and I'll show you."

"Not until you tell me what's going on."

His face reddened. "I can't, Eiryss."

The anguish in his eyes… She breathed out, deciding to let it go. For now. But she would make sure Dray had someone watching her brother at all times. She changed into one of her uniforms and cleaned herself up quickly. He led her to one of the receiving rooms. It was packed with members of her family.

Vicil stepped out from the others. He looked almost as bad as Ture—his eyes hollow and his skin pale—though he hid it infinitely better. "Another queen in the line," her cousin cried.

So Ture hadn't been the only man Hagath had released. *I haven't forgotten about you either, Haggy. I'm coming. Just hold on.*

Everyone cheered. She searched through the families, finding cousins, aunts, uncles. But there were obvious gaps. Missing faces. People who hadn't made it. People like her parents.

367

Then she caught sight of a wrinkled, dear old face. A cry left her throat and she was running, crossing the room in a few strides. She enveloped Belgrave's bony body. He winced, chuckled, and patted her back. "Oh, lady. To see you restored and then some; it does my heart good."

She pulled back to look at him, to search for injuries or weakness. Thankfully, he looked the same. "Belgrave, oh, how I've missed you."

"Marinda is here too," Ture said.

Before Eiryss could turn, their cook hugged her tight. "You've gotten too thin, lady. Oh! It's 'princess' now." She stepped back and whispered to Ture. "Am I allowed to hug her?"

Eiryss laughed. "Always." She embraced dozens of people as they milled about, eating a sumptuous breakfast. But her joy was tinged with sadness as she learned the names of those who had not survived or who were missing—she collected those names to give to Dray in hopes he could find them as he had her brother.

Ture trailed behind her, a shadow she didn't want to shake. Long after the servants had cleared the breakfast dishes away, he took her hand as he had when they were children.

"I never willingly betrayed my sister—" She opened her mouth to speak, but he held out a hand, his eyes begging her to let him finish. "But betray her I did. I can never truly make amends for what was done to her. What is still being done—" he choked off, his face going red.

"Ture," she said gently.

He finally met her gaze. "I wrote a song for you, Eiryss. A song for you to remember when I ask it of you. Remember when the shadow swarms thickest."

His earnestness took her back. She nodded.

In his deep, rich baritone, he sang,

Four ravens white and one silver queen
Bound by shadow darker than night,
But even darkest night gives way to daylight's gleam;
Defeat the dark king's wicked blight.

As his voice drifted away, her family cheered. She swallowed against the emotions scrabbling for purchase inside her. It was a gallant gesture. But it painted her as some sort of savior when all she'd done was run away and killed helpless people.

She was almost relieved when Dray slipped through the doorpane, his two boys in tow—a seven-year-old and a toddler. The oldest, Banner, was as rowdy as she used to be, and every bit as mischievous. She'd taken a liking to him immediately. Especially when he placed a snake in her bed, which he'd found in his own the next night.

He'd refused to meet her gaze at breakfast the next morning. She'd simply sat beside him. "Does he have a name?"

The boy had only glared blankly at her.

"Every snake needs a good name. I built a cage for him. Would you like to see it?"

The toddler, Vinwin, had been harder to win over. More apt to duck his head into his father's shoulder and stare up at her through his lovely dark lashes. Still, it had only taken an afternoon of reading in the nursery.

They all waited beside the door, clearly not wanting to intrude.

Ture leaned toward her. "Are you really going to marry him as part of some treaty?"

She wanted Ture's approval, but she did not need it. "He's a good man. And the children—they only want someone to love them. I think we'll be happy." She made to head toward her groom, but Ture caught her arm.

"Zannok—he's still out there."

She stilled at the mention of the traitor king's name. *Rule* was only a breath away from her collarbone. "Another few days, and it won't matter." Ture looked pained. She patted his hand. "We'll find him."

She smiled at her future husband as she strode over to him. Vinwin immediately reached for her. Banner held back but came when she held out her hand.

"And when you do?" Ture asked.

Something in her hardened. Darkened. "He will not have the honor of being laid to rest in the Silver Tree."

CHAPTER 35

DARKNESS FALLING

In the bride room in the high branches of the White Tree, Eiryss sat before a vanity on a padded stool. All the walls were mirrors that reflected Eiryss's image a thousand times over. A maid intricately braided her blonde and silver hair. Another placed a diadem of silver and diamonds on her head.

"The king is waiting, princess," one of her own Valynthian guards called from outside the room.

"Nearly done," one of the maids said around a pin in her mouth.

Designed by Trevo and Meyo, the glittering diamonds mirrored the plunging collar that revealed the monarch sigil spread across her chest. The full skirt mirrored the pattern of the neckline, deep V patterns of diamonds clustered so thick as to appear white. Hanging from a new silver chain was the amulet her mother had given her.

The maids laid the mantle over her shoulders. It had been special made so it wouldn't cover her monarch sigil. From it hung the fire opals Dray had originally offered to Ahlyn. She studied her reflection. Black wasn't her best color—it made her look wan and tired. It would have looked ravishing on Ahlyn.

Ahlyn, the perfect princess.

Only she hadn't been perfect. Any more than Eiryss was. She smiled at herself, for once not minding the crooked teeth.

When they'd finished, Eiryss rose to her feet. Hundreds, perhaps thousands of royal-black dresses reflected. Each one sparkled as she approached the archway before stepping through the only door.

She descended the enormous branches of the White Tree. Council members from both kingdoms thronged the upper and lower branches—Valynthian in silver and black, Alamantian in their rainbow of colors. Arbors Enderlee and Vesos stood before the font.

Dray waited at the top of the steps, his children lined up behind him, Vinwin hiding behind his brother's tunic, one thumb in his mouth. Ture and Vicil held the thorned cuffs woven fresh from the White Tree this morning. Once inserted, the thorns would form the marriage sigils that would bind her to Dray for life.

It was not the life she'd wanted. But it was a good life. A life that would bless their kingdoms for generations. Dray smiled at her. She returned his smile and stepped through the tunnel of soldiers lining the way.

When she reached the top of the dais, he took a gold cup, dipped it into the font, and swallowed. Then he held it out to her. Her fingers gripped the sticky sides. Something made her eyes shift over Dray's shoulder. Perhaps a flash of movement. Perhaps recognition piquing some unconscious part of her mind. Perhaps the magic itself. She zeroed in on a face in the crowd.

Ramass's face.

His gaze met hers. Long enough for her to be certain. A cry slipped from her lips as he ducked out of sight.

Dray gripped her arm. "Eiryss? What is it?"

She turned to him, sweat and sickness breaking out across her skin. "Ramass is here." And if Ramass was, so was Zannok.

Dray stiffened. "You're certain?"

Eiryss turned to Enderlee. "Get the council somewhere safe."

Enderlee motioned to Tria in the crowd. The two of them took off at a run. Vesos shouted out names from the Alamantian council.

"Clear the dignitaries," Dray said to Mav. He pointed to Habbia. "Raise armor and shields. Sound the alarm." Both started barking out orders.

Ture approached Dray. "He has to be hiding in the boughs. Send me with enough enchanters to imprison him."

"No." Eiryss gripped her brother's arm. "I won't let you." She couldn't lose everything. Not again.

Dray nodded permission to her brother.

Ture squeezed her fingers. "Remember what I told you." His gaze swung to their cousin. "Vicil, with me."

He pulled away from her. At Dray's command, a contingent of enchanters broke off to follow her brother and cousin. She watched them go; a warning in her heart thrummed that she would never see them again.

Dray positioned the children between them, his useless metal sword in hand. He played on a panpipe. A beat later, she followed suit. Threads of magic wove a dome around the four of them that nothing in the two kingdoms could break.

Dray grunted suddenly. He hunched over, his hand gripping his stomach. The look he gave her—of dawning horror and impotent rage. His gaze shifted to the font. The cup.

"Poison," he gasped.

No. This couldn't be happening. It couldn't! "Water!" she cried. "Charcoal!"

As if to punctuate his words, he leaned forward and vomited. Banner gaped at his father. Vinwin gripped his brother's tunic, his chubby fists white.

Dray spit out the last of his sick and said to his oldest, "Remember our plan?"

The older boy shook his head. "But that was for during the war!"

"Take your brother and go. Exactly like we practiced." Banner hesitated, expression conflicted, before he gripped his brother's hand tight.

Dray motioned to Eiryss. "Let them through."

She placed armor around the boys, herself, and Dray as she hurried to the edge of the weave. She took the ends of the thread in her fingers and spread them apart enough for the boys to squeeze through into the dissipating crowd, soldiers immediately surrounding them.

Enchantresses and enchanters layered domes around Eiryss and Dray, each filled with soldiers. Every moment they became more prepared. Yet no one moved against them. Why hadn't Zannok attacked yet? Had Vicil and Ture found Zannok and Ramass?

Out of all the many melodies of music commanding the magic, one thread had Eiryss turning, pointing, shouting a warning. It was already too late. Shadows shot out like ravens loosed from a cage. They attacked those fleeing first, shredding their magical armor and plunging into their mouths and up their noses. Lines of jagged black crawled up their skin. Screaming, people leaped from the platforms and stairs to their deaths.

Eiryss felt the ghost of shadow's touch against the shield she'd placed on Banner and Vinwin. So cold it burned. Her magic faltered, wincing back. But Dray's held sure and gave her something to hold onto.

The shadows pressed against the domes. Gaping, horrible faces screamed and chittered. Claws shredded through the magic like wet paper. They hadn't even finished fading to ash before the first layer of defense broke. Enchanters and enchantresses turned on each other. Brother and sister. Mother and Father. Silver against gold—all of it ended in dripping red.

Upon the dais, Eiryss watched as the smoke spread throughout the city, devouring light, twisting people's expressions into rictuses of hate.

Eiryss and Dray played, shifting the dome to a vault and expanding it to include those in the second circle. Enchantresses and enchanters desperately fed their magic into the gleaming sphere. Together, they shifted the weave from a dome to a vault and pressed it outward. Together, they drove the shadows back until the entire White Tree gleamed—a refuge in a sea of shadows.

Suddenly, the expansion halted. Dray collapsed. His magic slipped from the weave, the vault trembled, barely holding together. Eiryss knelt at his side and gripped his shoulder. Face flushed, he panted, his eyes unfocused.

"Dray," she begged. "You have to keep fighting. Together we can defeat him. I know we can." But if she lost Dray now... No. Hagath beat the poison. So could Dray. *But Hagath had the antidote,* a little voice in Eiryss whispered. She silenced it with a vicious shake of her head.

His gaze met hers. His sigil gleamed white and gold. "Help me up."

She braced under his arm and strained. He leaned against her until they reached the font. Then he pressed his palm onto the conduit thorn, blood swirling through it.

"Please. See what's happening. Help me. Let me fight." For a moment, his face was stark with determination. Suddenly, he relaxed. He turned to her, all his sigils alight. The apex of power and strength.

He dropped, the light going out like a spent candle. As the fledgling vault fell to starlight and ash around her, he gripped her hand. Between their palms, the last vestiges of magic flared, and blood ran between their entwined fingers.

"Light guide you," he gasped. Then his eyes rolled up and he went perfectly still.

Eiryss panted. In her hand, she held an amulet in the shape of an ahlea. She squeezed it and waited for a flare of power. None came. What good was all the magic in the world if it could not save him? She shoved the amulet into the pocket of her decadent gown.

All around her, people died. Shadows howled and gnashed at her armor with poisoned teeth. Their screeching filled her head to bursting. Eiryss wove the threads desperately, throwing a dome up around herself—a tiny bit of light in a world of shadow and blood, screams and screeches. Ture and Vicil were in that chaos. She had to find them. Had to protect them.

She pushed shakily to her feet. Through the dark mist, a woman approached. Jagged, forked lines pulsed beneath her skin.

"Wyndyn?" Eiryss barely recognized the girl. One of the copperbills was here? How?

Wyndyn's jaundiced eyes fixed on Eiryss. It wasn't a woman who looked back at her, but an evil older and deeper than any Eiryss had ever known. Wyndyn—the thing—staggered toward her, sword dragging behind her.

Wyndyn's disjointed movements shifted. Her sword struck against Eiryss's dome. A metallic screech echoed through her magic. Wyndyn's head cocked to the side like a bird. "No," her mouth said. "This one is for me."

Cowering on the opposite side of the dome, Eiryss didn't understand.

Behind Wyndyn, amid the dissipating shadow, King Zannok appeared, his son and daughter flanking him. His dark gaze fixed on Eiryss, eyes jaundiced and black as Wyndyn's.

"Go find another to kill," Wyndyn said, her lips matching the king's—a puppet to its puppet master. The creature turned and threw itself into the melee. Zannok strode toward Eiryss—toward the dome that would not hold. Not against a king.

Suddenly, Vicil and Ture slid down on lines and cut the king off. No shadows swarmed them. Not yet. But they were no match for Zannok.

"Run!" she cried.

But Ture's sword didn't even flare. Instead, he bowed, their cousin a beat behind. "The Alamantian Arbor is dead, Majesty. As are most members of both councils."

"Enderlee? Tria?"

"Escaped," Ture said. "Along with the boys."

The feeling came first. A rising tide of dread that choked her. Forced her arms to curl around herself. To stagger back.

Zannok nodded curtly. "And the city's defenses?"

"Our copperbills have broken through," Vicil said. "The gates have already opened."

Ture's boots—his boots were soaked in blood. Arcs of it had sprayed across his face. And she knew. This was how the enemy king had slipped into their most secure location. Her own brother and cousin had let them in. They had betrayed her. They had all betrayed her. Everything she'd ever known—ever believed, ever loved—had been a lie.

She screamed, the sound tearing something vital from her. She collapsed. Her head swaying. Darkness came for her. But if she passed out now, her dome would fall. The shadows would come. The two boys—Dray's sons—and their guards were still armored. Still safe. If she gave up now, they wouldn't be.

She pulled her own hair, hard enough to bring tears to her eyes. She wiped the spittle from her lips. Forced herself to. Look. Up.

Zannok's mouth tightened as he glanced over his shoulder at his son. At Ramass. "You let her see you. So you will be the one to kill her."

She'd been avoiding looking at him. Now she made herself see. See the king who had killed a princess. Her father. Her mother. A man who had begun a war.

And Ramass had known.

The man she had loved—still loved, burn it—stepped toward her, his sword flaring to life—silver sheathed in writhing shadows. His betrayal tore fresh through her. Burned and burned and burned. He had known when he'd touched her. Had known when he had made love to her.

Between them, her dome gleamed silver. Every ounce of magic at her command had been thrown into it and the boys' armor. She would protect Dray's sons to the last.

"Remember when the shadows swarm the thickest," Ture said gently.

Eiryss met his traitor gaze. He had the gall to look small. Wounded.

"Four ravens white," Hagath said in a small voice.

"Silence, all of you!" the king roared, his irises shifting to a sickly yellow, the whites of his eyes black. Before her, Ramass grunted in pain. Black lines pulsed through his skin. Black lines pulsed through all four of them.

Remember. Ture had begged her to remember. The song came to her in a rush. "Four ravens white and one silver queen," She looked upon her friends, dark shadows pulsing beneath their pale skin. Her own sigils, gleaming silver. "Bound by shadows darker than night." The shadows that bound all of them to Zannok. "But even darkest night gives way to daylight's gleam. Defeat the dark king's wicked blight."

"You will be silent and still." Zannok's eyes flashed and they all stiffened, the lines in their skin pulsing. He glared at Hagath. "If you hadn't convinced her to remove chaos, she would be mine by now. We wouldn't have to do this again."

Hagath didn't meet her father's gaze.

"Ramass, kill her."

Ramass had stopped moving when the king had commanded them to be still. Now he strode forward again. Tears streamed down his cheeks. The realization hit her in a burst. Zannok was controlling them. With the chaos sigil? For how long?

Zannok's shadow-wreathed sword flared in his hand as he lifted it two-handed over his head.

The song. Daylight's gleam.

Ramass struck. The pressure dug into her ears. She cried out in pain—she hadn't dared tie off the dome. But it held. Even against a shadow-laced sword. She wiped at the wetness running under her nose and down her lips. Blood.

Ramass's eyes begged her even as he thrust again.

Again her dome held. Her nose gushed. Blood seeped from her ears.

Cursing, Zannok shoved his son out of the way. "I am still the monarch of Valynthia. And now, I always will be." A sword forged completely of shadows formed in his hands.

Even the night must bend to daylight's gleam.

Before he struck, she released her dome. Shadows instantly swarmed her, nipping at her ears and hair. Briars tipped in poison dragging along her skin hard enough to draw welts. Her armor held by a thread. Her mother's amulet—the amulet Ture had made her swear to never take off—burned through her flesh to rest against her rule sigil. Her mother's magic lending strength.

Bend to daylight's gleam.

"Light save you," Dray had whispered as he'd formed the amulet.

Zannok charged her. Eiryss squeezed Dray's amulet, channeled her magic into it. Light burst from it, blinding her. So bright she could hear it—a high pitched whine that made her cry out. The light faded and then winked out.

The king lay on his back, his mouth open in a silent scream. The shadows embedded in his skin writhed like tortured vines desperate to be free. He hauled in a ragged breath. His twisted gaze fixed on her with a look of pure hatred. "Kill her!"

The others immediately charged.

But even darkest night gives way to daylight's gleam.

Eiryss squeezed her mother's amulet. She channeled everything she had into Dray's amulet. Every drop of the river of magic churning through her. The amulet flashed, so bright it blinded her. She staggered back and collapsed to all fours. Her hand went to her chest, to the empty space her magic had been. Even as she touched it, she felt the slightest trace returning.

When the light finally faded, Zannok lay on the steps of the font. Shadows seeped from him like blood. He twitched; his gaze fixed on her. Even as she watched, the shadows slowly crawled toward his body. She hadn't defeated him. Only stunned him. And she didn't have enough magic for another pulse. Wouldn't for a while yet. She looked helplessly at Ture.

He too was on the ground, shadows bleeding and crawling back to him like death. "You have to end him, or we'll all wish we were dead," he choked.

Some long-ago part of her quelled at killing a man who she'd once considered a second father. That part of her was long dead, and Zannok had been the one to kill it. She looked around for a weapon. There were none. Or at least, none she could wield.

Unless.

Praying for forgiveness, she broke off the conduit thorn, the base as thick as her wrist and wicked sharp. She stepped over bodies—people the king had killed.

Zannok crawled away from her, his shadows trailing him like broken wings. She forced her steps to steady, even as her ears rang so loud she couldn't hear the words coming from his lips.

She lifted the thorn. Hesitated.

"Do it," Hagath choked.

Switching to a two-handed grip to ensure she broke through his ribs, she drove the thorn deep into his chest. Something screamed. Something decidedly not human. Eyes closed tight, she staggered back. Something touched her with a cold so deep it burned. Something that felt and smelled like rotted cloth.

She gasped. Shadows, torn and writhing, flailed around her friends. Their backs were arched, their arms flung out, faces lifted to the sky in a silent scream.

They were dying.

Her hands flew to her mouth to hold back the cry that choked her throat. Unwillingly, her gaze went back to the king. Black blood dribbled from the corner of his mouth. His lung. She'd pierced his lung. Shadows seeped into him from all around, pouring into him from the besieged city. He looked at his son and daughter.

"You will not die," he commanded.

His voice resonated somewhere deep and private within her—a king to his vassals. And though *rule* flared, she could not dredge up the will to disobey.

She tripped over a body and fell onto her backside. Zannok's gaze caught on her. His sigils lit up, *chaos, break, repel, loose, and darken* painting garish lines across his skin. "I lay a curse upon the land. A curse of forgetting and shadows and barrenness. You, Eiryss, shall watch as shadow devours land and people, starting with your beloved Valynthia and ending here."

His magic pulsed, and shadows robbed her of sight.

CHAPTER

36

TRUTH AND LIES

Eiryss's armor shattered. The shadows dove down her throat. Her mother's amulet grew cold in her hand. The vision swarmed her. She was in a room with Ahlyn again. Only now she looked at the dead girl through Hagath's eyes.

Through their linked hands, Ahlyn's heartbeat stilled. Two more thready beats and then it stopped. Hagath wanted to rage. To cry for her friend to stay. Not to leave her behind. There wasn't enough breath for it.

Ramass did it for her. Both hands buried in her hair, he screamed in anguish. "I swear, I'm going to make Dray pay. I'm going to make his whole kingdom pay!" Settling Ahlyn back on the bed, he staggered to Hagath's side, gripping her hand in his. "Don't you leave me too. I can't bear it, Haggy, please."

One wheezing gasp.

She didn't have the breath to tell him goodbye. To tell him not to grieve too long. She didn't want that for her brother. But her heart crashed so hard against her ribs and the sweat drenched her and she was so dizzy and sick. Her stomach—she swore she could feel blisters forming and popping inside her.

Another gasp.

Her father pushed into the room, Marshal Undrad behind him. King Zannok 's eyes fell to the princess. "Is she dead?" Before anyone could answer him, he noticed Hagath and his face went white. "No."

He rushed to her side, shoving Ramass out of the way. He pulled a vial from his pocket, unstopped it, and poured the contents into Hagath's mouth. It had the sharpness of pepper and the earthiness of cheese.

She didn't want it. She wanted air. But she had no choice but to swallow. It cost her more air. Her lips, hands, and feet tingled, going numb. She sucked in a sip of air, knowing she was dying. Just as Ahlyn had.

Marshal Undrad leaned over her. "Calm down. You're working your body too hard. Breathe with me."

Her healer training kicked in. She forced her muscles to unclench. Fought against the panic. And she breathed. No more air entered her lungs than before, but she didn't need as much. She concentrated on relaxing every muscle in her body. On breathing in tandem with Undrad.

Father relaxed a fraction. "Milk. Get her milk."

"She can't keep anything down," Ramass said.

"Vicil, move," Marshal Undrad barked.

Vicil turned on his heel and was gone.

Hagath thought the next breath came a little easier.

"Has she vomited it all up?" Marshal Undrad asked.

"Yes," Ramass managed. "What did you give her?"

Father gripped Hagath's cheeks and looked into her eyes. "Why was she here? She was supposed to be working tonight." He glared at Ture. "You had specific instructions not to let anyone visit the princess."

"She said she needed a healer, sire," Ture said. "She requested Hagath."

Hagath took half a breath. The tingling in her limbs faded.

Vicil came with a pitcher of milk.

"Hold her head up," Father said.

Ramass got behind her and held her while Father put the drink to her lips. The smell made her bile rise. She turned her head away.

"Drink it, Hagath," Father begged. "Just a sip."

She did, swallowing making her raw throat burn.

The Arbor herself pushed into the room. Enderlee carried a tray with dozens of vials, which she set on the nightstand. "I need to know her symptoms to isolate the antidote."

Vomiting, stomach pain, sweating, flushed skin, racing heart, closing throat, *the healer in Hagath cataloged. She was too busy breathing to say any of them out loud. His face panicked, Ture did it for her.*

Enderlee leaned over Ahlyn's body, her fingers searching for a pulse. Her face paled when she found none. "It's too late," she said what everyone else already knew. Only then did her attention fix on Hagath. Her dry fingers pressed against Hagath's soaked neck. "I can give her something to slow her heart."

Enderlee poured in powder from two cups, mixing it will a little milk. They held it to Hagath's lips. It took everything she had to hold her breath for long enough to swallow. Blackness edged around from the outside of her vision. Enderlee mixed crushed lemon balm in oil and smeared it across Hagath's skin.

"Her stomach," Father said. "The poison is eating it away."

"Milk," Enderlee said.

"We have already done that!" Father said.

Enderlee stirred in another compound, one simply for sour stomachs. After Hagath had drunk it, Enderlee bowed her head.

"It could be so many things, Majesty. If I give her the wrong antidote, it will kill her."

"What can you do?" Father asked.

"Treat her symptoms. Try to make her comfortable."

"Get out!" Father roared.

Enderlee straightened, clearly affronted. "Sire, I—"

"Get out!"

Gaze sympathetic, Undrad motioned for her to go and shut the door behind her. Father rested his forehead against Hagath's, murmuring, "I'm sorry. Oh, child, I'm so sorry," against her hair.

Hagath stared at the body of her friend. If not for her unnatural stillness, Ahlyn could be sleeping. But she wasn't. She was dead. Yet Hagath wasn't. Her heart steadied in her chest. The sweating eased. She took her first deep breath. If not for the damage already done to her stomach, she would beg to be allowed to sleep for a week.

So why had Hagath survived when Ahlyn had not? She was tempted to blame it on how much more wine her friend had consumed. But Hagath was a healer. She knew death. Knew it had been coming for her. Until her father had given her a vial that looked exactly like the ones Enderlee had brought. As if he'd known exactly what antidote to give her when the Arbor herself hadn't.

He'd known to give her milk, though no one had told him her stomach hurt.

He'd known he hadn't needed Enderlee and her antidotes. He'd already given Hagath the antidote.

No.

Her father was a good father and a good king. He would never hurt anyone, especially not the princess. But no matter how hard Hagath fought off the truth, the truth didn't care. It crashed around her. Spun her until she was drowning in it.

Father gripped her, his tears dripping through her hair to streak along her scalp. "I'm sorry. I'm so sorry."

"You did this." The words hurt in more ways than one—her throat was burned too.

Her father brushed the hair away from her face. "Hush, darling. Save your strength."

She stared at the body of her friend, rage building inside her. "Why, Father? Why would you do this?" Speaking caused waves of pain to crash over her and drown her. She whimpered.

He held a cup to her lips. More milk. She drank, the action of swallowing making it so much worse. But then it was better again.

Ramass stared in horror at their father. "You didn't do this. You couldn't."

Father pointed accusingly at Ahlyn's body. "She was going to destroy our kingdom! We would have been absorbed into the Alamant—our ways and beliefs bred with theirs to create some vile mongrel!"

"You killed her," Undrad said in disbelief.

"What is the life of one girl compared to the fate of our people?" Father said.

"Or is it because she would have taken your place?" Undrad said quietly.

Hagath knew how much her father's swift fall from power had humiliated him. And she remembered a night not long ago when her father had told Ramass he should be the next king.

When Ahlyn had ended her relationship with Ramass, she'd also ended his chances of being consort.

"This isn't about our kingdom," Undrad cried. "It's about you retaining power!"

"I am king!" Father's face turned red. "Not that weak-willed slip of a girl!"

Undrad shook his head, his face a mask of pain. "King Zannok, you have committed murder and treason."

"Her death shall rally the council and enchantresses alike,"
Father said. *"They won't hesitate to declare war now."* He held
his hand out beseechingly. *"Undrad, brother, join me. Rule at
my side."*

Undrad stared at Zannok like he'd never seen him before.
"Ture, Ramass, bind him. The council must be informed." He
moved toward the door, his hand closing around the handle.

"Stop!" Zannok shouted. *"I command it!"*

Undrad pulled open the door and gasped. He glanced down
at the dagger in his side. In his liver. Her father had thrown it.
Undrad gripped the hilt.

"No!" Hagath cried.

"Father!" Ture cried.

Undrad jerked it free, blood instantly soaking him and
spreading on the floor. His knees buckled.

Ture caught him before he hit the ground. He pressed
against the wound, trying to staunch it.

Ramass's expression shifted from shock to disbelief and
then anger. Pivoting, he advanced on Father, his weapons
gleaming to life in his hands.

Hagath's love for her father felt poisoned, traitorous. A part
of her wanted to intervene, beg for her father's life. Another part
of her wanted him punished for what he'd done. The two sides
warred as she watched helplessly from her dead friend's bed.

"I loved her," Ramass said.

Father's steely expression softened. *"There will be others."*

"And what about Hagath?" Ramass cried. *"What about
Undrad?"*

*"She wasn't supposed to be here! Undrad—I didn't have a
choice. He didn't give me a choice."*

"Healer!" Ture cried. *"I need a healer!"*

This couldn't be real. It couldn't be happening.

Hagath took the paper and pen and wrote, *"Am I going to
die?"* she held up the paper.

His jaw working, Ramass pointed his sword at Father's throat. "Answer her!"

"It depends on how extensive the damage is to her stomach and throat."

Ramass drew his arm back and stabbed. A wretched sound worked its way up Hagath's throat. Pain clawed her from the inside out. Ramass's sword bounced harmlessly off Zannok's magical armor, fashioned by the strongest enchantress in the kingdom.

"You think you could possibly harm me?" Zannok said in a raspy voice. His shield flared, and he slammed it into his son's side, throwing him to the floor.

Ramass was back on his feet in a second. Blood soaking his clothes, Ture joined his friend's side.

"No," Hagath sobbed, the words hurting as much as the sight of her brother and friend contemplated killing her father. They all knew her father would win. As king, his magic was stronger.

Ramass stood, frozen with indecision.

Vicil walked into the room and saw Marshal Undrad in a pool of spreading blood, the princess dead in her bed, and his two best friends holding the king at sword point.

"What are you doing?" Vicil choked out.

"He killed them," Ture's voice was cold and hard. "He killed them both."

No! Not Undrad too!

Vicil stepped forward, hands out. "He's our king. Without Ahlyn, we have no one to lead our people."

"And you want him to lead you?" Ramass didn't take his eyes from their father. "He's a murderer."

"The tree chose Ahlyn," Ture ground out. "You have blasphemed."

Father didn't let his weapons fade as he eyed those in the room. "We worship the Silver Tree as a god, but it is no better than us. Simply a being with magic. Why should we let it dictate who rules us or who has magic? This is our kingdom!"

"The tree gives us everything," Ture said. "It could take it all away."

"It can't." Father pulled back his sleeves, revealing sigils over every inch of his skin—sigils twisted into patterns Hagath had never seen before. "I take the sigils I want. The tree cannot stop me or take them back."

Blasphemy. But the evidence was undeniable.

"Ahlyn was a good girl," Father said. "But she was no queen."

"Shut your filthy, murdering mouth!" Ramass said.

"And my father?" Ture asked.

Father faltered. "I offered him a place at my side. After everything we have been through." His gaze narrowed, and he pointed to Ramass. "You should be our next king! You have the most brilliant strategical mind in a century. People listen to you. Respect you. And you would never take the easy path and sell our people out because you were afraid."

Ramass shook his head in disbelief. "You want me to be the prince?"

"Why not?" Father spread his hands. "I am the king. I say what happens in this kingdom. If I name you prince, who is the Silver Tree to deny me?"

Ramass and Ture exchanged looks. "I refuse," Ramass said. As if on cue, they lunged forward, weapons attacking.

"Stop!" Father roared. His sigils flared, shadowy vines snapping around each of the men. Before Hagath could think to try to form armor around herself, the magic was inside her. But it was not her magic. This magic was deeper, so deep she could not see the bottom of it, and far older.

"You will not speak or even hint of anything that has transpired tonight." The words resounded through her, vibrating painfully. "Undrad was in league with the Alamantians. He

killed the princess. He tried to kill me. Ture stopped him. Ramass, Vicil, and Ture will command armies of their own. You will protect my life and obey my every command. And when the time comes, Ramass will become king in his own right."

Hagath's sigils buzzed painfully, glowed too bright, until she thought it would kill her. Just as a scream built inside her, the pain was gone. The others groaned from where they'd collapsed on the floor. Cold settled over Hagath from the crown on her head to the tips of her toes.

What had her father done?

"You think your magic can stop me?" Ramass cried. He called his blade, but it winked out as if it had never been. He stared at his empty hand in shock.

Ture lunged toward Father. He only made it a single step before his whole body locked up. He staggered back, disbelief written all over his face. "What have you done?"

Zannok pulled his cuffs over his sigils. "You'd be surprised what magic you can force from the Silver Tree when you start viewing it as a commodity."

There was no sigil that would allow her father to do this. At least, there hadn't been. This was something new. Something evil. Light, this couldn't be happening.

Ramass lifted his chin. "We may not be able to kill you, but I will tell everyone that you—" His voice choked off, his face going red. "You—" Ramass clutched his throat, eyes wide on their father. "Light save us."

"One day you and Hagath will understand. Even agree with me." Father straightened his jacket. "Vicil, you will come with me to the great room while my children say their goodbyes to their friend. And Ture to his... Ture will also say goodbye."

Ramass and Ture exchanged looks. But what could any of them do against the king and his magic? Head bowed in defeat, Vicil followed Father out.

Ture collapsed beside his father. "By the light, how will I ever tell my mother? My sister?" His shoulders bowed and shook with sobs.

Ramass stared at the useless weapons in his hands. "Hagath, what do we do?"

Frantic, she snatched a pencil and paper and wrote, "My father is a—" Murderer. Murderer. MURDERER! But her hand refused to form the word. No matter how she tried.

Enderlee hurried into the room, Father trailing her.

"He attacked me," Father said. "Tried to kill me. Ture saved me."

She knelt next to Undrad and pressed her fingers to his throat. "He's alive."

"What?" Zannok cried.

Ture had been wrong.

Her dearest friend leaned over his father. "Please. Help him."

"Bring me a stretcher," Enderlee called to someone out of sight. Healers bustled into the room, rolled Undrad onto the stretcher, and lifted it. "Take him to the healing tree."

Blood on her hands, she paused at the threshold and looked back, her expression carefully guarded. The Arbor couldn't know for certain that something was amiss, but clearly, she suspected it. Father studied her like he wanted to control her too— but he couldn't. Not without her knowing about it. Either he wasn't strong enough to use his dark enchantment on more people, or he dared not risk someone as powerful as Enderlee knowing. She left without a word.

Father cast them all a severe look before following Enderlee out. "I want to be informed the moment he wakes. No one else is to have access to him. No one!"

"Very well, Zannok," Enderlee said.

Hagath thought of her friend and Ture's sister, Eiryss. Undrad's wife, Emlon. They were both about to be told the lie that Undrad was a traitor. That Undrad would likely not survive.

Head bowed, Ramass said, "I'll find a way to kill him for what he did to you."

Tears filled her eyes. Her brother would do it—or at least he'd try. And he'd never live with himself after. Neither would she. "He's our father," she wrote.

He read the words. "Then it's our responsibility to make sure he never hurts anyone else."

Hagath sipped milk and battled the pain that carved her from the inside out. A battle she was steadily losing as her strength was whittled away one whorl at a time.

He gripped her cold hands in his warm ones. "Are you going to be all right, Haggy?"

She could not eat. Not with this much pain. And if anything grew infected or didn't heal... She sipped her milk. When she could, she wrote, "Don't call me Haggy."

For a moment, Eiryss felt her mother's amulet in her hand. Was aware of herself. And then she sank just as easily into Ramass's consciousness.

He turned to Ahlyn. To her body. By the light, how could he face the man who'd killed the woman he loved? Face him and do nothing to avenge her? And once he left this room, she would be whisked away by statesmen. And the people would see her. Like this. Covered in vomit.

He went to the common room. Father waited for him, his expression calm. "I've sent your friends to see to the announcement of the princess's passing."

Passing. Like she's merely slipped from one room into another. "She's dead, Father. You made—" Certain of that. But he couldn't finish the sentence. You will pay for what you've done. *He couldn't say that either.*

"What have you done to me? How?"

"I have learned how to create new sigils by combining the old. For example, if you take a dreamer and an emotive, you create chaos. *Combine* rule *and* bind, *and you create* thrall. *"*

Chaos? *Ramass didn't know what that meant. But he could guess what* thrall *meant. It meant his father could bend people to his will. "You're a dark enchanter."*

Father considered this. "Is the dark so bad, son, if it saves our kingdom?"

"You're not saving the kingdom. You're saving yourself."

"You'll thank me when you're a king in your own right."

"That's a lie."

Father took the remaining bottle of wine and poured it into the chamber pot. "You have to learn to stop thinking of the good of the one. Two deaths—by the light." He passed his hands over his face. "Two deaths are nothing when our whole way of life— our autonomy—is at stake." He sounded like he was trying to convince himself.

"I will never forgive you for this." Ramass couldn't stomach looking at him anymore. "I'm going to prepare her body. And you're going to make sure I'm not disturbed."

"Very well," Zannok said.

Back in Ahlyn's room, Ramass removed her soiled clothing. He washed the vomit from her skin and anointed her with fresh smelling oils. He dressed her in her finest gown, brushed her long hair, and plaited it in a braid over one shoulder. All the while he wept.

When he had finished, he pushed her mouth closed and kissed her lips one last time. "Say your goodbyes, Hagath."

All through his ministrations, Hagath had held Ahlyn's hand. Now she brought that hand to her cheek. For a time, the two of them cried. But their time couldn't go on. Ahlyn had a large family. Parents and siblings and aunts and uncles and cousins. Dozens of them. They deserved to know. The kingdom deserved to know.

Ramass took his grief, gathered it like broken shards of glass, and stuffed it deep. Then he gathered Ahlyn in his arms— she was still warm, her cheeks still pink, her body still giving. By the light, it was like she was sleeping. How he wished she was sleeping.

His emotions surged. With everything he had, he stuffed them back down. He stepped into the common room. The king rose to his feet and moved toward the door.

"You will remain here," Ramass said, voice hoarse with the effort it took to restrain himself.

Father arched an eyebrow. "Our people need to see their king."

"You will stay!" Ramass would not allow Ahlyn to be escorted to her funeral by the man who had killed her.

Zannok's sigils flared—a clear warning.

Ramass swallowed down every trace of his pride. "Please, Father." Zannok's expression shifted to one he wore around particularly stubborn council members. "Hagath needs you."

His father let out a long breath. "For now."

It wasn't good enough, but it was the best he would get. He stepped out, Ahlyn's head cradled against his neck. Vicil and Ture fell in behind him, Ture still covered in blood. Together, they made the long journey down the steps to the dock. Every step he took, he plotted his father's demise.

Word had spread about the Princess. Dozens and dozens of boats had already amassed. He chose one to row Ahlyn to the Silver Tree. Some of the men offered to carry Ahlyn for him, but Ramass would not pass on this burden. Arms aching, he climbed the stairs alone, hundreds of people trailing him, and laid Ahlyn out at the base of the font. He folded her hands over each other.

Her mouth kept falling open, so he rolled up a blanket someone had brought and placed it under her chin.

He knelt before her, head bowed, heart heavy. "I will find a way to avenge you, Ahlyn," he said so softly none could hear. "I swear I will."

Silence reigned until a shout came from behind him. A woman screamed, "No! Not my Ahlyn!" The crowd parted for her parents. Ramass moved aside, letting them grieve.

Tears streaking his cheeks, Ahlyn's father looked up at him. "Who did this?"

Ramass tried. How could he not? But the truth raging through him sputtered and died in his throat.

"King Dray of the Alamantians sent her a bottle of poisoned wine." King Zannok stepped onto the platform. Cries of dismay and anger rose around him. Zannok held up his hands. "She isn't the only one. My daughter, Hagath, has been poisoned. I'm not sure if she will survive the night."

Ramass didn't think it was possible to hate his father more. But this? Twisting Ahlyn's death and Hagath's near-death to gain support for his war? How could this be the man from his childhood? The man who'd gotten down on all fours, growling and laughing as he'd chased Ramass through their hometree. The man who'd come to each one of Ramass's tournaments. Who'd grieved still for his wife, so much so he didn't even notice the courtiers' suggestive glances.

Shouts rose from around them.

"This affront cannot be tolerated."

"The Alamant has gone too far!"

"They will pay for what they've done."

Zannok fell to his knees before Ahlyn's parents, arms outstretched like a petitioner. "What would you have of me. Ask, and it shall be yours."

"Avenge my daughter," the man said.

King Zannok rose to his feet. "Consider it done."

Ramass bowed his head as war cries rose all around him. He fixed his eyes on Ahlyn, knowing this wasn't what she'd wanted. Knowing there was nothing he could do to stop it. Hating his father for what he'd done. He bent over Ahlyn and pressed his forehead to hers.

Her cool skin shocked him. She was dead. By the light, how could she be dead? "I failed you," he whispered. "I'm so sorry."

A hand on his shoulder made him pause. "The guardsmen are going to search my hometree," Ture said.

Emlon and Eiryss. Oh, light, Eiryss.

Ramass motioned to the side. He and Ture slipped away from the mourning, angry crowd and made a run for the docks.

CHAPTER

37

TORN SHADOWS

Cold and light pulsed in each of Eiryss's hands and at her breast. That pulse ate away at the shadows until they resembled moth-eaten cloth. Her mother's amulet—somehow it had gleaned the memories from the shadows like it did from the dead.

She blinked, no longer in Hagath and Ramass's memories. She found herself in the White Tree. And now, she finally knew the truth. None of her friends or her father had abandoned her. They'd been spelled by a thrall. By a dark enchanter with all the magic and power of a king. She wanted to weep with relief, but she couldn't see anything beyond shadows still swarming her.

She had just enough magic for a flickering dome. Shadows boiled against the thin silver barrier. She called out to her friends; silence answered. She wasn't sure how long it went on—many long minutes. Perhaps an hour. Then the shadows retreated. The king breathed out his last and went still. Abruptly,

Ture, Hagath, Vicil, and Ramass ceased shaking. In the sudden silence, the king's curse resonated.

"I lay a curse upon the land. A curse of forgetting and shadows and barrenness. You, Eiryss, shall watch as shadow devours land and people, starting with your beloved Valynthia and ending here."

Hagath moved first, rolling over to her side and staring at her father. "She did it," Hagath breathed. "He's dead."

Vicil pulled up his sleeves and gaped at the shadows still etched in his skin. "Why aren't they gone?"

"The curse," Eiryss choked out. "What does it mean?"

On his haunches, Ramass clenched his fists to his thighs, eyes closed tight. He had tried—they all had—to protect her. She thought of the countless times they had tried to warn her with their eyes and their words. But how could she have ever guessed the truth?

Ture pushed to his feet, climbed over the bodies, and held his hand out to Eiryss. She stared at his palm, then back up at him. To go from being her brother to her betrayer back to her brother again...

He crouched before her. "Eiryss, it's over. You stopped him."

Then why did his curse still echo in her heart? Why did shadow still live beneath their skin? "You all lied to me."

"We didn't have a choice," Hagath said. "The king stole whatever thorns he wanted—he was a seer, binder, bearer, speaker for the dead, dreamer, and emotive. And a king besides. We could not disobey his commands—the worst of which was that we had to do everything in our power to protect him."

Light.

It was then that the body stirred. Namishka. She was not the only one. There had to be hundreds, perhaps thousands, of injured. Eiryss was a healer. She had to help them. She scrambled to Namishka and checked her throat for signs of a heartbeat.

Nothing. Barely fourteen, and already, she was dead. Her grandmother was alone now in the world, having lost the last of her family.

To her right, a man moaned and shifted. "What happened?"

Eiryss moved to help him. A hand grabbed her wrist. Namishka sat up. She was alive. Eiryss wanted to cry for joy. But there was something wrong with her. Tined lines traced her skin. And when Eiryss had felt for a heartbeat earlier... there hadn't been one.

Namishka's gaze snapped to Eiryss. Her eyes—her eyes were pure black. Inhuman. Eiryss screamed. Namishka lunged, teeth going for Eiryss's throat.

Ture pushed between them and shoved Namishka to the ground. "What are you doing?"

Snarling, she rose to a crouch. His sword appeared in his hand—only instead of silver, it was swathed in shifting shadows. Ture didn't seem to notice as he stared down at the waifish girl.

Eyes fixed hungrily on Eiryss, she tried to shift around him.

He blocked her. "Stop it!"

Namishka glared at him as if debating whether to obey. Behind her, a councilman cried out. Her movements unnatural and jerky, the girl lunged at the man, teeth sinking into his throat. Vicil hauled Namishka off. She scrambled back, blood dripping from her mouth.

"She's dead," Eiryss choked. "Her heart wasn't beating."

Namishka gathered herself and charged.

Eiryss dove to the side. Ture swung his sword, taking off her head. He didn't see Balendora creeping up behind him, eyes fixed on Eiryss—the same dead, black gaze her granddaughter had worn. Eiryss cried out in alarm.

Ture flipped his sword and plunged it backward, right into Balendora's middle. Her black eyes stared up at Ture with a look of betrayal. Ture jerked back. She slid off his sword and fell. Her back broken, she crawled over Namishka's body as if she didn't recognize her own granddaughter. As if she wouldn't have died for her a dozen times over. As if the girl was merely an obstacle to her quarry.

Ture decapitated her and staggered back. "What is this?"

More women were rising, women shaking out of their stupor. The women with black eyes attacked anyone without, using teeth and nails to rend and tear. Eiryss didn't understand. Not until she caught sight of Wyndyn, her eyes as black, her skin shadowed.

"They're copperbills," she murmured. Then loud enough for the others to hear, "They're the copperbills!"

Somehow the chaos sigil had turned against them. Turned them into these... things.

Unable to restrain them, Vicil and Ture began killing women—former enchanters who didn't seem to feel pain and died in utter silence. Fumbling for her flute, Eiryss played, her sigils lighting up. She wove the threads into a dome.

From all around rose the sounds of fighting.

All this time, Ramass hadn't moved. Now, he pushed to his feet and shouted, "Stop!"

The shadows in the copperbill's skin pulsed. As one, all of them froze. Ramass stared at his own hands, at the thorned vines twisting around his wrists like shackles.

"What kind of monsters are these?" one man cried as he wove a dome. Those still living flocked to him, the women brandishing swords.

Ramass's fists clenched at his sides. "They are what's left of the enchantresses of Valynthia."

"You mean the copperbills—" Eiryss began.

Ramass ignored them. Panting, Vicil and Ture exchanged baffled, frightened looks. Hagath rocked back and forth.

"What does this mean?" Vicil asked.

"It means we control them," Ramass choked out.

"No," Hagath moaned. "No, he's dead. He's dead!"

Ture marched to Ramass, gripped his tunic in his fists, and shook him. "It's over! We're free!"

The screams in the city grew louder. Ramass's sigils gleamed—obsidian instead of silver. His sword appeared in his hand—a sword now sheathed in torn shadows. Ture staggered back and braced himself against his knees, panting.

Vicil called up his own sword—an exact match for Ramass's. "Punishment," he murmured, his eyes slipping closed.

Were these the shadows the king had cursed them with? The shadows that bleed from the copperbill's skin to their eyes? The shadows that wreathed their swords?

Hagath began to cry. Her tears were black.

"The copperbills will obey your commands," Ramass said. "Go through the city. Command them to leave. Kill the ones you can."

Vicil was the first to obey, calling for the dead as he went. Moving in complete silence, the creatures stared hungrily at Eiryss, but they did not fight him as they shambled from the tree. They did not try to avoid his sword. Other than the splash of their blood and the thump of their bodies, they made no sound as they died.

Wyndyn was the last to go, her black eyes stark against her young face.

The wind tugging at her short red hair, Hagath stared at Eiryss. Black sigils pulsed beneath her scars—sigils Eiryss was sure Zannok had forced on her. "I can feel it inside me—the shadow. Growing." She turned to Ramass. "Will I even be me anymore?"

Ramass wouldn't look at his sister. "Go," he said gently.

Eyes heavy with sorrow, she stepped up to press her cheek against Eiryss's. "Forgive me?"

Eiryss's eyes fluttered closed. She squeezed her arms. "Yes."

Hagath turned without another word, grabbed a line, and zipped out of sight.

"One of us should be happy, Eiryss. Find a way." Ture turned without another word and took the line at a run.

And then it was only Ramass. He made no move to come toward her. To face her. "I don't know how long the four of us will be able to keep the shadow inside us at bay. But we will lose ourselves completely. You must defend the city."

Against them. "Can you kill the copperbills?"

He finally met her gaze and gave a sharp shake of his head. "My father captured many of our enchantresses. And he gave all of them chaos."

She thought of all her friends. She wanted to ask who. But a frightened corner of her soul couldn't bear to know. "Surely we can... heal them?"

He half shook his head. "They are more shadow than women."

She shivered and cupped her elbows. "I can vault the city, but the people beyond—all the other cities—Valynthia—what happens to them?" *You, Eiryss, shall watch as shadow devours land and people, starting with your beloved Valynthia and ending here.* Whatever the king had cursed them with, it had already begun.

He closed his eyes, his head tipped to the side as if listening to something only he could hear. "Hanama has already fallen to the heart of shadow." He looked at her chest, at the bloody sigil there. "You are all that's left of the light."

She pressed both hands to her mouth. "The shining city—all of it gone?"

He looked to the north, shadows dancing across his skin. "It will devour us all."

"Ramass," she begged. There had to be a way. Something they could do.

He hung his head. "All magic is light. If that light be darkened, shadow and punishment come." He staggered a step as if unable to bear the weight of it. "They are the shadow. I am the punishment." He finally looked at her. The quiet resignation in his eyes—the same look Dray had had moments before he'd died.

"What does it mean?"

"It means our people, Valynthian and Alamantian alike, will forget all of this—our history and our downfall. That we will never bear children. That before long, the shadow will destroy us."

This couldn't be. She wouldn't let it be. Her fists clenched at her sides and bumped against the amulet Dray had given her— the one she'd pocketed. "No. I'm going to stop this." She turned to the people cowering inside the dome behind her. "Raise the vault."

An enchanter gestured to the dozen or people inside. "There aren't enough of us."

"Then find more people," she snarled. Reluctantly, they dispersed the dome and moved out to do her bidding.

She rounded on the font. There might not be anybody strong enough to defeat the wicked king's curse. But there was a being strong enough. She squeezed Dray's amulet, not even flinching as the branches pierced her. Again. Nothing happened.

"I am not asking," she said through clenched teeth. "You will help me. Or by the light inside all of us, I will chop you down myself!" She visualized wielding an ax, the blade biting into the wood.

Something gave way. Her hand grew cold. She glanced at the amulet, at her blood running through the hollow core of it. Sap seeped through her veins. Suddenly, she wasn't standing on the platform of the White Tree. She was inside it. Memories and magic swirled around her, all controlled by an undercurrent of melody more vibration than sound.

There was no sight. No taste. No ability to communicate beyond a feeling of liquid light. But that light moved, her consciousness bobbing along with it. She traveled beneath the cool, shifting currents of the lake and into the roots biting through hard soil. Through branch and leaf. Every tree of the forest one vast organism with the White Tree their beating heart.

A memory surfaced. A man and a woman, naked, had climbed the first tree. Built a home there. First spilled their blood into one of the thorns. And the sacred trees had awakened to the magic of movement and sight and sound. To language and learning.

The trees had awoken. Unable to form words, the tree had communicated by the sharing of memories.

Eiryss finally understood. The trees were sentient but couldn't hear or speak. Trapped. In exchange for the magic of sight, memories, and movement, they traded their light with mankind. For centuries, the exchange had benefited both beings. Sacred trees and mankind flourished.

Until King Ramadal had awakened the tree to the evil committed with its magic. An evil that had snuffed out the tree's light, its goodness. And without the light, cold anger in the shape of shadows had come. Shadows and punishment. Ramass had given her that book to warn her what was coming.

Eiryss watched it happen. Over and over again. People and trees, whole forests, had been destroyed. Until only two remained.

"How did we not know?" she asked the light around her.

"A curse of shadow and forgetting," the king's voice echoed around her.

The truth had been forgotten.

She felt it then. From one direction, shadows writhed and clawed, killing the light as they went. The two trees were connected by tangling roots—where one began and the other ended was impossible to differentiate. They were mates—the silver and white trees. The last of their kind.

Sorrow and hopelessness spread from the Silver Tree's roots, infecting the White Tree.

You must cut yourself off from him, Eiryss thought. And then visualized the roots withdrawing.

The current of magic went perfectly still. The warmth turned cold and withdrew, leaving Eiryss adrift. When it returned, anger and resentment roared around her.

I'm angry too. She imagined herself screaming at the sky in fury.

The raging stilled. Finally, another image came to her. An enchantment from long, long ago. A memory handed down from one tree to the next. The ability to cut off life. An enchantment meant to kill a diseased branch before that disease spread.

Could it work to separate the two?

Eiryss wove the enchantment; the magic traveled the roots until it encountered shadow. She finished the enchantment. Everywhere it touched, trees died, until every tree along the border withered into a hollow husk in moments. Magic shimmered, a faint border that would keep anything from growing in the place between.

Memories of the dying suddenly burst in her mind. Blood stained the ground above her, soaking into the tree's roots. That blood told the story of people—Alamantians and Valynthians alike—killed by the not-quite-dead. Mulgars, they had been called. But there was no blood where the magic bubbled up.

Arbor rings, she realized. *Safe havens where the people have taken refuge.*

Magic gathered to her in response—a sensation of tingling light building all around her. Her distant body wove the magic with her hands—something the tree could not do, creating a vault. Another memory surfaced. Of a different weave. One she had not seen before. A weave that could be larger and last longer because it required less magic and was more permeable.

Using *rule* and the magic of the White Tree all around her, she immediately shifted the weave, drew the enchantment toward the Arbor rings, and let them rise and expand, forcing the darkness back. Blind as she was, and without more blood to tell her if it was working, she could only hope she had created the havens of safety she intended.

"How do we break the curse?" She imagined the shadow's vines fading to nothing.

Silence. No memories came.

Because no one had ever broken a curse before. Only delayed and contained it, as Eiryss had already done. But there had been more to the curse than shadows. "What about the forgetting and barrenness?"

More memories. Of the young growing old and dying with no children to replace them. After centuries, those ancient places of refuge had fallen, along with any trace they had ever existed.

Eiryss wept. "There must be a way." In answer, the tree released her. She fell backward, through light and magic. Until she emerged into her own body.

CHAPTER 38

PUNISHMENT

R amass held her in his arms, his gaze on the distant horizon. At the sun shifting toward night. His expression held a dark premonition. "I never should have let you be embedded. I thought I could keep you safe. And then you were the princess. I tried to hide the truth from my father long enough to marry you. Then you would be family. He would never hurt his family."

"Did you ever even want me?" Her voice hitched at the end.

He looked at her, his expression haunted. "I chose you before I ever knew you would be queen." He brushed the tips of his fingers down the side of her face. "Now I've lost you."

He choked back a sob. "I have to go. Dusk is coming."

"What happens at dusk?"

"I become your enemy—the shadows take over, the will of the Silver Tree driving me." He chuckled darkly. "My father made me a king of Valynthia, just as he always wanted. But now it is a land of death and shadow. He made me the king of the wraiths."

The breath left her body in a gasp. "You have never been my enemy." Light, even when she'd hated him—he'd been doing everything he could to save her. "I'm sorry."

"Don't." He took her hand in his. "The darkness is eating away at me like acid. Whatever is left... I won't be me anymore. Do you understand?"

How could she understand something so terrible? "What about the copperbills?"

"It's not just the copperbills. All the enchantresses my father trapped became mulgars. There are thousands of them. Far too many for us to kill before morning. They are the shadow."

And he was the punishment. A thousand memories of spinning—in the grass, and out over open water, and in each other's arms at the galas. They'd always been circling each other, their grip keeping them safe. She didn't know how to live without that. "We promised we'd never let each other fall."

He swallowed hard, and his voice came out scratchy, "I love you. I have always loved you."

He made to move away. She gripped his tunic and pulled his mouth down to hers. He resisted a moment before crashing against her. His arms pinned her against him as if he'd never let go. His lips devoured hers. Just as suddenly, he was sobbing. He held her tight, crushing her in his grip.

"Why?" she cried. "Why must I lose you?"

"Where the light is, shadow cannot go."

He released her. Shadows cloaked him, swirling around him like poisoned thorns. He took the line and rushed out of sight.

Unable to bear it, she ran after him. He landed at the base of the tree and cast his arm out. Shadowed briars boiled in a path across the waters. He crossed them, more shadows flocking to him. Mulgars streamed to him atop those shadows—an army of the dead.

Where the light is, shadow cannot go. Light and shadow. Male and female. Good and evil. Everything had its opposite. So if a curse was darkness, perhaps she could make a countercurse of light?

She played the flute her father had bought for her—the one Ramass had scoured her estate sale for. A river of magic coursed through her. The White Tree's amulet allowed her to see the shadows that lay like a snare over the land and people, a tangled briar woven of wicked thorns.

"Help me," she begged the White Tree. The amulet in her hand warmed. An enchantment came to her mind. As well as the cost. All the light of the Silver Tree now resided in her rule sigil. This enchantment would use it up to the last drop. Forever. Even the White Tree would be permanently diminished.

There wasn't a choice.

"Upon this land, I lay a blessing of memory and life and light." Magic raged from her, shining gold and silver filaments weaving nets around the shadow thorns. The curse split in two: the Valynthians were now cursed with lost magic and memory; the Alamantians faced barrenness and shadow.

She had not broken the curse. With the last of the full-strength monarchs dead, there wasn't enough magic for it. With the source of her magic—the Silver Tree—lost to shadows, perhaps there never would be again.

When every drop of her magic was gone, Eiryss sagged against the branch. Her hands ached where she held the now drained amulets. She released her hold and tugged the chain over her head.

Someone approached from her left. Eiryss turned to see Illin, a bandage around her chest and another around her head. "Where did you come from?"

"Just yesterday, I saw shadows of this day. I tried to enter the tree to warn you. The guards would not let me pass."

Light, the woman could have warned them not to trust Ture. That the Alamant had been infiltrated. Perhaps she could have saved them all from this curse. She looked over the dead and caught sight of Lord Darten's too-skinny body lying like a broken stick by the archway. A manic laugh burst from her.

"What is it?" Illin asked, bewildered.

"Nothing. Just that one of my suitors used to drone on and on about the cursed history of magic. I thought him mad. Turns out he was right." She gestured to him. "And now he's dead."

They were silent for a long time.

"You have diminished us all, Majesty."

Eiryss winced. "I'm not a queen anymore."

Illin watched the vault forming behind them. "The Silver Tree chose you. The last true queen in all Valynthia. You must travel your lands and gather your people to the safety of the Arbor rings. You will safeguard them as they build a new life—one without magic or memory. And you will plant seeds so when the time comes, the curse may be broken."

Eiryss shook her head. "You said yourself the magic is diminished. If I couldn't break the curse, who could?"

Illin laid her hand across Eiryss's stomach. "There are only two who escaped the curse—protected by your magic—you and this child."

Child? Eiryss gaped at the woman and staggered back. The maidweed tea hadn't worked. Nausea roiled within her. Ramass could never know he had a child—not with the evil he had become. Never. "You think my child could defeat the shadow when even I, with all my magic, could not?"

Illin frowned. "I believe in darkness. I also believe in light. That light will provide a way to escape the shadow."

"And the barrenness?" Eiryss asked. "None of this matters if the Alamantians will be wiped out in one generation."

Illin leaned over the banister as she stared into the distant forest. "Your countercurse weakened it so that the Alamantians will not be completely barren—only unable to bear daughters. So Valynthia will give us their daughters so we may continue to fight against the shadow."

But without memory, those daughters would never understand why they must leave.

The vault passed around them with the singing of crystals and the mineral tang of deep earth.

"And if we fail?" Eiryss whispered.

"If we fail," Illin said, "the wraiths and mulgars will have killed us all and it won't matter anymore." She pointed. Eiryss followed the gesture to the setting sun darkened by shadows. At a ridge along the edge of the forest, a man stood with arms outstretched as darkness devoured him.

"Ramass," Eiryss whispered.

The figure turned as if he'd heard her. Then the sun sank beneath the horizon, and he was gone.

EPILOGUE

TRAPPED IN AMBER

Sixty Years Later

Music wove through Eiryss's dreams. She was a girl again, dancing at one of the king's galas amid the Silver Tree's uncorrupted boughs. Everything was bright and silver. Ramass's arm was around her waist, her hand in his. He spun her about. Tucked behind her ear, the velvet petals of the lampent flower brushed her cheek. From one of the tables, she could hear her mother and father laughing at some joke Ture had told. Atop the dais, Ture sang beautifully,

> *Bound by shadow dark as night,*
> *A cursed queen, four ravens white,*
> *Must drive the shadow into light,*
> *Heal the darkness, cure the blight.*

Blood of my heart, marrow my bone,
Come hear saddest story e'er known.
A cursed queen, her lover lost,
A forbidden magic and dreadful cost.
Consumed by evil, agents of night,
Seek the nestling, barred from flight,
Midst vile king's curse of thorny vine,
Fear not the shadow, for you are mine.
In my arms, the answers lie:
A light that endures so that evil may die.

Ramass pulled Eiryss close, his cheek warm and soft next to hers. "You haven't much time left, love." Then he pushed her. Hard.

Eiryss's eyes snapped open and she was instantly awake, the music still ringing in her ears. One of the maids had left the lamp burning, but the shadows beyond were of the deepest part of night. Her hand was fisted around the amulet at her throat, the branch inside her skin. The curse hadn't left her sigils untouched. They had grown thick and unruly, covering her body in twisted vines. Every night, they wept, soaking her in sap that entombed her in amber by morning.

Eiryss flared her sigils and pulsed gently, shattering the amber. She sat up, her hips aching. The pain in her stomach that was her constant companion reminded her cruelly of its presence. Trying to ignore the pain, she pushed to the edge of the bed and rocked to her feet. She paused a moment, letting her aging body adjust. Letting the pain fade a bit.

She took her first shuffling, painful steps to her desk. She dipped the quill in ink and wrote down the last line of the song. The songs were messages—clues for how to break the curse.

The wind died, allowing the music from the Forbidden Forest, as it was now known, to sound louder. She went to her balcony, lifted the latch, and stepped outside. Beyond the city she

413

had helped design and build was the black, serrated shadows of the Forbidden Forest against the star-strewn sky. She didn't have to look to find him. She could feel the pull of his magic—stronger every day since her beloved husband had died, nearly three months past.

The music called to her. Sang of her blessed childhood. Of those she had loved and lost. Of the man who'd betrayed her—the wraith who haunted the woods and enslaved all those who failed to escape. Was there anything left of the boy she'd once loved?

Maybe it was time to find out. Ramass had been right. She didn't have much time left. Her body was failing—slowly starving to death. She couldn't eat for the pain in her stomach. She'd wasted away to sagging skin over aching bones. Her husband was gone. Her daughter Malia was queen now in all but name. Her other children were married with grandchildren of their own.

There was nothing left for Eiryss. Nothing, except the music Ramass played for her every night, and the curse she had failed to break.

She rang for her maid. Rubbing sleep from her eyes, the young girl helped Eiryss dress in tunic and trousers, careful not to tug on the cursed vines that grew over her skin—the sigils had turned against her decades before.

The girl laced up her boots. "Would you like breakfast, my queen?"

"Just some milk, if you would. And see my horse saddled and ready to ride."

The girl lifted wide eyes. "But, my queen, should you really be riding?"

Eiryss ran her fingers over the girl's smooth cheeks. Light, what wouldn't she give to be young again? To move without pain. To think without exhaustion clouding her mind. "I will live until I die, child."

"But it's still dark out!"

"Horses see well enough in the dark. And the stars will light my way. I wish to see my husband."

The girl bowed. "Yes, my queen." She hurried off to do as she was told, though no doubt she would report to Malia in the morning. By then, it would be too late.

After the girl had gone, Eiryss took her packet of letters from within her desk and laid them atop her journal. She wished she could say goodbye in person, but that would arouse too much suspicion. This was the best she could do.

Eiryss took her cane and started the long, long journey to the stables. Fortunately, the stable hand met her at the top of the stairs. He was a handsome boy, big and strong, his hair rumpled from sleep. He was sweet on Eiryss's maid. The two thought they were being discreet, but Eiryss had been young once and more than a little wild. She knew the signs—the way they orient-ed themselves around each other. The way their hands "acci-dentally" brushed. The smile that tugged at the corners of their mouths when looked at each other.

It was a dance. Awkward and lovely and full of hope.

It made Eiryss's heart ache with missing her husband.

The stable boy lifted Eiryss gently and carried her outside the palace. Her horse, a dappled gray gelding, waited placidly. Eiryss sipped at the cup of milk sweetened with honey. It both soothed and irritated her stomach, but she forced herself to finish it. Her maid gave her mint leaves to chew.

When she was done, the stable hand lifted her into the sad-dle.

It hurt—her joints didn't like being stretched. She waited a moment for the pain to fade and then nudged her horse to the other side of the palace. Two soldiers accompanied her—Malia insisted they were for her protection. They both knew Eiryss's magic was more than capable of protecting her. The men didn't even carry weapons, and one of them was a healer.

Eiryss sighed and rode down the hill toward the carved entrance to the crypts. They helped her down and handed her the cane and one of the lanterns.

"Wait for me here."

The men bowed.

She went into the crypts herself, the cold, mineral scent surrounding her—the womb of the earth. Not far from the entrance lay her husband's sarcophagus. It had been carved in his likeness from when he was young.

"Oh, Kit." She touched his face. She'd thought him dead when they'd left him that night so long ago, but the Alamantian healer had found him. He'd been their spy—had arranged for the Alamantians to attack their camp and assassinate King Zannok. Instead, Kit had been the one to nearly die.

He'd told her later that he'd overheard Zannok threatening Ramass, had seen the king use thrall on his son. Eiryss wished with everything she had that she'd failed to protect King Zannok that night—the night she'd first used chaos.

But she hadn't.

The Alamantians had taken Kit back and pieced his gut back together. And he had lived. A year after he'd found her, they were married. They'd had four children together. But now he was gone, and she would never see him again, for neither of them would ever be buried in the Silver Tree.

She touched his beloved face. "There's nothing more I can do for our children or our people. Except maybe this." She reached down and rested her flesh and bone forehead against his stone one. "I'm sorry I will not lay beside you, my love."

She pushed her creaking body up and left the crypt. It was a relief to breathe the crisp night air outside. She wiped the tears from her cheeks and let the men lift her into the saddle. "We'll go for a ride, the three of us."

The men exchanged glances, no doubt wondering if they should tattle on her to her daughter. She didn't wait for them to argue with her. She rode her horse through the city. The once golden sheen of new wood had long since faded to cracked, weathered gray. The ring of hammers and saws of long ago were silent. Now the people slept in their homes—having forgotten the lives they had once lived in the forest. Now, they only knew that a terrible beast stole their daughters in the dead of night. Whenever Eiryss tried to tell them the truth, her voice stopped up.

She left the city, her horse picking its way into the fields beyond, toward the shadows and songs calling her from the forest.

When it was clear that was her destination, one of the guards rode up beside her. "I'm sorry, my queen, but you are not allowed anywhere near the forest."

She smiled. "Long ago, I saved those I could and built us a city, but I never succeeded in banishing the shadow. I must try."

"I'm afraid I can't let you, my queen."

She smiled. "Silly boy. As if you could stop me. As if anyone could." She'd thought her magic gone the night she'd created the countercurse, but it had come back. At least a little. Her sigils flared. She wove a dome around him and the healer. The horses shifted uneasily. Animals weren't used to magic. Not anymore.

She met the guard's panicked gaze. "In the letter I wrote to my children, I asked that neither of you be punished." She turned her back on them and approached the dark line of forest.

"My queen!" one of the men called to her. "Please."

She ignored them, shifting down the hill. Morning wasn't far off—the sky had shifted to gray. The whisper of wind through the branches spoke to her of her childhood within the branches of her hometree. She closed her eyes, and for a moment, she was a girl again. She could feel her mother's fingers through her hair. Hear the ring of her father and brother's swords as they practiced their swordsmanship. The smell of allalla fish frying in Marinda's kitchen. Belgrave chiding the maids for missing one of the rooms.

She opened her eyes when the horse shifted nervously beneath her. Any closer to the wraith, and he would start fighting her in earnest. She tugged on her reins to still him and struggled to swing her leg over the animal's back. She half fell, managing to catch herself by a strap. *Curse this worthless body!*

She finally managed to extricate her foot from the stirrup. She stood for a moment, breathing hard, her head pressed against the warm leather. The guard had her cane, blast it all. She glanced up at the trees. She could see the wraith there, a darker shadow against the rest. He stood straight and tall—as if the last sixty years hadn't touched him at all. The black crown on his head trailed smoke. Though it was too dark to see the flute he played, she could picture it—the gilt carvings and black stain.

He was still fighting. Still killing.

She had thought she would feel fear. But really, what had she to fear anymore? If he killed her, he would spare her a much longer, much more painful death. And with her magic, she didn't think he could enslave her.

She straightened as much as her back would allow and moved through the meadow's grass. Beneath the torn shadows of his cowl, his shoulders were broad and his waist trim. What must he think of her after all these years? Her body stooped, her skin woven with lines, her once thick hair thin and frail as she was.

When she was a mere dozen steps from him, she paused.

He lowered his pipes and held out a hand. "Come."

That was not Ramass's voice. It was the voice of shadows and sorcery. She shuddered, suddenly cold. "For decades, you have called to me. Why?"

His voice changed then. Becoming the voice of the man she had known and loved. "Fear not the shadow, for you are mine."

The song Ture had sung over and over in her dream. "I don't fear you."

"Please, Eiryss." His voice shook, trembling with pain. "You can't die. Not before breaking the curse."

She looked at his hand, then back at her palace atop the hill. The sun lightened the sky behind it. She'd found happiness again, after being so sure that she'd lost it forever. But her long life was coming to an end—she felt it every time the pain in her stomach grew. She wouldn't ever have the strength to make the journey to the forest again—nor would her daughter ever let her.

Ramass panted hard. "I can't hold him off much longer."

The sun would rise in moments. Ramass would be banished. Before long, he'd be lost to her forever. She straightened her shoulders. She was the granddaughter of a queen and a queen herself. She was the blade of change—a blade that cut both ways.

Moments before the sun rose, she took the last few steps, her determined hand landing in his shaky one. The shadows drew her into what felt like black velvet cloth. Ramass pulled her through the thorned, shadowy vines that lay beneath the roots. She sensed movement, and then the cloth was eaten away. She found herself in the center of the Silver Tree.

Only it wasn't silver anymore. It was pure, glittering black.

Ture and Vicil and Hagath stood before the font as though they had been waiting for her. She took a step toward them, marveling that her body's movements were strong and sure. She looked down at her hands in disbelief. Gone were the liver spots and sharp bones. Her skin was full and plump, the veins delicate traceries.

She touched her cheeks, her hair—thick and lovely and still a bit too silver. She felt strong and healthy. Capable of anything. "How is this possible?"

Before she could think on it too much, Hagath and Ture wrapped their arms around her, squeezing her hard.

"Light, Eiryss, you came." Hagath burst into tears. She collapsed into Ture's arms. He hushed her with a kiss on her forehead, and the way he held her said they were far more than friends.

Ramass smiled shyly down at her. "We have a curse to break, but we can't do it alone."

She squared off before him. "I'm ready."

Here we find ourselves, dear reader, at the end. *Curse Queen* was not a book I ever intended to write. A third of the way through *Piper Prince*, I became stuck. For two months I fought against the story pounding at the doors of my imagination and distracting from the novel I needed to finish. I only gave in once I was sure I didn't have any other choice. I missed my deadline by a long shot. But in the end, Eiryss and Ramass deserved to have their story told.

If you've enjoyed the *Forbidden Forest* and would like to try another series of mine, *Witch Song* has been translated to three different languages and has over 1,500 five-star reviews on Goodreads alone.

You can snag it here:
https://amberargyle.com/witchsongseries/

Still not convinced? Keep reading for a sample…

GLOSSARY

Sacred tree: A magical, sentient being that communicates through memories.

Font: People who wish for magic come to the sacred tree. They approach the font, which grows from a dais where the trunk and branches meet. It's surrounded by thorns.

Conduit thorn: The largest of these thorns. It is hollow to allow human blood to mingle with the sap of the tree and therefore allow the tree access to the host's body to judge their worthiness.

Thorn: If the host is found worthy, the tree settles their blood in the thorns they may take. These thorns behave more like seedlings.

Embedding ceremony: The process by which the thorns are slipped into the recipient's skin.

Sigil: If the thorn takes root in the human host, it becomes a sigil, from which the user can now draw magic. The enchantress/enchanter trains the sigil to obey commands made of music.

Pipes: Magic wind instruments the enchanters/enchantresses use to communicate with their sigils. They must be made of the wood of a sacred tree.

Seers: Enchanter/enchantress whose sigil allows them visions of the future. These visions come in the form of memories that the seer must interpret.

Binders: Enchanter/enchantress who binds magic together. Binders bind the amulets to the hometrees, therefore creating homes. They also seal marriages and work the marriage cuffs.

Bearers: Enchantress/enchanter who bears the seeds of the sacred trees for replanting.

Speakers: Are given memories of the dead.

Dreamers: Can create illusions.

Emotives: Can manipulate the emotions of others through music.

Sigils come in two types: positive and negative. Positive sigils go on the right side of the body, negative on the left.

Types of sigils:

- **Build/break:** upper arm
- **Seek/repel:** forearm
- **Seal/loose:** thighs
- **Light/darken:** calves
- **Rule:** chest. This sigil is specific to monarchs. Only two people can have it at once—a king or queen and his or her heir. Once the prince/princess's magic surpasses the king/queen's, they become the new ruler. Their predecessor's magic fades to nothing.
- **Chaos:** A new sigil that combines the magic of a dreamer and emotive. Placed above the navel.
- **Speaker:** A sigil that allows vision of the dead.

There are two main types of magic: barrier and warrior magic. The trees always give warrior magic to those of the same sex as themselves. Hence, men in Valynthia and women in the Alamant have warrior magic, while barrier magic goes to the women of Valynthia and the men of the Alamant. Warrior magic creates shields and weapons. Barrier magic creates the barriers. Using the magic together creates the vault.

1

WITCHBORN

Brusenna's straw-colored hair felt as hot as a sunbaked rock. She was sticky with sweat that trickled down her spine and made her simple dress cling to her. Her every instinct urged her to run from the glares that stung like angry wasps. She had already put off her trip to the market for too long.

The merchant finished wrapping the spools of thread in crinkling brown paper. "Twelve upice," Bommer said sourly.

A ridiculous price, no doubt made worse by the drought. Had Brusenna been anyone else, she could have bartered it down to half that. Even though the villagers only suspected, it was enough. Careful not to touch her, the man's hand swallowed the coins she dropped in it. She wondered what marvelous things he ate to flesh out his skin that way. Things like the honey-sweetened cakes she could still smell in her clothes long after she'd left the marketplace.

As Bommer mumbled and counted his money, Brusenna gathered the packages tightly to her chest and hurried away. She hadn't gone five steps when a heavy hand clamped down on her shoulder. Fear shot through her veins like a thousand nettles. Here, no one ever touched her.

With a wince, she craned her neck back to see the merchant looming over her. "You tryin' to cheat me, chanter?"

This close, the smell of his stale body odor hit her hard. She swallowed the urge to gag. Her mind worked furiously. She'd counted twice. "I gave you twelve," she managed.

He yanked her around, grabbing her other arm and bringing her face next to his. She cringed as his large paunch pressed against her. Somewhere, a baby squalled. "You think I can't count?"

Brusenna tried to answer, but her mouth locked up. She should have been more careful. She should have stayed until he had finished counting her coins, but she had been too eager to escape. He shook her, his dirty nails digging into her skin. Her packages tumbled from her hands and hit the ground.

Taking shallow breaths and arching away from him, she squirmed, desperate to be free. "Please," she said, finally finding her voice. "Let me go!"

He laughed, his eyes gleaming with pleasure. "No. I don't think so. Not this time. You know what the punishment is for stealing?"

The stocks. Brusenna swallowed hard. Trapped for an entire day with the whole village taunting her. They'd throw things. Rotten food. And worse. She looked for help in the crowd that had eagerly gathered around them. Satisfaction shone plain on every face. She was suddenly angry with her mother for letting her face this alone. For refusing to come because someone might recognize her.

"I didn't steal," she whispered, already knowing no one would listen.

"You callin' me a liar?" Tobacco spit splattered her face. He backhanded her. Her vision flashed white, then black with stars, then red. She tasted blood. Her eyes burned with tears. She clamped her teeth shut against the pain, refusing to cry out.

Bommer half-dragged her toward the center of the square, where two thin blocks of wood were connected with a hinge. Three holes, one for her neck and two for her wrists. Remnants of rotten food, manure and rocks littered the base.

The sight of the stocks shocked Brusenna into action. She squirmed and struggled.

His hand on the back of her neck, Bommer shoved her throat into the largest, center hole. She tried to rear back. He pushed harder. The wood cut into her windpipe. She couldn't breathe.

"You let that child go, or you'll sorely miss your brain, my friend," said a feminine voice that was somehow soft and commanding at the same time.

Brusenna felt Bommer freeze, his arm still pinning her neck.

She strained against Bommer to see who had spoken. In front of her, sitting astride a glossy black horse, a woman glared at the merchant down the barrel of an expensive-looking musket. The wind picked up and her gleaming hair shifted like a field of ripe wheat. The woman's cobalt eyes met Brusenna's golden ones.

Brusenna gaped. She'd hoped for help, but never imagined it would come from someone both rich and powerful.

"What'd you say to me?" he asked the stranger.

The woman cocked back the hammer. "You heard what I said." Bommer didn't respond. Brusenna felt him shift uncertainly. When no one moved to support him, he growled deep in his throat. He pushed once more on Brusenna's neck, hard. But then she was free. She collapsed, clutching her throat and coughing violently.

When the spots stopped dancing before her eyes, she glanced up. The woman was watching Brusenna, fury burning in her eyes. The stranger let the barrel drop. "Where I come from, merchants ask for the missing coin before they accuse their customers of stealing. Especially a child."

A child? Brusenna bristled as she rose to her feet. She was nearly fifteen. Then, from the corner of her eye, she saw Sheriff Tomack pushing through the crowd. All thoughts of defiance flew out of her head. She tried to slip through an opening, but the press of bodies tightened into an impregnable wall. Arms roughly shoved her back to Bommer.

She shuddered as his hand clamped down on her shoulder again. "Sheriff, this girl stole from me and this," he worked his tongue like he had a bad taste in his mouth, "woman is interfering."

"I already heard it, Bommer." Sheriff Tomack studied Brusenna with an unreadable expression. "You trying to cause trouble, girl?"

Digging her toenails into the packed dirt, she shook her head adamantly.

He grunted. "Well then, give Bommer his upice or spend your day in the stocks."

Anger flared in her chest and died like a candle flame in a windstorm. It didn't matter that she'd already given Bommer twelve upice. It didn't matter that he was lying. She couldn't prove it and her word meant nothing to the villagers. Scrabbling in her money bag, she found an upice and held it out for Bommer.

The merchant slowly shook his head. "I don't want her money. I want her time in the stocks."

Brusenna's hand automatically moved to her bruised throat. Tears stung her eyes. She quickly blinked them back.

"Why?" Sheriff Tomack asked.

Bommer snorted. "You know why."

"You got proof?"

Bommer spit in the dirt. "None of us needs it. We all know what she is."

No one said it, but the word echoed in Brusenna's head, *Witch.*

"Has the girl ever stolen from you before?" Sheriff Tomack asked cautiously.

Bommer took a deep breath. "Her punishment is my choice."

With a click, the woman on the horse released the hammer on her musket. Dismounting, she strode forward. The crowd parted, half in fear and half in awe. She threw a handful of coins at Bommer's chest. The gleaming silver bits bounced off and scattered across the ground. Brusenna's eyes widened in disbelief. The woman hadn't tossed a few dirty upices; the coins were silvers.

Looking both beautiful and terrible, the woman straightened her shoulders. "Take your money, merchant. If you give this girl more trouble, I'll see that no one ever buys from you again."

Bommer spit a stream of tobacco juice dangerously close to the woman's foot. "Who're you to make threats?"

She smiled, a mere baring of her teeth. "Would you like to find out?"

Glaring, Bommer rolled his chaw around his mouth. Finally, his glower shifted to Brusenna. "You ain't worth it, chanter." He scooped up the coins and stomped back to his booth.

Hate filled Brusenna. She hated that Bommer's lies allowed him to abuse her without cause—had earned him ten times his due. She hated the crowd for hating her. Still, it could have been much worse. She could be in the stocks. Grim relief washed through her, cooling her anger. It was past time to be heading home. She twisted to disappear in the crowd. But the strange woman gripped the back of her dress with an iron fist. Knowing better than to fight, Brusenna stifled a groan. *Not again,* she thought.

Sheriff Tomack gave the woman a small nod before moving away.

Brusenna turned a pain-filled glance to the marketplace. Though the crowd had grudgingly moved on, people still shot suspicious, hateful glances her way. Their tolerance of her had taken a dive since the drought had worsened. They blamed her and her mother for their dying crops, simply because they were Witches.

She forced herself to unclench her fists. The breeze felt cool against her sweaty palms. She turned toward the woman, though she dared not look at her face. "Thank you," she murmured.

The woman cocked her head to the side. "Why do you buy from him?"

Brusenna shrugged. "The others won't sell to me. And Bommer needs the money."

"So he resents you for it." She released her grip on Brusenna's dress. "What's your name, child?" Her voice was as sweet and lingering as the smell of the honeycakes.

"I'm not a child. My name is Brusenna."

The woman sighed in relief. "Ah, Sacra's daughter. I thought so."

How could this woman know Brusenna's name? Her mother's name? Her ears buzzed. She managed to bob her head once. She began gathering her scattered packages. The paper scraped loudly against the packed dirt.

The woman crouched beside her. Picking up the last package, she brushed it off and handed it to Brusenna. "My name is Coyel. Will you take me to your mother?"

Brusenna's stomach clenched. There were two iron-clad rules—one: never let them hear your song; two: never lead them home. She swallowed hard. "Thank you, Coyel, for helping me. But I'm not... I mean, I shouldn't... I mean—"

Coyel cocked an eyebrow and pitched her voice so no one else would hear, "I'm the eldest Keeper of the Four Sisters."

Brusenna blinked in confusion. Coyel's statement seemed to hold a deeper meaning, but for all her searching, she couldn't understand it. "I... I'm an only child. My sister died before I was born."

A look of disbelief crossed Coyel's face and Brusenna knew she had missed the mark entirely. "Take me to your home. I must speak with your mother."

She bit her bottom lip. Coyel had saved her from the stocks, so if she wanted to speak with her mother... well, Brusenna owed her that much. With a nervous glance at the townspeople, she nodded then scurried through the streets. Almost as soon as the village thinned behind them, they crossed into fields flanked by deep forests that grew over the gentle hills like a furry blanket over sleeping giants. Usually, those forests were deep green, but the drought had caused weaker patches to give up the season, trimming themselves in golds and reds.

Brusenna's shoulders itched for the cool, comforting shadows of the trees. She felt naked out in the open like this, where hateful villagers could scrutinize her. She felt even more vulnerable with the echoing clop of the horse's hooves to remind her of the woman and her cobalt eyes.

Nearly a league from the marketplace, Brusenna waited while Coyel tied her horse to a nearby tree. The path wound through thickets as dense and tangled as matted cat fur. She and her mother made it this way to keep strangers out.

Just as she moved to enter the forest, Coyel placed a hand on her shoulder. "This is your home. You should be the one to sing the song."

Brusenna's eyes widened in disbelief. Another Witch? It couldn't be.

Coyel lifted an eyebrow. "Unless you'd prefer me to sing?"

Brusenna didn't understand. Coyel was beautiful and powerful. Not skittish and weak. How could she be a Witch? "At the marketplace, you knew what I was. How?"

Coyel shot a glare in the direction of the village. "I heard someone saying the Witch was finally going to the stocks."

Brusenna folded her arms across her stomach. It made sense. Who else but another Witch would have helped her?

Coyel must have sensed her hesitation. "Are you unable?" There was simple curiosity in her gaze. As if she wanted to see if Brusenna could do it.

Of course she could sing the pathway clear. She'd been doing it for years. But Brusenna hesitated. It went against years of training to sing in front of a stranger. She was nervous to perform in front of another Witch who was everything Brusenna wasn't.

Before she could change her mind, she squared her shoulders and started singing.

Plants of the forest make a path for me,
For through this forest I must flee.
After I pass hide my trail,
For an enemy I must quell.

The underbrush shivered and then untangled like it had been raked through by a wooden comb. As they walked, Brusenna continued her song. As soon as their feet lifted, the plants wove behind them, tangling and knotting themselves into a formidable barrier nearly as tall as a man's chest.

What was nearly impossible without the song was fairly easy with it. In no time, they left behind the last of the forest. Brusenna stepped aside, giving the woman a full view of her home. Drought left the whole countryside brittle. And yet here, their lush gardens thrived. The house and barn were neat and well tended. The milk cow lazily munched her cud under the shade of a tree. With a fierce kind of pride, she watched for Coyel's reaction.

Coyel took in the prolific gardens with a sweep of her gaze. But the woman didn't seem impressed. As if she'd expected no less. And maybe she had.

Brusenna wanted to ask why Coyel had come, but her tongue dried in her mouth. Her mind shouted it instead, *What do you want with us?*

Bruke, Brusenna's enormous wolfhound, noticed them from his position in the shade of the house and bounded forward, the scruff on the back of his neck stiff with distrust. They'd purchased him as a guard dog after someone had shot their old plow horse. His wary eyes shifted to Brusenna in question.

Brusenna blinked rapidly. She suddenly wanted to explain why she'd broken the rule before the stranger breezed into their house. She darted past Coyel and up the worn path. "Bruke, heel."

With a glare at the stranger, Bruke glued himself to Brusenna's side.

She pushed open the door to the house. "Mother!" she called, pulling some clinging hair off her sweaty forehead.

Sacra's head popped up from the floor cellar. "What is it, Brusenna?"

"A woman named—"

"Coyel," the woman finished as she stepped up behind her.

For the longest time, the two women stared at each other. The charge between them made the tiny hairs on Brusenna's arms stand on end. Coyel stepped into their home. To Brusenna's knowledge, she was the first outsider to do so.

"It's been a long time, Sacra," Coyel said.

Brusenna's gaze flitted back and forth between her mother and Coyel. That they knew each other went beyond her comprehension. In her fourteen years, Brusenna had never seen her mother converse with anyone other than an occasional trouble-making villager—usually one of the adolescent boys who had taken on the challenge to kill one of their animals as a dare.

Sacra stepped out of the cellar and lowered the door as gently as if it were glass. Slowly, she straightened her slender back. "Brusenna, leave the things on the table and go check the corn."

Brusenna's disbelief rose in her throat, nearly choking her. "But, Mother—" At her mother's glower, she swallowed her words, dropped her purchases on the table and ducked out the door. Bruke followed. Careful to keep her stride even, she waited until she had rounded the corner of the house before peeking back. The way was clear.

"Bruke, stay," she whispered. With a disappointed whine, the dog sat on his haunches.

Hunched over, Brusenna retraced her steps. The soft grass felt cool under her hands and the sun was hot on her back as she crouched on one side of the doorway. There were no sounds from within. She waited until her knees were practically numb. She'd almost determined to chance a peek through the window when their voices halted her.

"What brings you, Coyel?" her mother asked warily.

"The Keepers need you, Sacra. There are precious few of us left and signs of the Dark Witch increase daily. The Circle of Keepers must be complete if we are to recapture her and stop the drought."

Brusenna's eyebrows flew up in wonder. It had never occurred to her that Sacra could have been a different person before she became her mother. Mustering every ounce of bravery, she peeked through the corner of the window.

"Calling Espen the Dark Witch only increases her power over us." Sacra's gaze remained fixed on the floor. "Find another Eighth."

Coyel pressed her lips in a tight line. "The others are gone."

Her mother's head came up slowly; she blinked in surprise... and fear. "I have a daughter. You have only yourself."

Coyel pointed toward Gonstower. "They call us Witches. But long before that, the Creators named us Keepers. It's what we are. Keepers of the Four Sisters—Earth, Plants, Water and Sunlight. And as a Keeper, you can't deny that all are floundering. If we don't act now, it'll be too late."

Sacra stood rigid and immovable. "No."

Coyel's voice flared, "You know what the Dark Witch will do if she succeeds? Your daughter is Witchborn; even worse, she's the child of a former Head of Earth." She shook her head in disbelief. "She doesn't even know our signs."

Her mother turned away and stared blankly at the trees behind the house. "The less Brusenna knows, the safer she is."

"Safer?" Coyel spat. "You haven't taught her to protect herself. She's terrified of those *villagers*." The last word sounded like her mother's voice after she'd found rats in their oats. "What chance do you think the girl will stand when Espen finds her?"

Her head in her palms, a moan escaped her mother's lips. Coyel stepped forward and rested her hand on Sacra's shoulder. "I've heard her. When she's fully come into her own, I wouldn't doubt she'll be at least a Level Four. But right now, she's… immature. And not just her song. Keeping her isolated will only make it worse. She needs to be around other Keepers her own age. Learn."

Brusenna's cheeks flamed with shame, partly because she suspected Coyel was right about her immaturity. Whenever she was around strangers, her tongue dried up in her mouth and her stomach felt full of writhing snakes.

Her mother jerked away as if Coyel's touch had burned her. "Coyel, no. Espen won't find her. I've been careful. Gonstower is isolated. No one knows I'm here. And we're not completely without friends."

Friends? Brusenna mentally flipped through the faces of the villagers who would have gladly seen her in the stocks. What friends?

Coyel's gentleness vanished, replaced by disbelief and anger. "I found you. And if you think those villagers will protect her identity, you're deceiving yourself. The ignorant fools would gladly turn her over. Never understanding the very Keepers they hate are all that stand between them and—"

"I said no!" Sacra shouted. Brusenna jumped. She'd never heard her mother shout before. "Get out!"

Coyel backed away, her jaw working as if she might chew through Sacra's resistance and then her head dropped. "We're gathering at Haven. I'll wait in the village for three days." Her fervent gaze met Sacra's smoldering one. "Please, Sacra. We can't do it without you."

Not daring to linger another moment, Brusenna scampered away from the door and pressed herself flat against the smooth boards on the other side of the house.

"Please, Sacra," Coyel asked again. And then all Brusenna could hear was the sound of footsteps that grew fainter within moments.

She barely felt Bruke nudge her with his wet nose. Her chest rose and fell as her mind reeled with unfamiliar names. Circle of Keepers, Level Four, the Dark Witch? Surely her mother had no understanding of such things. Surely, she'd lived here for generations.

Hadn't she?

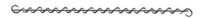

If you love unique magic, sweet romance, and daring adventure, you'll adore WITCH SONG.
Don't miss this bewitching read that will keep you up all night.

Read your copy today!
(https://amberargyle.com/witchsongseries/)

ACKNOWLEDGMENTS

Thanks go out to my amazing editing team: Charity West (content editor), Jennie Stevens (copyeditor), Cathy Nielson (proofreader); and my talented design team: Michelle Argyle (cover designer), Julie Titus (formatter), and Bob Defendi (mapmaker).

My everlasting love to Derek, Corbin, Connor, Lily, and God.

ABOUT THE AUTHOR

Amber Argyle is the best-selling author of numerous fanta-
sy and romance novels. Her award-winning books have
been translated into several languages and praised by
such authors as *New York Times* best sellers David Farland and
Jennifer A. Nielsen.

Amber grew up on a cattle ranch and spent her formative
years in the rodeo circuit and on the basketball court. She graduated cum laude from Utah State University with a degree in Eng-
lish and physical education, a husband, and a two-year-old. Since
then, she and her husband have added two more children, which
they are actively trying to transform from crazy small people into
less-crazy larger people. She's fluent in all forms of sarcasm,
loves hiking and traveling, and believes spiders should be rele-
gated to horror novels where they belong.

To receive her starter library of four free books,
simply tell her where to send it:

http://amberargyle.com/freebooks/

OTHER TITLES BY AMBER ARGYLE

Forbidden Forest Series

Lady of Shadows
Stolen Enchantress
Piper Prince
Wraith King
Curse Queen

Fairy Queens Series

Of Ice and Snow
Winter Queen
Of Fire and Ash
Summer Queen
Of Sand and Storm
Daughter of Winter
Winter's Heir

Witch Song Series

Witch Song
Witch Born
Witch Rising
Witch Fall

Lightning Source UK Ltd.
Milton Keynes UK
UKHW022218120822
407249UK00003B/108